A Pound of Flesh

Also by Alex Gray

A Pound of Flesh

A DCI Lorimer Novel

ALEX GRAY

WITNESS
IMPULSE
An Imprint of HarperCollinsPublishers

This book is dedicated to Nanette Pollock,
formerly Detective Chief Inspector of Strathclyde Police

Excerpt from *The Swedish Girl* copyright © 2013 by Alex Gray.

A POUND OF FLESH. Copyright © 2012 by Alex Gray. All rights reserved. Printed in the United States of America. No part of this book may be used or reproduced in any manner whatsoever without written permission except in the case of brief quotations embodied in critical articles and reviews. For information, address HarperCollins Publishers, 195 Broadway, New York, NY 10007.

Originally published in Great Britain in 2012 by Sphere, an imprint of Little, Brown Book Group.

Digital Edition NOVEMBER 2017 ISBN: 978-0-06-265922-4
Print Edition ISBN: 978-0-06-265923-1

Cover art by Guido Caroti
Cover photographs: © April30 / Getty Images (street); © RyanDeanMorrison / Getty Images (background); © DenisTangneyJr / Getty Images (snow)

WITNESS logo and WITNESS IMPULSE are trademarks of HarperCollins Publishers in the United States of America.

HarperCollins is a registered trademark of HarperCollins Publishers in the United States of America and other countries.

18 19 20 21 LSC 10 9 8 7 6 5 4 3 2

What do you think a man does who has a hundred sheep and one of them gets lost? He will leave the other ninety-nine grazing on the hillside and go and look for the lost sheep. When he finds it, I tell you, he feels happier over this one sheep than over the ninety-nine that did not get lost. In just the same way your Father in heaven does not want any of these little ones to be lost.

St Matthew's Gospel, Chapter 18, verses 12–14

Chapter One

IT WASN'T ALWAYS easy to see the moon or the stars. This city's sodium glow rose like yellow fog from its streets, blotting out any chance of star gazing. But she knew it was there. That cold white face dominated her thoughts tonight and she shivered as though it already saw her flesh naked and exposed to its unblinking watchfulness. Perhaps it was because she was trying to be seen that she felt such awareness. The red jersey pencil skirt folded over to create a too-short mini, those agonisingly high-heeled sandals cutting into her bare toes; spread across the bed back in the hotel they had seemed the garb of an adventuress. Now, revealed in the glare of the street lamp on this corner she felt a sense of . . . what? Shame? Perhaps. Self-consciousness, certainly. But such feelings must be overcome if her plan was to work.

She had already overcome the blank indifference of the girls down in Waterloo Street, their body language both defiant and compelling. Her hips shifted, one slender foot thrust forwards, as she remembered how they had stood, languidly chewing gum, waiting for their punters. Their desperation drove them to return night after night, the price of a wrap of drugs equating to an hour with some stranger.

Her own need was just as strong, fuelled by a passion that would not be spent until she had fulfilled her desire.

It was warm in this Glasgow summer's night and her black nylon blouse clung to her back, making her uncomfortably aware of her own flesh. The thin cotton coat she'd worn to conceal these trashy clothes as she'd tapped her way across the marble foyer of the hotel was now folded into the black bag at her feet, along with her more sober court shoes. When it was over she would slip them on and return the way she had come, hair clipped in a businesslike pleat. She smiled thinly. Being a woman had some advantages; the facility for disguise was just one of them. Her carefully made-up face was stripped of colour in the unforgiving lamplight, leaving only an impression of dark eyes, darker hair tossed back to reveal a long, determined mouth. She recalled what Tracey-Anne, one of the girls at the drop-in centre, had told her: *I get through it by pretending to be someone else for a few hours, then I can be myself again.*

Tracey-Anne was lucky, though.

After tonight *she* could never again be the person that she used to be.

Glancing at the elegant façades around the square, the dark-haired woman suddenly saw these city streets through different eyes: the shadows seemed blacker, the corners harbouring ill intent. Her chin tilted upwards, defying those inner demons tempting her to turn back.

After tonight things would change for ever.

WHEN THE CAR slowed down at the kerb her heart quickened in a moment of anticipation that astonished her. She had expected the thrill of fear, not this rush of excitement sweeping through her blood.

The man behind the wheel had bent his head and she could see his eyes flicking over her hungrily, appraising his choice. He gave a brief nod as if to say he was pleased with his first instinct to stop. Her lip-glossed mouth drawn up in a smile, she stepped forward, willing him to reach across and open the window, ask her price. For a moment he seemed to hesitate and she could see tiny beads of sweat on his upper lip, glistening in the light. Then the door of the big car swung open noiselessly and she lowered herself inside, swinging her legs neatly together to show as much thigh as she could. But the gestures were still ladylike, almost reserved, as if she knew that would quicken his senses.

'How much?' he asked. And she told him, one shoulder moving insouciantly as if to declare that she wasn't bothered whether he could afford her or not: someone else would pay that price if he wouldn't. She glanced at him briefly, catching sight of the tip of his tongue flicking at his lips like a nervous lizard, then he made a gruff noise of assent, looking at her again, as though to be sure of his purchase, before accelerating into the night.

Chapter Two

DETECTIVE INSPECTOR KEITH Preston listened patiently as the scene of crime manager took him through the morning's work. A patrol car had found the Mercedes abandoned beside a train station half an hour's drive outside the city. The white car had been parked just under the railway bridge well away from the prying eyes of any CCTV camera. The victim's body was still where they had found it, slumped over the steering wheel, a gathering posse of flies buzzing around the dark stain on the man's shirt.

'Matthew Wardlaw,' the DS told him, 'lived in Solihull. From the contents of his briefcase it seems he'd been staying up here on some sort of legal business. Was booked into the Crown Plaza hotel.'

'Pathologist on his way?'

'*Her* way. Doctor White.' The DS grinned.

Preston nodded. Jacqui White was one of Glasgow's more recent celebrities, due to her part in a documentary series about facial reconstruction. Forensic anthropology had been her initial career choice before she had switched to medicine and so the pathologist had been selected to appear in a series of programmes around the country featuring universities like Dundee and Teesside. Preston guessed that the programme's ratings success was probably down to her milk chocolate voice and a face that the camera just loved. Whatever, *Under their Skin* had made Jacqui White a household name on both sides of the border as she travelled around talking to the forensic anthropologists whose work was an integral part of criminal investigations. Today, though, she was here in her capacity of consultant forensic pathologist.

Both men looked up as the charcoal grey Porsche Carrera parked behind the two police vehicles. One door was pushed open and in a matter of minutes the pathologist had donned her white boiler suit, picked up her medical bag and was heading towards them. She would examine the corpse, estimate the time of death and tell them what they already knew: that the victim had been shot through the heart, the scorch marks around the entry wound testifying to the fact that the bullet had been fired at close range. Finding out why he'd been there and who had reason to kill him were not within Dr White's remit, however. She would examine him more fully down at the city mortuary, leaving Preston as Senior Investigating Officer to work out these sorts of problems.

'Someone knew what they were doing,' Jacqui White commented as she snapped off her surgical gloves at last. 'Bull's eye, in fact,' she added with a fleeting smile.

'Or they just got lucky,' the DS suggested.

'Well, *he* didn't,' Preston pointed out, nodding back towards the Mercedes. They watched as the scene of crime photographer prowled around the car, leaning in to take shots from various angles, one more stage in the piecing together of just what had taken place under this railway bridge. Matthew Wardlaw's body would soon be zipped into a body bag and transferred to the waiting van. But for a time this cordoned off area would continue to be forbidden territory to any curious eyes.

Overhead a train rumbled on the tracks, its brakes suddenly shrieking as it drew closer to the platform. Preston looked up and nodded thoughtfully. Perhaps this wasn't such a random location after all, then. Whoever had pulled that trigger might have waited for such a moment, the deafening noise on the bridge obliterating the sound of gunfire. Well, they would have to wait for forensics results before anything could really push this one forward. It was an isolated spot, far from any domestic habitation, just a couple of shops and a post office-cum-general store nearby. Still, the station would have CCTV that could be looked at, though Preston had a bad feeling it would be of little use to them.

He turned away from the scene of crime with a sigh. Once an incident room had been set up he'd have his team look into the victim's background. It would be a starting point at least. The DI's brow furrowed as he frowned. First, though, he'd have to make contact with the police in Solihull, get someone from their family liaison out tonight to break the news of Wardlaw's death to his family. It was one of the least pleasant tasks in this job, but at least whichever officer rang that doorbell would have been spared the sight of the victim's body, and could refer to the man's death as an 'incident' for now, at any rate.

Chapter Three

SHE PICKED UP the croissant, surprised at the steadiness of her fingers. The perfectly manicured nails sank into the burnished crust, tearing it apart and revealing layers of soft yellow pastry. She broke off a piece and chewed thoughtfully.

Her act of killing seemed to have given her strength. She had expected to feel some reaction, weakness or trembling, but there had been nothing. Not even the satisfaction of a job well done. Perhaps, she thought, taking a sip of the hotel's very good espresso, it was because it was only the beginning.

She had chosen to sit facing the windows, her back to the waiting staff in the dining room, looking out at the trees and grass of Blythswood Square. This was possibly the most upmarket hotel in Glasgow, formerly the home of the Royal Automobile Club and the historic setting for the start of many a famous rally. Glancing at the scarlet lightshade suspended in the long window, she wondered if whoever had been commissioned as interior decorator for this place had had any notion of its less salubrious history. Not only was it part of the notorious square mile of murder, it had been known for decades as the red light district. At each window looking out onto the square there was a similar red lamp. And, directly opposite the main door, were two deeply recessed seating areas in plush red velvet, reminiscent of a nineteenth-century bordello. Was that a deliberate joke on the part of the firm contracted to give the hotel some cachet? Or was it only an ironic coincidence?

There was something missing from the place, however classy it might be. It was too quiet, that was it. No trace of music gave any comforting layer to the atmosphere, though what sort of music could be pleasing after last night was questionable. And that quietness brought her a sense of unease rather than solace. Noises from her fellow guests as they clattered cutlery and chattered to their breakfast companions seemed to be magnified in this place with its minimalist decor, making her feel exposed, somehow. Even as she sat facing away from them she wondered who might be looking at her and speculating about this solitary woman. What was she to them? Surely just another guest breakfasting quietly before whatever work had brought her to the city, her laptop case placed strategically against the table legs like a *keep off* sign to guard her privacy. Today her demure charcoal business suit and smart cotton blouse proclaimed her for what she really was – a businesswoman.

But nobody glancing her way would ever suspect that her business was murder.

She picked up the linen napkin, wiping away some stray crumbs from her lips just as effectively as she had disposed of the bloody garments several hours earlier. There was not a trace of her on his body or in the car. She was certain of that. She allowed a small smile of satisfaction to play about her lips.

There had been no smile on her face that night in the hospital, just a dry gasp as she had entered the cubicle where the dying woman lay. The memory could sweep back into her thoughts at the most unexpected moments, like a harsh black outline against the lemon light of dusk.

She was alive, she reminded herself, sipping the last of her coffee. It was Carol who was gone, far away from the pain and bloody shambles that had taken her. But the horror of her leaving repeated itself night after night, images of what must have happened endlessly reverberating in her mind. She'd thought to quench it with that other, noisier, death. But that hadn't happened. Nothing would bring Carol back and nothing, it seemed now, could relieve the painful recollection of her last moments. The cruel point of that turning knife (she knew all about that from the pathologist's report: she'd spared herself nothing); the samples of sweat still waiting for a match in the lab; Carol's endless cry as the pain shot upwards, fearing she was about to die. Sometimes it seemed that it was Carol's scream she heard, tearing her from sleep; often it was her own.

It might take days before she knew if she had been successful, and she wasn't stupid enough to believe in beginner's luck. It might take several nights standing beneath that street lamp before she found the man she sought. And until then she would have to content herself with the fact that there was one less kerb crawler littering up the streets of Glasgow. If that were the case, it might prove to be a small consolation, rubbing balm into the sore place of failure.

Chapter Four

DC BARBARA KNOX was nothing if not thorough. It was, she reasoned, the only way to obtain useable information and she didn't care a toss if the others on the team thought her completely anal in her working methods. Besides, hadn't she already uncovered bits and pieces that had helped in previous cases? Her SIO had meted out sufficient scraps of praise to encourage her dogged approach to investigations, though Barbara knew fine that she would work things her own way even without such encouraging words. Take this one, she smirked, pressing the print button to churn out hard copy to take through to her boss. HOLMES had come up with a nice parallel case that was not only in their region but remained satisfyingly unsolved. Satisfying, at least, for a young woman like her who was hungry to prove what a great officer she was going to be. The Home Office Large Major Enquiry System had provided information on past cases in the UK for more than two decades now and was a primary tool in any ongoing investigation. What Barbara found most satisfying was its ability to process and prioritise information, something she wished every one of her fellow officers shared. It would be a great start to the New Year if she could impress the SIO.

Barbara lifted her ample bottom off the computer chair and marched through to Mumby's room, only pausing briefly to give his door a swift rat-a-tat-tat.

'Think you'll want to see this, sir,' she said gruffly, stepping towards the desk. A balding man with a round, rosy face looked up at her. DCI Mumby's mouth hung open ever so slightly, giving him the look of a startled child.

'It came from HOLMES,' Barbara added. 'Case last summer that was never solved. Guy shot dead in his own car,' she added, nodding at the paper now in Mumby's hand.

'Hmm, found slumped across the steering wheel . . . neat hole drilled in his chest . . . found under a railway bridge . . .' Mumby muttered, reading from the report. 'Good Lord! Looks like we may have the same killer on our own patch, Knox. Well done. Hmm, well done indeed.' DCI Mumby nodded his head at her.

'There are other similarities too, sir,' Barbara insisted, coming around the side of her boss's desk and pointing at a paragraph halfway down the page, oblivious to the proximity of her large breasts to the DCI's reddening cheeks. 'Both men were strangers in the city, both of them up on legitimate business.'

'Meetings noted in their BlackBerrys.' Mumby nodded again, trying hard to keep from staring at his junior officer's expansive bosom. The faint smell of lavender filled his nostrils; a very feminine scent, somehow at odds with this large, plain woman whose stubby fingers were drawing his attention to a particular part of the photocopied page.

'And no connection with any sort of organised crime,' Barbara pointed out. 'Pure as the driven snow, or so it would seem,' she added darkly, cynicism having coloured her outlook ever since that very first week at Tulliallan Police College.

'Coincidences do happen, of course,' Mumby said, then sighed and shook his head as he caught sight of DC Knox's sceptical expression.

'Two men driving white Mercedes S-class cars found shot dead under railway bridges?' Her scorn was almost palpable.

'Well, yes,' Mumby admitted. 'Perhaps we ought to see what this DI Preston has to say about the first case.'

Barbara Knox nodded her satisfaction. The body of Thomas Littlejohn might even now be laid out on the cold steel of the mortuary table. There was no apparent reason for his death, no connection with the sorts of people who meted out summary execution. But that was exactly how this murder had appeared.

Okay, the two killings might be several months apart, but DC Knox was willing to bet a chunk of her monthly salary that it was the same person who had picked off these apparently innocent men.

Chapter Five

DETECTIVE SUPERINTENDENT WILLIAM Lorimer turned over the calendar so that the month of January was showing. It was a snowscape of Rannoch Moor, one single wind-bent tree standing starkly in the foreground, the Black Mount a brooding presence against the cold blue sky, misty wisps of cloud hovering balefully above. Despite its bleakness, the moor was a place that beckoned to the policeman, making him want to be there, his climbing boots sinking into the snowy approach to the hills, a pack on his back. Instead he was here in the red brick sprawl that was police headquarters, his only view the streets and buildings of Glasgow. This was Lorimer's first day in the job here at Pitt Street and he still had to come to terms with the new regime. Being in charge of such an important department as the Serious Crimes Squad had afforded him the dubious luxury of an office overlooking the back courts of other buildings in the city. The SCS existed to filter out the more difficult cases throughout the Strathclyde divisions, murder being one of the main crimes investigated by the hand-picked team. And Detective Superintendent William Lorimer was well qualified in such inquiries. It was, he supposed, a good step up from being in a Divisional Headquarters, though he already missed the buzz of voices from the open-plan offices he'd worked in during his last post as Detective Chief Inspector.

He had arrived earlier than necessary, partly to see where he could park his battered old Lexus and also to steal a march on the officers who comprised this elite squad.

After the official interview Lorimer had been taken to meet his new colleagues and had been surprised by how few officers were actually in the building.

'The squad is at the disposal of every division in Strathclyde,' Joyce Rogers, the deputy chief constable, had explained to him when she had first mooted the idea of Lorimer taking over the running of this regime. 'Officers can be seconded to any serious crime at all, but it will be entirely at your discretion which officer goes where and why and for how long. Man management is the name of this game,' she'd told him with a grin.

That was all very well, but with more than half of his team away on cases elsewhere, how was he meant to become familiar with their skills and their personalities? Tomorrow, he told himself. He would book one of the larger rooms in this building and have them all meet after their working day was over. It might not go down particularly well with those who'd been sent away further than the confines of the city, but it had to be done. How could he do this job if all he had was a list of names to which he was unable to put faces? That wasn't his way of doing things and they had better know that from the outset.

He had taken leave after his wife, Maggie's, operation, so that leaving his old division and beginning his post at the Serious Crimes Squad had proved to be less of a wrench. It was pretty normal for officers to be posted from one division to another following a promotion but Lorimer had been the DCI in a Glasgow division just down the road from police headquarters for a goodly length of time and he knew he would miss his fellow officers there. Niall Cameron was moving on, too, becoming a DI out in Motherwell this month; it would not be his final posting by any means, Lorimer thought. The tall young man from Lewis would go far by his reckoning. But it wasn't only the officers that he would miss. Wee Sadie Dunlop, the mouthy woman who served in the police canteen, was someone who had been special to him as well. Wee Sadie told it as it was, he recalled with a smile, addressing the most junior recruits right up to the Divisional Commander as 'son' or 'hen'. Still, it wasn't too far away for him to pop in and have a bite to eat now and then, was it? The canteen here was far noisier than the one at his old headquarters and Lorimer would have to become accustomed to the press of folk at lunchtimes, forensic scientists and a large civilian population sharing the facilities with the officers from Strathclyde Police. He'd have a look in the canteen for some decent Danish pastries, the sort that wee Sadie used to keep for him.

As if by thought transference, a knock came at the door and a smiling, grey-haired woman appeared, bearing a tray with coffee and a plate of chocolate biscuits.

'Good morning, sir, here you are,' she beamed. 'Thought you'd like something to warm you up. Isn't it a chilly one this morning?' She cocked her head to one side, beady bird-like eyes twinkling at him as though something amused her.

Lorimer came forward as the woman laid the tray on a low table next to the window. Shaking her hand, he scrutinised the woman's face. A nice homely sort of woman, he thought, with her green tweed skirt and a thick jumper that looked hand-knitted, but for the life of him Lorimer could not recall having met her before.

'And you are . . .?' he asked, hoping she would give him some sort of clue as to her position in the administrative hierarchy. Was she a secretary? Or part of the civilian staff?

'Don't think you remember me, do you?' she laughed. 'We met once, a long time ago when I was on a course at Tulliallan. I'm Rita Livingstone, your IO,' she smiled.

Lorimer's mouth fell open for a moment. How could he have made such a mistake? Wasn't he always lecturing other people about the need to distinguish a person's appearance from the realities of their character and abilities? Rita Livingstone, he remembered the name now, but could not recall any previous meeting. His intelligence officer! And here he had been thinking she was some wee Glasgow wifie bringing in his coffee. *Rapped knuckles, Lorimer*, he told himself, noticing the two cups and saucers laid out on the tray.

'Shall I be mother?' Rita asked as Lorimer noticed the corners of her mouth turn up in a smile of mischief.

'Thanks,' he said weakly. 'Please, sit here,' he added, taking a seat on one of the easy chairs that flanked the coffee table.

'I'm sorry,' he said, picking up a cup of steaming black coffee. 'I really didn't remember you from that course.'

Rita shook her head, still smiling. 'No worries, sir. And sorry I missed you when you came in with Joyce Rogers. I was in and out of the office that day. You'd hardly have had time to take in who you'd met and who was missing amongst your new colleagues. Plus the fact that some of them were skiving off doing last minute Christmas shopping,' she added, her eyes crinkling up at the corners. For a moment Lorimer smiled as Rita suddenly reminded him of a favourite aunt of his who had been a mine of information about so many things, both fascinating and completely trivial.

'Did you have a nice time, yourself? I love Christmas, don't you?' she rattled on, eyeing him all the time as though she were here to take the measure of this tall man who had been appointed head of their department.

'Yes, thanks. Probably quieter than for most folk,' he told her. 'We have no children,' he added. Better to get that out in the open from the start, he thought, Maggie's recent hysterectomy having sounded the knell on any fleeting hopes they might once have had.

'They're a mixed blessing,' Rita told him with a canny look in her eye. 'Better none than ones who go astray,' she added in a certain tone that gave Lorimer the impression that his IO's home life might not be picture perfect, despite her comments about loving the festive season.

'I was thinking of having the entire team in tomorrow evening,' he said, deciding that this was a woman he could confide in.

'Good idea,' Rita answered. 'Tom and Duncan are away on that case down at Gairloch but most of the others should be able to make it for, what time did you have in mind? Seven-thirty, maybe?'

LATER, ONCE SHE had left, Lorimer drew out the personnel file from his desk drawer. Tom Armstrong was one of three detective inspectors on the team. Lorimer had met *him*, at any rate, he remembered, casting his mind back to a thick-set man with receding hair. Armstrong had greeted him in a friendly enough manner, he thought, recalling the day they had met. The others were DI Duncan Sutherland and DI Monica Proctor. His memory of Proctor was of a sharp-suited blonde who had seemed pretty young to be already at that rank. Sutherland he had yet to meet. Four detective sergeants and the same number of detective constables, plus the IO and several civilian staff that they shared with other departments brought the total of his working colleagues to more than a dozen.

He flipped over the pages, reading their résumés and wondering about the different skills each had brought to the job. It was interesting to note how few of them had been fast tracked after university. Most had chosen the police as a career in their twenties, having had different jobs elsewhere. Martin Gray, one of his detective sergeants, had been a PE teacher in Ross-shire before educational spending cuts had forced him to choose between leaving the area and finding an alternative career.

Lorimer sighed. There was something disquieting in having all of these officers off on cases while he was here inside this building, waiting for something to happen. *Be careful what you wish for* was a cliché with some modicum of truth, he reminded himself. Hadn't he wished for promotion before now? Stepping into his old boss's shoes had once been the height of Lorimer's ambition, and he'd seen his chance when George had retired. But it had been Mark Mitchison, a man with whom Lorimer had never rubbed along, who had been granted that particular appointment. Now he was here, with several high-profile cases to his name, not just having attained the rank of detective superintendent but with this prestigious department under his control. And yet he was restless already.

Slipping the file back into his desk drawer, Lorimer spotted a hard backed black notebook. It was a brand new diary with the crest of Strathclyde Police embossed on its cover. A slip of paper fluttered towards the floor. Swiping it with the toe of his shoe, Lorimer retrieved the bit of paper and saw immediately that it had his name on it. Someone had probably put them into all the desk drawers of senior officers before the year's end. The book had clearly not been opened so there was probably nothing yet written into his day. Lorimer flicked the thin pages just in case. No. Today's date was still pristine. He leaned back, wondering how to spend the rest of his first day when there had been no commands from on high nor even any need for him to remain in the office.

After tomorrow he would be getting to know his new colleagues, though over his term of leave he had already familiarised himself with the current cases in which Serious Crimes were involved. But perhaps this might just be the opportunity he had been looking for, he thought. Could he take a wee trip over to the Lexus dealership, see what they had on offer? Maybe he could surprise his wife with the news that he had at last decided to trade in the ancient dark blue car that had taken him on so many investigations.

Today Maggie was finally returning to work, her GP having advised that she take several weeks off to recover from her surgery. Lorimer wondered how she was coping after so much time away from school. Perfectly well, most likely, he told himself. Maggie Lorimer was well thought of in the secondary school where she taught English and well liked by her colleagues. There had been a flurry of Christmas cards from staff and pupils alike, many of the latter expressing how much they missed their favourite teacher.

Lorimer's smile widened as he remembered Christmas Day. They had spent the afternoon with Rosie, Solly and baby Abigail in their large, airy flat overlooking Kelvingrove Park. It had been a day quite unlike any other Christmas that he and Maggie could remember, Abigail being passed from one to the other, her little face lighting up in a grin as he dandled her over his knees. It was something of a privilege to have this little girl in their lives, especially as they knew now they would never have a child of their own. He and Maggie had spent a fortune buying baby clothes and gifts, but that was okay; godparents were allowed to indulge their little ones, weren't they? Rosie was still on maternity leave but had warned him that she intended to return to her post as consultant forensic pathologist by the summer. Jacqui White was doing a reasonable job of covering for her but Rosie fretted that too much of that young woman's time was being taken up in front of the television cameras. And not for the right reasons.

When the telephone rang, Lorimer blinked away the vision of Professor Solomon Brightman's flat with its massive Christmas tree and returned to the room he must call his own as head of Serious Crimes.

'Detective Superintendent Lorimer speaking,' he said, realising suddenly that he was not completely accustomed to stating his new rank.

The voice on the other end of the line belonged to DCI Mumby from K Division out in Paisley. Lorimer listened carefully as the man outlined a recent murder case and the parallel with one from Dumbarton that still remained unsolved.

'Certainly sounds like the same MO,' Lorimer agreed. 'What does DI Preston make of it?' He listened, doodling on a pad in front of him as Mumby explained that Preston had requested that both cases be assigned to him as SIO. Yet, as his senior, Mumby felt that he should be taking control of a case that fell within his own jurisdiction.

'Quite a while apart, though, aren't they?' Lorimer told him, playing devil's advocate to see how Mumby would react as much as anything. 'Late summer and now the middle of winter.'

He could hear the exasperation in Mumby's voice as the DCI strove to explain just how many parallels there were in the two murders: both men came from south of the border on business, had driven the same make of car (a white Mercedes SL); and had parked below railway bridges several miles from the city centre where they had booked into hotels. And, of course, there was the MO, a shot at close range to the heart. So far there had been no forensic evidence to give a clue as to the perpetrator of either killing, suggesting that they had been carried out by someone who was forensically aware.

'So, what are you looking for?' Lorimer asked. 'A mediator between yourself and DI Preston, or someone to take the entire investigation off your hands?'

Everyone in the force knew that Serious Crimes existed to conduct investigations into a range of criminal activity throughout Strathclyde region. Their caseload at present included a drug cartel and an investigation into money laundering activities as well as an internal inquiry into possible sabotage at the Ministry of Defence at Gairloch.

The first day into the job and murder was already knocking on his door, he thought wryly, acknowledging that his own time in the force had brought him investigations into several high-profile serial killings.

'There's no apparent reason for these men's deaths,' Mumby began slowly and Lorimer could hear a wheeze in the DCI's voice, suggesting he was suffering from a bad cold. 'One of my officers suggested that a night-time watch be made on railway bridges across the city, but of course that's out of the question given the current budgetary constraints,' he continued, pausing to cough away from the telephone.

'And there's no connection at all between Wardlaw and Little-john?' Lorimer wanted to know.

'None that we can find, sir,' Mumby replied. 'My officers have been over all of that ground with a fine toothcomb, believe me,' he said firmly.

Lorimer thought for a minute. 'Okay,' he said at last. 'Send the files over and we'll have a look at them.'

He put down the telephone. There had been no promises made to the officer and no decisions taken. Whether this particular pair of shootings found its way under the auspices of the Serious Crimes Squad remained to be seen.

DCI MUMBY REACHED into his desk for a honey and lemon pastille. It was as much as he could reasonably expect from Lorimer. Could twice amount to more than a coincidence? he asked himself, echoing the words of DC Knox who had wanted officers posted at a series of railway bridges *just in case*. A third time would look like sheer carelessness on the part of the police, the young woman had insisted. She had enthused about local squads making detours from their routes to look out for any parked cars under the bridges' shadowed arches. Far too time-consuming and expensive, Mumby had snorted, and he knew he was right.

What neither the detective constable nor the DCI could have known, however, was that the killer's next location would be well away from the echoing embrace of those curving stones below a railway line.

Chapter Six

THE GARAGE WAS situated near St George's Cross, a five-minute drive from Pitt Street. Lorimer parked his old Lexus by the edge of the MOT bay, feeling the driver's seat give a little, and hearing a creak, as he got out. A new car would take a while to become as familiar as this old friend, he thought, shaking his head at his foolish sentimentality. The midnight blue car had received its fair share of scrapes and scratches over the years and had recently developed a taste for oil on an alarming scale. It was time, long past time, Lorimer told himself, to trade it in for a newer model with a lower mileage.

He walked through the showroom, admiring the huge four by fours and wondering what Maggie would say if he rolled up in one of those. The price tags were far beyond what he wanted to pay anyway, he told himself, moving out into the yard where there were rows of second-hand saloons and hatchbacks. A black Mercedes caught his eye and he walked around, admiring it, wondering if he wanted a complete change. It was a chunky beast, built for durability rather than the good looks of the S class, he thought, wandering along the rows, looking out for the familiar Lexus logo.

He found it at the very end of the row, parked slightly at an angle from the rest of the cars as though someone had recently driven it there. Lorimer nodded, a smile forming on his lips. The silver car had the sleek lines that he liked and, peering into the interior, his smile broadened into a grin as he caught sight of the walnut fascia and polished metal gear stick. It was lust at first sight, Lorimer knew, and any misgiving he might have had about relinquishing his old faithful vanished as he was filled with a sudden desire to drive, no, to *own* this car.

There was no sticker across the windscreen and for a moment his heart sank. *If you have to ask how much it is you can't afford it*, his old dad used to tell him sternly. But that was when he was a boy, wasn't it? Now as a man of almost forty, recently promoted to a senior position in Strathclyde Police, he might well be able to afford this lovely set of wheels.

'Can I help you, sir?' A young man was suddenly at his side and Lorimer smiled, recognising him as one of the fellows who sometimes booked his Lexus in for its service.

'DCI Lorimer, isn't it?' the man smiled, putting out a hand.

'Detective Superintendent since the beginning of this year,' Lorimer smiled, shaking his hand.

'Congratulations, sir,' the salesman said. 'Thinking of trading the old girl in?'

Lorimer sighed. 'Aye, it's well past time I did that. Been too busy,' he shrugged. 'But since I had a little time to spare this morning . . .' He tailed off, looking back at the silver Lexus, his expression betraying naked longing.

'That's a lovely car,' the salesman said, walking around and nodding in admiration. 'Just came in last night on a trade-in and we haven't even had it valeted yet.'

'Any notion how much . . .?'

'Depends on what we give you for yours, of course, but tell you what. Why don't I get the keys and some trade plates and we can go for a test drive. If you have time, of course.'

Less than half an hour later Lorimer found himself seated in front of the salesman's desk, his signature already on several different documents.

'Should be able to collect it by the end of this week,' the salesman said, smiling happily. 'And we'll have it taxed for a full year as discussed.'

'What about the old car? Do you think you'll be able to find a buyer for it?'

The salesman shook his head. 'It'll most likely go to one of the car auctions.' He shrugged and gave a sympathetic smile. 'Big mileage like that. We wouldn't be able to sell it on from here, I'm afraid.'

LORIMER SAT AT a set of traffic lights, his eyes wandering over the old car. Somehow the things that had spelled familiarity now looked simply dusty and worn and his mind shot back to the silver 300 series that he had just purchased. It was the start of a new year and a new job. Time for a change, he decided, accelerating across the junction and heading back to work.

MAGGIE LORIMER PULLED the handbrake and sat back against the driver's seat with a sigh. A few moments of stillness were what she wanted, just a few moments sitting there, letting the noise and tension of the journey drift away as she listened to music. The CD had been played to death but Nicola Benedetti's recording of the Mendelssohn concerto still had the power to make her feel that life was good and some things worth the effort. As the rain streamed down the windscreen, she could see a blur of yellow amidst the green; winter jasmine cascading across her doorway, its tiny star-shaped flowers winking beyond this downpour, sheltered by the roofline.

As the last strains of the violin ceased, Maggie smiled and leaned forwards to press the off button then thrust open the door, ready to make a dash for the house. Shaking the water off her rain-coat, she hung it across the line of hooks in the hall before turning into the open-plan room that led to her kitchen. A cup of decaf and a wee scone, she thought, her eyes flicking towards the blue flowered tin where she kept her home baking.

Inside, everything was just as she had left it that morning, with one exception. Curled into a round ginger ball, Chancer the cat was asleep on top of the pile of fresh laundry that Maggie had taken out of the tumble dryer that morning.

'Oh, Chancer!' she sighed, noting the paw prints all over a cream-coloured fitted sheet; but the cat simply opened one eye, stretched out a front leg then curled back to sleep, a deep purr expressing his satisfaction at her return.

'Bad puss,' Maggie scolded, not really meaning it, her fingers already caressing the cat's soft fur.

Later, sitting in her favourite rocking chair, her hands clasping the steaming mug of coffee, Maggie reflected on her first day back at work. When Bill came home she would tell him that everything had gone well, not wishing to bother him with things that had been less than pleasant. Like the new woman in their department who had come to provide cover for her during her absence and had somehow managed to inveigle her way into staying on for the remainder of the term. She'd been given Maggie's room and had taken down all of her favourite posters, leaving them to gather dust in an untidy heap on top of the cupboard.

Maggie felt her cheeks burn with indignation as she remembered how Lena Forsyth had slapped down her diary on her desk (*her* desk, not Lena's!) and made her look at the class lesson plans that had been created, as though Mrs Lorimer were a probationer who didn't yet know the ropes. The woman's effrontery had continued as Lena had suggested (no, not *suggested*, thought Maggie, *insisted* was a better word to describe her manner) that Maggie continue to follow her recommendations to the letter. From the first glance Maggie could see that this teacher had been chancing her arm, failing to follow several guidelines as well as having done very little in the way of issuing and marking written work. Her mouth narrowed as she remembered how she had sidestepped the woman's commands. She would drop a hint to her head of department when the time was right but for now Maggie knew she would simply have to put up with Lena's strident manner, especially since they were to share the responsibility for two first-year classes. It had irked her to see that Lena would have use of her classroom during some of Maggie's non-teaching periods. To make matters worse, the new member of staff had spent what seemed the entire lunch break talking in a loud voice about her Christmas skiing holiday in France. At least Maggie would only have to endure her till the end of term. Then she could regain total control of her classes and her beloved classroom.

Pity she didn't manage to break her leg, Sandy, Maggie's friend, had muttered. Ah, dear Sandy! It had been good to catch up with her pal again. Sandy, one of the Business Studies teachers, had an acerbic tongue that made Maggie chortle with glee whenever a few apposite words were thrown out to describe one of their fellow colleagues. She was an excellent mimic, too, and could give a few of the staff a red face whenever they became too full of themselves.

Maggie yawned, suddenly wearied by the day's events. She closed her eyes, stretched out her feet and, in a matter of minutes, was fast asleep.

THERE WAS NO reply to his usual 'Hi!' as Lorimer stepped into the house and locked the door behind him, shutting out the biting wind. Shrugging off his winter coat, the policeman listened intently for the domestic noises that usually came from the kitchen at this time of the evening, but there were none.

'Maggie?' His voice held a note of anxiety as Lorimer walked through the doorway into their study-cum-dining room. He stopped next to her rocking chair, his expression softening as he spotted his wife lying asleep. Reaching down, he smoothed her unruly dark curls away from her face, but that small movement disturbed her and Lorimer felt a pang of regret as she blinked and yawned, wishing he could have let her rest a little longer.

'What time is it?' she asked sleepily, gazing up at him.

'It's gone seven,' Lorimer replied.

'Oh dear. Sorry about that,' Maggie yawned again. 'Haven't even started dinner yet.'

Lorimer hunkered down at her side. 'Tell you what. How about a fish supper, eh? I can be at the chippie and back by the time you've got the kettle on and warmed the plates. Okay?'

Maggie smiled and nodded, taking his outstretched hand in hers. 'Ooh, you're cold. Sure you want to go back out there again?'

'No worries.' He hesitated, looking at her sleepy eyes.

'What's your first day been like?' she asked, stroking his fingers.

'Tell you all about it later. There's an interesting double murder case but I don't know if we'll take it on,' he added with a wry smile. He dropped a kiss on her forehead. 'See you in a bit,' he told her, then straightened his long frame and stood up. He'd save the news about his new car for later.

Outside the wind had gathered strength; the trees in next door's garden were being whipped sideways and Lorimer struggled to button his coat as he headed towards the Lexus. It wasn't a night to put a dog out but in every part of this city there would be officers driving or on foot, their job taking them into some of the seediest parts of Glasgow as the offices closed and the night life began. He'd done his share of foot slogging as a young uniformed copper and could still remember how his trousers would turn stiff and hard with hours of constant rain lashing against them. As he drew in to the kerb by the chippie he spotted a young girl shivering in an office doorway, her short jacket barely covering a flimsy dress and sparkly tights. Her pallid complexion and stick-thin arms were a dead giveaway. Was she waiting for a punter? Or simply craving her next fix? Location seemed of no importance now; even in what was considered respectable suburbia there were lassies who had succumbed to the relentless pull of some drug or other. Tonight there would be young policemen and women walking around their beats, some of them taking in the pends and cobbled lanes that comprised the red light district, or drag, as it was usually called. Not his business, he told himself, heading into the shop. But the image of the girl outside in the rain stayed in his mind.

As Lorimer stood waiting for his order in the steamy warmth of the chip shop he thought about these women who sold their bodies for a quick fix of heroin. Over the years, thanks to schemes like Routes out of Prostitution, Strathclyde Police had helped to reduce the hundreds of prostitutes on the streets and now there was barely a tenth of the number that had been on the game when he had been a new recruit.

'Three fish suppers,' he said, wondering if he was daft and if the lassie would even be there when he emerged from the shop or if Chancer would be getting an extra special treat tonight.

Lorimer held the vinegary parcel close to his chest as he left the shop, his eyes immediately drawn to the empty doorway.

So, she'd gone.

Looking up the street he could see two figures, one whose skimpy dress was blowing all ways in the vagabond wind; the other the dark-coated figure of a man clinging to her as if for support. Her pimp? A punter? Her dad, perhaps? Telling himself once more that it was none of his business, Lorimer shoved the food onto the passenger seat and drove off into the lashing rain.

Chapter Seven

IT HAD BEEN a night like this when she had died. A bleak night of wind and rain battering against the sheets of corrugated iron that had served as a backdrop to the crime scene. Carol's body had lain for ages, soaked through, until those police officers had found her and called for an ambulance. *Amazing that she had been able to survive for so long*, one of them had remarked later, as though it was the junk in her veins rather than her own resilience that had kept her lingering for those few hours.

The injuries did not bear thinking about, but she had made herself look and learn them by heart, as though remembering was the single most important thing to do. When that call had come she had hurried out right away – a night-time scurried panic through near-empty streets, leaving the car parked any old how, running, running through the hospital corridors until she came to that small cubicle with its dingy yellow curtains drawn around the bed. It had afforded Carol scant privacy, especially with the constant noise of trolleys being wheeled past and some man in the cubicle next to theirs yelling in drunken incoherence.

Carol had woken just once, her head turned so that she knew who was sitting next to her, holding her hand. She would never forget that ghost of a smile under the dim lighting; it was as if the dying woman knew that it was only a matter of time before she would slip back into an unconsciousness from which she would never awaken.

'Who did this to you?' she had whispered, aware of the uniformed police officer standing just feet away from them, listening beyond the curtain.

A slight rise in her eyebrows was probably answer enough but Carol had managed to utter a few words. 'Some punter,' she'd said, the words hardly audible as her breath came in painful gasps. 'Picked me up at Blythswood . . .' Tears had filled her eyes as she remembered. 'Stranger . . . Not from here.'

'Can you tell me anything else about him?' she'd demanded, squeezing Carol's hand as tightly as she dared, urging her to give her something, anything that would help to nail the bastard.

'Hurt me,' she'd whispered, her eyelids flickering. Was she sinking rapidly into that darkness? But, no, she had opened her eyes, looked straight at her, focusing on a different memory. 'Tell my . . . mum . . . I'm sorry,' Carol had wheezed, then that bubble of blood had appeared at her mouth and the terrible sound deep within her chest as though some subterranean creature was trying to escape from her ruined body.

Then the alarm bell had begun its insistent beeping and she had been ushered out firmly, several white-coated professionals filling that tiny space around Carol's bed.

It was still strange to recall how quickly it had all been over. The next time she had seen Carol there was a clean white sheet drawn up to her chin, hiding those other horrific knife wounds, and she appeared to be simply asleep, her face turned slightly to one side, mouth half-open as though she still had things to say.

Later, as she sat in the Accident and Emergency waiting room clutching a cardboard cup of milky tea, she had overheard two of the uniformed policemen talking about Carol. *That prostitute*, one of them had said and she had seen the indifferent shrug of the shoulders by the other. That was all she had been to them: a woman from the drag, a junkie out for her next fix, the dross of society that they had to sweep away as part of their bloody job.

She'd set down the tea on the floor by the metal chair, then turned deliberately on her heel and left, a rage boiling inside her that made her want to smash her fist into someone's face. And what had transpired afterwards? Not a hell of a lot; the senior investigating officer had made lots of noises via the press but they'd never found Carol Kilpatrick's killer. She'd given up on the police eventually, doing her own investigation, talking to folk like Tracey-Anne who had been with Carol that night. Listening as the girl had told her things she hadn't mentioned to the police. *A white Mercedes, big sports job*, Tracey-Anne had told her. *Aye, that wan*, she'd said, her finger jabbing on the brochure she'd picked up from the dealership in Milton Street. The SL, a sporty car that had been the rich man's favourite for decades. Anger had energised her, made her seek out things she feared the police had overlooked.

Well, she thought, listening to the rain beat down on the skylight window; that anger was controlled now and had a direction and focus that would eventually bring Carol's killer to the sort of justice he deserved.

Chapter Eight

'HELL'S TEETH!'

DCI Helen James grabbed her stomach and lurched forwards. The nagging pain that had resisted several packs of Rennies over the past week was now tearing into her guts with a ferocity that took the senior officer's breath away.

'Ma'am?' One of her detective constables was approaching her, an expression of alarm on his face as Helen staggered from her office, one hand waving feebly to warn him off.

The projectile vomit was nothing short of spectacular, splattering a vast swathe of the floor outside her room as well as catching the unfortunate officer's well-polished shoes.

'Get me an ambulance,' Helen croaked, doubling up once again as the pain creased her insides.

It was only later as she was being wheeled to the operating theatre that Helen remembered where she should have been and what she ought to have been doing, but by then the pre-med had taken effect and she could only pray that Tracey-Anne would be sensible and do what she had advised.

THE DROP-IN CENTRE was a haven for girls like Tracey-Anne who used it at night. The older women with more experience tended to keep to the evening hours of seven till eleven, though desperation for a fix sometimes forced them back out in the wee small hours of darkness. Tracey-Anne sat swinging her leg up and down, up and down as the jitters began to take hold. She shivered under her fake fur coat, wishing that she had put on a few more clothes, but hey, the punters couldn't be bothered to unwrap layer upon layer as they searched for their honey pot.

'You awright, hen?' A dark-haired woman lurched towards Tracey-Anne, the mug of tea in her hand threatening to tip sideways. 'C'n I sit here?' the woman added, plonking herself down on the chair opposite without waiting for a reply.

'Aye,' Tracey-Anne nodded, her leg action becoming faster and faster as her agitation increased. In truth she didn't care if someone sat beside her. Sometimes it paid to hear what the other women said about their punters. They'd moan about ones to avoid, those who threw you out of the car as soon as they'd done the business or the big bruisers who'd had too much to drink and were little more than brute beasts by the time they'd pulled you in.

'Ur you no' the lassie that wis gassin' tae that polis woman?' The woman's thick accent wasn't local, reminding Tracey-Anne of a woman she knew as mad Moira. Falkirk, maybe? Or some place the other side of Edinburgh?

'Aye,' Tracey-Anne agreed, though most of the girls who came here had talked to Helen James at one time or another. So many of her mates were dead and gone, three of them murdered; others lost to the drugs; it was no wonder the polis kept an eye on them all. Helen was there to warn them, she always insisted, wanted

them to avoid dangerous situations, as she put it, so yes, she let
the policewoman buy her the occasional cuppa. But she'd never
spoken again about the night that Carol had been killed. Couldn't
bring herself to go over any of the details, she'd told her, crossing
her fingers under the table. There were some things she'd been
warned to keep entirely to herself. But, aye, the polis wifie was
okay, spoke nice to you an' that. It didn't make you a grass or anything to have a wee blether. Not when the woman was doing her
best for you, handing out leaflets about getting off the game and
into a better place.

'Och, she's awright,' Tracey-Anne shrugged, her eyes passing
over the woman for a moment. She was older than most of the
others, probably somewhere in her forties, her dark hair crimped
around a thin narrow face, shards of rainbow light flashing from
her dangling earrings as she shook her head uncertainly. It was
odd that she had never set eyes on this one before, but then perhaps she was new to the city?

'Are ye not from around here, then?' Tracey-Anne asked.

'Naw,' the woman replied, fixing her with a gimlet stare that
seemed to say that no more questions were welcome.

A tap on the window made both women turn to see who was
there. A man's pale face stared in at them, his breath fogging up
the glass.

Wearily Tracey-Anne rose from her seat, picked up her handbag and headed for the door. Tam was peering at her through the
window, one hand beckoning her over, making it clear that she
should get out of there pronto and go and find her next punter.

'C'mon, hen. C'mon. Whit's keeping' ye?' he demanded, jerk-
ing her from the doorway so that her coat fell open revealing the
thin blouse and short lycra skirt. Tracey-Anne hardly had time to

pull it back around her before he was urging her along Robertson Street.

Tracey-Anne just kept her head down and let him lead her up through the city to her pitch. It was better not to cross Tam when he needed to score. Usually he was too out of his head to be a threat, but sometimes, like tonight, she'd glimpse a mean streak that gave her the feeling he might turn nasty. Just get him the money and he'd leave her alone for the rest of the night. She'd be back at the flat some time, hoping he'd left enough for her. What was it Helen had told her? A vicious circle or something. Well that was right enough, Tracey-Anne thought as they headed up the hill towards Blythswood Square. There was never a good time to come off this drug that held her in its grasp. Never a good time to leave Tam either. Besides, where would she go? Helen's other warnings faded from her mind as she tried to concentrate on the here and now.

The red lights from that fancy hotel twinkled as they approached. Funny how so many posh folk in their big cars came after the likes of her, Tracey-Anne often thought. But then punters were men and men all had that desire between their legs that needed to be satisfied. She felt a jab on her back through the fur coat as Tam staggered suddenly, pushing her against the railing.

'See and get back tae me within the next hour, d'ye hear me? Ah'm jist aboot ready tae top myself,' he warned her, releasing his grasp on her arm at last.

Then, slouching off into the night, Tam left her to shiver once more as she stepped to the edge of this pavement that had become more familiar to her than any home Tracey-Anne really knew.

Be careful, Helen had warned her. *Remember what happened to Carol and the others.* The policewoman's voice came back to her now in the silence of the night.

Tracey-Anne had listened and nodded, hoping that Helen would stop going on about the dangers that certain predatory men posed for a vulnerable woman like herself. Och, but who really cared? So what if someone was to end it all tonight? Nobody would miss her, would they? Not even Tam, who would just find another junkie woman to scrounge off, she thought wearily. Her thoughts were interrupted as the big car rounded one side of the square and slowed almost to a standstill.

Tracey-Anne was at the door, her best smile directed towards the driver, before she had time to consider any of the consequences. It was a punter. He was asking *How much?* And she was already getting into the car, thinking about how easy this was, how soon she could be back at the flat and how marvellous she would feel again when this deadly cold was stopped for a while by the fire rushing through her veins.

THE WOMAN STANDING on the steps of the hotel wrapped her black cashmere coat around her more closely as she watched the car's tail lights vanish over the hill. She had recognised the prostitute, known that she might be recognised herself had she stepped further into her orbit. Maybe it was a good thing that poor, junked-up Tracey-Anne was now using Carol's old pitch. Any punter comparing her to the attractive dark-haired woman who sometimes stood across from her on Blythswood Square would find it easy to choose between them, wouldn't they? But that other woman was not coming out to play tonight, she thought, turning back into the warmth of the hotel. She was biding her time. And it paid to be patient, didn't it? The police inquiries were simply all over the place, officers at a loss as to who had dispatched those two men in their fancy white cars.

She smiled as the duty manager nodded at her. She hadn't been here often enough to have become a familiar figure, a business-woman who patronised their establishment, sometimes staying over, coming and going at odd hours of the night when different members of staff would simply glance as she went past. Had they ever noticed the changes that she went through? The sleek night clubber returning as an insomniac jogger? Possibly not. But per-haps she might think of shifting her custom a little way down the hill to the Malmaison. After all, it paid to be cautious.

TRACEY-ANNE STOOD WITH her back to the road, wiping her hands furiously with the antiseptic wipes she kept in the bag at her feet. Just a hand job. Only a measly tenner, not enough for either Tam or herself to score a bag of gear. And she needed that fix. Oh, dear God how she needed it!

The white car rounded the corner of the square as she straight-ened up. Could her luck be in this time?

For a moment she froze, striving to remember something Helen had told her. Or was it something she had meant to tell Helen? A fugginess like the mist around the lamp post swirled in the young woman's brain. The white car. She should step back and wave it off, shouldn't she? Make that phone call, like she'd prom-ised. But the thought of a whole bag of gear and being back at the flat instead of standing here for hours in the cold made her shake her head as if to dispel any residual fears.

Stepping forward, Tracey-Anne saw the tinted window being rolled down, the shape of a man's head leaning towards her, an arm being raised to open the door.

'Want tae do the business?' she asked, trying to make eye con-tact with the driver.

'Get in,' a heavily accented voice told her. 'I pay double your usual. Okay?'

It was hard to keep the grin off her face as she climbed into the car, taking in its warmth, the rich leathery scent of its interior. She knew a classy car didn't always mean a nice punter, but this one didn't even look at her as she buckled on the seat belt.

Chapter Nine

'WHITE FEMALE. No vital signs. Request doctor at scene and mortuary van.' The officer who stood at the edge of the pavement tried not to look back into the cobbled lane as he spoke into his radio. Finding the woman's body had not been part of his plans for tonight's shift. All he'd expected was a quick recce round the drag, shining his torch into the pends and back courts, then down to the chippie to chat up that new bird, Patricia, who'd been allocated as his neighbour on the beat. Now he was virtually on his own as the rookie cried her eyes out over the road, the victim his responsibility until the duty doctor and the scene of crime officers arrived.

'Sooner the better,' Fraser MacDonald whispered under his breath as he listened to the voice from the control room.

The ground glistened under an early morning frost as PC Mac-Donald turned back to the lane. His boots slipped on the shining cobblestones and he put out one leather gloved hand to the wall beside him to steady himself. They'd almost passed her by, he thought, glancing at the bundle in the corner beside the red industrial garbage bins. A heap of rags, he'd presumed at first, seeing the curled shape, not recognising it as anything human.

What the heck's that? Patricia had asked, waving her torch at it.

Fraser had been on the point of hurrying her on when something had stopped him; some instinct that told him to take a second look. He'd only seen the coat at first; a discarded old furry thing thrown over a heap of other rubbish.

Only it hadn't been a litter dump. When Fraser had lifted the coat he had seen the woman's naked body curled, foetus-like, underneath, the stab wounds livid even in the weak lamplight, blood darkening the ground where she lay. He'd felt for a pulse, knowing as he did that it was a waste of time. Poor bitch was as dead as a doornail. She wasn't anyone he knew, but then, Fraser had reasoned, it was only the second night shift he'd done on this particular beat.

'Get your arse over here,' he growled under his breath at the police officer who stood shivering across the road. 'You'll be expected to be at the scene when the van arrives,' he called louder, so she could hear him. 'You need to have some clue what's going on in case you're cited as a witness later,' he reminded her as she re-entered the lane, still sniffling into a paper hanky.

'I . . . I've never seen a dead body like this before,' the girl mumbled, her eyes flicking over the dead woman in the corner. 'Just the ones in the mortuary,' she added quietly.

'Well you've seen one now,' Fraser snapped, growing increasingly impatient with his colleague. What had she joined up for if she hadn't expected to see things like this? he wondered.

'Look, you need to have a note of the time we arrived here and the actions undertaken. Okay?'

The girl nodded and stuffed the handkerchief back into her uniform pocket.

'Now can you take a look at her? There's nothing to be scared of,' Fraser said, a more gentle tone creeping into his voice as he saw the girl take a deep breath. 'The dead cannae do you any harm. It's the living you need to be wary of,' he told her, touching her sleeve. 'All right?'

The young policewoman drew her torch out once more and shone it over what was now officially a crime scene. Fraser had not replaced the coat and Patricia couldn't help thinking that the dead woman's body looked far too small to be human. As she took a few tentative steps towards it, she saw the open gashes on the sides and back. Blinking hard to focus on what she was seeing, Patricia tried to remember what she had learned in basic training about knife wounds. But her mind refused to let her remember the dispassionate facts that she had written up in her notebook. This was a real person, had been a real living woman just a few hours ago before someone had ravaged her poor body, cutting into vital organs, perhaps. Patricia saw each entry wound, wondering at the kind of person that could harm a poor wee woman like that.

'Don't get too hung up about her,' Fraser said suddenly. 'Remember she was only a prostitute. They're all oot their heads on dope. She probably didn't even feel a thing.'

'How can you say that?' Patricia protested suddenly. 'A prostitute and a junkie she may have been, but once upon a time she was someone's wee girl. Maybe she was even some fellow's wife or girlfriend.'

'Look, hen,' Fraser sighed, 'you need to try to distance yourself from this. Take in the facts. Do your job. That's all. If you get all emotional about every victim of crime you see you'll never be able to cope.'

Fraser saw the look in the woman's eyes as she struggled to reply. There were tears of what? Righteous anger? Self-pity?

'We'll find out all about her in due course. But for now we've got a job to do here. DCI James will want a full report given the other women in her case load. Okay?'

The rookie cop nodded, knowing that what he said was right. The unsolved deaths of several street women had been taxing their Senior Investigating Officer for months now, long before Patricia Fairbairn had joined the force. Patricia raised her head as a squad car appeared at the mouth of the lane then looked up at her neighbour, noting the sense of relief on his face. So he wasn't immune to the total horror of this either. Fraser MacDonald wasn't that much older than she was. Maybe blokes were just better at hiding their feelings. Or maybe she wasn't cut out for this sort of job. Was this really what she had been expecting? The training at Tulliallan had been such fun, a bit like school, really. And she'd been good at school too, hadn't she, with that dream of becoming a police officer always at the front of her mind.

She shrank back against the wall as several officers emerged out of the darkness. Some were clad in white boiler suits, their breath making small clouds in the frozen air. A blue light beating behind them made the figures seem like something from a science fiction movie, the sort that gave her the horrors.

This was the stuff of nightmares, Patricia told herself, shivering. Not the stuff of her daydreams after all.

Chapter Ten

'LORIMER.'

The detective superintendent listened, nodding from time to time as the voice on the other end of the line explained the situation. Not only had DCI James been rushed into hospital for an emergency gall bladder removal but there was one more street woman dead on her patch.

Lorimer knew Helen James. She was the sort of police officer he liked, firm but fair. They had been at Pitt Street together a few months ago, watching the demonstration of some high tech stuff that he'd subsequently used in a case. James had been a mite scathing about the device but it had proved its usefulness after all. How long had it been since that first prostitute murder? A year? Eighteen months? The press coverage had been relentless and he recalled the DCI's drawn face and air of determination. It was something that every senior officer experienced during a murder case. Lack of sleep, lack of evidence, lack of witnesses to come forward, but no shortage of column inches decrying the police for getting nowhere with any of those cases. It was little wonder the woman had suffered some sort of internal disorder. Stress took its toll on so many cops. Ulcers, heart attacks, sudden bouts of depression – these, and James's gall bladder removal, were hardly the stuff for the features pages of the popular press, were they?

Lorimer's frown deepened as he considered the latest in the four murders. Tracey-Anne Geddes had been stabbed in what one of the officers described as a frenzy, a similar MO to that first one, Carol Kilpatrick. There had not been any suggestion until now that the killings could be related even though the girls had all worked on the drag. Miriam Lyons, the second victim, had been pulled out of the Clyde down near Bowling, while Jenny Haslet had been strangled with her own tights and thrown into a back court in Cathcart. Was there enough to justify calling his old friend in on this case?

The policeman's face softened as he thought about Solly. He was Professor Brightman now and father of little Abigail, their god-daughter. Their friendship aside though, Lorimer respected Solly as a professional, and the psychologist's input on a case such as this could make a real difference. Budgetary constraints were worsening by the month but perhaps an initial appraisal by Solly might be justified? Whatever, it looked like this particular lot of murder cases was also to be placed squarely at the door of Serious Crimes. Well, he decided, Mumby and Preston could just battle it out between them over the murder of those two businessmen.

SOLOMON BRIGHTMAN SMILED and sighed as he heard the last of the footsteps receding from his door. It had been a productive morning with interesting classes and this recent tutorial but now he was alone and free at last to pursue his own work. As he gazed out of the tall windows at the road that sloped down past the old university buildings, a gothic statement in darkened sandstone, his eyes searched out a paler block. There was a gateway where, if one turned and walked a few yards, one would come to an insignificant-looking door and a vestibule where a porter might ask what business took one to that particular establishment. But Solly did not need to be asked why he went there or whom he wished to see; everyone in the Department of Forensic Medical Science knew that the professor was the husband of Rosie, one of their very own consultant pathologists. Solly's smile deepened. She was not there right now, of course, but back home caring for baby Abigail, yet the very sight of his wife's place of employment still served to give Solly a warm glow.

Solly turned at last and let his eyes roam over the extensive library that covered an entire wall of the spacious room. There was something he needed to look up, a chapter he had marked with a lurid pink Post-it note somewhere along the shelf third from the top. It was in one of that collection of stiff-backed books with the bevelled spines he had bought at auction, their faded gold lettering meaning he had to peer more closely to see which one he wanted.

Having researched and written a book, albeit a fairly slim volume, about female serial killers, the professor was hoping to follow it up with a history of British crime relating to underage killers. The Jamie Bulger case might seem an obvious one to begin with, given that it had generated more media coverage than any other, but Solly wanted to go back a lot further than that and his reading currently included material from as long ago as the early nineteenth century.

He was nodding with satisfaction as he selected the text that he wanted, his benign smile changing instantly to an expression of mild annoyance as the shrill noise of the telephone interrupted his train of thought.

Placing his book carefully on the huge table that dominated the room, Solly headed towards his desk, anxious to silence the insistent ringing.

'Hello?' he queried politely. 'Professor Brightman speaking.'

'It's me, Lorimer. I've got something that might interest you. Any chance we could meet up?'

Solly blinked, taken by surprise. It had been some time since his friend had asked for his help in a professional capacity. Indeed Strathclyde Police had warned Solly that his services might not be required for future cases. But, he reasoned, that had been before his involvement with the case last autumn, hadn't it? Now the parameters had changed. He was a professor and Lorimer a detective superintendent, the promotions bringing each man some further respect from the police as a whole.

'Solly? Are you still there?' Lorimer's voice sounded impatient and Solly smiled once more. Theirs was an unlikely pairing; the policeman had little time for the lengthy pauses that his friend tended towards, preferring to come straight to the point whenever they discussed a case.

'Yes, still here. What can I do for you?'

'I've got authorisation to have you on a case,' came the reply. 'So it's official, this time.' Lorimer hesitated, knowing as he spoke that Solly would be aware of every nuance of his speech, every tiny space between his words. 'It's the murder of four known Glasgow prostitutes. That's how the press will see it. I'd rather think of it as the brutal murder of four vulnerable young women.

'It's looking a bit complex,' Lorimer went on in a lighter voice, 'so you're bound to like it.'

Solly nodded, responding to the seriousness of his friend's tone. He could imagine the tense expression upon the policeman's face as he spoke.

'Well, as it happens I'm finished with classes for today so ...'

'Good. See you here in half an hour?'

Solly put down the phone, shaking his head slightly. So much for his plans for spending time reading this afternoon, he thought with a sigh. Yet as he packed some papers into his satchel there was a gleam in his dark eyes. A new case with Lorimer: the first since his appointment to the Serious Crimes Squad. Solly locked the door behind him and hurried down the stairs, his mind already on what lay ahead. *A bit complex*, Lorimer had said. Well, that remained to be seen.

HELEN JAMES OPENED her eyes and blinked. It was all over then, she thought. A collage of images filled her mind: the siren sound of the ambulance, the overhead lights in the corridor as she was wheeled into the operating theatre and the man in the blue mask and matching cap who had assured her that everything was going to be fine ...

It was strange how relaxed she felt now after a night of unbroken sleep. Her lips moved towards the semblance of a smile as she caught sight of the drip, felt the drain in her right arm. Well, maybe not that strange after all if they were pumping some nice drugs into her. She sighed but it was not a troubled sigh, more an exhalation of all the worries and troubles that had dogged her for the past months. There was nothing she could do about any of it and the knowledge that someone else must be taking over from her was surprisingly good.

Closing her eyes once more, Helen slipped into a dreamless sleep, happily unaware of the latest in the series of murders that had taken place on her patch.

Outside the hospital room the uniformed police officer glanced at her watch, checking it for the umpteenth time against the clock on the wall above the nurses' station. It was funny to be here, PC Patricia Fairbairn thought to herself. The word was that Serious Crimes was supposed to be taking over and she might have been seconded to Pitt Street as part of the team, yet here she was, waiting for her DCI to waken so she could bring her up to speed with this horrible prostitute killing. Sighing heavily, Patricia stepped across to the glass door, peering in at the figure lying on the bed. No, she didn't seem to be awake yet. She bit her lip. Over and over Patricia had rehearsed the words she would say when her boss was finally awake. If only she would open her eyes so she could get it over with.

Hearing her stomach suddenly rumble, the police constable decided that a visit to the canteen downstairs was in order. With one final glance at the woman who appeared to be sleeping peacefully, Patricia slipped off down the corridor, her thoughts already on a cup of black coffee and whatever calorie laden stuff the hospital canteen might provide.

'You're awake, ma'am,' Patricia said, putting her fingers to her mouth, nervously wiping away any traces of her latest snack.

'So it would appear, Fairbairn,' Helen James said dryly, eyeing the rookie cop who had been landed in her division so recently. 'Nice of you to visit, but perhaps you'd care to tell me why you're here.'

'It's not good news, ma'am,' Patricia said, all her carefully rehearsed speech flying out of the window as she looked down on her boss's pale face. 'There's been another prostitute killing. Just last night. I . . . I was one of the officers on duty who found the body,' she continued, tightening her lips to keep them from betraying her inner trembling.

Helen's fingers gripped the bedclothes and a sharp crease appeared between her eyes. 'Who?'

'Tracey-Anne Geddes, ma'am. She was found when we were patrolling the drag.'

'Oh, God.' Helen turned away so that her young colleague could not see the sudden tears. She blinked rapidly before facing the girl once more.

'Who's the SIO in charge?'

'That's just it, ma'am,' Patricia told her. 'It's gone up to Serious Crimes. Detective Superintendent Lorimer has taken it on now.'

'Lorimer . . .' Helen sighed heavily, sinking back into the comforting softness of her bank of pillows. 'Well, that's some relief.'

'Who *is* he, ma'am?' Patricia Fairbairn asked, coming forward to scrutinise her boss's face. She'd expected a sudden fury from the SIO, outrage at the very least that the case that had commanded so many man hours was being shipped off to Serious Crimes.

Helen James turned to the young policewoman and gave a smile that lit up her face, softening all its harsh lines and angles. 'William Lorimer is one of the best senior officers around,' she said. 'And you'll find that out, young lady, if you're ever lucky enough to be part of his team.'

'Professor Brightman,' the officer behind the desk smiled at the bearded man standing waiting for his security pass. 'Good to see you, sir.'

Solly nodded and smiled. The officer had recognised him from the previous visits he had made to this building, often to discuss the finer points of a case with the hierarchy that comprised the top brass here in Pitt Street. But now he was here at the behest of the man who was heading up the Serious Crimes Squad.

'Solly!'

He turned to see a tall man who was crossing the foyer and, before he knew it, his hands were enfolded in a firm grasp.

'Lorimer. Hello,' Solly said, smiling as he nodded at his friend.

'Come on up,' Lorimer told him. 'See my new domain,' he chuckled. The two men chatted as they ascended the stairs to the upper floor where the Serious Crimes Squad had its share of a long corridor.

DETECTIVE SUPERINTENDENT LORIMER was emblazoned in gold lettering on the wooden door, Solly noticed. He nodded to himself, recognising that this man's promotion was well deserved given his track record. And, he thought to himself, who better to head up a unit devoted to serious crimes than the man whose determination and skills had solved so many of them?

'Not bad,' the psychologist smiled, looking around the room. It was fairly large and airy, given that the blinds were pulled all the way up and the winter sun was making a valiant attempt to penetrate this side of the building. Two easy chairs flanked a low coffee table and the detective superintendent's desk dominated one end of the room, its blond wood already piled with papers and files.

'Hard at it already?' he asked, pointing at the mass of paperwork.

'Aye, plenty for me to do and, as usual, never enough time in which to do it, but at least I've got my own manpower and the ability to call on various divisions within the force.' Lorimer grinned.

'You haven't put up any pictures yet,' Solly remarked, his eyes scanning the walls that were bare of any decoration save a large calendar depicting a Scottish scene.

'Michael MacGregor?' he asked, recognising the photographer who had taken the snowy landscape.

'Yes,' Lorimer replied. 'Once again my dear wife has given me something for Christmas that she knows I'll enjoy. He paused for a moment, looking at the photograph of Rannoch Moor. Mac-Gregor was his favourite Scottish photographer, his ability to capture the magical qualities of a landscape something that the policeman greatly admired. 'Och, I'll get around to putting up my prints sometime,' he told Solly, cocking his head at the stack of pictures propped up in a corner, still in their brown paper wrappings. 'Have to make do with this and the charts for now.'

He strolled over to a large map of Glasgow taped to the wall to one side of his desk and indicated four red rings. 'These are all scenes of crime,' he told the psychologist. 'I want you to have a copy of this,' he added. 'So you can do all your stuff with locations and whatever.'

'Perhaps we could begin with a discussion about the victims first,' Solly remarked mildly.

'Aye.' Lorimer ran a hand through his dark hair, letting it flop over his forehead. 'Four victims,' he nodded, taking a file from the desk and coming to sit beside his friend. With a sigh that told Solly more than mere words would allow, he began to outline the young women's murders.

'Such a waste,' Lorimer murmured. 'Wee lassies on the game because they had to stick that stuff into their veins.' His voice was low but Solly could hear the outrage in his tone, an outrage that any right-minded citizen would surely share.

'Were they all very young, then?' Solly asked, the phrase *wee lassies* commanding his attention.

'It began more than eighteen months ago,' Lorimer said, choosing not to answer that particular question directly. 'First victim was a twenty-year-old woman name of Carol Kilpatrick.' He held out a photograph and Solly looked at the picture of a thin girl with badly dyed blonde hair, dark roots showing either side of her parting. She was smiling at the camera, pink lips curled as though saying *cheese* for the person behind the lens, but that smile had not reached her light blue eyes where an expression of sadness made Solly wonder what sort of suffering this girl had endured in her young life.

'She was found in a lane just along the road.' Lorimer jerked his finger at the door. 'Less than five minutes' walk from this place.' He let the implication of his words sink in. Pitt Street might represent the bastion of law and order but there were plenty of dodgy areas close by; the juxtaposition of light and darkness, good and evil, in this city was something that was not lost on the detective superintendent. Nor was the savagery of some of the city's killers.

'Raped and then stabbed several times. But she was still alive when she was discovered at the scene,' he added, taking more photographs from the file and handing them over to Solly. 'Died in hospital later that night.'

Solly took the copies of the various photos, blinking at the images of a young female: some were close-up shots taken by the pathologist, a ruler placed strategically to show the extent of the stab wounds and vaginal bruising, while others depicted various angles of the cobbled lane where the attack had taken place. There were no aerial shots, he noticed, probably too difficult to obtain in a narrow alley like that.

It was a horrific way to die; alone, vulnerable and no doubt gagging for her next fix. He made himself examine the photographs once more, concentrating on what she must have felt as much as who had wanted to make her suffer like this.

'Any leads at all in this case?' Solly asked, looking up.

Lorimer shook his head.

'No. But not for lack of hard graft on the part of DCI James and her team, I can promise you that. Still, there isn't much in the way of forensic evidence. The killer had evidently worn gloves and taken the precaution of using a condom.'

'There was nothing useful at all, then?'

'There were traces of sweat found on the victim's body that might be useable should we ever find a suspect,' Lorimer conceded.

The psychologist nodded his dark head, his bushy beard giving him the look of an Old Testament sage. He knew what the detective was thinking. Making a match was what this particular science was all about. Even if they had found loads of useable DNA it amounted to nothing until that vital equation was made. Now his own branch of scientific thought would have to come into play as he sought out something that might have been missed, or strove to see a picture that might have been obscured by other matters.

'You can have a copy of the crime file notes,' Lorimer told him. 'See things like the history of the victim and where she usually stood waiting for punters.'

'And where she lived,' Solly added.

Lorimer gave a grimace. 'Afraid that was a women's hostel. They come and go in places like that and according to the files there was nobody who could tell the investigation team very much about the victim.'

'What about her family?'

Lorimer shook his head again. 'That's another tragic thing. Her family apparently disowned her when she became a heroin addict. Even the formal identification was made by another woman from the drag. So there is very little in the way of information about the victim's background. Parents didn't even attend the funeral,' he added, pointing to a paragraph in the notes.

'But surely . . .?' Solly bit his lip. What had he been about to say? Surely anyone would want to see their loved one put to rest? Well, perhaps all this family had wanted was to block out the horror, especially in the wake of what publicity there had been.

'DCI James was quite sure there was no reason for thinking that the second and third victims were killed by the same perpetrator,' Lorimer continued, passing over the case files about Miriam Lyons and Jenny Haslet.

'You might find this one a bit close to home,' he went on, nodding at the file marked LYONS. 'Girl was a well-brought-up lassie from Newton Mearns. Family were devout Jews,' he said, with the hint of a smile. Lorimer knew fine that Solomon Brightman no longer visited the synagogue as part of his Jewish faith, but the religion was something he could respect and understand, especially as his own parents were still practising Jews.

'Miriam,' Solly said softly, 'the older sister who put Moses into a basket in the water. How sad that she should have been left to die like that.'

'Hope you're not going to start seeing obscure symbolism in this,' Lorimer said darkly. 'Miriam was on the game for the same reason as Carol and the others. Got hooked on junk and had to fund her habit,' he said, his mouth twisting in distaste.

'You disapprove of the street girls?' Solly asked, his bushy eyebrows raised in surprise.

'I'd like to see every last one of them off the streets, same as Helen James wanted,' Lorimer muttered. 'Somewhere they could be safe from any predatory males. It's a damn sight better than it used to be,' he added, 'but while there is still one wee lassie out there selling her body for a fix then we're not doing our job properly.'

'We?'

Lorimer sighed. 'Och I don't just mean the police. It's society as a whole. Nobody wants to think about things like that going on under their noses. At least till something like this happens,' he said, tapping the photo of Miriam Lyons after she had been taken out of the Clyde by the riverman.

'What would you like me to do?' Solly asked, suddenly aware of the passion in his friend's voice.

'I know exactly what I'd like you to do,' Lorimer answered. 'See if Helen James was wrong. There's way too much similarity in the MOs of Geddes and Kilpatrick. The other two girls worked the drag as well. It's just the way they died and the place where their bodies were found that set them apart.'

'What about DNA traces?'

Lorimer shook his head again. 'None on Lyons due to the length of time she had been in the river and, according to her notes, Helen James thinks that whoever strangled Jenny Haslet must also have been forensically aware.'

Solly put his fist to his lips, pondering. Lorimer was already involved in this in a big way, he thought. Was it to do with it being his first major case in this new job? Or was the policeman's natural instinct for justice asserting itself? Lorimer was a man capable of feeling great pity for murder victims, Solly knew, and would treat these poor, vulnerable women with as much compassion as any other girl who had been brutalised.

Chapter Eleven

THE MALMAISON HOTEL was a short walk from the red brick building that comprised police headquarters, a fact that amused rather than intimidated her. It was in direct contrast to the large façade of the Blythswood where she had spent these other few nights, being tucked away on the sloping hillside, though in truth both hotels had been landmarks in the city for quite different reasons in the past. While the Blythswood owed its history to the Royal Automobile Club, this smaller place had once been a Greek Orthodox Church. Any religious connotation seemed long gone, however, as she stepped into the foyer, noting the chequered carpet in purple and beige.

'Any chance of a coffee?' she asked the couple behind the desk.

'Certainly.' The girl looked up from the papers she had been discussing with her colleague and came around to where the tall, dark-haired woman was standing. 'Just through here to the brasserie. Down the spiral staircase,' she added, showing her the way.

Light flooded down from a glass roof to the enclosed courtyard below the wrought iron stairs. She glanced to one side at a pink checked chair, its back rising up into one curved point ending in a black tassel like a jester's cap. It was a quirky bit of styling that made her smile as she walked delicately down to the coffee parlour below. Here there was further evidence of the chequered theme with three small tables topped with chessboards, empty of their playing pieces for now. She was just sliding into a comfortable seat when a blonde waitress approached, pad and pen in hand, a smile on her face that looked totally genuine rather than pasted on for the benefit of the clientele.

'Cappuccino, please,' she said, glancing around at the other tables. Not many people were here at a quarter to midday; a bit too late for morning coffee and not quite time for lunch, she decided. From the adjoining restaurant came the faint sound of saxophone music, a soothing undercurrent of noise to blunt the edge off clinking cups and glasses. She sighed, stretching out her legs. For the first time in days she felt relaxed. It had been a good decision to come here, she thought, gazing up at the sky through the glass roof. White clouds scudded across it, blown by an easterly wind that had made her glad to leave the windy street and retreat into this welcoming place.

The coffee, when it came, was the best she had tasted anywhere in the city. And the home-baked gingerbread man on the side made a refreshing change from the familiar plastic wrapped biscuit. A small smile made her mouth twitch as she picked it up. One bite and its head was gone. The spicy fragrance curled around her mouth as she chewed and swallowed, breaking off bits of the body until there was only a scattering of brown crumbs left on the plate.

It had tasted good but had given her an entirely different sort of satisfaction from polishing off these men in their posh white cars.

'Can I get you anything else?'

The nice waitress was back again, breaking into her reverie.

'Yes,' she decided. 'Do you have a room?'

THE BEDROOM HAD a stylish interior that echoed the main parts of the hotel, she noticed once the porter had taken his leave. Flinging herself down on the comfortable bed, she smiled and sighed deeply; her decision to stay here had been spot on. Her eyes strayed to the remote control for the television that was within reach and her fingers moved towards it as though by habit.

The BBC news programme showed a familiar female presenter sitting against the backdrop of the river Clyde. As she watched, the woman's carefully lipsticked mouth changed shape from her usual smile and her voice dropped a couple of tones as she began to describe a particular item of news.

'The body of a young woman discovered in the early hours of this morning in a back alley close to the main shopping area of Sauchiehall Street has been identified as that of Tracey-Anne Geddes...'

Both fists grabbed at the silken counterpane as she sat up again, back suddenly rigid as she listened to the rest of the news. A photograph appeared, filling the screen, then the alley where the murder had taken place – an alley that was in easy walking distance from this very hotel... Her heart began to beat faster as she heard the story unfolding.

'Police are appealing for anyone who saw Tracey-Anne in the hours leading up to her death to come forward.'

The thin sound that began somewhere in the back of her throat ended in a howl of anguish as she let the pain and horror consume her once more, then racking sobs made her whole body judder.

A MAID, WALKING by in the corridor outside, paused. For a moment she stepped closer, one hand poised to knock and enquire if everything was all right. She bit her lip, wondering. Was it just a television programme, perhaps? But the wails that sounded from behind this locked door sounded like real, grief-stricken cries. She stepped back, her mind made up. The guests deserved their privacy, no matter what had happened to them. Maybe the woman was here in Glasgow for a funeral? She had been wearing a good black coat, after all. Yet, even as she continued along the corridor the maid shuddered, remembering the unearthly quality of that outpouring of anguish.

BEHIND THE WOODEN door the woman was now sitting on the edge of the bed, tears drying on her pale cheeks. The fingers that gripped each other tightly betrayed an inner anxiety. Tracey-Anne was dead. And that might just be a threat to her own safety. No longer would there be any midnight calls alerting her to the man she sought, nor any more meetings with the woman who had befriended Carol. No. She was on her own now.

She glanced down at her handbag lying open on the floor beside her, the mobile phone peeking out of its tiny pocket. For a moment she blinked, her mind trying to focus on what she was seeing, what it meant.

Hands trembling, she reached down and took the phone out of her bag, swiftly removing the SIM card. They would try to call her, wouldn't they? But whatever number Tracey-Anne had stored on her mobile would soon be impossible to reach.

Chapter Twelve

'I WANT AS much of our resources put to this case as possible,'
Lorimer said, eyeing the group of officers assembled in the room.
It was not the assembly he had anticipated: some of them had been
seconded from DCI James's team, others were his new colleagues
from Serious Crimes. Becoming acquainted with this latter group
would either have to wait now or happen on the job.

'Professor Brightman may not be known to many of you,' he
continued, one hand raised to acknowledge the bearded man
standing slightly to one side. 'But let me assure you he has been of
great use to Strathclyde in many cases of multiple murder.'

There was a murmur at that, some of which Lorimer hoped
was approval.

'Tracey-Anne Geddes's murder may well turn out to be the
work of the same person who killed these other girls.' He turned
to the huge screen behind him and pressed the switch that made
the faces of Carol Kilpatrick, Miriam Lyons and Jenny Haslet
appear.

'You'll notice I have kept the images of Tracey-Anne separate from the others. Maybe you'll be thinking *is he hedging his bets*?' The laugh that followed made Lorimer relax a little.

'Well, perhaps I am,' he continued. 'Nobody should ever be guilty of making assumptions at the beginning of a case and I can assure you that DCI James did not fall into this trap and neither will I.' He paused to let his words sink in. This was something that every officer knew fine but it was all too easy to let initial intelligence gull even the best cop into haring off down one particular route. He didn't want to insult his audience by spelling it out, though. These were all hand-picked officers who had great track records in helping solve crimes of a serious nature.

'We are fortunate to have some of DCI James's team here with us for the duration of this investigation. Manpower within the force has never been more severely challenged and I am accordingly grateful that they have agreed to work with us on this.'

Lorimer paused again. Was this the time to drop the bombshell? Hints that Serious Crimes was going to enjoy a limited shelf life had been going on for years; part of his own hesitation in accepting the post had revolved around that fact. But budgetary cuts were going to be made in the coming weeks by the Scottish Executive and rumours included the mothballing of this very sector of Strathclyde Police or, at best, the reorganising of it out of existence. Joyce Rogers wanted him here for now, heading up the team, but it would only be a matter of time, she had explained, till he was moved on again. No, he decided. He was the man in charge of this unit and, as far as anyone was concerned, in charge of this ongoing series of cases. He would just have to hope that they could find Tracey-Anne's killer before any police politics took him off the case.

'One of the things that I want to insist upon in this case is the way we treat any potential witnesses,' Lorimer said. 'I believe it is hugely important to call back any witnesses who come forward. They need the reassurance that their information is important to us. And we need them to be on our side at all times.'

A good few nodding heads showed that they were on his wavelength.

'It's inevitable that as overall SIO I will be at the mercy of our friends from the press each and every day.' He smiled as he heard the collective groan.

'You know what they all say,' he continued ruefully. 'You've got to feed the bear or it'll bite you.'

It was true. The press could be helpful or frustrating in equal measure in their headlong rush to sell stories.

'Instilling public confidence is always one of our top priorities,' Lorimer went on. 'And I want people to feel that they can walk about our streets without fear.' He turned again to the wall behind him. This time the visual of Tracey-Anne dominated the screen.

Human beings less inured to the disturbing images of women stabbed to death might have drawn a collective breath. This lot, Lorimer was pleased to note, didn't react at all. Instead every officer's attention was focused on the pictures as he took them through the discovery of the body and the initial post-mortem examination.

Jacqui White had done a decent job, he thought, as the pictures moved from the pend where the victim's body had been found to the city mortuary.

'Sixteen stab wounds, all inflicted with a sharp instrument,' he went on. 'The pathologists have given measurements that suggest the weapon may have been some sort of sword.' He paused again to let this new detail impinge on their minds. 'This was exactly the same suggestion given after Carol Kilpatrick's murder,' he told them. 'Obviously one of our major lines of enquiry is going to be into the sale and possession of such weapons.' He enlarged the image of one of the stab wounds, a lengthy gash in the abdominal area.

'I have to tell you,' he continued, 'the severity of this was much worse than any of the wounds inflicted upon Carol Kilpatrick.' He hesitated for a moment. Even these battle hardened men and women were going to react to this one.

'This particular wound penetrated the victim's body and came out the other side,' he said. 'The pathologist's report tells that the victim was probably standing against the wall. There's blood on the bricks at just the height of the victim's waist,' he went on, pulling the image back once more to show where the weapon had been thrust. 'Carol Kilpatrick also had wounds to her stomach and abdomen but none as deep and penetrating as these,' he went on.

'Once again, we cannot afford to make any assumptions, but it's hard to ignore the glaring similarities in the deaths of these two young women.'

This time there was an undercurrent of murmurs as they concurred. It was going to work, he thought. They were already on his side, united in the search for this girl's killer.

He took a deep breath.

'I'm going to ask as many of you as possible to delegate your current cases in favour of this one,' he said quietly, staring out at them with a determination that he hoped they now shared. He let his words sink in, then, 'Any questions?' he asked, scanning the group of men and women, turning at last to include the bearded psychologist who was beginning to look a trifle queasy.

'Who's going to mind our ongoing cases if we're to drop them for this . . .?' someone asked.

Lorimer stared at the big red-haired man who had spoken, wondering at the way his question had tailed off, at the nod he had given towards the pictures on the screen. Had he really detected a note of disgust in this man's voice? And, anyway, who was he? Not one of Helen's . . . then it came to him. This must be DI Sutherland, one of the men who were currently pursuing inquiries into the delicate area of the Ministry of Defence. He might not share it, but Superintendent Lorimer could see things from this man's perspective. *Why muck up an important government inquiry just to root around into the deaths of four prossies?* Without allowing his expression to change, Lorimer nodded towards the man.

'DI Duncan Sutherland?'

The answering grunt that was given for affirmation was so breathtakingly rude that he could hear Solly's sudden gasp of astonishment. Sutherland was showing remarkable gracelessness, something Lorimer knew was quite deliberate. Was he trying to wind him up? And if so, why? For a few seconds the rest of the officers assembled in this room appeared to be holding their breath.

'I didn't hear a *sir* after that inaudible response, DI Sutherland. Something stuck in your throat, perhaps?' Lorimer asked smoothly.

The man stared back defiantly, arms folded across his black leather jacket.

Lorimer took a step forward, his blue eyes raking the man's face. When he spoke again, there was no mistaking the venom in his tone.

'Perhaps it's the search for the man who has murdered four street women that sticks in your craw? Hmm? Don't see the point of wasting police resources in chasing after the killer of four wee junked-up lassies that nobody's going to miss? Is that it?'

Every officer watched, mesmerised, as Sutherland continued to stare back at the tall man who was slowly bearing down on him. For a moment the tension in the air was almost palpable, then a collective sigh could be heard as the red-haired officer seemed to sag before the intensity of Lorimer's glare.

He took one more step towards the man, pleased to see that Sutherland had not only unfolded his arms but had dropped his gaze. 'Well, DI Sutherland, to answer your question; you *will* be part of this team and you *will* relinquish your current case to the local police, is that understood?'

'Yes, sir,' he mumbled at last.

'Right,' Lorimer said briskly, addressing the entire room once more. 'Any other questions or can we get on with the business of finding this killer before he selects his next victim?'

'THERE'S PLENTY TO do,' Lorimer said, sinking into the easy chair in his new room at last. Solly had followed him back here and now he was enjoying a few minutes alone with the psychologist.

'And not only in the investigation, it would seem,' Professor Brightman replied, a tiny smile hovering across his lips. 'You'll have your work cut out just running this unit,' he murmured.

'Well, each of these officers maybe sees himself or herself as pretty special just by virtue of being in Serious Crimes,' Lorimer conceded. 'Still, I hate to hear anyone denigrate the street women just because of who they are and what they do. They're entitled to the same level of justice as any other citizen.'

'Not everyone is going to share your opinion,' Solly continued mildly.

'No, I suppose you're right,' Lorimer sighed, running a hand through his thick dark hair. 'But I just can't stand that kind of attitude, you know?'

'I know,' Solly agreed, his dark eyes bright behind his horn-rimmed spectacles. 'Anyway, to return to the object of my being here,' he continued. 'I think I would like to talk to the families of the victims.' Then, before Lorimer could reply, he continued briskly, 'Would there be anyone from family liaison to accompany me on such visits? I don't recall much of the media coverage except for the Miriam Lyons case. Wasn't her father a lawyer?'

'Aye, that's the one.' Lorimer heaved a sigh. 'Poor guy was hounded by the press, of course. They made hay with the fact he was a solicitor and his girl had been soliciting. You know the kind of thing they love to do in headlines; it's either a play on words or alliteration.'

'Is Mr Lyons still in practice?'

Lorimer shook his head. 'No. He retired from his firm shortly after Miriam's death. But our intelligence suggests he is still at the same address. Why? Do you want to begin with him?'

'I don't think so,' Solly replied. 'I think beginning with the first victim and looking at them all in chronological order would be the most constructive approach.'

'Well, best of luck with the Kilpatricks,' Lorimer told him. 'According to Helen James's reports they were pretty offhand with her officers first time around.'

Chapter Thirteen

PROFESSOR SOLOMON BRIGHTMAN sat awkwardly on the edge of the armchair trying not to spill the tea from the exquisite little floral cup that he held gingerly between his fingers. His discomfort was not about taking tea from something that resembled a delicate antique, however, but from the man and woman who sat facing him. He had decided that he had to make these two people his priority, not only because their daughter's death had begun what might be a series of killings, as he had told Lorimer, but also because of the similarities in the MO.

Robin and Christine Kilpatrick had agreed, albeit reluctantly, to permit this visit but Solly wondered if they were having second thoughts now that he and the family liaison officer were actually here in their home. The house was off a road that ran between two villages in West Renfrewshire, easier to see from the M8 motorway that whizzed past the foot of their garden than from the overgrown lane. Solly's first impression of the place was that it was unloved and neglected. Waist-high weeds obscured half the

gable end and there were greenish lines from the tiled roof running down the once-white roughcast walls where moss and water
had gathered in the sagging gutters. Even the stone steps leading
to the front door were a slick dark green.

Once inside, though, things were rather different. Someone,
Mrs Kilpatrick perhaps, had continued to make an effort to keep
the place decent; logs crackling in the grate gave the place a warm
glow even though his welcome had been a tad frosty.

'You may remember my colleague, PC Bryant?' Solly smiled
and nodded towards the middle-aged officer sitting next to him
as they sipped their tea. Connie Bryant was a motherly looking
woman, slightly overweight with thick corn-coloured hair. Solly
had taken to her immediately, realising she was well suited to her
job; those large blue eyes held an expression of sympathy that was
more friendly than pitying.

'You came to see us afterwards,' Robin Kilpatrick acknowledged, giving a stiff nod in the family liaison officer's direction.
Mrs Kilpatrick said nothing, her eyes cast down to her cup and
saucer.

She's still in denial, Solly thought. But was it denial of her
daughter's death or of the way she had lived? A discreet look
around the room had shown no evidence of any family photographs, though Solly knew from the records that the couple still
had another daughter.

'What I am actually here for,' Solly began, laying the cup back
gently on its saucer, 'is to ask you about Carol.'

'Already told the police everything we know, which is nothing,'
Mr Kilpatrick said brusquely. 'We had a daughter. She chose a . . .
a . . .' he frowned, as though struggling for a word, 'a *route* that
was alien to us. We don't have anything to do with people like

that,' he added, as though the entire matter was closed to further discussion.

'Sadly my own profession sometimes takes me into the worlds of many different souls,' Solly told him quietly. 'I see things that I would hate any of my loved ones to see. So I do understand what pain you must have experienced, and not just when Carol died.'

'Do we have to go through this all again?' Robin Kilpatrick demanded.

'I wish I could spare you,' Solly said, 'but it is not just Carol's death that is being investigated.'

'Oh?' The man's head went up and Solly could see that he was suddenly curious in the way that most humans are when other people's tragedies impinge upon their own.

'Another girl was attacked in the same place where your daughter met her death.'

'So? It could have been a coincidence, couldn't it?' Kilpatrick blustered.

'This girl was one of Carol's friends,' Solly continued, his eyes never leaving the man's face. 'And I have to tell you that the method used by the killer was identical to that used on your daughter,' he added.

'Another street girl?' the father asked, his face twisted into a mask of disgust. 'Why should we care about her?'

'Because some evil bastard is out there and we want to catch him before he sends another unfortunate victim to her death!'

All three of them turned to stare at Connie Bryant, whose mild manners suddenly seemed to have deserted her.

'You're not the only parents who have lost a child to heroin, you know,' she continued heatedly. 'There are hundreds like you all over this city and every city in the country. We try to stem the tide but it's not easy,' she went on. 'So many young girls are lost to their families and friends then turn in desperation to selling their bodies on the streets for the price of a fix.' She paused for breath, cheeks flushed. Then her voice dropped and her tone became gentler and more persuasive. 'The police have done a sterling job of cleaning up the streets, protecting the girls as best they can, but until we have help from people like you two then we're not going to change the public's perception of prostitution.'

There was silence in the room but Solly still felt the woman's words reverberate in the air around them. Robin Kilpatrick was staring at Connie Bryant, his lips parted as though to speak, but it was his wife who spoke first.

'How can we help?' Mrs Kilpatrick said, raising her head at last.

'Tell us about Carol,' Solly told her gently. 'What she was like as a girl, why you think she went off the rails. What contact you had with her after she left home.' He paused then stared into space, wagging his dark beard thoughtfully. 'That would be particularly helpful to begin with.'

'Carol left home when she was sixteen,' Mrs Kilpatrick said, her lip suddenly trembling. 'We had no contact with her after that.'

Solly frowned. 'Did Carol leave home because she had an addiction to heroin at that time?' he asked. Sixteen? It seemed so young to be leaving her family. A quick memory flicked into his brain of himself at that age, steeped in his school exams, home and family a secure and loving support. How different Carol Kilpatrick's experience had been!

'Why?' he added, shaking his head slightly. 'Why did Carol leave home then?'

There was a silence that he longed to break, an uncomfortable minute when things that had long been hidden were coming close to the surface for this mother and father. Things, Solly felt sure, that would give him more insight into the woman that Carol Kilpatrick had been.

Robin Kilpatrick gave his wife a swift glance but once more she had elected to disappear into some world of her own, her head bent so that she was staring at a spot on the carpet. The psychologist wanted to take her to a place where he could talk to her alone, search her soul for whatever was troubling her, driving her deep into herself. Something, he felt certain, that had to do with their daughter.

'She left home because she wanted to live with her friends,' Robin Kilpatrick said, in a voice that sounded suddenly weary. 'That's all we can tell you.' He rose stiffly and glanced at the door. 'Do you mind? I think my wife and I would prefer to be left alone now.'

'FUNNY COUPLE,' CONNIE Bryant muttered as they drove away from the house. 'Never did find out much about Carol from them.'

'Was it assumed that Carol left home because of her drug habit?' Solly asked.

'Hmm. Well, you've seen what they're like. Nobody on the investigation team ever doubted that they'd kicked her out. Did you hear what they called her? An alien!' Bryant's voice quivered with indignation.

'No,' Solly corrected her. 'What they said was that she had chosen a way of life that was alien to them.' Still, the family liaison officer's words remained with him, troubling him. Was Mrs Kilpatrick now riven with guilt and regret that she had chosen to cut all ties with her child? Or was there still something else that he needed to know about the relationship she had had with the teenager who had become a heroin addict and prostitute?

'. . . Daddy's coming home, bringing pockets full of plums!'

'Hello, you two. Here I am,' Solly beamed at his wife and baby daughter as he closed the door behind him.

'Hiya,' Rosie smiled back at him then held the baby up. 'Go to Daddy, you wee rascal. Let me get dinner sorted while you give her a bath, eh?' She handed over baby Abigail who gave a delighted chuckle as Solly swung her high above his head then let her little fingers pluck the end of his beard. All around him lay the chaos that only a young baby can create: soft toys littered one corner of the elegant drawing room, Abby's bouncer sat in the cradle of the bay window, where Rosie had placed it earlier in an attempt to catch the last warm rays of the sun, while evidence of a busy mother could be seen in a discarded muslin dropped on the floor. Solly smiled, seeing past the untidiness, imagining instead the shared moments mother and child had enjoyed throughout the day. He carried Abby through to the bathroom and his smile grew into a chuckle as he noticed that one of his beloved paintings in the hall was slightly askew. This, Solly thought to himself, was as it should be. The days of living here alone with only his artworks for company were gone; now this place was filled with the love and laughter of his little family.

A few minutes later he was holding Abigail's shoulders, gently whooshing her back and forth in the warm water, grinning as she gurgled and laughed. Once upon a time Robin Kilpatrick might have done just this sort of thing with his own baby daughter, Solly suddenly thought. When at last he gathered Abigail up in a fluffy towel, the psychologist held her close to his chest and sent up a silent prayer that his little girl would never come to such terrible harm.

THE PLACE WAS in darkness when she awoke, only the light from a distant street lamp letting her see the dim shapes of this unfamiliar room. Somehow she had slept here, glad to be away from her own place, thoroughly exhausted after that storm of weeping, but now the facts of Tracey-Anne's death came back at her and she shuddered, remembering the words from last night's television report and the scene where Carol's friend had died.

Her fists still clutched the edges of the silken counterpane, the tips of her fingers pulsing blood red with rage: how could she have got it so terribly wrong? She had seen Tracey-Anne get into that car last night. Not a white Mercedes sports car. If only she had kept a lookout at that corner of the square . . . Then a queasiness began to fill her stomach as the doubts formed. Had Tracey-Anne been lifted by another punter later on? That had to be it, surely?

She had dispatched two men to their death. *Two innocent men*, a small voice suggested. The deepening pain in her belly made her want to retch. Trembling, she rose from the bed and staggered towards the adjacent bathroom. The black and white tiles were chilly under her feet as she leaned over the washbasin and turned on the cold tap to splash water on her hands and face.

She stood up, shivering now, and grabbed the fluffy towel that someone had placed on the heated towel rail. A huge sigh seemed to ripple through her whole body as she buried her head in the warm towel. It was a small comfort.

What had she done? How had she got it so wrong? She'd been so certain each time . . . As she took the towel from her face she looked at the mirror above the basin. A dark-eyed woman frowned back at her, hair straggling over pale cheeks, mouth open as though to utter some words of disparagement. And didn't she deserve them? Didn't she deserve to be cursed for these dreadful mistakes? For deciding that these men had to die? For condemning their loved ones to the same sort of suffering that she had endured for so long?

As she looked at the woman in the mirror she saw the mouth close in a tight line. *Don't be so stupid*, the voice scolded her. *They were never innocent, trawling the streets for the flesh of young women.* And then the face before her dissolved as the tears began to fall once more.

Back in the bedroom she sat at the dressing table and lifted a hairbrush. As each stroke pulled the tangles straight she began to relax once more. She had done nothing wrong but rid the city of some of its vermin. Her only guilt lay in failing to find Carol's killer. And Tracey-Anne's.

She frowned again as a thought came to her. Tracey-Anne had known about the white car. The girl had made those two calls to let her know it was around the drag. Why would she have endangered her life by choosing to get into that particular vehicle? She blinked away the thought, remembering that the poor junked-up girl had not always behaved in a rational manner.

What was important now was to find the right man. Her eyes fell on the unopened case. Somewhere in its depths lay the pistol wrapped neatly inside a cashmere sweater. It was waiting for her. Just as it had been the night she had found it, tossed under that wardrobe in an east end flat. She had picked the Starfire up in one gloved hand, its silver blue steelwork winking at her, daring her to take it for herself. And she had. Her fingers curled more tightly around the hairbrush, recalling the feel of the gun in her hand as she pulled the trigger, hearing again that awful blast, seeing the expression of shock on the man's face.

Yes, she told herself, smoothing down her hair and noting with satisfaction that her cheeks were dry: yes she could do this thing again, even though there was nobody to tell her when a white car might be circling the city streets. She could do it again. And again – until she brought Carol's killer to a justice of her own.

Chapter Fourteen

EDWARD PATTISON SMILED to himself, blissfully unaware that it was only a matter of hours from now when *all smiles would stop together*, as the poet, Robert Browning, had put it, the expression of murderous intent hedged about with cunning euphemism. Pattison was no poet, however, nor a lover of poetry. Politics had thrust him into quite a different sphere of creativity and now, as Scotland's newly appointed deputy first minister, he was enjoying the sort of power over his peers that the 'Last Duchess' of Browning's poem would have recognised. Sitting here, on the front row of the debating chamber, Pattison knew that he was a presence to be reckoned with, his smile more for the cameras that were recording the debate than for any of his colleagues. Changing his colours for those in the current ruling party had been seen by the media as pure opportunism and Pattison had never denied it; well, not in so many words. And he had a way with words, was able to charm most of the reporters who came into his orbit with titbits of parliamentary gossip and free tickets to red carpet events. (*Don't tell the others*, he'd whisper as he sat with them in the Garden Lobby. *Just make them jealous.*)

So far Pattison's progress had been remarkable. From being one of several Labour Party members of the Scottish parliament, he had defected to the Nationalists and found his reward in the upward curve of success. Deputy Leadership was not enough, however, and as Pattison let his eyes slide across to the woman who currently headed up both party and country, he considered his next step towards the ultimate goal. Felicity Stewart's ruddy complexion, weathered by years of country pursuits, was not going to grace the press pages for much longer if he could help it, Pattison told himself. He'd already dropped hints about their leader's drinking habits, some of which had been taken up by the redtops. A canny word here and an allusion there had sown seeds that were beginning to bear fruit.

Glancing at his diary, Pattison read what his agenda consisted of for the remainder of the week. A meeting in Glasgow with Visit Scotland personnel then a dinner at the City Chambers tomorrow for a delegation on educational business that would take him through until later that evening. He'd already told his wife, Cathy, he'd be staying over in the west and his long suffering secretary had booked him into the Central Hotel as usual. His smile deepened as he considered his options: an hour or so of forbidden fruit in the city, perhaps? He was taking the Merc anyway, so why not? It was risky, of course it was, and tomorrow was Friday the thirteenth, his diary told him, but Edward Pattison had never really been a superstitious man, trusting instead to his own abilities.

Pattison uncrossed his legs as a familiar warmth stole through his nether regions, his mind now completely distracted from the facts and figures being thrashed out by the Labour member currently on his feet. As the clock on the wall measured its relentless progress towards Pattison's final hours, the man himself could only wish that time would pass more quickly so that he could indulge his hidden desires.

It was an irony that would never be discovered, however, by those who were to report on his death, or by the ones who were left to ruminate over what might have become of his life.

IT GAVE HER a frisson of pleasure to create her disguise. Gone was the serious-faced professional, a brittle frown scoring lines between eyes the colour of faded leaves. In its place she admired the curving brows above eyelids painted like an Egyptian queen's, haughty yet provocative. She'd dressed with her customary care, zipping the pelmet of skirt against her bare thighs, feeling the metal teeth cold and ragged upon her skin. After the first night she had chosen to wear black. That red skirt had beckoned like a flag but now she wore confidence as though it were a primary colour.

Tonight boots replaced the sandals, their thin metal heels beating a sharp rhythm across the marble tiles of the hotel bathroom. Killer heels, she thought with just a hint of a smile. Slung across her low cut blouse the fashionably large bag held everything she would require. It had been easy to find a taxi back to the city centre from the vicinity of a railway station but she knew better than to lead her next victim to a similar place. That was why her bag contained a pair of well-worn running shoes. Together with the gun that was now nestling between the folds of a rolled-up tracksuit.

THERE WAS A dent in Edward Pattison's lower lip, bitten into a dark pink tooth shape of indecision. Would he or wouldn't he? It was a question he asked himself purely because of an irritating conscience, not from any worry that it might prove a matter of life and death.

Pattison could almost read the thought bubbles emanating from his head.

'Go for it,' the horned beast leered at him.

'Think of Cathy back home,' countered the one with the halo.

Pattison gave a defeated sigh. He'd never been one for harps and nightgowns. And Cathy wasn't exactly a saintly wife either, he reminded himself, eyes narrowing in a bitter little frown. With a tilt of his head the second bubble burst into the ether leaving only traces of what he imagined to be a diabolic chuckle.

HE SPOTTED HER under the lamp, a slim girl, taller than Cathy (he cursed himself for making comparisons) with luxuriant shoulder-length hair. Something about the way she held herself made him drive around the square for a second look. It was running the risk of being caught on any CCTV cameras that might be working, Pattison knew, but risk served to add an extra spice to the thrill of it all. Under the street light he noticed the raw carelessness of her expression as if she was daring anyone to stop. Daring them to ask, to do what it was she knew they wanted. It was at once seductive and compelling. Even as he let the window open silently he could feel a swelling in his groin.

When she turned to him with a proper smile, not the junked-up glassy stare of so many of the women he'd been with in this city, he knew that this one would be special.

'I know a place,' she told him, her voice tantalising the erogenous zones, making him feel that surge of male power, that urge to dominate one of those girls in the street.

He jerked his thumb, a command to get in, then, as soon as she'd clicked her seat belt in place Pattison drove off, head held high as the big car leapt into the night. Another conquest was beginning; another woman was fit to be given a doing.

After giving him a few directions she didn't speak again until the city had fallen behind them, its myriad lights cast off like a spangled garment.

'Next left,' she intoned, one hand placed for a second upon his thigh.

He risked a glance at her and she smiled encouragingly.

'Not far now,' she assured him, her fingers sliding slowly up the webbing strap of her seat belt.

The country lane by the wood looked safe enough, Pattison told himself as his foot pressed the brake. There was a double click as they undid their seat belts and he reached across for her, hungry to begin.

'Wait.'

The word made him back off as she rummaged in the bag at her feet. He thought he understood, heart beating with anticipation. They all used protection after all. And it would have been crass stupidity on his part not to be careful. Never knew where they'd been.

When she straightened up again he saw her hands full of a dark shadow that became an explosion of light and pain.

Then total darkness as his heart burst into shattered pulp.

THE NIGHTLY GARBAGE collection cleared Glasgow city streets of more than the usual detritus that night. The woman added the clothes she'd worn, rolled tightly in a double layer of supermarket carrier bags, to the pile lying in the doorway of the cobbled lane.

Any residue from the gun or contact traces from her victim might have found its way onto her hair and clothing, traces that she was keen to destroy.

It was a place she knew well. And somehow it was fitting to leave the evidence (that would never be found) in the very spot where two women had been brutalised, the place no longer cordoned off by police tape. If she could have taken any of her victims there she would have enjoyed some dramatic irony in the situation. But it was too much of a risk. Thrusting her tart's clothes deep into the heavy-duty bin liner was as near a twisted joke as she could contrive.

Walking slowly uphill to Blythswood Square and the hotel, she was already planning her next outing. Not this week, though, and probably not the next. She would watch the aftermath of the shooting impinge itself on the city's consciousness. And, above all, she would follow the progress of the senior investigating officer's investigation. Or rather, she smiled to herself as she asked for her room key, the lack of it.

Killing time, she told herself, liking the phrase so much that she spoke it out loud as she walked up the back stairs:

'Killing time.'

There was the semblance of a day job, of course, and what it entailed, but she could pretend to herself that there were shift patterns; days off and the need to maintain an appearance of normality. Washing the car, shopping for groceries, doing the laundry; all the things that filled in the space between the day-to-day obligations and what had become more than a duty. This was no mere act of revenge on her part, she told herself. Revenge was mindless and all her actions had been well conceived, purposeful. If he'd been caught, Carol's killer would be serving some piffling sentence in Barlinnie, Saughton or wherever they could squeeze him in. Then, early release. Always early release. She ground her teeth in silent rage. No. Revenge was far less sweet than what she would ultimately feel when he finally fell into her trap. It would be a vindication, a meting out of justice. She'd be the one to apprehend him, try, sentence and execute all on one starlit night. Meanwhile she killed time, taking pleasure in watching as the media's interest in the shootings quickened.

Chapter Fifteen

He had passed the junction for Erskine hundreds of times in the past, but now Detective Superintendent Lorimer was taking the turning near the Erskine Bridge. The call had come some time after two a.m. with a barked instruction from the chief constable to get his arse over to Renfrewshire asap. Hearing the victim's name had galvanised him into action and now he was here on this darkened stretch of road, flicking his lights on to full beam.

The presence of a police car let Lorimer know to swing left off the main road and slowly follow the narrow track that led into woodland. The thermometer in his new car registered minus one but there was no wind and the thick pine trees ahead glistened with frost, illumined by his headlights. He stopped the silver Lexus round the next corner behind a line of other cars, the familiar blue and white tape some yards ahead barring further entry, and lifted his kit bag from the passenger seat beside him.

'Detective Superintendent Lorimer, Serious Crimes Squad,' he told the uniformed officer standing guard at the side of a muddy path. The man looked at him warily so, suppressing a sigh,

Lorimer flipped open his warrant card and the officer immediately stepped aside.

'Just watch your feet, sir, it's a bit icy further along,' the man told him, pulling his coat collar up around his ears.

Lorimer edged carefully over the hard ground, almost slipping once or twice as his feet connected with a frozen patch. The scene of crime was a few yards further along the narrow track and Lorimer could make out several white figures moving about in the swirling gloom. As he drew nearer a pale shape flew silently past, a barn owl hunting for its prey. The arcs of torchlight up ahead had done nothing to deter this bird from its usual nocturnal habits, Lorimer thought, his eyes trying to focus on what was happening. He peered into the darkness, looking for the victim's car. Was that it? A white blur partly obscured by dense foliage?

'Can you keep back please?' A thick-set man suddenly stepped towards him out of the darkness, torch in hand. 'Only official personnel allowed.'

For the second time Lorimer whipped out his warrant card and held it close to the man's torch beam so that he could read it.

'Sorry, sir, we weren't expecting you this soon. Scene of crime personnel are still attending the scene and we're waiting for the pathologist. I'm DS Jolyon, scene of crime manager from K Division.'

'Good to meet you, Jolyon,' Lorimer said, giving the man a brief handshake. 'Just let me get geared up will you?' Turning aside to a patch of dark grass that looked reasonably flat, Lorimer laid down his kit bag and took out the regulation garments that were essential to protect a crime scene from any contamination. Soon he was clad like the others in a white hooded suit and latex gloves, his shoes encased in bootees to prevent any contamination of the soil around the crime scene.

The slam of a car door made Jolyon and Lorimer turn around and they waited until another figure appeared, similarly geared up and carrying a medical bag, stamping along the path to join them.

'Doctor White,' Lorimer nodded at the pathologist who was serving as Rosie's locum.

'Lorimer,' the dark haired woman nodded briefly then strode past them both as if she had no need of torchlight to see the locus of this particular crime.

The victim was lying slumped to one side; the hole in his chest black against his white dress shirt. Headlights from nearby patrol cars had leached all sense of colour from the man's face. Lorimer looked once, then looked away. It was true, then. Edward Pattison, deputy first minister for Scotland, was dead, shot in this quiet woodland, far from his Edinburgh home. The first officers on the scene had identified him from the bank cards in his wallet, then the call had gone out, wakening even the chief constable who had then instructed Lorimer to attend the scene as SIO.

'Near contact wound?' he ventured as the pathologist turned to look at him.

'Possibly,' she said and smiled. But there was no warmth in that smile and Lorimer had the feeling that the woman would be happier to talk to him once the body had been examined on her surgical table. The gunshot wound was almost certainly near contact like the others but the pathologist was obviously refusing to commit herself in any way at all right now.

In truth there was little for him to do here. Dr White's examination would continue later in the mortuary; much later, he thought, since they had decided to leave the scene intact until daylight. Sometimes it paid dividends to work at the scene before shifting the body since a wealth of evidence could be gathered by scene of crime officers and the forensic services. And this was a case that he couldn't afford to mess up in any way, Lorimer told himself. The terse call from the chief constable had made that much clear.

Daylight would bring more officers to this woodland spot and, he acknowledged, the ever eager press pack. He was already composing a brief statement that would go out to their own press officer; finding the right words was of paramount importance if he was to have the papers and the public on his side. But right now he had to work with the scene of crime manager to ensure that everything was done as efficiently as possible.

Lorimer's expression was sombre as he thought of the scientists who would be involved; a forensic chemist, biologist, firearms examiner and mark enhancement officer as well as the usual scene of crime officers would be grumbling as they feigned exasperation with his orders to obtain a full forensic. The press would just have to wait their turn.

The Gazette
Saturday 14th January

TOP POLITICIAN SHOT DEAD IN GLASGOW

Deputy First Minister Edward Pattison was found dead in his car in the early hours of this morning. Pattison, who had been part of a delegation at Glasgow City Chambers yesterday evening, was discovered by a young couple walking through a woodland track near to the Erskine Bridge. Early reports suggest that the politician had been shot at point-blank range and police and forensic experts are currently searching his white Mercedes sports car and the surrounding area for clues.

This is the third shooting of a middle-aged man in a white Mercedes that has taken place on the city's perimeter in recent months, sparking off two manhunts, and police may be considering the theory that the victims were the target of a serial killer with some peculiar agenda. In September last year Matthew Wardlaw, from Birmingham, was the first victim, followed in January by fellow Englishman, Thomas Littlejohn. Each of the three men was away from home on business but the most notable thing they seem to have had in common was the make and colour of their luxury cars.

The deputy first minister leaves a wife, Catherine, and three children who are at the family home in Edinburgh being comforted by relatives.

A full report on Pattison's life and career can be found on page 12.

'PATTISON IS NOT to be treated like some ordinary person who happened to be in the wrong place at the wrong time!'

The chief constable's words rang in William Lorimer's ears even after he had replaced the telephone. A high-profile murder like this one was always going to be a bit of a nightmare and handing it over to Serious Crimes was one way of dealing with it, the detective superintendent supposed, absently chewing his index finger. That he already had intelligence about the first two cases under his jurisdiction was helpful to say the least. It let Mumby and Preston off the hook at any rate and he could almost imagine their sighs of relief that they wouldn't have to deal directly with the press pack right now, something that had fallen to him as SIO. The *Gazette* and other papers had the bones of the story but Lorimer knew he would have to keep them updated on a daily basis.

The entire day was going to be taken up with Edward Pattison's death. Just as the early evening news would devote extra space to the dramatic developments surrounding the deputy first minister's killing, so Detective Superintendent Lorimer's officers had all weekend leave cancelled and were now being expected to drop everything else to concentrate on this high-profile murder. Lorimer ground his teeth in hopeless rage. The fact that he had already diverted so much of Serious Crimes' resources into the prostitute murders had been brushed aside by the chief. These young women who had been so horribly brutalised were to be of lesser importance now that this public figure had been found dead. He remembered the smirk of satisfaction that DI Sutherland had given when he had broken the news to them. The street girls' investigation was to be scaled back for now, though he had allowed Professor Brightman to continue his inquiries. Maybe they'd find Pattison's killer pretty quickly, Lorimer told himself. After all, he had been promised all the resources he wanted.

From just after two a.m. when his car had been found out in that lonely Renfrewshire wood, the police hunt had spread across Glasgow and was now making its way to the capital where Pattison had lived. By midday Lorimer was heading along the M8, the motorway that cut Scotland in two with Glasgow and Edinburgh at either end. Throughout the journey he had kept in touch with what was happening back in the woods near Erskine Bridge and the beach, a popular spot for courting couples. The scene of crime lads and lasses had been and gone but there was still a strong police presence there, the usual blue and white tape keeping dog walkers and nosey parkers from contaminating the site.

Now, as the police car swung around the roundabout that led to the city's perimeter, Lorimer wondered just what he was going to say to Catherine Pattison. More to the point, he wanted to know what she would say to him. Rumours had already reached his ears via the chief constable's office that the Pattisons' marriage had been a stormy one, to say the least.

'Good-lookin' fella,' the chief constable had commented. 'Bags of charm. But tended to play away from home, if you get my drift.'

Lorimer wondered if that throwaway remark had been intended to give him some insight into the victim's character. It wasn't really helpful, he thought. If every guy who strayed from the marriage bed was shot in his car, the population would be severely depleted.

His head lifted for a moment as a familiar malty smell wafted into the car. Lorimer inhaled deeply, enjoying the old-fashioned scent of a brewery that was now no more. Only the smell lingered in this particular spot. Then the moment passed and his driver was turning into the heart of the city. Lorimer glimpsed the castle on its plug of volcanic rock, an austere and forbidding pile of grey stones built into grey slabs of hillside. Before Christmas he and Maggie had enjoyed an evening in Edinburgh at the German markets, the lights from trees glittering all around, the big wheel turning and the carousel music melding with voices full of Yuletide cheer. Today, under grey skies and a thin, bitter wind that came directly from the River Forth, Edinburgh seemed far less welcoming.

Their first stop was at the Scottish parliament at the foot of the Royal Mile and as the driver slowed to a halt, Lorimer couldn't help but stare at the modern building. It had been designed by an inspired Catalan for Scotland's people, but the building had divided the opinion of its citizens, not least for the cost that had escalated almost out of control. It was a place that Lorimer loved although he couldn't quite say why it moved him. Maggie liked the lines of poetry etched into the wall round from the Canongate, of course, but what was it that lifted his own spirits every time he entered the doors of this place? Was it the feeling that it belonged to the people of Scotland? And that for once they deserved something so spectacular? Or had he been beguiled by the clever use of stone and wood, reminding him in some subliminal way of ancient castles screened by the old Caledonian forests?

In minutes he was taken through security by a nice young woman who introduced herself as Grace, whisked upstairs in a private lift then taken into the room that was reserved for the first minister, Felicity Stewart.

'Detective Superintendent Lorimer,' the woman in the purple tweed suit said, as she rose from her desk.

'Ma'am,' Lorimer replied, taking her hand and noting the firm handshake as well as the fact that in real life Felicity Stewart looked smaller and more careworn than she did on the television screen or in press photographs. Her steel grey hair was smooth and sleek and her make-up had been applied carefully to conceal her naturally ruddy complexion, but nothing had been done to take away the frown lines from around these penetrating grey eyes or the wrinkled flesh on her ageing hands. She had twisted a green and blue silk scarf around her neck, and, apart from her trademark pearl earrings, there was little other concession to fashion or femininity.

'Sit down, Lorimer,' she said, ushering him towards a chair. 'Now, I don't know what you expect me to say, but I'm not going to utter meaningless platitudes about Edward's death. I'll save those for the press.'

Lorimer's raised eyebrows elicited a small smile from the first minister.

'You said on the telephone that you wanted to let me know more about Mr Pattison, ma'am,' Lorimer began. 'And I'll certainly welcome any background information you can give me.' He looked at her, wondering just what was going on inside the first minister's mind.

'You're shocked that I don't put on a long Presbyterian face and say how awful Edward's death is for us all, admit it.' She gave a mirthless laugh. 'Why do I say that? Well, I'll tell you because you will want to know the truth about this man.' She leaned forward, one finger shaking at the policeman as though he were being given a lecture. 'Edward Pattison was a conniving bastard who would gladly have seen me sacked from this office.'

'The press always described him as an ambitious man,' Lorimer said tactfully.

'Ho! Ambitious doesn't cover it, Superintendent. Edward was totally ruthless and would have stopped at nothing to realise his plan to run the country.' She smiled again, sitting back and folding her arms. 'Suppose that gives me a motive for wanting to see him dead,' she chuckled. 'Lucky for me that I have an alibi for all of last night.'

'Are you trying to suggest that there may have been a political motive behind Mr Pattison's killing, ma'am?'

'I have absolutely no idea, Lorimer. All I want to do is to give you the facts. I knew Edward Pattison as a colleague and, yes, as a rival. I cannot tell you everything about his personal life, of course. What Edward did in his own time was none of my business. What he did in parliamentary time certainly was and I want you to be clear about the sort of man he was, not what the papers will have you believe.' She snorted. 'I expect they're already making him out to be some sort of Braveheart who would have led the country to independence. He wanted to project that image when it suited him, of course.' She stopped, her eyes sliding away from his, her expression thoughtful. 'It was something we all wanted at one time,' Felicity Stewart remarked. Then she sighed and shook her head. 'Edward was good at rallying the people. That was why I didn't make any attempt to block his political career. But I want you to know, Lorimer, there are several people within this building who would happily have seen Edward come to grief. Now whether any one of them would have stooped so low as to take his life is something you have to find out. But he certainly had plenty of enemies, both within the present government and in the Labour Party.'

'You think there might have been someone bitter enough about his defection to have had him killed?' Lorimer's tone held a note of scepticism.

'Stranger things have happened,' Felicity Stewart replied. 'Though I admit it is more likely that someone would have brought him down by rumour and innuendo.' She grinned, showing a set of perfect teeth. 'After all, that's exactly what he was trying to do to me.'

'Really?' Lorimer could not stop himself remarking. But there was a steeliness in those grey eyes that made him believe her.

'It would be very helpful, ma'am, if you could give me the names of any persons who might have had reason to harm Mr Pattison,' he continued, deliberately trying to keep the conversation on a formal footing.

'Hmm, where do I begin?' She leaned back, her cheek resting against her hand as she considered his request.

THERE WAS A glimmer of sunshine as Lorimer was driven away from the Scottish parliament building and, as he looked up at Arthur's Seat, the hill behind him, misty clouds above its rounded top parted to reveal patches of blue sky. *Enough to mend a sailor's trousers*, his mum had been fond of saying. That thought brought him back to his next visit. Edward Pattison had been a husband and a father. His loss was going to be something quite different for his wife and kids. There would be none of Felicity Stewart's straight talking; that was for sure.

What had he made of the woman? Lorimer wasn't a particularly political animal, police politics having been enough to stomach in his career, but he did have a fondness for the history surrounding the ideals of Scottish independence. Ms Stewart was one hard woman, that was evident, but perhaps having a steely core was a primary requirement for trying to run the country whilst fending off an opposition party like Labour, who were traditionally at odds with the SNP. That she had been honest was admirable, but Lorimer felt she had lacked something. *The milk of human kindness*, he thought, remembering Lady Macbeth. Surely it wouldn't have hurt the first minister to utter one kind word about Pattison? Still, she had given the detective some names, in complete confidence, of course. Lorimer frowned, wondering if the men whose names he had written into his BlackBerry had really been the dead man's bitter enemies. Or was Felicity Stewart using him to undermine the credibility of these politicians for her own ends? He had a duty to investigate them now, of course, but why did he feel that he had just escaped from a sticky web of intrigue?

The house where the Pattisons lived was not too far away, probably a ten-minute journey at rush hour. Murrayfield was an upmarket area, not only because of its proximity to the famous rugby grounds, but also due to the large and solid properties marching in rows away from the main road. It was easy to spot the Pattison home. Across from the grey stone detached house a knot of reporters were stood, and they began to rush the police car as soon as it turned into the avenue.

The uniformed driver and his escort stood their ground, however, ushering them back to the opposite pavement, despite their shouts for information. Lorimer heard cameras clicking and he had no doubt that his profile would be gracing the *Edinburgh Evening News* later in the day. A tall young copper from Lothian and Borders standing outside the garden gate of the house sketched a salute as the detective superintendent passed him. Lorimer gave him a nod in reply. It was to be expected that a police guard would be put upon this place given Pattison's public persona. He only hoped it would keep the worst of the press at bay for the family's sake. It was a short walk to the front door, past well-tended lawns and a row of blue ceramic containers filled with rich dark soil. In a few weeks the first bulbs might help to cheer this entrance, but for now this garden was still in the grip of winter.

His office had made the call for him, letting Mrs Pattison know that Detective Superintendent Lorimer from Strathclyde Police would arrive some time in the early afternoon. Now, as he stood in the porch, one hand ready to ring the doorbell, Lorimer wondered how that news had been received. Bad enough to have to deal with a sudden death, but murder and the intrusion of the police must surely compound the grief and confusion of any newly bereaved woman. After ringing, Lorimer waited, watching for shadows behind the glass door with its etchings of a Greek-style vase and plaited laurel wreaths. He had brought bad news to people's doors plenty of times in the past and was able to empathise with them, understand their shock and horror. It wasn't the first time he had been involved in the murder of a man with such a high public profile but death had no consideration of class or status and Lorimer expected this widow's reaction to be similar to those he had seen so often before.

A figure approached the glass door and it opened with a click and a rattle, the tell-tale sign that a security chain had been unfastened.

'Detective Superintendent Lorimer?' An older lady stood by the half-opened door, looking at him uncertainly. She had the voice of a well-educated woman, deep and clear, with that cultured accent he associated with Edinburgh gentlefolk.

'Yes, ma'am,' Lorimer replied, holding out his warrant card so that she might be able to verify that he was indeed a policeman.

'I'm Mrs Cadell, Catherine's mother,' the woman told him. 'Please come in.' She closed the door firmly behind them and replaced the chain.

'Can't be too careful,' she remarked, her voice betraying the first signs of nervousness, but she gave the ghost of a smile, as if it was important to keep one's spirits up. 'Catherine asked me to take you through to the drawing room. She'll be right down.'

Lorimer followed Mrs Cadell through the reception hall and into a bright airy room that looked out onto the street. He was not surprised to see cafe curtains at each pane of the bay windows, keeping any prying eyes from seeing into the Pattisons' home. His own mum had always kept her *nets*, as she'd called them, up at the front windows and Lorimer could still recall summer days when they had billowed from their washing line before being given a quick iron and put back onto their wires. It was a pleasant room, its walls painted pale yellow to tone with the ochre tapestry cushions on the occasional chairs surrounding a large oak coffee table. As always, Lorimer's eyes were drawn to the paintings, his history of art training making him notice anything that was in a decent frame; two were landscapes that he recognised as the work of the Scottish artist Tom Shanks, but the third was a full-length portrait of a young woman in a black evening dress, her long dark hair wound around one side of her neck in the manner of an old Gainsborough. She seemed to look down at him as he gazed, her eyes following him as he stood to one side then the other, trying to catch the light properly. The pale face was tinged with just a hint of pink on the cheeks and the laughing mouth was outlined in scarlet. It might have owed something to the old masters but this was certainly a modern portrait and he was curious to identify the artist: a Robert Mulhern, perhaps? Just as Lorimer was approaching to see if he could make out a signature, the door opened and the subject of the painting walked in.

'Mrs Pattison?' Lorimer stepped towards Edward Pattison's widow, one hand outstretched.

Catherine Pattison glanced up at her portrait and then back at the tall policeman from Glasgow. Her long hair was tied back in an elastic band but there was no mistaking that pale face with its high cheekbones and those dark eyes. Instead of the formal black evening clothes, the woman was dressed in tight-fitting blue jeans, a navy cashmere sweater and a pair of red leather loafers.

'Ed had it painted after we were married,' she said. 'Don't know why he bothered, really,' she added in the same clipped tones as her mother.

'It's a lovely picture, Mrs Pattison,' Lorimer said gently.

They were silent for a moment as Catherine Pattison chewed her lip and looked away from him.

'I'm sorry to have to come today, so soon after you've received this terrible news,' Lorimer said at last. Then, as she made no reply, he took her gently by the elbow and steered her towards one of the chairs. 'Better to sit here while we talk,' he added, hoping that she was going to be able to speak to him.

'My husband,' she began, turning to Lorimer. 'He . . .' Her voice tailed off in a note of despair, then she thumped the arm of the chair, her face twisted into a mask of fury. 'Oh God! What the hell was he doing in that wood? Can you tell me that, Superintendent? Why wasn't my husband in his hotel room where he said he would be?'

Lorimer noticed the unshed tears in those dark brown eyes, but it was her expression of hatred that gave him pause for thought. He had been expecting grief but instead it was pent-up anger that seemed to be spilling out.

'We're following every possible lead, Mrs Pattison, and I can assure you that the police will do everything in their power to discover why your husband was out in Renfrewshire. That,' he added more firmly, 'is one reason why I'm here. To see if you can shed any light on this for us.'

'Me?' Catherine Pattison's mouth fell open for a moment in genuine astonishment. 'How on earth would I know what he'd been doing or who he'd been with? I'm only his wife,' she added with a bitterness that made Lorimer's eyes widen.

'You think that your husband was with another woman?'

'Oh, probably. Ed was one of those men who simply can't . . . sorry *couldn't* keep his trousers on . . .' She tutted, as though annoyed with herself. 'God, I've got to get used to referring to him in the past tense, haven't I?'

'Was there anyone he knew in that area?'

'In Erskine? Not that I know of,' Catherine Pattison replied. 'Though he had been out at that hospital for the ex-servicemen once or twice and he'd stayed over at Mar Hall on several occasions. Even took me there once,' she added.

For the first time, as she smiled at the memory, Lorimer saw the young woman through the artist's eyes. Young, lovely and with a suppressed passion that was at once appealing and erotic. What the hell had Edward Pattison been thinking when he had abandoned his wife for casual affairs, if that was what they really had been?

'Did you consider these other women any real threat to your marriage?'

Catherine Pattison smiled again but this time her mouth was twisted in an expression of cynicism. 'Ed would never have left me. He was always far too aware of his public face, you know: the happily married man with three gorgeous kids who adored him. And they did, you know,' she added, suddenly serious. 'It's going to be very hard for them. Ed might have been a philandering bastard but he was a good father.'

Then, as though she had held them back for too many hours, Catherine Pattison let the first tears trickle down her cheeks.

For a few minutes Lorimer let her weep, even handing her one of his own well-laundered white handkerchiefs to blow her nose.

'I said there were several reasons why I had to speak to you, Mrs Pattison,' Lorimer said at last. 'And I do have to ask you if you know of any reason why someone might have wanted your husband dead.'

'Apart from me?' She smiled through her tears, then bit her lip as she saw the policeman's unflinching expression. 'Shouldn't have said that, even as a joke, should I? After all it's usually the spouse that commits the crime, if all these TV shows are to be believed.'

'Statistically speaking, they are correct,' Lorimer told her. 'And so, yes, I do need to know where you were yesterday evening.'

Catherine Pattison heaved a sigh. 'Well, I was at home all of last night. Peter, Kim and Lucy were in bed and I read a book till after twelve o'clock. The police phoned just after breakfast. She paused. 'And my mother came straight over, of course.'

'But there was nobody else with you last night?'

'No.'

'And did you receive any telephone calls during the course of the evening?'

'No,' she frowned. 'What are you asking me all this for?'

'As you said yourself, you need to give an account of your whereabouts in order to be eliminated from our inquiries.'

She looked at him, suddenly surprised at the idea of being regarded as a possible suspect. 'I wouldn't have murdered him, Superintendent. Even though he might have deserved it. I know I have a temper but I couldn't do a thing like that.'

'Well, can you think of anyone else who might have been capable of killing your husband?'

Catherine Pattison looked at him intently. 'Actually,' she said, 'I can.'

Chapter Sixteen

'PRIORITIES, LORIMER, PRIORITIES,' the chief constable said, nodding, hands behind his back as he paced the room. 'Pattison was possibly in line to become the most important figure in Scotland. Whereas . . .' He shrugged his shoulders in a gesture that said more than mere words allowed.

If he kept grinding his teeth together like this as he struggled to keep his temper he'd strain his jaw, Lorimer thought, trying to maintain as bland a countenance as he could. The latest killing of a prostitute was of very little significance compared to Edward Pattison's death, wasn't this what the chief constable was telling him? Okay, so the public would expect a high profile with this one, but to practically shelve Helen James's cases was wrong. Lorimer's face must have expressed something of his inner feelings as the chief constable turned to him, eyes boring into his own.

'You don't like it. Well, that's not my concern right now. You'll do what you're told by myself, Chief Constable Turrell in Lothian and Borders and of course by Felicity Stewart.'

He smiled, scratching the side of his nose. 'What did you make of her, by the way?'

Lorimer raised his eyebrows, wondering if he was genuinely being required to state his opinion or if the chief was trying to search out his political leanings.

'Fairly sharp, sir,' he replied, hoping that this answer would be non-committal enough for now. *A hard, unforgiving sort of woman*, he had thought to himself, though he'd never utter such words outside his own four walls.

'Aye, she is,' the chief nodded again. 'And she'll be expecting you to find Pattison's killer as soon as possible. The longer all this goes on, the worse it will be for the current administration. So, prioritise all of the existing cases in the squad, Lorimer. You hear what I'm saying?'

IT WAS, HE thought grimly, like being given a taste of his own medicine. Was this how DI Sutherland had felt when he had given him no option but to obey his orders? Perhaps. Well, there was maybe a lesson in this for him. He was always going to be accountable to someone higher up the chain of command, Lorimer thought. And even the chief constable probably had to do whatever the first minister demanded. The case files he'd given Solly suddenly came to mind, images of the Geddes woman in death making him tighten his lips in a moment of pity. He had wanted to take that case and shake it by the scruff of its neck, not because he'd had doubts about Helen James's capabilities as an SIO, but simply because it seemed to matter so much. And, he acknowledged to himself, he wanted to find the person who had murdered these women and bring them to justice. Well, the street girls' murders might have to be delegated to someone else now, but he was determined to keep an eye on whatever developments happened in that investigation. He thought of Helen James for a moment; pity she'd been unable to have keyhole surgery. The recovery time from her operation would be at least six weeks. Well, perhaps he'd have the Pattison case done and dusted by then, though something told him that wasn't likely.

Lorimer sat still for a moment, considering his options. Creating a special unit drawn from Mumby and Preston's officers and the task force that he now ran here was one possibility. It would certainly make sense to utilise the men and women who already knew the first two cases inside out. But he guessed that given Pattison's position as the country's deputy first minister the inquiry was going to require quite a different approach. The chief constable's demands were perfectly reasonable, after all. Pattison had been a very important man and one who may well have had enemies within political circles. A niggle of suspicion made him frown: was this all to do with Pattison? He had come across sick-minded killers before who had carried out several murders simply to obfuscate the one that really mattered. And, if ballistics came up with a different sort of weapon, could this possibly be a copycat killing? Felicity Stewart had given him a few names, one of which was the same as that supplied by Catherine Pattison; a disaffected Labour party member who had been heard threatening Pattison on more than one occasion. The others were SNP colleagues who, she claimed, had resented the late deputy minister's meteoric rise to power. Somehow though, Lorimer felt it unlikely that any of them would have stooped so low as to actually kill their rival. Still their alibis for the night of Pattison's death would have to be checked out and Lorimer found himself hoping that each of these politicians had been far from the scene of the deputy first minister's murder.

Lorimer let his gaze pass from one photograph to the next, willing something to ignite a spark in his brain to show him a connection between each victim, not that he lacked faith in the officers who had been down these roads before. Until now all they had were crazy things: they'd all owned luxury cars in the same dazzling showroom white, they'd been staying just for a few days (or overnight in Pattison's case) in the city centre. And the first two men had been killed by the same gun, according to ballistics. So far, questions asked in Glasgow's shadier corners had failed to turn up anything, but there was still plenty of time for that, especially with the lure of a substantial reward in the wake of Edward Pattison's death, something that had already been promised by the Scottish government. None of the informants questioned in the first two cases could supply the name of any pro that had been hired for the jobs. In fact there had been a distinct sense of unease coming out of the Glasgow underworld. Word had it that whoever was carrying out the killings had no previous connection with anyone in the network either up here or south of the border. But now things had changed. With the death of this high-profile figure surely something would emerge?

Edward Pattison's death had begun to intrigue him. Despite the other cases that demanded Lorimer's attention he admitted to himself that he wanted to know more about this man and what he had been doing out in that remote woodland area. Forensic reports still had to come in and perhaps then he would be able to make more sense of this bizarre killing. He'd already spoken to several journalists as well as allowing a press notice to be circulated with the grave warning to let the police get on with their investigation without interference. There were times when the press could be positively helpful but Lorimer knew this case would be plastered over every paper in the country, with speculation running high; and some journalists could and would write things that were counter-productive in a case. Well, at least it helped to have the authority of government to rein them in for now, he thought grimly. Politics came in handy sometimes after all. Tomorrow there would be more meetings with government figures and Pattison's friends and family but for tonight he might just allow himself the luxury of a few hours away from here.

As Lorimer closed the bulky file and thought about going home to Maggie, he suspected that he was probably facing a sleepless night full of unanswered questions.

MAGGIE LORIMER SHUT her book with a bang. What a stupid ending! The characters' actions had been utterly predictable but she had read on, hoping against hope for some twist in the tail. The book fell onto the floor and she left it there, too annoyed to be bothered to place it back on the bookshelf. Maybe she'd put it into the bag in the hall cupboard that she kept for the charity shop, she thought to herself with a smile of satisfaction. If Lena Forsyth thought that was a suitable text for Advanced Higher pupils then she really was off the wall, Maggie thought, remembering the supply teacher's strident tones at that afternoon's departmental meeting.

Outside darkness had fallen to an inky black and rain battered against the windows. Shivering suddenly, Maggie got up and went to close the curtains against the winter's night. Bill had told her a little about the latest prostitute murder but not much more than she had gleaned from the television and newspaper reports. What a night for any young woman to be out, standing waiting for some man to use their body! And all because someone had lured them into the world of drug abuse.

Maggie's mind slipped to the wall outside the school's medical room where posters urged the pupils to shun any form of drugs. The messages were hard hitting all right, but did they ever hit home with the kids? There were a few pupils that worried Maggie Lorimer, the quiet ones who seemed withdrawn and anxious as well as the wee neds who slunk into corners of the playground at break times, shuffling stuff in their pockets that might have been bits of hashish or something worse.

The sound of the new car turning into the drive banished her dark thoughts and Maggie felt her whole body relax as she waited for Bill to turn the key and come through the front door. It was, she admitted to herself, the best time of the day when he arrived home, no matter how late the hour. And, as Maggie waited, she experienced a moment of sheer pride in her husband. He was *detective superintendent* now, the man heading up this important unit at Pitt Street, whose face was all over the newspapers and TV with this high profile murder case. He had deserved to buy himself this new Lexus, she told herself.

'Hi, gorgeous.' Lorimer was suddenly there, his coat wet from the rain outside. Then, as Maggie found herself folded into his embrace, Lena Forsyth and her stupid book were banished completely from her mind.

'I've had dinner but there's plenty left for you. Made that Sophie Dahl asparagus soup you like so much,' she murmured. 'And there's some chilli as well. Just need to warm it up in the microwave.'

'Ach, you spoil me, woman,' Lorimer said, holding her still and stroking her hair gently. She felt his sigh against her body. Maybe he would tell her what had been happening in his world, maybe not. Maggie smiled to herself, leaning her head against her husband's chest. He was home now and whatever lay outside could wait for tomorrow.

Chapter Seventeen

TRAVELLING BY TRAIN at rush hour was not perhaps the most likely place to find love. It was certainly not what Barbara Knox was expecting to find that morning, looking through her copy of the *Metro* and glancing at her travelling companions. A middle-aged man directly across from her sat slumped in his corner next to the window, eyes half-closed, ears full of goodness only knew what sort of music from his iPod. Or was he listening to something work related? Barbara looked covertly at him again from the shelter of the sports pages. Nah, she told herself. Probably not music. Didn't look the type, and wasn't she always congratulating herself on being able to tell a person's character from the little clues about their appearance? She smiled quietly to herself. Maybe that was an attribute she would bring to the team that Detective Superintendent Lorimer had asked her to join?

Barbara Knox felt a warm rush of pride as she remembered the article in the police magazine. The photo had been horrible, her face grinning out at the photographer from Pitt Street, but the feature itself had given her a glow of satisfaction as it outlined her short biography and the fact that she was to join this prestigious squad. And there would be new people there – people who might become friends, she thought, feeling a little wistful.

The squeal of brakes drowned out any further thought as the train slowed to a halt at one of the busier stations on the route into Glasgow, several of the passengers already on their feet, queuing to reach the doors. DC Barbara Knox gave a sigh and returned to her reading as the man with the MP3 player rose from his place and joined the others who were silently filing off the train. Barbara felt her coat being dragged slightly as he swept past so she rummaged into the pocket, her hand feeling her warrant card. She was pulling it out and trying to find an inside pocket in her jacket when more passengers began to enter the train. Mr MP3's place was taken by an attractive dark-haired woman who sat down carefully as though she were taking special care not to disturb Barbara as she shuffled the card to a safer place. For the briefest of moments their eyes met and Barbara was surprised into giving one of her rare smiles. The other woman smiled back then turned away to look out of the window, as though suddenly shy of human contact.

But it was there, Barbara was sure of it, that little frisson of recognition, one girl to another. A surreptitious glance at the other woman's ungloved fingers told Barbara what she had hoped to find out: no rings on the third finger of her left hand. Something caught at her throat as she continued to observe the woman and Barbara felt the familiar sense of excitement at anticipating a new conquest. She was undoubtedly a businesswoman; that much Barbara could tell from her thick black coat and expensive-looking leather boots, plus the well-groomed air that she had. It was classy, not overdone like one of these girls from the perfume counters, all blusher and false eyelashes, but subdued and elegant like the profile that was turned as if to let Barbara see just how exquisite she was.

The carriage was plunged into gloom as the train entered a tunnel and for a moment each woman gazed at the other in the reflection of the darkened window. This time the gaze was held and Barbara's smile grew warmer.

As the train journeyed on through the approach to the city Barbara could see the woman's smile still fixed on those reddened lips, lips that she suddenly yearned to kiss. *She was, she was, she had to be*, Barbara told herself, closing her eyes for a moment and imagining the touch of the woman's hand on hers.

When she opened them, the woman was looking right at her, a curious expression on her face that made Barbara blush. Surely she couldn't see into her mind? No, that was ridiculous!

Then the train was slowing down and everybody was rising to their feet, some straining their eyes to see on what side the platform would appear. Barbara and the dark-haired woman rose together and Barbara automatically ushered her out first before leaving the train herself.

It seemed the most natural thing in the world to strike up a conversation as they walked along the platform, side by side. The weather was the first topic, obviously, but then the woman cocked her head to one side and said, 'You're a policewoman, aren't you?'

'Yes,' Barbara replied. 'How did you know?'

'You've got that clever air about you,' the woman said, a smile on her half-parted lips that seemed to be keeping back something else that she wanted to say, some secret she wanted to share.

It was madness, of course it was, speaking like this with a perfect stranger. But at that moment Barbara Knox found herself beguiled by a smile and the soft timbre of the woman's voice. In a sudden rush of pride, she found herself telling this stranger about the call to join Lorimer's team and how she hoped to gain some experience and eventually promotion. The dark-haired woman was an easy listener and there was something more, Barbara sensed; a warmth that was greater than the interest of a mere passer-by.

'What is it you do, yourself?' Barbara asked as they waited to cross Hope Street. She expected she was a lawyer, or maybe an accountant; the offices between here and Pitt Street were full of businesses like that.

The enigmatic smile made Barbara eager to know more about this woman as she turned away. 'Ah,' she said, 'that would be telling, now wouldn't it?' and the laugh she gave was husky, almost sexy, deepening the policewoman's curiosity.

'Go on, let me guess,' Barbara began, deciding that a mildly flirtatious approach would do no harm. 'You're an international lawyer of some sort, or, no, let me think, you work for one of those global corporations.'

'You shouldn't be able to guess,' the woman told her, a serious note creeping into her voice. 'Actually, I'm a journalist.'

'Ah.' Barbara's face fell and she quickened her step. What the hell was she playing at, trying to charm one of the press pack?

'Oh, it's not what you think,' the woman replied quickly, one hand on Barbara's arm, slowing her down. 'I'm freelance. In fact,' she turned around, a furtive gesture as though to ensure that nobody was listening, 'I work mostly undercover. On really important cases.'

DC Barbara Knox found that they were standing at the corner of Bothwell Street now, outside Starbucks. Her eyes travelled towards the door, wishing she had the nerve to ask, biting her lip in sudden confusion. She always turned up far too early for work and there was time today . . .

'Coffee?' the woman asked and before she knew it, Barbara was inside the place, its familiar smell of coffee overlaid with cinnamon and vanilla tickling her nostrils.

It was easy after that, talking about work, telling her new friend about the case she'd been on with DCI Mumby and how Lorimer now had her up at Pitt Street to help out with this work, keeping the details deliberately vague.

The amazed expression on the journalist's face had made her falter for a moment. 'What?' she'd asked, puzzled.

'But that must be the case I'm working on too!' the other woman had whispered, drawing her seat closer so that their knees met under the table, giving Barbara a fluttery feeling deep within her stomach. 'The story of the men killed in their white cars!'

AFTERWARDS BARBARA WONDERED what sort of fate had led Diana Yeats to sit opposite her on that particular morning. That was her name, the woman had confided, but she had uttered it in a manner that made the policewoman wonder if it was a pseudonym of sorts, something to be used in her profession or with a stranger met on a train. She had left her there quite reluctantly, a smile between them and a promise to meet up again after work.

And, as Barbara Knox turned up into Pitt Street her feet seemed not to notice the steep incline. A red letter day, some folk called it; a day when good things happened. And beginning to work with Lorimer and meeting Diana all on one day surely justified that expression?

Thoughts of the woman were kept to a secret corner of DC Knox's mind, however, as she entered Strathclyde Police headquarters, the word for *welcome* etched on the double glass doors in more than a dozen different languages. The commissionaire nodded as she showed him her warrant card and directed her upstairs away from the small foyer with its empty black seating.

THE WOMAN WHO had called herself Diana sat on in the coffee house, her second latte still untouched. Was there such a thing as coincidence? Or were the fates that had driven her to seek out Carol's killer bringing her more help in the rather unlovely shape of this lesbian police officer? Spotting that article in the police magazine had been a piece of complete luck. The feature had been more about the Serious Crimes Squad itself and the woman had sensed the politics behind the editor's desire to elevate the squad's profile when she knew fine the department was going to be mothballed. It had paid off having contacts in the right places even after all this time. And one of them had even tiptoed around the matter of Barbara Knox's sexual orientation. Then it had been a matter of catching the right train at the right time, looking for the face that matched the photo in the magazine, hoping that she could ingratiate herself with the police officer. Forging a liaison with this Barbara person was immensely risky, but then perhaps the final consequences would outweigh the risks.

'I WANT EVERY car dealership and every paper that advertises private sales to be contacted,' Lorimer said. 'And don't forget these car auctions places either,' he added, remembering the fate of his old Lexus. 'It stands to reason that anyone owning a white car of that particular make is going to become jittery, so expect a small flood of car sales or trade-ins.'

'What about the owners?' DI Sutherland wanted to know.

'I was coming to that,' Lorimer told him. 'We could work on the theory that there is some obsessive killer on the loose who is randomly targeting men in white Mercedes sports cars. Professor Brightman will bring us up to speed on that one,' he added. 'But we cannot rule out the possibility that whoever has been luring these men to their deaths actually has some prior knowledge of the victims.'

'But surely Wardlaw and Littlejohn were just in the wrong place at the wrong time?' Sutherland protested.

'Could be,' Lorimer agreed. 'Or it could also be the case that there is a link between all three men that we have yet to discover. A link,' he added, turning to the rest of the officers assembled in the incident room, 'that may be shared by other Mercedes owners and that could possibly give us some sort of clue about these deaths.'

The expressions on the faces of his officers were far from happy, Lorimer could see. The nitty-gritty business of police investigation was always laborious and time-consuming but they had no alternative but to throw all their resources at this case, given the third victim's public profile.

'Delegate as much as you can to Mumby and Preston's officers but it is imperative that every single one of you report even the smallest finding back to me. This is a team effort and I don't want any mavericks looking for glory,' he added sternly. 'You're part of an elite squad so you don't have to prove yourselves to me or to anyone else. Okay?'

As he left them to carry out their various actions, Lorimer felt a pang of envy. His present remit was to go downstairs and face the group of journalists who would no doubt be already assembled and waiting for him.

PROFESSOR SOLLY BRIGHTMAN smiled to himself as he typed in the information to his preliminary report. Cases of obsessive personalities fixating on one particular set of circumstances or objects that led to murder were actually quite rare and it intrigued the psychologist to think that there might be someone of that description out there in the city who needed to be taken into custody. Solly was the sort of person who was able to look at the facts dispassionately, however. Three men had been lured to their death by a person or persons unknown. Each had been found in a quiet place, far from main roads, the first two beneath railway bridges, suggesting that the killer may have made his way back to the city by a late train. Whoever had murdered Edward Pattison had had to leave the scene on foot, however. There were no buses from Erskine at that time of night so either the killer lived in the vicinity or had simply walked away. Unless there had been another person waiting for them in those woods, of course.

The police would be able to examine any CCTV footage of the Erskine Bridge itself. It was a magnet for suicides, Solly knew, recalling the Samaritans placard on the approach to the footpath. But he felt intuitively that the killer would have taken a less public route from the scene of crime, losing themselves in the labyrinth of housing estates that comprised the town of Erskine. He was not much given to using his intuitive powers, though, preferring to look at the facts in a logical manner.

He blinked as he continued to type, remembering the family of Carol Kilpatrick. Their home was only a few miles from the scene of crime; a walk that might take a fit man less than an hour. And then there was the death of Miriam Lyons, whose body had been found on the other side of the river that separated Erskine from Clydebank and Bowling. Could there be a link between the death of the deputy first minister of Scotland and these poor street girls?

Solly shook his head, smiling once again. No. He was being fanciful, seeing things that simply weren't there. Coincidences did happen and, sadly, murders took place all over the city and its environs. For now his remit was to examine everything he could about the possible type of mind that had planned and carried out the killings of these three men. Heaving a sigh that Lorimer would have recognised as pity for the women whose cases were being regarded as of secondary importance, Solly continued his work, frowning in concentration as the words continued to grow on the computer screen.

Images of these lonely places loomed up in his mind as Solly tried to visualise the cars and the bodies that had been left for some unsuspecting person to discover. A frown formed as he pictured each scene. The men had been sitting in the driver's seat, hadn't they? So, he wondered, what had taken place before the shots that had killed them? Had they been coerced into driving to these out-of-the-way spots, a gun forced against their sides, perhaps? Or had they known their assailant? Trusted them, even? Solly removed his spectacles and rubbed his eyes as though that small action would aid his thought processes. If each of these men had been abducted, he reasoned, it would have taken at least one strong man to have overpowered them. But that did not make sense if he was looking for someone who fitted an obsessive disorder of this sort of magnitude. The assassinations had to have been carried out by a single killer. Someone who had cowed the men into meekly obeying orders to drive into a quiet and dangerous location. Solly stroked his beard thoughtfully. All three victims had been big men, physically, and surely strong enough to have at least tried to fight back against a dangerous gunman? Solly only had photographs and written descriptions of the first two victims but since his death images of the deputy first minister had been plastered over every newspaper and television screen until he could conjure up his face at will.

For a long moment the psychologist stared at his computer screen, not seeing the paragraphs he had already written but a vision of Edward Pattison sitting at the wheel of his white Mercedes, his familiar smile directed at an unseen companion.

'AYE, I KENT her,' Doreen Gallagher nodded, her dangly earrings bouncing off each pale cheek as she took the cigarette from the other woman. They were standing on the pavement outside the drop-in centre in Robertson Street, *having a friendly chat* as the woman who had identified herself as a journalist had put it. 'Ta,' she grunted, leaning forwards to get a light. 'Aye, Tracey-Anne wis a regular here a'right. Pair lassie didnae ken whit time o' day it wis half the time, mind.' Doreen blew the cigarette smoke upwards then fixed the other woman with a stare. 'Whit's it tae youse anyhow? Thought ye'd be all ower that ither murder. Big cheese in the Scottish parliament.'

'Someone else is dealing with that,' the dark-haired woman told her. 'I've been assigned to this one. So,' she continued, 'what else can you tell me about poor Tracey-Anne Geddes?'

BARBARA KNOX SMILED wryly at the report in front of her. Detective Superintendent Lorimer had not been wrong on this one, she thought, reading the statistics that told of several white Mercedes sports cars suddenly being offered as trade-ins around the country. Her smile widened as she remembered how the SIO had asked her directly to take on this particular action. Working here in the Serious Crimes Squad was not only better than being at Mumby's beck and call, it would surely look good on her CV and improve her chances of promotion. Okay, it was only temporary but Barbara was relishing the chance to work on this case, particularly with Lorimer in charge. He had . . . how could she describe it? The kind of authority that made you want to do your best for him. And he cared, he really cared about the victims of crime, something that DI Sutherland seemed to have forgotten how to do, she thought darkly.

She pressed the print button, telling herself that she needed to re-read hard copy before she forwarded this information to the rest of the team. It had to be good, to read well, and, most important of all, it had to impress that tall man with the piercing blue eyes. Two copies of the information slid onto the feed tray and DC Knox pulled them off, separating them quickly. One copy she shuffled into a card file, the other she folded twice then, hesitating for just a fraction, stuffed it into a pocket of her handbag.

'GENTLEMEN,' LORIMER SAID, turning slightly to one side and smiling, 'and ladies,' he added, nodding to the female journalists who were present for this press conference. 'Thank you all for coming to police headquarters. I intend to give a short statement regarding the progress of this case after which I can give you all time to ask questions.'

A murmur of appreciation rose from the men and women facing Lorimer in Pitt Street's assembly hall. The detective superintendent wanted nothing more than to be left to get on with the case right now, but he acknowledged that this time with the press pack was invaluable if he were to get them onto his side.

'There is as yet no suspect for the murder of the deputy first minister or the two men who were killed in sports cars identical to Mr Pattison's. We are throwing massive resources at this case, however, and hope to have reports from the forensic services very soon. Officers from each of the divisions investigating Mr Wardlaw's and Mr Littlejohn's deaths have been seconded to this squad meantime.' He paused and looked out directly at them all before continuing. This next point might prove controversial but it mattered to him.

'Serious Crimes have enlisted the expertise of Professor Brightman from the University of Glasgow,' he said slowly. 'We hope that he might throw some light on the personality of the killer. Professor Brightman has assisted Strathclyde Police most successfully in previous cases and we are very lucky to have someone of his calibre working with us.'

Several of the people in front of him turned to their neighbours, a questioning look on their faces. Solomon Brightman's services had been suspended for a time following a debacle south of the border when an experienced psychologist had made a colossal error, throwing the entire science of criminal profiling into doubt. Lorimer realised, however, that this was his chance to reinstate Solly in the most public of ways.

'I would be pleased to take any questions for the next thirty minutes,' Lorimer said firmly.

IT WAS IN fact considerably more than half an hour later that Lorimer was walking hurriedly across the street to where his driver was waiting. Once again he had to make the trip across to the east of the country, this time to talk to Pattison's colleagues and friends. Thinking back to the way both Felicity Stewart and Catherine Pattison had described the dead man, Lorimer wondered if in fact the late deputy first minister had had anyone who might recognise themselves as his friend.

A thin sleet had begun to cover the city rooftops as they made their way from Glasgow past the tall forbidding chimneys of the Royal Infirmary and out along the motorway. Sitting in the rear of the big car, Lorimer had time to think over the press conference. There had been, inevitably, questions asked about the wisdom of using a profiler, particularly at a time when police budgets had been so severely constrained. His reassurances about Solly and reminders of his past successes had hopefully served to assuage any lingering doubts about his friend's abilities. But it had been the questions about Edward Pattison that had troubled him most.

Not being one to follow gossip columns in the tabloids, Lorimer had never really picked up on details of Pattison's personal life as portrayed by such papers. It had come as a surprise then, to find that his teetotal lifestyle had once been overshadowed by a predilection for cannabis in his student days. One older reporter had quizzed Lorimer about a possible drug connection in Pattison's death but Lorimer had replied blandly that inquiries were still ongoing whilst furiously trying to recall anything that Rita Livingstone had turned up about the deputy first minister. His former boss, Detective Superintendent Mark Mitchison, had always been one for trying to link sudden deaths with drug abuse. Sure, the prevalence of drugs in their city meant that many incidents had them at their source but statistics showed that drunkenness was a far greater contributing factor to a fatal stabbing or the like. His gut feeling was that Pattison had been squeaky clean, especially in the light of Felicity Stewart's comments. *He doesn't drink, do drugs or drive over the speed limit,* she'd told Lorimer with more than a hint of disgust, as though a real man should at least be able to incorporate one of these vices into his lifestyle. Ms Stewart's own liking for a tipple was well documented, though, and she had hinted that Pattison had been using that to bring her down.

Well, he might ask a few searching questions of the three people who had agreed to meet him at the Scottish parliament.

Chapter Eighteen

'RIGHT, MISS, GO to sleep,' Rosie whispered, laying the baby down slowly and gently so she would not waken. The wisp-thin muslin awnings on either side of the baby's cradle quivered as Abigail sighed once, her feathery lashes lowering as her blue veined eyelids closed. Rosie stood still for a moment, wondering at the miracle of motherhood. Yes, it was exhausting, but there were times, like now, when she wanted nothing more than to stand and stare at her little daughter, counting the blessings that had come her way since the day she had met Solly. It was three months since Abigail had come into their world, destroying almost every night's sleep with her constant demands, but Rosie had treasured every moment, knowing that her own career would have to be resumed long before the baby's first birthday.

Jacqui White had agreed to be her locum for six months only and part of Rosie was glad that she hadn't asked the woman to continue for longer than that. Yes, she was looking forward to returning to work and yes, she felt that the celebrity pathologist didn't really have the same commitment to her work as she did, but then there was another huge part of her that longed to stay home and watch as Abby grew up. Wasn't it a subject that came perennially into every woman's magazine, this wrench between nurturing one's offspring and making a career? Well, her career was certainly established and Rosie had no doubts that returning to work was what she should do. Still, finding a carer for their daughter was uppermost in Solly and Rosie's minds and not just anyone who happened to be available; whoever looked after Miss Abigail Margaret Brightman would have to be a very special person indeed.

Maggie Lorimer had asked if she could help out at weekends, especially as Rosie would have to be on call some Saturdays and Sundays. Before Abby's birth this hadn't been a problem but now she was grateful for Maggie's offer. Spending time with her godmother would be good for their little one, and looking at things another way, might even help to make up for the Lorimers' own lack of family.

Rosie slipped out of the nursery at last, certain that Abby was sound asleep. If she were to repeat the pattern of previous days then she might be able to have a whole hour to herself.

'Asleep?' Solly asked as Rosie came up behind him and placed her arms on his shoulders.

'Yes,' she answered, then looked beyond him at the computer screen. 'How's it going? Any clues about Pattison yet?'

'Ah,' Solly smiled at her, stroking the hand that had wound its way to find his own. 'Don't tell me you're looking for that elusive magic that so many people think is bound up with profiling.'

'Nope,' Rosie replied. 'Not only do I know you better than that, I'm cynical enough to believe that Edward Pattison wasn't just unlucky,' she said darkly. 'He was up to something. And I bet it involved a woman.'

'How do you make that out?' Solly murmured.

'Well, stands to reason, doesn't it? He'd been busy all evening with a delegation or something and should have been getting down to his beddy-byes in some nice hotel or other. So what else could have taken him out in his fancy car at that time of night? Eh? Tell me that!' she said, nodding her head as though this should have been the most obvious thing in the world to ask.

'Now if we knew the answer . . .' Solly began.

'Well, what about the doorman at the hotel, or the night manager or . . . or . . . the guy who looks after the cars down in their garage? Has anyone asked them that question yet?'

'Actually, yes,' Solly said, turning around in his chair and catching his wife around her waist. 'All of them are co-operating with Lorimer's team.' He smiled at her. 'Are you so desperate to get back into harness, my lovely?' he asked wistfully. 'Sure you don't want to give it a rest for a couple of years?'

'Oh, don't, Solly, please,' Rosie replied. 'It's going to be hard enough, but you know my mind's made up. Once we find a good childminder it'll all work out, you'll see.'

'And meantime you want to know more about the facts of a murder case than when to give our daughter her first solid food?' he teased.

'Aye, too right,' Rosie laughed. 'Let me get back to my department and I'll appreciate that wee lady next door all the more, I promise you. Anyway, see this case. D'you think it's all about Pattison or is there really some nutter running around looking for guys in their Mercedes sports cars?'

'Hmm,' was all that Solly would give as a reply. Then turning back to his computer he began to re-read what he had written so far.

Rosie waited for a moment then shook her head before leaving him to it. She could hardly complain that her husband was busy at work now that she was thinking ahead to the resumption of her own career. Still, maybe she had struck a chord with her remark about Pattison. If she had been away from home at a conference she'd either have been in the bar talking to her colleagues or else telephoning Solly from her hotel room. Why Edward Pattison had been doing neither of these things but had chosen to drive away from his hotel late at night was not just a mystery, it didn't make any sense; unless, as she had hinted, he had been up to something that his wife didn't know about.

SOLLY FROWNED, LOOKING intently at the words on his computer screen. Rosie was absolutely right. Of course Pattison should have been at the hotel, not gallivanting about Glasgow at that time of night. His diary had made it clear that he was expecting a full workload the next day and any hard-working politician would have been glad to have a good night's sleep before returning to the Scottish parliament and his other duties. So, what had he been doing? What attractions had the city for a man with a reputation for clean living? Or, he wondered, had it been one particular attraction? And, if so, should Lorimer and his team be looking for what Glasgow folk would call Pattison's *bit on the side*?

Chapter Nineteen

LORIMER WATCHED AS the snowflakes whirled faster around the windows, obscuring the landscape on either side. Even the dark rows of pine trees on this stretch of the M8 had been obliterated by the whiteout and his driver had slowed down, warned by the overhead gantry signs that there was an accident ahead. It was, he thought, the law of natural cussedness that, at a time when he needed to act swiftly, his day was being held up, first by that press conference and now by the vagaries of the Scottish weather.

A small noise from his inside pocket made him take out his BlackBerry and read the latest message. He grinned when he saw Professor Brightman's name appear at the top.

Cherchez la femme was all it said, but Lorimer knew fine what Solly was hinting at. Despite the fact that he hadn't yet told Solly about his conversation with Catherine Pattison, the psychologist seemed to have reached the same conclusion about the dead man. He'd spent time during this journey trying out ways of asking questions of Pattison's closest friends and family. But how did you frame a sentence that asked if a man had been cheating on his wife? As the wind whipped the snow in drifts across the road, the driver turned around, shaking his head.

'Sorry, sir, think we'll have to turn off at the next junction. The road's totally blocked after Harthill. I think it would be best to call up a Land Rover if you still want to get to the capital today.'

'Do what you can to have a vehicle standing by,' Lorimer told him. 'I need to be in Edinburgh today and back tonight if that's possible. By train if need be.'

Then as the car slithered to the inside lane, skidding slightly on the impacted snow, Lorimer sat back, calculating how late he was going to be for his first appointment.

THE TALL MAN reached up as his scarf threatened to unwind itself, caught by a blast of icy wind that seemed to come straight from the Russian Steppes. Tucking it into his dark tweed overcoat, he stepped gingerly across the forecourt of the garage, aware that any dark patch might cause him to fall. He blinked as the snowflakes began to quicken, landing on his eyelashes and dampening his hair.

Once inside the warmth of the car showroom, he turned back his coat collar and glanced around him. Every new car gleamed in the overhead spotlights as he moved from one to the next, savouring the more conventional saloons and dismissing the Grand Editions despite their tag of *more leg room more luxury*. Yes he might be a big man, but he didn't require a car with that much space.

When the inevitable 'Can I help you, sir?' came from the smart-suited smiling young man, he was ready with a reply.

'I have a car that I would like to trade in. Perhaps we could discuss terms?' he said, his voice smooth, but with an Eastern European accent that told the salesman that this customer was not from these parts.

'Yes, of course, sir. If I could have a look at your current vehicle?' The young man's smile stayed glued in place as the tall man nodded to the window where the snow was now falling heavily from a leaden sky.

'That is it there,' the tall man replied, pointing to a white Mercedes sports car that was parked a few yards across the forecourt.

'I'll just grab my jacket, sir,' the salesman said, turning into an office behind the curved reception desk.

'White Merc. Punter here to trade it in,' the young man hissed at the girl behind a computer screen. 'We've to call the police, remember?'

'Well, just get his name and address. What's all the fuss about?' the girl drawled, shrugging one shoulder as if to say that her colleague was dramatising the affair.

'Okay, okay, I will,' he replied sourly, pulling on a padded navy jacket emblazoned with the Mercedes logo.

'Right,' he said, rubbing his hands and striding towards the automatic doors, not forgetting to fix his smile back on again. 'Let's have a look at your car, shall we?'

As the white car purred away from the forecourt, Alan Jackson grinned widely. That would take his monthly bonus up and no mistake! Making the sale of that brand new CLS Class Coupe, Champagne Silver this time, for a new customer was a success indeed. So many of their existing clients were choosing to trade in and buy second-hand in these difficult times, so a sale like this was a genuine reason for Alan Jackson to grin. The guy was in a hurry for it, right enough. Wanted the paperwork done today and could he pick up the vehicle by tomorrow. Alan's smile had faltered just a tad as he had explained the necessity of arranging insurance and road tax as well as getting the gentleman's bank details, necessities that would, regretfully, take a little longer than a mere twenty-four hours. But the buyer should have known that, surely?

Smoothing his hair and giving a mocking glance at Estelle, the girl with whom he shared an office, Alan sat down at his desk and pulled a card towards him. Moments later he stopped swinging his chair from side to side and sat up a little straighter as the voice from Strathclyde Police headquarters came onto the line.

'FIRST ONE!' DETECTIVE Constable Barbara Knox crowed triumphantly, though there was in truth nobody to hear the delight in her voice. Her part of the office was empty at that moment, most of her colleagues either out on separate actions or upstairs in the canteen having lunch. But that did not matter to the stout young woman who was busily typing details into her computer.

Mr Vladimir Badica, with an address in the west end of Argyll Street, was a new client, Alan Jackson had told her.

How did he seem? Barbara had wanted to know and was gratified when Jackson had replied, *in a hurry.* Aye, there might be a few rich punters with white sports cars wanting to offload them as fast as they could after all the media coverage about Pattison being found shot dead in his big white Mercedes-Benz. The dealership where Jackson worked was the main one in the city but Strathclyde Police had put out the same message to Mercedes dealerships throughout the country: all possible trade-ins of white Mercedes sports cars had to be reported back here to Glasgow. As the woman shifted her gaze to the window and saw the falling snow she let her gaze linger, lulled for a few moments by the hypnotic quality of the huge snowflakes constantly falling out of a cold white sky. Then blinking as though to clear her head, she had a sudden thought: who in their right mind would want to drive to a car showroom on a day like this? Pulling her chair closer to the desk, DC Knox began to type in her own little note about Mr Vladimir Badica and why he might want to take all that trouble to get rid of his car.

'Facts, Barbara, facts,' she whispered to herself as unfounded suspicions began to rise to the surface. Just because the owner of this car had a foreign sounding name didn't mean he was Russian mafia or anything, did it? No, the politically correct brigade would delight in telling them that this man deserved the same attention as any other law-abiding citizen in this part of the world, wouldn't they? Still, she grinned to herself, it would be nice if she were to be given the role of interviewing Mr Badica, wouldn't it? The DC gave a nod of satisfaction as she finished typing up the information.

For a moment the woman's eyes darted to the printer next to her computer. Her finger hovered above the button then she breathed in sharply, wondering for a moment what the consequences of this small action might be. It was completely against all the regulations that had been dinned into her from the beginning of her career.

Rubbing the palms of her hands together, Barbara felt the unfamiliar sweatiness. She swallowed then glanced around the room, listening for footsteps outside. There was nobody about, she told herself, nobody to see two copies being made.

Taking a deep breath, the policewoman pressed the button. She watched as the sheets of paper shot out onto the tray then changed the command back to a single copy.

The second sheet of paper was folded twice, and once more hastily tucked into a pocket of her handbag that she zipped tightly shut. It was done. She would leave the office later today carrying information for her friend. No one would need to know. And, besides, surely it would help this investigation in the long run?

The sense of triumph was overcast by a lurking feeling of guilt, however, as DC Knox attempted to resume the task she had been given.

'DETECTIVE SUPERINTENDENT! GOODNESS. I really didn't expect to see you today,' Felicity Stewart declared, tossing a cashmere wrap across her left shoulder then offering Lorimer her right hand in a firm grasp. As before, the first minister was dressed in severely cut tweeds, her sensible flat-heeled shoes a gesture towards the weather outside the parliament building. 'Lots of call-offs in the diary, as you might expect,' she went on as they walked through the corridors. 'Jimmy's in, though.' She stopped and looked up at him, her eyes narrowing a little. 'I'd be interested to know how your little chat with him goes,' she said, smiling a crocodile smile that was all teeth.

'I think Mr Raeburn will be hoping for the same discretion that I afforded you, ma'am,' Lorimer replied, the hint of a smile hovering around his mouth.

Felicity Stewart threw back her head and hooted with laughter. 'Oh, you would have made a smooth politician, Lorimer,' she chortled. 'Telling me off but still polite with it. I could always do with a man who isn't afraid to treat me like that,' she added with a grin. This time her smile was genuine and she regarded the detective superintendent with an expression that made him feel both flattered and uncomfortable.

The first minister's laughter had alerted the occupant of the office which they stood outside; the open-plan offices were like a visual metaphor for political transparency, Lorimer thought. Nobody in this place apart from the first minister had the luxury of a wooden door that was closed to prying eyes. Every one of the small offices was identical; a minuscule glass fronted area where the secretarial staff worked leading to a narrow room ending in the famous pod by the window. The detective superintendent saw a short, stout man approaching and as he drew closer Lorimer noticed that he was wearing a tartan bow tie and a mustard-coloured checked suit. The effect of his choice of garments could have made the man appear clownish, but there was nothing in the least comical in his grave expression as he regarded the man and woman outside his office.

'Jimmy, this is Detective Superintendent Lorimer from Strathclyde Police,' Ms Stewart said. 'I'll be in my office should you need me, Lorimer,' she added then, giving them both a perfunctory wave of her hand, she turned on her heel and left the two men together.

'Amazed you made it across here today,' Raeburn began, then stepped aside and ushered Lorimer into his office. 'Come in, come in. It's not very big in here, more of a den, really, but at least it's warm.'

Lorimer walked into the room, surprised by how tiny it was, but then perhaps the clutter of books and files spread across the strip of mottled carpet made the place appear smaller than it really was. As Raeburn bustled about, attempting to tidy things away, Lorimer had time to absorb the man who had been, if one believed the media reports, Edward Pattison's closest friend and political ally. Raeburn was a man in his late fifties, his soft white curls around a balding pate giving him a scholarly look. Lorimer had seen the politician on television but here, in the flesh, he was different somehow. It was odd, almost ironic, Lorimer told himself with a puzzled frown, that here in real life Raeburn seemed more like someone acting the part than the man he recalled from several late night TV programmes.

At last the politician appeared to have cleared away sufficient documents to create a space on two modern-looking chairs around a small wooden table. For a moment Lorimer was nonplussed. Had James Raeburn really been so busy all morning, sorting out paperwork? He had been expected, after all, Lorimer reasoned, telephoning to alert the people he had arranged to meet that he might be a little late, that was all. Perhaps Raeburn lived in a perpetual state of chaos? Or had he been looking for something in particular, Lorimer wondered: something to do with the death of his friend?

'Sorry about that, Lorimer,' Raeburn said, pulling one soft-looking earlobe as though it were an unconscious habit. 'Now,' he said, pulling his chair sideways so that he was facing the policeman. 'What can I do for you?'

Lorimer crossed then uncrossed his legs, feeling the dampness from the melted snow that had seeped onto the edges of his trousers. 'I'm here about Edward Pattison, of course,' he began. 'In any murder inquiry there is a need to clarify much about a victim's personality and social habits,' he said carefully. 'So I may have to ask you some rather personal questions. He was your best friend, was he not?' He paused, seeing the nod of agreement and that unwavering stare in the other man's eyes. Whatever he suspected about Pattison, Raeburn's body language was not giving much away.

'You were with Mr Pattison in Glasgow at the delegation on the night he died, I believe?'

'Indeed,' replied Raeburn. 'But I left to catch the late train back to Edinburgh. It'll be in the diary if you need to verify that,' he commented dryly, indicating the lady sitting with her back to them, her tiny workspace practically out in the corridor. He shrugged and smiled. 'Afraid I can't help you very much. You see,' he added, 'as far as I knew Ed was going back to his hotel for the night.' The smile slipped as he blinked, as though remembering. 'The last I saw of him was when we were putting on our coats before I left to catch the train from Queen Street station.'

'Did Mr Pattison have any particular friends in the Glasgow area he might have decided to see that night?' Lorimer asked smoothly.

Raeburn's eyes flickered and Lorimer could see that the implication behind his words was not lost to him.

'Had Edward Pattison been seeing some woman behind his wife's back? Is that what you're really asking me, Lorimer?' Raeburn bit his lip suddenly. 'Well, perhaps he had been. But if that was the case, nobody knew about it. Not even me!' He looked straight at Lorimer, meeting the policeman's blue gaze with a stare of his own. 'If Ed *had* been seeing someone then it was done so discreetly that no mention of it would ever have come out. No matter how thoroughly the press pack raked in various middens,' he added sourly.

'But he did have friends in the Glasgow area, surely?' Lorimer persisted. He was aware that the man's feathers had been ruffled. The detective superintendent, however, was determined to remain as impassive as possible. 'Didn't he use to visit Mar Hall sometimes for dinner?'

'Perhaps he did,' Raeburn countered, looking at Lorimer with suspicion. 'But not with me. I'm an Edinburgh man, myself,' he added. 'Most of my socialising is done here in the capital,' he went on. 'And I can tell you,' Raeburn lifted one finger and began to wag it as though he were giving the policeman a lecture, 'Edward Pattison enjoyed this city more than any other in Scotland. Glasgow is all very fine, I suppose,' he conceded, the finger still raised, 'but unless he had a reason to go there, Ed was happy to spend his leisure time here among his friends and family.'

'What do *you* think he was doing out in his sports car in the woods of West Renfrewshire, Mr Raeburn?' Lorimer asked suddenly, sitting forward a little so that the smaller man shrank back, clasping his hands tightly.

'I don't know.' Raeburn shook his white curls sorrowfully. 'Truly I don't. And,' he continued, rubbing his thumbs together, 'it pains me to think that there might have been some area of Ed's life that he kept secret from me.'

The silence that followed this remark was probably his cue to get up and leave, Lorimer thought, but, as he bent forward to rise, his eyes were caught by one of a pile of books that lay askew on the carpet.

'A hobby of yours?' he asked, pointing towards the 2010 edition of *The Standard Catalogue of Firearms: The Collector's Price and Reference Guide.*

'Yes, as a matter of fact. I'm a collector,' Raeburn told him, straightening his back. 'Not a passion that Ed shared, I'm afraid, and before you ask, no, I have nothing missing from the locked case where my guns are kept. Lost quite a lot of them after Dunblane,' he said ruefully. 'And the ones that remain are all licensed. You can do a check on me if you like,' he added testily, lifting up the book and placing it in his desk drawer. 'I have nothing to hide.'

THERE WAS LITTLE more to be had from Raeburn after that and Lorimer had left the MSP at the door of his office, wondering at that tone of regret. Did Raeburn suspect that his friend had had a secret that he had chosen not to share with him? And, Lorimer thought, what sort of secret would a man in Pattison's position wish to keep from his closest friend? Somehow the idea of a sexual liaison as suggested by Solly seemed more and more likely. *Cherchez la femme*, the psychologist had written in his text message. Well, perhaps his team would begin to do just that. And, he smiled grimly to himself, maybe the next person he was going to see would have a different sort of slant on this particular theory.

Zena Fraser was seated in her pod, a quiet sanctuary that each member of the Scottish parliament had been given, conceived as a place of contemplation by Enric Miralles, the clever architect of this marvellous building. It was, in truth, only a raised seating area set at right angles to the narrow little room and next to a window barred with rounded poles of what might have been beechwood. Yet, as the word came to his mind, Lorimer dismissed it. Barred was the wrong term to apply to these spars that reminded him of waving lines of bamboo: there was certainly some movement suggested by that simple design.

She looked up at Lorimer as he strode into the room, knocking on the glass door that was, he assumed, permanently ajar. Despite the room being a mirror image of the one he had just left, Zena Fraser's was far neater and it was evident that she had made an effort to personalise her limited space. This room had a woman's touch here and there: a vase of winter leaves and scarlet berries was arranged on the small desk, almost hidden by an enormous anglepoise lamp that dominated the surface, and the coat stand held a cream-coloured wrap with a large furry collar. There was a plant on the steps within the pod, albeit a sad-looking orchid with one fragile bloom still clinging to its narrow stem. The whiteboard to his right held a garish calendar with African tribal figures dancing in the heat of this January month. He blinked as he entered the inner office, surprised at the bleakness of the decor: one wall was like a wooden jigsaw, panels open to reveal the shelves of files within; the other simply looked as though the builders had upped tools and left, the white wall surrounded by greyish concrete that had the look of slightly ageing chipboard.

Lorimer's first impression of Zena Fraser as she stepped off the pod and came to greet him was of a pretty, middle-aged woman who might easily have graced the fashion pages of a classy magazine in her earlier days. Her blonde hair curled softly just above shoulder level and, as she removed a pair of rimless spectacles, Lorimer noticed that her blue eyes had been skilfully enhanced by muted shades of blue and grey make-up. As she stood up and smoothed down her short skirt Lorimer was afforded the sight of a pair of very shapely legs and slim feet clad in expensive-looking high-heeled shoes, the sort that Maggie sighed over but had never actually bought.

'Miss Fraser, Detective Superintendent Lorimer, Strathclyde Police. I spoke earlier to your assistant,' Lorimer began, smiling politely as Zena Fraser looked him up and down.

'Hello, Detective Superintendent Lorimer.' The woman's smile lit up her face and Lorimer could see at once the keen intelligence in those baby blue eyes. 'Rather a mouthful,' she said teasingly. 'Is it all right if I just call you Lorimer?'

'Everybody does, ma'am,' Lorimer replied.

'Oh, Zena, please,' she laughed. 'Let's not be too formal, shall we? And I can't stand being called Miss. Makes me sound so spinsterish.' She smiled again, her cheeks dimpling as though she was perfectly aware that the man before her had no such thought and was in fact regarding her right now with a modicum of male appreciation.

'We'll have to make do with my wee office, I'm afraid,' Zena said, pulling out the two chairs tucked into the circular table that seemed standard issue for these politicians. 'It's not very big,' she apologised, 'but we'll be left in peace with nobody to interrupt us.' She closed the glass door firmly, shutting out sound but not sight: every person who passed along this corridor would be able to note exactly who was in the room. There was certainly no space for any clandestine activity within these offices.

'Now, have you had a cup of tea or coffee since you arrived? No? Well, what's your poison?' she twinkled, moving towards a small refrigerator that had an electric kettle jug and a cafetière placed on top.

'A coffee would be fine,' Lorimer replied. 'Just black, no sugar, thanks,' he added as Zena Fraser lifted a pair of china mugs from somewhere behind her desk.

'Ed liked his coffee like that,' the woman murmured. She was crouched down beside the refrigerator so that Lorimer was unable to see the expression on her face but he could hear a note of wistfulness in her voice that made him curious.

'You were good friends?' Lorimer asked.

'Oh, yes,' came the reply. 'Our friendship goes back . . . sorry *went* back . . . to our childhood days.' She stood up to fill the kettle with a bottle of water that she had taken from the fridge. 'Our parents were next-door neighbours. Ed and I were both only children and we used to play in one another's gardens. I was a year older than Ed so perhaps that's where I got my bossy attitude from.'

'Mr Pattison was known for his own strength of character,' Lorimer countered.

Zena Fraser frowned. 'Later, perhaps, but as a wee boy Ed was a camp follower, trust me. I was a real little tomboy in those days, always up to some mischief or other. Poor Ed,' she sighed. 'I was the one who made the shots for him to fire. Oh!' Zena's hand flew to her mouth as she realised the gracelessness of her choice of words. 'Why did I say that?' Her blue eyes teared up suddenly. 'Sorry, it's so hard to think about what happened,' she sniffed, reaching for a tissue from a flowered box on her desk.

'Cath . . .' she broke off to blow her nose loudly then turned away as the kettle began to boil.

For a few moments there was only the soothing noise of cups being filled and stirred, then the MSP handed Lorimer his coffee and sat down behind her desk, cupping her own mug between her hands as though to warm them. It was interesting how things in the room had suddenly changed: Lorimer was seated at a psychological disadvantage, as if he were the interviewee and Zena Fraser the person in charge. Now, with that physical distance between them, Lorimer wondered if the intimacy of their conversation would be resumed.

'You were about to say something,' Lorimer began. 'About Mrs Pattison?'

'Was I?' The blue eyes turned to him appeared guileless but Lorimer knew fine she was prevaricating.

'I thought we were talking about Edward,' she said, regarding him thoughtfully.

'You were obviously close to Mr Pattison,' Lorimer continued smoothly. 'Were you perhaps close enough to know if he had been seeing someone in Glasgow on the night he died?'

Zena Fraser laid her mug carefully on a slate coaster before replying. 'I think I would already have told the police if I'd known anything about Edward's death,' she said.

'That's not quite what I meant,' he said. 'May I be blunt?'

A rise of her finely plucked eyebrows was all the answer he required.

'Was Edward Pattison having an affair with somebody in Glasgow or the Glasgow area?'

'That's blunt all right,' she said. 'Asking if poor old Ed was up to no good.'

'Having an extra-marital relationship isn't a crime,' Lorimer said gently.

'No, maybe not,' she replied, then added with a touch of bitterness, 'but the press would have treated him like some sort of a social pariah if they had found out something like that. A man in his position . . .' She shrugged, leaving the rest of the sentence unsaid.

'Ed and I . . .' Her voice faltered for a moment and Lorimer saw the uncertainty in Zena Fraser's face. And, in that moment, he became aware of several things. Why this lovely woman had never married, why she had chosen to follow her childhood friend into politics and why Catherine Pattison had insisted that the MSP was a person capable of killing her husband.

Lorimer stared at her for a long moment until she finally looked away. 'You and Edward Pattison,' Lorimer said slowly. 'You were more than childhood friends, weren't you?'

Zena Fraser shot him a look then glanced beyond him to the door of her office. 'I'm very much aware that this is a murder inquiry,' she said. 'But I need to know that anything I tell you will not go beyond these four walls,' she added, glancing at the glass partition beyond them.

'If you have had nothing to do with Edward Pattison's death then you have my assurances that anything you say to me here will be kept completely confidential.'

She gave a huge sigh then licked her lips as though wondering how to begin.

'Ed and I were lovers. Off and on,' she said. 'He'd been my first proper boyfriend and even after he and Cath were married we continued to have the odd weekend away together. Nobody knew about us, not our friends or our family. Though I often thought that Cath had her suspicions.' She looked up as if to see some sign of confirmation in the policeman's face but Lorimer's expression remained one of mild interest.

'What did she tell you? That I had wanted Ed to marry me? That I was the scorned woman?'

Lorimer did not immediately reply, but his thoughts turned to the old adage that *hell hath no fury like a woman scorned*. Was she a woman scorned? Not only for the wife of the man she had loved but possibly for a string of mistresses?

'Where were you on the night that Edward Pattison was killed, Miss Fraser?' he asked at last.

THIRD TIME LUCKY, Lorimer told himself as he approached the corridor that held the offices of most of the Labour party members of the Scottish parliament. Both Raeburn and Zena Fraser had been able to supply alibis for the night that Pattison had been killed, though these would of course have to be corroborated.

'You're Lorimer, I suppose?' A Glasgow accent made the detective superintendent whirl around to find a stockily built man with untidy dark hair who was wearing a brown tweed overcoat and a striped scarf.

'Coming to see me? Frank Hardy,' the man said, shooting out his arm and giving Lorimer a swift once up and down handshake.

'Come on, let's get out of here. Don't think I'm paranoid or anything, but walls have ears, know what I mean?'

His grin was infectious and Lorimer found himself smiling as the man tilted his head towards the row of glass and wooden structures that served as offices.

Before Lorimer had time to answer, Hardy was off along the corridor and heading for the stairs that would take them back out of the parliament.

This time Lorimer noticed things that had not caught his attention on the way in. There were several pictures upon the walls and one in particular made him stop and stare, Hardy lingering at his side as he gazed. It was an enlarged photograph of a woman and her goat inside what could have been a 'but and ben', the ancient style of rural cottage that served as shelter for both man and beast. The woman, however, was looking askance at the goggle-eyed creature as though wondering what had possessed her to let it in. Lorimer gave a tiny smile, remembering the story of the discontented old woman who had asked a wise man how to make her house bigger. The wise man's advice had been to take in her animals one by one, causing her to doubt the man's alleged wisdom. He had, of course, eventually told her to let them all out, at once transforming the house into a larger space.

The smooth feel of wood beneath his fingers as he trailed them on the banister was pleasing to the man who had forsaken art history for a career in the police. As were the polished granite floors and slate steps. It was, Lorimer thought, a great attempt to marry so many of Scotland's natural resources into this building.

'Bit of a nip, eh?' the man said, turning his collar against the wind that was blowing straight off Arthur's Seat. He looked up at the darkening clouds approaching from the east. 'Maybe a good idea to find somewhere we can get ourselves some central heating before the next heavy shower, eh? Any particular howff you fancy?'

Bemused by the man's eagerness to depart the Scottish parliament, Lorimer shook his head. 'Don't usually drink on duty,' he murmured.

'Ach, one wee dram'll no' do you any harm,' Hardy replied, grinning. Then, looking down at Lorimer's thick-soled shoes he added, 'Come on, the pavements shouldn't be too bad up the Canongate and there's a nice pub with a good fire that I know.'

Lorimer fell into step beside the man who, he noticed, was wearing stout boots, as though he had decided beforehand that Lorimer would acquiesce to his suggestion of marching through the snow-covered streets of Edinburgh's old town.

'You represent one of the West Renfrewshire constituencies,' Lorimer said.

'Aye, it takes in Erskine, Bishopton and Langbank,' Hardy replied. 'Nice and handy seeing as I live in Erskine myself. Been there since I was a wee boy back in the seventies when the Scottish Special Housing Association built the place. Was a councillor for Bargarran before I became elected,' he added, puffing slightly as the hill began to rise before them.

'Were you at home the night that Edward Pattison died, then?'

'Uh-huh,' Hardy nodded, fishing in his coat pocket and drawing out a packet of cigarettes. 'Do you smoke? No?' he asked, offering the packet to Lorimer who shook his head. 'Cannae think that Ed was just along the road from our part of Erskine when . . .' He stopped for a moment to light his cigarette then blew out a plume of smoke that lingered in the frosty air. 'Terrible thing to have happened, eh? And him that well thought of, too.'

Lorimer glanced at him, trying to detect any trace of sarcasm and wondering if the words were at all sincere or merely an empty platitude. Frank Hardy's quarrel with Pattison had been well documented in the press after Pattison had defected from the Labour party. The things that Hardy had uttered then had been far less gracious, Lorimer remembered.

'Over there,' Hardy said at last when they had marched well up the hill and past the crown-steepled church of Saint Giles. The politician was nodding to a pub on the corner diagonally opposite the crossroads where they now stood waiting for the traffic lights to change.

Deacon Brodie's Tavern was, thought Lorimer, an interesting choice of pub for the MSP to bring the policeman. He knew most of the story: Brodie had been an Edinburgh worthy back in the eighteenth century, a town councillor and supposedly wealthy cabinet-maker by day but a housebreaker by night. His double life had ended when he'd been caught and he had been condemned to death on the gallows.

The warmth hit them right away as they stepped inside the pub. Almost every table was surrounded by men and women drinking and enjoying a late lunch and the vinegary smell of chips began to waft temptingly around Lorimer's nostrils.

'Bet you havenae had anything to eat,' Hardy asked abruptly. 'Listen, I'm not like these Edinburgh folk. *You'll have had your tea?*' he said in a high voice that was intended to be a mimicry of an Edinburgh matron that made Lorimer grin despite himself.

'I could murder a burger and chips,' he confessed.

'Well, come on upstairs. There's a nice warm fire up there too,' Hardy assured the policeman. Then, 'Hey, Chloe, hen, can we have a couple of menus for the restaurant?' he called to a young girl in black who was polishing glasses behind the bar.

'Sure, Mr Hardy. Here you are,' she said, picking up a couple of hefty leather-bound menus from a pile at the end of the counter. 'Be with you shortly,' she said, smiling.

'You're a regular here, then,' Lorimer said as they headed upstairs past prints of Lord Byron and Robert Burns, poets both, perhaps favourites of the legendary Brodie.

'Aye, your powers of deduction are just brilliant, Detective Superintendent,' Hardy laughed as they settled at a table by the window. 'Wee Chloe works here during the week so she knows all the punters that come in. See that new place across the road?' he said, pointing at a modern building that stood out against the older, more gracious architecture on either side. 'Well there used to be one of the ugliest buildings in the city right on that spot, before they knocked it down and built this new hotel. That was where we all worked before they created that money-sponge down at Holyrood. Brodie's was a dead handy place for members of the Scottish parliament. And I kind of like it. So,' he shrugged and grinned, 'I see no reason not to keep on patronising their illustrious establishment.'

Perhaps the man's patronage was indeed pure altruism, for the upstairs restaurant was completely empty except for themselves; or was he in the habit of coming here for peace and quiet, Lorimer wondered.

'Deacon Brodie was supposed to have been the inspiration for Robert Louis Stevenson's *Dr Jekyll and Mr Hyde*, wasn't he?' the policeman asked.

'Is that right?' Hardy shrugged. 'Not a great reader myself,' he added.

'My wife is an English teacher,' Lorimer told him. 'And a big Stevenson fan. The book was about a man who had two sides to his personality, one moral and the other evil. Wasn't Brodie a little bit like that?'

'Och, Brodie was a pure chancer,' Hardy replied. 'Oh, Chloe, right hen,' he said as the waitress approached. 'A couple of pints of Stella and two drams of Macallan. That okay with you, Lorimer?'

'Just the whisky, thanks,' Lorimer replied.

'Are you ready to order your food, gentlemen?' the girl asked politely, taking her little notebook and pen out of a black wrap-around apron.

'Burger and chips twice?' Hardy asked, looking at the detective who nodded hungrily.

After the girl had gone through the usual rigmarole of sauces and sides, the two men were left alone, the only sound coming from the fire that was crackling and hissing as the rain began to pour down against the windows.

'You were telling me about Deacon William Brodie,' Lorimer reminded Hardy.

'Aye, so I was. Seems he was a terrible gambling man. That's how he got into the housebreaking game. Lost all his family's money. They say that Brodie got off by bribing the hangman. Was supposed to have been seen alive and well in Paris.'

'Must have been a bit of a character to have had a place like this named after him,' Lorimer mused. 'Wasn't Edward Pattison rather a colourful character too?' he asked mildly.

'Pattison? Colourful?' Frank Hardy looked doubtful for a moment. 'Don't know that I'd call him that. Bit of a chancer like

Brodie, though,' he said, leaning forward then lowering his voice. 'You want to know what that man was really like, Lorimer? Well, you've come to the right man to tell you— Thanks, lass.' Hardy sat back as the waitress placed their drinks on the table then waited until she had left the room and her feet could be heard clattering on the wooden staircase.

'Edward Pattison was a shit of the first order,' Hardy growled. 'See if he'd been an Edinburgh wifie, you'd have said he was all fur coat and nae knickers. Pretended to be all lah-de-dah with that big hoose of his and the fancy sports car. The wife's money, of course,' he added, pausing to take a swig of his lager. 'Pattison came from an ordinary background but that was never going to be good enough for him. He was the sort of man who had to *be* some-one, know what I mean? A right wee social climber. Why he even joined the Labour party I cannot imagine. Didn't have a socialist bone in his body!' he finished in a tone of disgust.

'Why do you think he joined the Scottish Nationalists?' Lorimer asked.

'So he could get ahead. That was Edward all over. He wanted to be part of whatever was successful at the time,' Hardy snorted.

'Politics aside,' Lorimer said, 'what can you tell me about Edward Pattison's private life?'

'His women, you mean?' Hardy gave a lopsided grin but his eyes had narrowed and there was a sly look on his face as he regarded the policeman. 'Oh, I can tell you plenty.'

'I've already spoken to James Raeburn and Zena Fraser,' Lorimer told him.

'Och, James knew nothing about what Edward got up to in Glasgow. But I guess Zena may have had an inkling,' Hardy said, lifting his glass for another mouthful of beer.

'And what was that?'

Hardy grinned, his green eyes twinkling under his bushy eyebrows.

'Poor wee Catherine was never enough for that big man,' Hardy said. 'She'd given him her family's fortune and three nice wee weans. And in return her man went off with anything in a skirt that took his fancy.' He looked sharply at Lorimer. 'Paid for it too, from all accounts,' he added quietly. 'At least he did back in *our* home town.'

'How do you know this?' Lorimer asked.

'Edward Pattison wasn't always the clean-living boy he was made out to be,' Hardy began. 'Truth was he couldnae hold his drink, that's why he gave it up. Terrified he'd make a fool of himself in public.' He leaned forward again, his voice lowered. 'See, one time when we were a lot younger, me and Edward were out on the batter and he told me some things that would make your hair curl. Things about what he did to girls, street girls, you know?'

'When was this?'

'Och, years ago, before either of us was married,' Hardy admitted. 'But I know fine he was still at it,' he continued. 'Saw him driving round Blythswood Square a couple of times, on the lookout, y'know?'

'And you never told anybody about this?'

Hardy shrugged. 'None of my business what the man got up to, was it? And I'm not the type to go bleating to the papers about another bloke's weaknesses.'

Lorimer frowned. 'But it was well known that you couldn't stand the man,' he began.

Hardy straightened up, his face reddening. 'Now listen, Lorimer, I might have had a grudge against the wee shit, but I would never have stooped so low as that. Some of us MSPs do have principles, you know, despite what the journalists would like the public to believe. Plus,' he mumbled, 'what do you think that might have done to Cathy and the kids?'

THE RETURN JOURNEY to Glasgow began much more quickly, snow ploughs having cleared the earlier blizzards and a heavy rain washing the residual slush to the sides of the M8. As the afternoon closed in and darkness began to fall, Detective Superintendent William Lorimer had a lot to think about, mainly from what Frank Hardy had revealed about his erstwhile colleague. The chief constable of Strathclyde had hinted that Pattison had been a bit of a ladies' man, but surely he had not known that he had been a regular along the drag? Perhaps, Lorimer thought to himself, it was time to see if anyone else had knowledge of Pattison's nefarious activities.

Chapter Twenty

MAGGIE HUMMED ALONG to the Vaughan Williams variation of 'Greensleeves' on Classic FM as she flicked through their ancient address book. A hundred guests was not an unreasonable number, she told herself, ticking off yet another name on her list. She smiled as she thought of her husband's reaction when she pulled the surprise on him. Turning forty was a landmark for anyone and, though *she* would happily settle for a week or so in Venice when it was her birthday, a party with all his old friends and former colleagues was just what her husband would most enjoy. To turn up at a restaurant when he was expecting to dine alone with her and find his best buddies was the treat that Maggie had in mind. Okay, so his work could still wreck all of her plans, but why should that stop her, she thought, a determined expression hardening her jaw.

The rattle upon the window panes made Maggie Lorimer turn to see the hail slanting sideways and she rose from her cross-legged position on the couch to pull the heavy winter curtains, shutting out the black night. Bill would be late again, meetings at HQ taking precedence over a peaceful night at home. Glasgow and Edinburgh weren't that far apart but the weather had played havoc with his plans and everything in his diary seemed to have been pushed back so that Maggie didn't know when to expect the sound of his key in the lock. Still, it gave her an opportunity to organise this party while he was out, didn't it? She consoled herself with the thought that the Malmaison was near enough to Pitt Street that he could come straight from work, and they had been very nice about fixing her up with a lovely room to stay the night in as well. Bill's birthday was on a weekday this year, she knew. The seventh of February seemed quite far off still and hopefully these major murder cases would be over by then or at least taking up less of his time.

William Lorimer had been born under the auspicious sign of Aquarius, and although Maggie derided all that star stuff in women's magazines she had to admit that her husband did fit the profile of an intellectual whose honesty, loyalty and deep desire to right society's wrongs were his greatest strengths. Maggie had never seen her husband in action very much, but on those rare occasions she had seen a darker side to him, qualities that seemed to be intractable and unpredictable. He had, too, a propensity to appear unemotional and detached, though Maggie knew that was a skill he had learned over the years of interviewing men and women who had been suspects for a variety of crimes.

As the radio changed to the more poignant tune of 'The Ashokan Farewell', Maggie curled into a corner of the settee, shivering as though something unseen and unearthly had crossed the room. Why, when she should be having fun preparing this party, was she suddenly having a strange feeling that it would all end in tears? As the wind gathered strength and began to moan, she gave a jump, her heart beating faster.

'Stop being so silly, woman,' she said aloud, as if to utter words would break this malignant spell that seemed to be creeping over her.

The sound grew louder but then turned into the more familiar noise of the Lexus, and Maggie breathed a sigh of relief. He was home! Shoving the notebook under a seat cushion, she smiled once again. It would be fine. He'd have a lovely party, she was determined to make sure that happened.

THE MORNING SKY was streaked with pink as Lorimer looked out of the kitchen window that faced east. He'd slept soundly despite all the thoughts fighting for attention in his brain and now, at this early hour, ideas about Pattison's death seemed to be more clearly in focus. That he had arranged to see some woman or other was possible. Of course it could have been a man, he thought, remembering James Raeburn's wistful tone as he realised his old friend had hidden something from him. As for Hardy's innuendoes, well maybe the socialist politician had been closer to the mark. Blythswood Square was part of the drag, and a well known place to pick up a better class of street girl, if in fact that was what Pattison had been doing.

There was something . . . Lorimer frowned suddenly, taking a sip of his scalding hot coffee as he stared unseeingly at the garden outside the window. A pair of redwings foraging at the holly berries in next door's tree failed to grasp his attention for once as he considered a possibility that had occurred to him. If Pattison had indeed been in the habit of soliciting prostitutes whenever his business took him to Scotland's largest city, then was there a chance that he was already known to some of the girls who plied their trade there? The frustration of leaving Helen James's case to concentrate on Pattison's murder could be allayed if he had a legitimate reason to ask questions that might help find Tracey-Anne's killer as well. It was something of a coincidence that a top politician (who might or might not have been soliciting prostitutes, Lorimer reminded himself) had been killed so soon after the murder of Tracey-Anne Geddes. He wasn't a great believer in coincidences and on this occasion there was absolutely nothing to link the death of a poor, junked-up street girl with Pattison's shooting. Three businessmen in white Mercedes cars had been shot at point-blank range, all in lonely places far outside the city, whereas the murders of Carol Kilpatrick and Tracey-Anne Geddes had been vicious stabbings committed within its heart. Miriam Lyons and Jenny Haslet's deaths had not fitted the same picture, although what Solly might come up with could change the perception that the two girls had been murdered by other hands. It was a sad fact of life that such vulnerable young women were sometimes targets for the more horrific excesses of violent men. Helen James's file would undoubtedly show lots more examples from cases over the years.

A familiar ring from his BlackBerry alerted Lorimer to an incoming email and he turned from the window, his concentration broken.

It was, he was surprised to note, from that big girl, Detective Constable Barbara Knox, who had seemed so eager to join the team at Pitt Street. He read the email, amused to see that the DC had been keen to relay this information to him. One Mercedes dealer had already had a firm trade in and there had been two telephone enquiries from an out-of-town dealership from owners of white Mercedes sports cars.

DCI Mumby had been uncharacteristically effusive about Knox's capabilities and Lorimer had wondered if the senior officer had been hoping to offload the woman permanently onto his team for some reason. It happened in all walks of life, this kind of promotion in order to be rid of an abrasive element within a team. But if Barbara Knox had a fault it was that she was super efficient. Emailing him routine information at this hour seemed a bit unnecessary and he couldn't help but wonder what it was that could not wait until his arrival at Pitt Street in less than an hour's time.

SHE LISTENED TO the message once again, drawing in her breath as the woman's voice became edgy. Barbara was useful, that was true, but she wasn't quite the pushover that she had expected. Sex, or at least the anticipation of it, was a powerful weapon. She had lured three men to their death like one of the sirens from mythology, the promise of sex leading them to their doom. But the policewoman posed more of a threat. She could keep her at bay for now but eventually she might have to give in to the younger woman's sexual demands, a prospect that did not fill her with any sort of joy. So far she had learned what she could about the investigation under her chosen guise, a freelance journalist. Barbara had laughed with a childlike glee when *Diana* had told the policewoman that undercover work forbade her from keeping a website, an excuse she had thought out carefully beforehand. Anything that smacked of cloak and dagger stuff tended to be a turn-on for that girl, she thought, her lip curling in distaste. But it relaxed into a smile again as another thought entered her mind: DC Barbara Knox had no inkling whatsoever that she was being seduced by the very killer she sought.

DC KNOX HAD come in early as usual, a habit that was partly to do with the fact she was fastidious about starting up her computer in complete privacy and logging on to a variety of websites before her colleagues arrived. But then, if she was absolutely honest, the lack of a social life was possibly what made Barbara immerse herself in work. The policewoman grinned as she considered this thought. Perhaps having a social life like most of her colleagues would be a possibility now that she had met her new friend.

Call me Diana, the dark-haired woman had said, a quiet smile upon her face as though they both knew that her identity was something worth hiding. This investigative journalist who had worked on so many top secret missions was not going to endanger her very existence by blurting out her real name to a stranger in a coffee bar, now, was she? But they were no longer strangers to one another, Barbara told herself, remembering the other woman's distinctive scent and the delicious feel of those fingers tracing a line across her cheek. So, *Diana* was her secret, a secret that she was happy to hug to herself. That Diana was eventually going to be running a story about the case was a thought that Barbara Knox pushed to the back of her mind. Weren't they both working for the same outcome, after all? It was well known that undercover journos sometimes helped the police, so why should it be any different to assist Diana in her investigation if, in the long term, their aims were the same? And it wasn't as if she had accepted a bribe, was it? Keeping her friend abreast of what was going on had not compromised her position here at HQ. No, Barbara told herself; if anything, her liaison with the dark-haired woman might even result in new intelligence being passed back, with DC Knox gaining even more plaudits from her new boss.

As though the thought had conjured him up, Barbara saw the tall figure of Detective Superintendent Lorimer through the frosted glass panel that separated her part of the office from the corridor outside.

'Good work, Knox,' he said, looking down to where Barbara sat at her desk. 'Let me know if any other cars turn up, won't you? I've arranged for officers to visit the owners,' he added, dashing Barbara's hopes of interviewing the mysterious-sounding Badica. Then, giving her a smile that lit up his blue eyes, he added, 'See you're an early bird like me,' before heading back along to his own office.

'Aye,' Barbara whispered under her breath, 'and we'll see how many nasty wee worms we can catch between us, eh?'

PROFESSOR SOLOMON BRIGHTMAN was also an early riser but for the simple reason that baby Abigail demanded her feeds at regular intervals and some inner body clock seemed to have selected five-thirty a.m. as her first meal of the day. Warm baths and a cosy room had done little to solve this problem and both Solly and Rosie were resigned to early nights simply so that they could have sufficient sleep to keep going through the day.

'She'll be better once she's on mixed feeding,' Rosie had sighed.

'All my babies were the same,' Ma Brightman had laughed, as though her son was making too much of a fuss when he had mentioned the baby's constant wakefulness. 'Sign of a clever child,' his mother had added consolingly.

The problem of broken nights was one that all parents had to endure, but the psychologist allowed his thoughts to wander during these nocturnal strolls rocking the baby up and down, cradled in his arms, until she went back to sleep again. Now, Rosie was asleep too, the baby tucked into the crib by the side of their bed, contented at last.

The psychologist had spent much of the night thinking about what Lorimer had told him following his visit to the capital. Zena

Fraser he could dismiss right away as she appeared to have a cast-iron alibi in the form of an old school chum who had been staying overnight with her. Hardy's tale about seeing the deputy first minister kerb-crawling was more interesting. The socialist politician had had a grudge against Pattison and he lived in the area where the body had been found. Yes, the forensic experts might eventually be looking to match trace evidence found at the scene with Hardy, but something told Solly that this was not the man they were looking for.

Of the three, Raeburn interested him most. Why should Catherine Pattison have named the best friend of the victim as his potential killer? An ageing bachelor, Raeburn was known as a patron of the arts in Scotland as well as a hard-working politician who had defended his party's lack of progress in achieving independence for Scotland. And that was not all; of the three of them, Raeburn was the only one who had had any previous experience with small firearms. But logic dictated that everything else was wrong about the man as a potential killer, Solly told himself; unless Mrs Pattison knew more about the politician than she was letting on.

Solly was standing at the large bay windows that looked down on Kelvingrove Park and across the city to its western edges. It was still dark outside and he could hear a fierce wind blowing. The lights from the street lamps outside seemed to waver and sway, blurred by the rain falling across his window. It was like a parody of his mind, he thought; wasn't he trying to see through a sort of darkness? There were some things that were obscuring his vision, too; these three politicians amongst them. He had seen them all on television at one time or another and could remember the attractive woman, the Glasgow man, Hardy, and James Raeburn whose programme on contemporary art Solly had also followed at one time. The psychologist rubbed his eyes with both hands as though to erase the pictures of them from his mind, then turned from the windows to concentrate on the day ahead. He was still pursuing the case that Lorimer had been forced to abandon, meeting with any friends and family of the murdered street women, and today he had an appointment with Miriam Lyons' father.

I'll come to your office, Jeremy Lyons had said when Solly had called up the number Lorimer had given him. *Give me a time,* the solicitor had added in a brusque tone that sounded as if he were already looking at his diary to check a slot that was free.

Solly, who knew his own university timetable off by heart, had offered the man an hour mid-morning that he could fit between lectures. Now, in this time before dawn when sounds from the city were beginning to drift up to the houses above the park, Solly wondered why Miriam's father had insisted on seeing him on his own without Miriam's mother present and not at their address. Perhaps anyone who had business with their daughter's death brought with them a sort of violation of their home. What sort of striving for normality must these poor parents have had? Not only coming to terms with Miriam's death but its aftermath, the media poking and prying into every crevice of their personal lives. You didn't have to be a psychologist to work that out, Solly reminded himself grimly.

THE JEWISH LAWYER was right on time, Solly thought, seeing the man in the dark overcoat who stood on the corner of University Gardens checking his watch. His navy scarf was wound several times around his neck, the fringed ends flapping as the wind caught it and Solly wondered how long he had been standing there in the cold. He came away from the window and, leaving his door ajar, headed down the flight of stairs, ready to greet his visitor. Lyons looked up from where he stood on the pavement outside the Department of Psychology and, catching sight of Solly, he nodded as though recognising something reassuring in the psychologist's appearance.

'Mr Lyons.'

'Professor Brightman.' Gloved hands closed over Solly's for a moment as the two men regarded one another. Jeremy Lyons was a man of around fifty, Solly guessed, noticing the dark hair receding and greying at the temples. But those deeply set brown eyes pouched with heavy folds of skin suggested someone much older. Solly knew that look; it was a look of grief beyond normal suffering that Jeremy Lyons shared with others in the aftermath of violent death.

'Please come up.' Solly waved a hand at the open door and ushered the man into the building and upstairs to his capacious office.

'Sit over here by the radiator,' he urged, nodding towards the pair of comfy chairs that flanked the heater. Lyons sat down on the edge of the seat without unbuttoning his overcoat, the scarf still wound around his neck.

'Would you like some tea?' Solly asked, lifting up a box of assorted teabags that he kept for his students.

'No, no, I must get back . . .' Lyons hesitated.

'A herbal tea, perhaps? Just to warm us up? I have some nice camomile,' Solly said, flipping the switch on the kettle and pulling a pair of mugs off a shelf.

'Well, all right, then,' Lyons said. Solly turned away with a smile as he saw the lawyer take off his leather gloves then begin to unwind the dark blue scarf. A cup of tea to ease any tension in a subject was always good psychology. And this man looked as if he had long forgotten how to relax.

'Thank you,' Lyons said as he took the mug and looked up at Solly, his mournful eyes full of much more than mere gratitude for a warming cuppa. 'You have a daughter?' he began, after taking the first sip.

'Yes,' Solly told him.

'I thought as much. You have a sympathetic manner, Professor Brightman. You understand about fathers and daughters, then?'

Solly smiled. 'She's only three months old,' he said.

'But that bond of love . . .?' Lyons tailed off, looking at Solly as though no more words needed to be said.

Solly nodded, wagging his beard sagely in agreement.

'I've been asked by Strathclyde Police to talk to the families of four victims of crime, your daughter being one of them,' Solly began softly. 'Miriam's death was not like the other three,' he added, 'but it's my job to look for any points of similarity in case we can find a pattern that might suggest the same perpetrator.' He chose his words carefully, not just to keep the conversation on a more formal basis but to avoid any mention of violence that could disturb this already harrowed father.

'What do you need to know?' Jeremy Lyons asked, his voice suddenly low and weary as though he had told this story over and over countless times, which perhaps he had.

'Tell me about Miriam,' Solly said.

The psychologist listened, sipping his tea, as the story of a young life wrecked by drugs and wild excess was imparted. Miriam had been a studious girl at school, all set for a career in dentistry, when she had met up with a *bad lot* as Lyons referred to them. Then almost overnight it had seemed their perfect girl had become a rebellious teenager, staying out all night when she felt like it, missing school and eventually leaving home altogether to set up home with her newfound friends. Lyons had stormed at her, cajoled her, then in desperation offered her anything she wanted to come home to a mother and father who were at their wits' end. But it had been futile. Miriam had changed so much, he told Solly with a heaviness in his tone that spoke of a final relinquishing of his beloved girl to the life she had chosen. On the few occasions when she did come home (always looking for money) they had been shocked at her appearance, how thin and gaunt she had become.

'She only came home looking for money to spend on drugs, of course,' Lyons told him sadly. 'And one day I simply said *no*.' He passed a hand across his eyes. 'We never saw her again until . . .' He stopped suddenly, biting his lip to prevent a sob issuing from his throat.

The rest of Miriam Lyons' history was known to Solomon Brightman. How she had become a prostitute to fund her drug habit, how the hostel where she had stayed had thrown her out and how she had been found, floating in the murky waters of the Clyde. But the final chapter was still unclear. And that was something Solly needed to know.

'You stopped working after your daughter's death?' Solly said at last, changing the subject to bring the conversation back to a semblance of normality.

'I resigned from my practice,' Lyons admitted. 'But I still work,' he said. 'Actually I work for nothing these days. Not the stereotypical image of a Jew, is it?' he said, the ghost of a smile appearing on his face.

'What do you do?'

'After Miriam died my wife and I wanted to find out much more about prostitution in the city.' He shrugged. 'It probably began as something that was purely cathartic, maybe still is if I'm truthful,' he said. 'Anyway, nowadays I'm a volunteer on the Big Blue Bus, have you heard of it?'

Solly nodded. The project of the Big Blue Bus served to give street women advice and help about coming off drugs and finding places of safety to live. It had begun as a Christian outreach but was now funded by several different religious organisations. The prostitutes knew the bus would pick them up at various points along the drag during the wee small hours, times when the drop-in centres were normally closed.

'Funny old world,' Jeremy Lyons mused as he set down his mug on the floor by his chair. 'There's that politician been shot and I was only talking to him on the bus about three weeks ago.'

'Edward Pattison?' Solly asked, trying to conceal his amazement.

'Yes, the SNP man. I'd had a meeting with him at Holyrood to discuss the possibility of government funding for a women's refuge. He asked if he could come over to Glasgow and see what the project was doing.'

'Pattison visited the Big Blue Bus when it was doing its rounds?' Solly asked.

Lyons nodded. 'He was great with the girls. Chatted away to them quite happily.' He shook his head. 'What a waste,' he said, 'a man with gifts like that. He had such charm, what is it they call it? Charisma, that's the word. He had these girls quite enthralled, you know.'

'You liked him?' Solly asked.

Lyons frowned suddenly. 'Funny you should ask that. I feel that I *should* have liked him but . . .' He broke off, shaking his head. 'He was a bit overwhelming for me, professor. A bit *too* charming, if that's possible.'

Jeremy Lyons looked up at Solly and his dark eyes widened. 'He was the sort of man you and I might have warned our daughters to avoid,' he said slowly as though the idea had only just occurred to him.

LATER, AFTER HIS second class of the morning had trooped out of the lecture theatre, Solly had time to think over his meeting with the lawyer. Not only had Edward Pattison had contact with prostitutes but he had also been invited to assist the project that was designed to help these women come off drugs and leave the streets for good. Solly did not believe in coincidences any more than his friend, Lorimer, up at Pitt Street: Edward Pattison's death seemed to be linked with more than those of the other two businessmen whose bodies had been found in their white Mercedes cars.

Had Solly now found a link between the two major cases that had been taken over by the Serious Crimes Squad? The chief constable had issued a command to Lorimer to concentrate on the senior politician's murder. So, Solly mused, perhaps it was time to talk to someone who knew more about the deaths of these street girls than anyone else.

Chapter Twenty-one

HELEN JAMES PUT down the phone with a sigh. The days since her operation had merged into one, with sleep and more sleep as the combination of anaesthetic and the recent punishing regime at work took their toll. He sounded nice, this professor. She'd heard of him, of course. Who in Strathclyde hadn't? 'Solomon Brightman,' Helen said aloud, relishing the psychologist's name. 'Solomon the Wise.' She smiled as she thought of the Old Testament king whose sagacity had earned him universal fame. Well, it would certainly be a diversion for the DCI in her enforced recuperation. She had nobody now in her division that she really wanted to see. Fairbairn had given her a ring, right enough, she admitted grudgingly, but that was out of courtesy, not friendship. And right now she would have welcomed visits from some old friends.

A sudden sigh came as Helen James recalled one of her favourite detective sergeants, a blonde lass with a sharp wit who had been hounded out of the force some time back by the anti-gay brigade. A high-profile case had resulted and Helen had been unable to do anything but watch helplessly from the sidelines. Claire had won it hands down but had then left in disgust. Such a waste of a good polis, she thought, shaking her head. Claire would have made senior rank no bother. Och, well, at least some of her officers were being usefully deployed with Lorimer. And being introduced to Solomon Brightman. Helen smiled suddenly. Perhaps being at home wasn't such a bad thing if it brought the opportunity to discuss a case with the celebrated professor.

VLADIMIR BADICA SLAMMED the metal door behind him, creating a draught of frozen air in the vast space that housed his fleet of cars. The weather had brought a spate of cancellations and as a result this side of his business was deathly quiet. Not so the concrete garage that lay beneath the Glasgow streets: the sound of metal banging against metal and rap music from a transistor radio drew his eyes to the mechanic under one of the luxury cars. All Badica could see was a pair of stout black boots sticking out from under the chassis but he knew those feet.

His hands twitched by his sides as he listened to the man whistling tunelessly to the music. If he could grab hold of those boots, pull him out and . . . and what? What would he really be able to do to this man who had brought such grief into his life?

Badica clenched his fists, struggling to control the urge to do damage to the young man below the car. Better to leave it. He was a good mechanic, he thought grudgingly, watching as the feet shifted under the car; knew these Mercs inside out.

The Romanian shivered suddenly, but it was not a sensory reaction to the cold outside but a chill that came from deep within his heart.

'THANKS FOR THESE,' Helen James said, sipping her coffee and eyeing the lovely M&S chocolate biscuits that the professor had brought with him. Should she try one? Would it hurt her delicate insides? The district nurse had urged Helen to try different foods bit by bit to see if things were back to normal. Sod it, she thought, picking up her favourite cream-filled biscuit, might as well enjoy it while I can.

'You're all right now to eat them?' Solly asked anxiously, noting the police officer's hesitation.

'Och, why not,' Helen replied, grinning and biting into the biscuit with relish. 'Right, professor, nice of you to visit but I'm sure you have lots of questions for me, eh?'

'I want to ask you about the prostitute murders,' Solly said.

'Of course you do, professor. Who else would you come to?' she replied, still smiling. But the smile did not reach Helen's eyes as she regarded the psychologist thoughtfully.

'I visited the parents of Carol Kilpatrick,' he began, looking at her intently. Helen nodded and grimaced as if to show she understood what his reception had been like.

'It was hard to fathom such animosity, especially now that she is dead,' he ventured.

'Aye, they were bitter, bitter people, those Kilpatricks,' Helen admitted. 'Couldn't hack the fact that their wee lassie swung the other way.'

'*That*'s what it was all about,' Solly said and heaved a sigh.

'Aye, Carol was a lesbian long before she went on the game. Parents kicked her out and she found some *friends* who made her feel better about herself. In a chemically induced way,' she added, her voice laden with sarcasm. 'The parents can't accept that they were in any way to blame for their girl becoming a druggie.'

Solly looked away, saddened that such a thing could have happened, yet telling himself that it happened all the time. And this policewoman with anger in her eyes knew all the background of stories such as Carol's. Could she help him to join up the dots in these four murder cases?

'Miriam Lyons and Jenny Haslet do not at first appear to fit any kind of pattern,' he began slowly. 'But I did wonder what you thought about their deaths.'

'I know what you're asking, professor. Do I think the same person killed all four of my girls? Well, the MO might be different but each of them was brutalised by someone. Some man who overpowered them.' She paused, her eyes dropping to a point somewhere on the carpet. 'All of them are . . . were . . . extremely vulnerable young women, but there was a toughness about Tracey-Anne . . .' Her voice tailed off and Solly saw her biting her lip as though to conceal some emotion.

'She put up a fight, didn't she?' Helen asked at last, her eyes boring into Solly's own, defying him to deny it.

'The post-mortem suggests as much,' he said, nodding. 'Dr White's report includes details of defence wounds.' The psychologist blinked, trying hard to blot out the memory of those photographs of slash marks on the young woman's arms, images that could make him feel distinctly queasy.

'What I don't understand,' Helen said slowly, 'is how anyone could have got to Miriam and Jenny.'

Solly frowned, unable to see where she was going with this. 'But if they were as vulnerable as you say they were . . .?'

'Aye, they were, but if my information about them is accurate they were also both off the streets by the time of their deaths.'

'But I thought . . .?'

'You assumed they were all working the drag, is that right? Well,' Helen pointed a hectoring finger at the psychologist, 'those two girls had been working in a sauna for weeks before they were killed. And there was no sign of them back out on the streets. That,' she said firmly, 'is something they had in common, even if their deaths were different.'

'So, you saw no pattern linking all four of the women, then?' Solly asked after a moment's consideration.

'I wish I had,' Helen replied. 'There was something wrong with it all,' she added with a frown. 'Carol's death was a shock to everyone. So brutal, so . . .' She searched for the right words to describe the girl's murder. 'So *vicious*. Look, we all see terrible things in our line of work, but that was the worst any of my team had ever experienced. How she stayed alive for those few hours, only God knows. Then when Miriam was found in the Clyde . . . well she'd been strangled and dumped, you know that, yes?'

Solly nodded as she continued.

'Maybe it was because her murder was different, but I felt at the time that it could have been the same person who killed them both. George Parsonage, the Glasgow humane society officer, told me at the time that her body was probably pushed into the Clyde near the city centre. He knows all there is to know about tides, currents and stuff,' she added.

'And Jenny Haslet?' Solly prompted.

'Aye, wee Jenny. Poor wee lassie. Had been trying to get off the drugs with help from the folk in the Big Blue Bus. You've heard of that, I assume?'

'Yes, I have.'

'As I said, Jenny and Miriam had both found jobs in a sauna. Same one as it happens. Place called Andie's. We thought we'd found a link at first.' Helen shrugged. 'But nothing came of it. Owner told us later that Jenny had simply failed to turn up for work one day. Seems their girls can be a bit unreliable that way,' she grimaced.

'And Jenny Haslet was strangled, like Miriam,' Solly said slowly.

'Aye. Not far from where she lived in Govanhill. If any of them was the odd one out then it would've been Jenny. Away from the city centre, maybe pulling punters near where she lived. Who knows? Forensics found she'd been choked to death with her own black tights. Someone had raped her first. Some big ugly brute, if the pathologist's report was right. Hey, hold on,' she said suddenly. 'That was Dr Fergusson, wasn't it? Your . . .'

'My wife,' Solly said. 'Yes. That's right. I do remember Rosie telling me about that particular case. She was so sure that someone would be found and that she would have to give evidence in court.' He shrugged. 'But it didn't happen.'

'Well perhaps if we put our heads together and find some common strand in all of this then something will come of it,' Helen James replied, but there was such doubt in her voice tinged with bitterness, that Solly Brightman wondered if the DCI was already resigned to these murders remaining unsolved, at least by her own team of officers.

ANDIE'S SAUNA WAS located in a side street off Govan Road. It was less than a mile away from the BBC and STV studios and the luxury flats that had sprung up on both sides of the Clyde, but it might have been on a different planet. That, thought Solomon Brightman, was one of the more fascinating aspects of Glasgow, where those who had plenty of life's riches rubbed shoulders geographically with those who had nothing. At first glance the sauna might have been a launderette, its double-fronted glass windows showing a couple of blonde women sitting with their backs to the street, mugs of something hot clutched in their hands looking for all the world as though they were passing time waiting for their washing to be done. But, crouching a little to peer inside, Solly saw that they were sitting reading magazines, their bare legs crossed, spangly stiletto sandals revealing garishly painted toenails.

'Looking fur a quick ride, pal?' A voice behind Solly said with a guffaw, making him straighten up in alarm.

A short man with grizzled grey hair and yellowing teeth leered up at him then nodded towards the door. 'Awright if ye can afford them sort of prices, eh? Eh?'

Solly opened his mouth to speak then thought better of it as the smell of drink wafted off the old man. 'On ye go son, dinna mind me,' the man said, then, giving Solly a swift dig in his side, he staggered off cackling to himself.

As Solly opened the door he noticed the two women looking up at him as soon as they heard the tinkle of the door chime.

'I'm looking for the owner of the, um, establishment,' he said brightly. 'Andie?'

'S'no' in the noo,' one of the girls replied, looking at Solly with thinly disguised interest. 'If ye're wantin' a session see an' phone fur an' appointment, okay?'

'I'm Professor Brightman,' Solly said. 'I'm actually here on behalf of Strathclyde Police.'

The reaction was immediate. Both women sat up straight, uncrossed their legs and tugged at what passed for their skirts. If it hadn't been part of a serious case, Solly would have burst out laughing as he observed their body language.

'Andie's away over at the other place, far as I know,' the younger of the women told him. 'We're jist keeping things tickin' ower, isn't that right, Jessie?'

'Aye,' agreed the other, churning a wad of gum around in her mouth while looking at Solly as if she had found some new species of humanoid. 'Yer no' wantin' a session then, mister?' she asked regretfully, her eyes slipping over him in a way that made his face burn with embarrassment.

'No thank you. Maybe you can help me, though,' he said suddenly, squashing the urge to back out of the place at once.

'Oh, aye, sure we can,' the girl called Jessie giggled as she stood up.

'Miriam Lyons and Jenny Haslet,' he said quietly, looking intently at them from behind his horn-rimmed spectacles with an expression that he hoped was sufficiently professorial. Hearing the names had an immediate effect on the women whose faces both became suddenly serious.

'Mind the names,' one of the women said with a frown. 'D'you 'member them, Francine?'

'Aye,' the younger woman said shortly. 'Knew them from before . . . used to see them both down in Robertson Street.'

'And on the Big Blue Bus, perhaps?' Solly asked gently.

'Aye, there 'n' all. Whit's with the questions, Sherlock? Jenny an' Miriam are both deid,' Jessie protested.

'I know that,' Solly said. 'That's why I'm here. You see, ladies, I'm a psychologist and I'm trying to create a profile of whoever killed these young women.'

The nervous glance that passed between the two women gave Solly the idea that some revelation was about to be produced. But he was wrong.

'Better come back anither time, son,' Jessie said, walking towards him so that Solly had to back towards the door again. 'An' make a proper appointment tae see the boss, okay?'

'Aye, an' we wisnae here when ye called, right? Got that, professor?' Francine insisted. The timbre of her voice had heightened and Solly knew that, if he were ever asked, he would admit that he was hearing a young woman who was now under a good deal of stress.

THE WHISTLING STOPPED as soon as the man heard the door slide closed once more. Stuffing the oil-soaked rag into a pocket of his dungarees, the mechanic shuffled his body from under the Mercedes-Benz and emerged from his prone position beneath the luxury car. Anyone seeing the big man would be surprised at how nimbly he sprang to his feet, smiling as though there was a secret joke he was keeping to himself. He stretched upwards, flexing his muscles after their confinement below the car, making him appear even taller than his normal six feet and five inches. Then, looking around at the cars parked in a careful row, he nodded to himself as his glance rested on one particular model. The white Merc was due for its trade-in, Vlad had told him, in clipped tones that made the mechanic aware that the boss was less than well pleased at having to part with this particular model.

The big man shrugged. It would be one less car to wash and polish for weddings, he supposed. Pity, though. There were still a few white Mercs but there was something alluring about the sporty model that made customers want to take it out for hire. *A babe magnet*, he'd heard one of them call it. The mechanic turned away, still smiling as he wiped his hands on a fresh piece of paper towel. He liked that idea. A magnet attracted metal to metal, didn't it? His grin widened as he looked in a rectangle of mirror that someone had placed by a shelf near the wooden staircase that led to the offices above the garage. A dark-haired man with deep brown eyes stared back, his finely chiselled cheekbones giving just a hint of his ethnic origin. He'd been told more than once what an attractive man he was. *A throwback*, Vladimir had called him once, and, though he did not fully understand what that meant, he took it to be a compliment, however grudgingly given.

As he made his way upstairs he could hear the woman in the office speaking in the tone of voice she reserved for customers. Only this was not a customer. A uniformed police officer stood patiently by the reception desk as the mechanic passed him by. There was not even the flicker of a glance towards him as he walked through reception to the small side room where he would wash and change before eating the lunch that had been prepared for him. Nobody, after all, noticed a mere mechanic in greasy overalls within the precincts of a garage, did they? Even though this particular mechanic had a handsome face that might attract attention.

'So, let me get this right,' the officer said. 'You hire out these Mercedes-Benz cars for weddings and for general use?'

'Well, *general* covers a lot of things, constable,' the woman replied starchily, drawing herself up as far as her five feet two including sensible court shoes would allow.

'These are luxury cars,' she told him reprovingly. 'Not the sort of vehicles available to every Tom, Dick and Harry,' she sniffed.

'So,' the police officer continued, 'what sorts of people do hire them out?'

'People with good taste,' she fired back. But seeing his eyebrows draw together in a frown of disapproval hastily added, 'Business-men usually. The sort who are used to good quality and don't wish to compromise when they're away from home.'

'Do you have records of everyone who has hired a car from here in the last two years?'

'Well, I don't know,' she said doubtfully. 'I suppose so. I could check, perhaps.' Then, turning away from her desk, she took a few steps towards a half-glazed door marked PRIVATE and pushed it open.

Watching her closely, the officer thought he could discern a certain timidity in her approach as she looked around. It was, he realised, unfamiliar territory. The boss's office, he guessed; somewhere sacrosanct, or a place where secrets were hidden?

On the desk beyond the door lay an opened laptop and the woman stood before it, making a show of clicking on buttons, her tongue nervously darting in and out over her lips. There was an old-fashioned high-back chair, ornately carved, but the receptionist chose to remain standing as though to sit in her employer's place was a breach of protocol.

'There's a diary here of transactions going back to 2009,' she said at last. 'What exactly was it you wanted?' She looked up but her eyes were not on the policeman, they looked beyond him as if to check that her boss was not going to come in the front door and interrupt them.

BARBARA KNOX TAPPED the information onto the page, nodding silently to herself. This was good stuff. Not only had they found a series of Mercedes owners (all men, she thought with a grin) who wanted to offload their white sports jobs, but now there was this company who actually hired them out. Vladimir Badica was the owner of these hire cars, many of them white ones used for weddings. She grimaced as she read the list of couples that had hired the larger and more expensive ones for their big days. Waste of money, she thought. Better to spend it on a holiday somewhere like Mauritius. Barbara's face became thoughtful again. Diana hadn't exactly said they should take a holiday together, but had hinted that something like that would follow as a reward for their joint efforts.

She shrugged the idea away. Probably wouldn't happen, knowing her luck. Better to concentrate on the job in hand. See who had hired the white Mercedes during the past couple of years in case there was some sort of tie-in with the three shooting victims.

LORIMER READ THE report for the second time. It simply didn't make any sort of sense that the three people named by Catherine Pattison had reason to murder her husband. One of them, Zena Fraser, was out of the picture anyway because of her alibi. Raeburn had no apparent motive for killing his close friend and somehow Lorimer could not believe that Frank Hardy would have been so forthcoming to a senior police officer had he had anything to hide. Why, then, he thought to himself, had Pattison's widow been so adamant that these people had been worth the time and effort it had already taken to check on their backgrounds and their whereabouts on the night of the murder?

She may well have been aware of the liaison between Ms Fraser and her husband. *Hell hath no fury like a woman scorned,* he reminded himself. Had it been some sort of female spite to name Zena Fraser as a possible killer? His frown deepened. There had been something in Frank Hardy's words that had suggested that the Labour MSP's sympathies lay *with* not *against* Catherine Pattison. So what on earth would make the woman suspect that man of killing her errant husband? *Cherchez la femme,* Solly had told him, meaning something quite different at the time. But, he wondered, was there something worth searching for in Catherine Pattison née Cadell's own background? Picking up the telephone, Lorimer dialled the 0131 ex-directory number.

CATHERINE PATTISON PUT down the telephone, her fingers trembling. Had Frank said something? She bit her lip as she turned towards the window. Outside the snow had stopped falling and the garden was shrouded in silence. Once she would have gasped in girlish delight at the frosted leaves on her holly trees or the bare branches covered in glittering white against that powder blue sky. But years of waiting and wondering had robbed her of the capacity to enjoy such simple sights as this. She rubbed her thumb repeatedly across her forefinger as though to warm it against the chill outside, but her eyes had taken on a faraway look as if her thoughts were somewhere other than this Edinburgh suburb and its winter landscape.

She had given Detective Superintendent Lorimer Frank Hardy's name as a double bluff. That was what they had agreed, after all. What had Frank told that policeman? She shifted restlessly as she recalled the tall man with those piercing blue eyes that had seemed to gaze into her very soul. Or, was that simply something she had made up since then? A false memory born of a conscience that one could only brand as guilty?

She turned at the sound of a door opening and blinked as her mother entered the room, bearing a tray laden with home-baked marmalade loaf and a small pot of coffee. Catherine looked up as the older woman laid down the tray and began to fuss with the pair of folded linen napkins.

'Don't,' she said, more sharply than she had intended, seeing the shadow that crossed her mother's face. 'Leave it just now, will you?'

'Thought you said you were hungry,' Mrs Cadell murmured. 'Who was that on the phone just now?' she added.

'Lorimer,' Catherine answered, turning away from the buttered loaf that had been made as a treat for her. It was all she needed to say; one single word to explain why her appetite for her mother's home baking had suddenly vanished.

'Well,' the older woman said, folding her arms across her chest. 'Did you tell him what really happened?'

'Of course not,' Catherine replied crossly. 'What sort of fool do you take me for?'

'The sort of fool that makes most women wish their husband was gone so they can make the same mistakes all over again,' Mrs Cadell sighed, shaking her head wearily.

Chapter Twenty-two

ROSIE LIFTED THE lid of her husband's laptop and was soon keying in his password. It was something that they had agreed on when they had moved in together, even before their marriage. No secrets, shared case studies, the lot. If Solly chose to ignore the gorier aspects of forensic pathology, that was up to him, Rosie thought with a grin. But the no-holds-barred policy meant that she had access to all his ongoing cases and she was curious to see what her beloved had made of the four prostitute murders. Reading through them on screen was like being back at work, Rosie told herself; or at least it felt like that while Abby was slumbering soundly in her crib. And, besides, hadn't she performed the post-mortem on at least one of the women?

The telephone ringing made her shoot out of her chair and grab the nearest handset, panic filling her lest the sound wake her baby and make her lose this precious time she had set aside for herself.

'Maggie!' she gasped, hearing the voice of her friend. 'What a surprise! Shouldn't you be at school this afternoon?'

'We were all sent home early yesterday because of the snow and the council has decreed in their wisdom to keep the schools shut until at least tomorrow,' Maggie said, the unconcealed glee in her voice making Rosie smile. Outside the huge bay windows that overlooked Kelvingrove Park Rosie could see children playing on sledges, some of them little more than tin trays.

'Ah, right, so you're footloose and fancy free,' Rosie said. 'Don't suppose you'd like to come across town to see your god-daughter?'

'I'd love to,' Maggie replied, 'but it's only Bill's car that's going anywhere in this weather. Mine's well and truly stuck in the garage, I'm afraid. What are you up to yourself? Abby being a good wee girl?'

'She's asleep, actually,' Rosie said, trying not to whisper.

'Oh, sorry, hope I haven't woken her up.'

'No, don't think so. I was just trawling through that case our husbands were both working on, the prostitute killings, you know?'

'Aye, something nasty in them,' Maggie said. 'Not that I'm given all the grisly details, mind.' She paused. 'See if I was in Solly's shoes, I'd be looking for a class one nutter, you know? Someone who howls at the moon.'

'Best not let him hear you refer to the mentally unstable like that,' Rosie chuckled. 'Listen, why not come over this weekend if you can thaw out that car of yours? We could take the wee one to the park if it's not too cold. Wrap her up in her sling.'

'Okay, but I'll let you go now in case Abigail wakes up. Speak soon. Bye.'

Rosie put down the telephone, listening hard for the sound of a baby's plaintive cry but there was nothing. Breathing a small sigh of relief, she returned to the laptop, pressing the space bar to make the screen re-appear. It would be funny if Maggie was right, she thought, then, more to amuse herself than anything else, Rosie jotted down the four dates when each woman had been murdered then Googled them to see if there had indeed been any planetary influence.

A few minutes later she stared at the notes she had scribbled on a pad, blinking in disbelief. The very thing that Maggie Lorimer had uttered in jest had actually taken place. Carol Kilpatrick, Miriam Lyons, Jenny Haslet and Tracey-Anne Geddes had all been murdered on the night of a full moon.

'WHY WASN'T THIS picked up before?' Rosie asked accusingly as she rocked the baby back and forth in her arms.

'It isn't something that most people would think to do,' Solly answered quietly. 'In fact I might not even have thought of it at this stage. Thanks to Maggie, however, we now have something that links all four of these girls, albeit,' he smiled ruefully, 'something that might not be looked upon by the police or even the courts of law as anything more than a strange sort of coincidence.'

'But Lorimer . . .'

'. . . doesn't believe in coincidences,' Solly finished for her. 'No more than I do, darling. No, what we have here is the possibility of a psychotically motivated series of killings. But what else must we see in this picture?' he murmured, no longer looking at his wife but rather talking to himself. 'Remember Lorimer's mantra: means, method and opportunity,' he said, counting them off on his fingers. 'Opportunity might have come easily enough either from someone frequenting the sauna or out on a familiar patch of the streets – all the victims were vulnerable young women. The methods tended to differ inasmuch as two were strangled and the others stabbed in something of a frenzied attack, but we still have to keep an open mind about that. Then the means. Someone,' he said slowly, 'had a way of attracting each of these girls into a situation where they could be overpowered and murdered.'

'A drug dealer, maybe?' Rosie suggested, breaking in on his train of thought. 'They were all on the game to feed their habit, remember.'

'But Jenny and Miriam had got work in a sauna. Doesn't that indicate that they were making some attempt to clean up their act?'

'Aye,' Rosie said sceptically. 'If you believe that you'll believe anything, love. Don't think the owners of these places are all that particular about what their girls get up to.'

'I'm not so sure,' Solly replied. 'There was mention of the Big Blue Bus project. These people go all out to get the girls off drugs, don't they?'

Abigail, who had been content to listen to the voices around her, let out a familiar whimper.

'Oops, sorry, wee one, time for your feed,' Rosie said, patting her baby's back and making shushing noises as she walked into the nursery.

Solomon Brightman stood watching as Rosie set Abby gently against her breast. It was an age-old gesture that spelled out the wonder of motherhood, something that was a privilege to behold.

Had someone else's mother held her son to her like that, a son who was destined by dint of some abnormality in his genetic make-up to become a cold-blooded killer? Perhaps, Solly told himself sadly. All the joys and tender moments of motherhood would be destroyed watching one's beloved child grow into some sort of monster. And, if he were to be instrumental in any way in finding this man, then that mother too would become a victim.

Back in his study, the psychologist lifted his desk diary, hearing the creak of the still-new spine as he turned the pages. Blinking owlishly, Solly stopped at a particular date. Scribbled under the seventh of February he had written *Lorimer's party. Keep free. Babysitter?* But above the date, floating quietly on a white space were the words: full moon.

THE WOMAN WHO sometimes called herself Diana walked slowly towards the red brick building, her heavy boots slipping in the slushy snow. She paused for a moment to peer in at the entrance, curious to see what she could see, but it looked simply like any other reception area of a big organisation, though the familiar badge of Strathclyde Police dominated the view for any passersby. Detective Superintendent Lorimer worked somewhere up there, she knew. Barbara had been fulsome in her praise of him and something had drawn her here, wondering just what this man was like. Yet caution prevailed over womanly curiosity and she walked on, smiling a little to herself. If only they knew she was here, she thought, walking past their front door like any ordinary citizen!

UP THERE WITHIN the myriad offices of Strathclyde Police headquarters the detective superintendent in charge of the Serious Crimes Unit was indeed in situ, frowning over the email that Solly had sent him. He'd be much happier if he could devote some of his time to Helen James's cases, he thought, instead of being sent on what he now believed were wild goose chases to Edinburgh. That Catherine Pattison had her own agenda, he was now certain. Her voice had given her away, even though her words had striven to reassure him. *James has all of these dreadful guns,* she'd told him, faltering slightly as though she was perfectly aware that her accusation against the MSP was ill founded. And yet, and yet . . . the memory of Raeburn's words had come back to him time and again. *Nothing to hide*, the man had told him. And that gun book had been there for all to see. Had it been a deliberate show, perhaps?

Lorimer shook his head wearily. How many man hours had been spent collating the background checks on those three people, officers struggling through these hazardous conditions over in the capital where the snow had become so bad that the army had been called out to clear main roads like Princes Street? Perhaps, he thought, it was time to delve into Mrs Pattison's own background. Frowning again, Lorimer realised that this was an action that would be delegated to a more junior officer. Being in charge of this department had meant more paperwork and meetings, not the sort of day-to-day work that he really enjoyed. His naturally restless spirit made him want to be out and about, the way he used to be as a detective inspector; tramping the streets, asking questions, meeting up with his own snouts.

He sighed. He was not quite forty and yet had already gained this rank, this prestigious appointment to Serious Crimes, so why was he feeling such a sense of detachment from the cases under investigation? Was it being here at HQ in Pitt Street, away from the cut and thrust of a division? And there were killers out there on these mean streets, he told himself, biting his lower lip; killers that he wanted to catch before any other innocent victims became their prey.

Standing up, he wandered over to his window and looked down on the snowy street below. There were a few people about and he could see their figures walking gingerly on the filthy pavements

where ice had formed under layers of compacted snow. Suddenly
the room was too warm, too confined and Lorimer felt that old
sensation of claustrophobia that had dogged him from childhood.
He had to get out, even if it was only to walk around the block for
ten minutes. Looking at his watch (a Christmas gift from Maggie)
he saw that his next meeting with the press was not for another
half an hour, plenty of time to breathe in the cold air and clear his
head.

The road outside led upwards to Blythswood Square and its
patch of gardens surrounded by elegant Georgian buildings. As he
approached this city centre oasis of greenery he looked up at the
façade of the Blythswood Square Hotel, a luxury establishment
that dominated one entire side of the square. Perhaps he could
take Maggie there some evening for a meal, he thought idly; she
might enjoy a bit of high living.

The sound of birdsong made the policeman stop suddenly at
one corner of the gardens and look up. He blinked then blinked
again, hardly daring to believe what he was seeing. There, fluttering
from one bare branched tree to the next, were several small buff-
coloured birds, their tiny crests making them easily identifiable.
Lorimer stood gazing upwards as the high pitched notes floated
down, the little birds hopping from branch to branch before taking flight, displaying the blobs of red on their open wings, and
making for the original tree once more. Waxwings! Here in the
city centre, he thought. The severe weather must have made them
rest there to feed on the plentiful berries in the trees and bushes,
he told himself. Slowly he walked to the opening where a path led
around the interior of the gardens, taking care not to slip on the
patches of ice. Overhead the grey skies had begun to clear and
there were swathes of blue making a backdrop for the silhouettes

of leafless trees. He stood still, watching the birds, then inhaled a deep draught of frosty air, his warm breath forming a cloud around his face.

The walk back to Pitt Street took only minutes but it seemed to Lorimer that he had been away from his office for far longer, such was his feeling of liberation. As he entered the building he reminded himself that his tenure here was not for ever. Serious Crimes would be shelved eventually, and then he would be looking for a new challenge, something that would hopefully take him back to a more hands-on role in policing. Smiling at the thought, Lorimer took the stairs two at a time, ready for the more imminent daily task of facing the journalists, this time expecting their endless questions about the murder of Edward Pattison.

THE IDEA HAD been growing slowly in her mind ever since Barbara had mentioned the daily press conference. Watching from behind a parked car, she saw them entering the red brick building, some singly, some in pairs, as though they were familiar with each other; the press pack, gaining entrance to this place and ready to question the man who had all knowledge of the ongoing investigation. Drawing a deep breath, she willed herself to follow them, fingering the laminated badge in her pocket. *Diana Yeats, freelance journalist*, had made a good job of faking the ID, but just how good a job was about to be tested. Would anybody recognise her? Hopefully not. The fluffy blonde that she had been all those years ago had been transformed dramatically into someone entirely different. Besides, there was something else, a feeling that she had carried with her ever since that first shot had been fired; it was as though she was invulnerable, safe from discovery.

The dark-skinned man behind the desk looked enquiringly at her as she stepped towards him.

'Press,' she said as brightly as she could, her confident smile belying the nerves that were making her stomach turn over. What did this police officer see? A woman smartly dressed in a black, fur-trimmed coat carrying a leather briefcase as she waited for the plastic pass that would allow her to follow the others down to the press room.

'First time here?' the officer said, taking her business card and turning to his computer to type her name onto a piece of card.

'Yes,' she replied, watching as he slipped the card into its clip-on holder and handed it to her.

'Just go downstairs and you'll see them all gathering in the main hall,' he said, leaning forwards and indicating the staircase opposite.

'Thanks,' she said, still forcing herself to smile as she clipped on the badge and headed towards the darkened stairwell.

THERE WERE PERHAPS forty people assembled in the hall waiting for the detective superintendent to make his entrance. Someone had failed to put on all of the lights and the large room was shadowy and cold as Lorimer walked on to the stage. The murmurs of talk from the assembled journalists ceased immediately as all eyes turned towards the tall figure spreading his notes upon the lectern.

To someone who had never seen him before, Detective Superintendent Lorimer was an imposing man. He might have been a sportsman, had in fact played rugby rather well as a young man, but the strength of his physique was more than matched by a different sort of power; those unsmiling eyes and that granite jaw came from a man whose experience of life had hardened him into a formidable opponent of the worst sort of criminal. When he began to speak it came as no surprise to hear a clear, deep voice in an accent that was securely rooted in his native Glasgow. And, as he spoke about Edward Pattison, the ongoing investigation and the need for journalism to help and not impede the case, his eyes were roving over each and every member of the pack. Yet some of the seated figures had deliberately chosen corners that were in shadow, watching while not being watched in turn.

When the question and answer session began it surprised the woman sitting at the back to hear how polite most of the journalists were to this man who was now gripping the lectern and leaning forward slightly as though to catch every word that was being said. There were none of the recriminations that might have been expected in a case that had not seen much progress. That, she thought, was some relief. Having Barbara as her *deepthroat* was one thing, but she was never completely sure if she was being fed useless titbits by the detective constable or not. Glancing round the room, the dark-haired woman knew that was an added risk of coming here. Okay, Barbara believed her story about being a freelance journo, but she still didn't want to run into the girl.

As she listened it was all about the deputy first minister. *Pattison, Pattison, Pattison.* She could have told them all they ever wanted to know, couldn't she? But why was there never a mention of Tracey-Anne? And what about these other victims? The sensation in her chest that she had thought to be nerves deepened into a pain as she fought the desire to stand up and demand that the officers in this place get off their backsides and find these women's killer. The rage inside her screamed so hard to be released that she turned her head a fraction, wondering if the man next to her had sensed it.

Then suddenly the meeting was over and Lorimer was striding off the stage, as if to demonstrate that he was eager to be off to some other area of the investigation. The babble of talk resumed as they filed out, lining up at the front desk to leave their security passes.

Once outside she walked smartly away from the building, not even turning to look behind her, and headed up towards the Malmaison. The hotel was becoming something of a refuge, she thought, as the twin bay trees flanking the main door came into sight. It was not until she was settled in the brasserie with a coffee that the woman who called herself Diana took out her reporter's notebook and flipped it open.

What had she written on that lined page? One short sentence that, reading it now, made her mouth turn up into a secret smile: *He doesn't know.*

LORIMER CLOSED THE door behind him, glad that the daily task of facing the press pack was over. It had been a much more subdued meeting than usual, perhaps the intense cold had made them want to scurry back quickly to the warmth of their offices. And there had been a new one in their midst, that dark-haired woman sitting silently at the back, listening but not asking any questions. That in itself had drawn him to regard her with a flicker of interest. Perhaps she'd been sent by her editor as a substitute for the regular news reporter; this weather was playing havoc with everybody's travel arrangements, after all.

Then, as the telephone rang, commanding the detective superintendent's attention, all thoughts of the strange woman disappeared.

Maggie Lorimer listened as the rain pattered onto the skylight window. It was well after two in the morning and the thaw that the weather forecasters had promised seemed to have arrived. If only it didn't turn to ice afterwards, she thought, shivering as she closed the bathroom door behind her. At least the schools would be back today and they could catch up with all the missed lessons. Padding quietly back to bed, she paused for a moment, looking down at her sleeping husband. He'd not missed a single day at work despite the dreadful weather. Crime didn't take off snow days, did it? Especially crimes like the vicious murders that concerned Detective Superintendent William Lorimer.

Slipping into bed, Maggie let her thoughts wander. What would life be like if Bill hadn't joined the police force? Would he have become an art historian as he had always intended? She closed her eyes, willing sleep to come, and drifted into a half-dream about pictures in a gallery, but they were all the same subject; a woman lying in the snow, blood spilled artistically from a wound beneath her curvaceous body. Then they were not flesh and blood people at all but pictures of a broken statue and the blood was not that bright red colour at all but a sickly brown as water coursed past, leaving the marble muddied and wet, its surface gleaming in a chiaroscuro light coming from somewhere that only the artist could see. Then she was falling off the edge of a pavement . . .

Maggie woke up suddenly, aware of the dream but with it already slipping from her consciousness. She heaved a sigh, turned on her side and let her head sink deeper into the pillow.

The Glasgow streets had been washed clean by the rain but there were still lumps of brown-tinged snow in car parks and untreated side roads where huge drifts had been piled up by the relentless snow ploughs. Lorries with their flashing lights had been a familiar sight, scattering their ever-diminishing supplies of grit like pebble dash onto the icy roads, sometimes flicking the tiny particles onto other vehicles as they made their lumbering night-time way along motorways and city streets alike.

Jim Blackburn was listening to the request programme from Radio Clyde as his gritting machine moved slowly along Sauchiehall Street. He signalled right as the pedestrian area loomed ahead, then turned the wheel and headed uphill, across Bath Street and upwards into the shadows of the buildings that lay on either side of Blythswood Street.

His eye caught the figure hovering near the corner of the pavement. She was not quite close enough to the kerb to be making a move to cross, yet neither was she lurking in the shadows, since the light from a street lamp let Jim see her clearly enough. In the moments it took for his gritter lorry to pass her by, he saw a skinny wretch of a girl. She was clad in a black jacket, a pale blue miniskirt that barely covered her decency (a phrase his granny had sometimes used in an offended Presbyterian tone) and knee-length boots. Jim's glance took in the white of her bare legs. He swallowed, realising just what she was and why she was standing there at this hour of the morning. Not only would her legs be bare, he thought, but she wouldn't be wearing knickers either. Somehow the thought did not arouse any other feeling than pity in the man; as he saw her in his wing mirror he realised she was about the same age as his own wee lassie, Kelly, a schoolgirl who was strictly forbidden from going into the town after a certain time of night. Jim's mouth tightened in a grim line. What sort of life led a young lassie like that onto the streets? He sighed and gave a shake of his head at the thought, leaving the girl behind as he drove up to the square, letting the grit scatter over the icy tarmac.

Jim Blackburn did not think much more about the prostitute that night but later she was to haunt his dreams for many months to come.

LILY SHIVERED AS she stood on the pavement. *It'll be fine*, the other girls had told her, *you'll make a fortune*. For the first half-hour Bella had waited just across the road, nodding encouragement whenever she had looked up. Lily had smiled back but inside she'd been hoping against hope that it wasn't really happening and that she might just be allowed to go back home again. But home wasn't on the agenda any more, was it? Not since her mother's boyfriend had come on to her . . .

This bit of pavement was special, one of the others had told her; it had been another girl's pitch. Lily thought she knew who they had meant: the dead girl whose face had been in all the papers. Her shivering became so bad that her teeth began to chatter. A spiteful little wind had begun to lift the debris from where she stood, swirling it into crazy patterns as Lily stared into the cobbled lane. That was where her body had been found, wasn't it? She wrapped her arms around her chest, wishing she'd remembered to bring a scarf. *You look the part*, one of them had told her after they'd chosen her outfit and made her twirl before that big mirror in the bedroom three of them shared. The approving glance in her eye had made Lily smile then, basking in the glow that the pills had given her. The clothes had seemed quite glamorous, certainly a lot more expensive than anything she had ever owned before. But that feeling had dissipated as the night had worn on and now she saw herself for what she really was, a fifteen-year-old girl who had run out of options and needed to sell her flesh to survive.

A car had stopped opposite and taken the other girl away so now Lily stood on her own, waiting and wondering. Would he be nice to her? Would he be gentle? *Some of them were old enough to be her father*, one of the girls had giggled. *Her grandfather more like*, another had hooted and back there in the flat it had all sounded like a bit of harmless fun. But there was nothing nice about being out here at the mercy of the elements, waiting for a stranger to offer her money for sex.

Only the gritter lorry had passed in the last half an hour and Lily had begun to wonder if it would be safe to return to the flat, telling them she'd not had any custom, when a sleek grey Jaguar turned into the street and began to slow down. Lily stepped forward. Maybe he was a stranger in this city? Perhaps all he was going to do was ask for directions?

A middle-aged man wearing an open-necked shirt smiled at her as though he could see what she was and didn't mind. Lily could see a thick gold chain around his neck and a heavy gold signet ring on the hand that was beckoning her closer.

She was supposed to ask him if he wanted to do the business, but the cold seemed to have frozen the little speech that she had been rehearsing all night.

'Get in, girl,' the man said, looking at her as though she was a girlfriend he'd been expecting to pick up. Some of them had that sort of fantasy, Lily had been told.

'Car's nice and warm,' he added, patting the leather seat next to him.

The door was open and she hesitated for the merest fraction of a second before scrambling in beside him.

'Fasten your seat belt. Don't want the cops to catch you,' he told her with a complicit grin that made her smile back at him. Then, as the car accelerated into the night, Lily knew it was going to be okay after all. Perhaps it would only take a quick half an hour, maybe even in a nice hotel room? She pictured herself stuffing a wad of notes into her handbag. Easy money, the girls had told her, and maybe it was, Lily thought, settling back against the soft leather, glancing at the man who was to be her very first customer.

Chapter Twenty-three

THE DAY BEGAN frosty and cold, ice concealed by the slick of rain that had cleared away the snow. A sliver of crimson peered over blue-black clouds in the east, then tentacles of flame spread across the sky heralding another day, but with the warning of further poor weather to come.

Maggie filled the kettle at the sink as Chancer wound his furry body around her legs, his meows becoming more urgent as he waited for his breakfast. The central heating had been humming nicely for over twenty minutes and the kitchen was warm enough, but as Maggie opened the blinds she saw the morning's rosy glow and shivered. These ink-black clouds surely held more snow? Well, Muirpark Secondary School was opening its gates once more and she'd just have to get a move on, have breakfast ready for them both and make time to defrost her car.

Since Bill had been at Pitt Street, Maggie had tried to make this hour a time for both of them. Even having something as simple as breakfast together was a bit special after all the years of early morning rises and very late homecomings that his job had demanded. Maggie Lorimer had hoped that the new post might have given her husband more of a steady routine to his day but with Edward Pattison's murder such hopes had been severely dashed. Bill's face had appeared regularly in the press and even on television where he had made a statement following the politician's death. Once such matters would have caused a frisson of excitement and led to remarks in the staffroom, but nowadays Maggie took them for granted, more used to her husband's high profile. Sure, there had been a bit of chat amongst her colleagues, but Maggie's reticence always stopped too much speculation. Even Lena Forsyth had kept her mouth shut for once. They all suspected that she knew much more than she was letting on, but in truth Maggie was not always given the details of every case. She smiled as she laid the two places at the kitchen table. If Bill wanted to tell her anything then he would, but sometimes she felt as though he wanted to spare her the grislier side of such crimes as murder, especially since it had touched their own lives. The smile slipped as Maggie remembered the case that had brought so many police officers into her home . . .

Chancer reared up against her dressing gown, a gentle pat from his paws reminding her that his bowl was still empty.

'What would I do without you, eh?' Maggie grinned, bending down to stroke the soft fur on the cat's head. 'Okay, okay, I'll get it right now,' she added as he began to purr loudly.

'Hi, you.' Lorimer was behind her and his arms around her just as Maggie stood up from retrieving the cat's bowl.

'Hi, yourself,' she grinned, then slipped out of his grasp to wash the bowl as Chancer's meows became more frantic.

Once the cat had been fed Maggie let her husband's arms encircle her once more, closing her eyes for a moment, her head nestled in against his chest, luxuriating in the feel of his warmth, knowing that such caresses were fleeting as the clock ticked inexorably towards the time when they would both have to leave for work. But in that moment Maggie Lorimer felt completely safe and calm as she allowed her body to relax into his.

Words from a poem she was teaching to her third-year class for next week's Burns Supper came to mind, causing her to whisper them aloud:

'But pleasures are like poppies spread,
You seize the flow'r, its bloom is shed;
Or like the snow falls in the river,
A moment white – then melts for ever,
Or like the borealis race,
That flits ere you can point their place;
Or like the rainbow's lovely form
Evanishing amid the storm.
Nae man can tether time or tide:
The hour approaches Tam maun ride.'

Her sigh deepened as she extracted herself from his arms.

'Neither time nor tide waits for any man or woman,' she sighed. 'Not that rascal, Tam O' Shanter, or your good wife who has to be in Muirpark to teach her classes in just over an hour.'

'Right, woman,' Lorimer laughed. 'And I'm at the beck and call of our first minister again this morning. Maybe see you later on tonight?' His wry smile said it all. This life of his with long hours spent away from her side was so at odds with Maggie's ordered day. While she was busy with classes that came and went according to bells ringing every fifty minutes, Detective Superintendent Lorimer could be asked to get himself over to the Scottish parliament at Holyrood or attend a crime scene anywhere within the vast region of Strathclyde. Yet somehow they managed to make it work, she thought, watching as he left the room.

Maggie's smile deepened as she thought about her preparations for the seventh of February. Bill being away so much had had the advantage of helping her bring her plans to fruition. She had invited most of his old colleagues from the city centre division as well as friends like Rosie, Solly and Flynn. Even the deputy chief constable had been invited, something Maggie had decided on so that Joyce Rogers would ensure the party was not spoiled by work. Maggie suddenly thought of another woman whose stern face appeared so often on the television screen; no, she certainly wouldn't be inviting Felicity Stewart to Bill's fortieth. And, hopefully, this case would be finished by then. Glancing at the calendar on her kitchen wall, Maggie realised that Burns Night was drawing closer and after that there would be less than two weeks until her husband's party and the surprises she had planned.

THERE WERE NO surprises in Edinburgh by the time Lorimer's driver drew up outside the massive building at Holyrood. The snow on this side of the country was taking longer to clear and there were still piles of frozen ice caught in the angles between pavements and gutters. Although the paths outside the parliament were well swept they were gritty underfoot as Lorimer strode into the warmth of the building and made for the reception desk to collect his security pass.

'Back here again, Superintendent?'

Lorimer spun on his heel at the Glasgow accent behind him.

'Mr Hardy,' he said, slowing down to let the other man approach. 'Yes, I have a meeting with Ms Stewart.'

'Wonder she finds the time, what with her Russian delegation arriving today,' Hardy muttered sourly. Clearly there was no love lost between the nationalist leader and the socialist MSP.

'Russians? Any special reason why they're here?' Lorimer ventured.

'Aye, her ladyship's Burns Supper up at the castle on Wednesday night,' he said, raising his eyebrows. 'Even the dear departed aren't going to stop her holding that particular event,' he continued as they walked up the staircase, side by side. 'This lot are from St Petersburg. She went over there last year and is ostensibly returning the compliment. We usually have an event like that here but Felicity's pulled strings to have it up at the castle instead. Making a big show of it. Fact of the matter is she's desperately trying to negotiate a trade deal.' Hardy grinned. 'Maybe she'll invite you to attend.' He dug Lorimer in the ribs then passed him by, whistling a Scottish tune that was vaguely familiar.

It was not until Hardy had disappeared out of sight and Lorimer was standing at the entrance to the first minister's private lift that he recognised it as Burns' own 'Oh whistle and I'll come tae ye, my lad'. Was the Glasgow MSP insinuating that the detective superintendent was some kind of government lackey? Lorimer bristled at the thought. Yet perhaps that was just what he had become in this case, running back and forth from Glasgow to Edinburgh at the woman's bidding when, if truth be told, he would have preferred to delve more deeply into the case of the street girls' murders.

LORIMER'S KNUCKLES WERE white from gripping the file that lay across his knees as he sat in the back of the police car. To bring him all the way over here simply to enquire about the progress of the case was unforgivable and the detective vowed that he would ignore any further such requests from Ms Stewart. Bloody waste of my time! he'd wanted to shout as he got into the car, but caught sight of his driver. Instead he fumed inwardly and waited for the next vibrant ring on his BlackBerry that would doubtless keep him company all the way back along the M8. He could just imagine the conversation Felicity Stewart might be having any time now with her colleagues or the gentlemen of the press: *Oh yes, Lorimer keeps me informed of everything. Comes here to brief me on what's going on.* No wonder Hardy had whistled that tune.

Frank Hardy had been right, too, about an invitation to the Burns Supper, for himself and Maggie. His icily polite refusal had included the excuse that his wife already had plans made for her school's event and he had just stopped himself in time from telling the woman where she could stuff her Burns Supper when he had two separate cases of multiple murder to deal with. What the hell was she playing at? He was a working cop, not a social butterfly. And for the next few evenings he expected to be putting more hours in with his team in Pitt Street while the rest of the country was eating its haggis, neeps and tatties.

As he read his text messages, Lorimer put the wasted morning behind him and tried to concentrate on what his next plan of action should be. His eyebrows rose as he saw that there was a forensic report waiting for him back at headquarters; the results of the extensive examination of Pattison's Mercedes were now complete and Lorimer was keen to know what had been found. A huge amount of work had been going on behind the scenes by several experts: the forensic chemist would have been examining the Mercedes for firearms discharge residue, taping surfaces that might hold such traces. Then the firearms officer himself would be the one to examine the vehicle to determine the angle of the shot as well as trying to determine the type of weapon used. Surfaces inside and outside the car had been taped to search for DNA and fingerprints as well as hairs and fibres, especially from places like the seats and headrests.

As the scenery rushed past him Lorimer found his eyes closing on the grey day outside but his thoughts were still very much alive as to what was happening in Glasgow. *Every contact leaves a trace*, Locard had said, establishing once and for all the principle by which all forensic work was done. Even the tiniest samples of hair, fibres or materials that might have been stuck to the sole of a shoe or boot could be of use in tracing Edward Pattison's murderer. The initial lots of fingerprints that had been taken from the car had so far been matched against family members and of course Pattison himself. Yet even if the geniuses at Pitt Street could amass a wealth of trace evidence it was only worthwhile when matched against the clothing or hair of a suspect. And so far, as Detective Superintendent Lorimer was woefully aware, he was short of even one person to fit that frame.

And it was not just the press but the first minister of Scotland who kept reminding him of that particular fact.

Suddenly the car stopped, making Lorimer open his eyes. There were flashing lights ahead, signalling some sort of accident on the motorway. His driver glanced just once behind him and Lorimer gave a nod. Before long the big police car had manoeuvred its way onto the hard shoulder and was at the scene of the crash, Lorimer letting down the window.

'What happened?' he asked the uniformed officer who had approached his car. He could see a blue Fiat that was on its side, a white van askew across one lane.

'Probably a poor judgement on overtaking,' the officer said. 'Driver must have copped it on impact,' he added shortly. 'The other one's too far gone to tell us anything,' he added.

Lorimer nodded. There had been several fatal accidents all during this long hard winter but sometimes it was sheer idiocy rather than icy conditions which brought such lasting grief to the victims' families.

The siren sound of an ambulance from the Edinburgh direction gave Lorimer all the excuse he needed. One more vehicle here was only going to cause more problems.

'Well, you won't want us hanging around, officer. We'll be on our way,' he said, giving only a cursory glance towards the blue car. A quick nod from the yellow-jacketed policeman soon saw Lorimer's driver ease his way past the wreckage and head towards Glasgow, no doubt leaving behind a trail of frustrated motorists in their wake.

Sitting back in the car, Lorimer's mouth was a grim line. The driver of the Fiat was a definite fatality, the passenger unconscious and in pretty poor shape. Why did people take such foolish risks in this weather?

Why take a car at all if you don't have to? a little voice asked him. Yes, he thought. Why had Edward Pattison driven from Murrayfield to Glasgow in his Mercedes when he was staying overnight in the Central Hotel and could easily have taken the train back to Edinburgh next morning? The service between Glasgow Queen Street and Edinburgh Waverley ran every quarter of an hour and only took fifty minutes, whereas the journey on the M8 was always an hour and usually more, with tailbacks and delays a common occurrence, especially at peak times. Why had Pattison bothered to drive at all? After all, Raeburn had returned to Edinburgh by train, hadn't he? Ordinarily it didn't make sense but, if Solomon Brightman was correct, the murdered man had needed his own car to pick up some woman or other after the meeting in the City Chambers. Some woman who couldn't or daren't come into Glasgow to meet Pattison? Was the location of Erskine woods closer to the mystery woman's own home, then? Had Pattison been driving to a romantic rendezvous of some sort? Then who had been with him in that car, gun ready to kill the deputy first minister just as he had killed two other men already? And why would Pattison have given anyone a lift if he was off on a secret assignation?

Lorimer's brows were drawn down as he frowned, puzzling out the problem. It simply didn't make sense. Unless . . .

He tried to imagine the politician cruising around the darkened streets in his big white car, peering out to see what he might pick up from the choices on street corners. The idea that had been relegated to the back of his mind was brought out and re-examined. Was it possible that the politician had been on the hunt for a prostitute? Certainly someone as high profile as Pattison had been could not afford to risk a call girl coming to his hotel room. Lorimer picked up his BlackBerry again. It was time to translate this particular thought into action.

'Check all the CCTV camera footage round the drag on the night of Pattison's death, will you?' he asked the person on the other end of the line.

This wouldn't take too long, Lorimer thought. By the time he was back in his office the information he had just requested might well be on his desk, such was the efficiency of modern technology.

WHAT THE HELL was he to tell the press pack this time, Lorimer asked himself, watching the footage that had been emailed to his computer.

There it was, the big white car, its registration number showing as it moved slowly around Blythswood Square. The shadowy figure of Pattison in the driver's seat might be anyone, but once the boys in the lab had hold of this they would be able to work their magic and bring that blurry image into a sharper focus to enable better identification.

Lorimer could anticipate the sort of headlines in tomorrow's papers: *Pattison found seeking prostitutes. Deputy first minister in sleazy street.*

Oh, they were going to have a field day, weren't they? That is, *if* he decided to spill the beans. Then again . . . he drummed his fingers on the desk, thinking hard. Perhaps it was time to summon the troops, alert only the officers who were dealing with this case, keeping from more senior members of this establishment the new information he now had?

DETECTIVE SUPERINTENDENT LORIMER regarded the men and women assembled in the muster room. Some of them were slouched by radiators or bent over their chairs, obviously pretty weary, having spent hours on this case already. But there was that keen light in every pair of eyes that looked his way; for, with every meeting, there was the hope that the boss might have come up with something that could push things to a good conclusion.

'Good news and bad news,' Lorimer began, looking at them to see the effect of his words. Some sat up a little straighter, others simply stared.

'Good news first,' he continued. 'New CCTV footage of Pattison has been found from the night that he was killed.'

There was an immediate reaction from the officers; not yet a full-blooded cheer but a loud enough sound of appreciation that at last this case was getting somewhere.

'Now for the bad news,' Lorimer told them, his hand up to quieten them. 'Pattison was last seen in Blythswood Square and it was pretty obvious from the way he was driving what he was up to.'

'Looking for a whore!' Sutherland's voice came loud and clear.

'Yes, that's the most likely explanation,' Lorimer said. 'We don't have any footage of him actually picking a woman up but the time on the film shows that it was well after he had left his meeting in George Square.' He turned to Barbara Knox who was standing beside a laptop that was connected to a screen behind him.

'Okay, DC Knox, let's see it.'

Soon the entire room was silent, peering at the images of a pale car cruising around the drag, the different shades of grey picking out skeletal trees and darkened basements.

Then there was a collective gasp as one of the images showed the face of the murdered man leaning forwards as though he needed to see something or someone that was out of the camera's view. As the car disappeared off the screen for a moment the officers' murmurs became louder but the next image silenced them all.

The tail lights of the Mercedes could be seen as the car accelerated over the hill and it was just possible to make out a second figure seated in the passenger seat.

There was a moment's silence as they digested what they had seen, then Rita Livingstone's voice piped up, 'What are you going to tell the press?'

THE TEAM HAD seen the sense in keeping a lid on this new piece of evidence, even Duncan Sutherland had nodded his approval as Lorimer had outlined the need to keep the press away from the possibility that Pattison had been out looking for a prostitute on the night he had died.

What would not have gone down so well would have been any suggestion that the three men who had been killed might somehow be linked to the ongoing prostitute murder case. That was something that Lorimer kept to himself for now but it was a matter he felt needed urgent discussion with the one man he knew would not rubbish the idea.

SOLLY RUBBED HIS eyes then replaced the round horn-rimmed spectacles that gave him the appearance of a wise old owl; at least that had been the caricature some wag of a student had drawn in the *Glasgow Guardian* and somehow the perception had stuck. For once the psychologist was looking forward to the weekend and the chance to catch up on some much needed sleep. Baby Abigail was his heart's delight but after yet another broken night, Solly wished that his little daughter would not wake quite so often between midnight and six in the morning. So it was that he arrived in his large office overlooking University Avenue each morning almost glad of the peace and quiet that pervaded this part of the building. And, if he did have to stifle a few yawns by late afternoon, these were shared by many of Solly's students whose lives were bound by the frantic need to cram as much activity into each of the twenty-four hours in a day as they could possibly manage.

It was fortunate for the psychologist that he was in between classes when the call came from Pitt Street.

'Solly, I need to talk to you about this case. Something's come up. Are you free any time later this afternoon?'

Solly glanced at the clock on his wall. There were two classes left today: a lecture and a seminar. He had planned to leave right after the latter and walk home through the park, but he recognised a quality of urgency in Lorimer's voice and his curiosity was aroused.

'Do you want me to come into town?'

'No. I'd rather we met somewhere outside headquarters. This is really big stuff, Solly, and I don't want the press to get wind of it.'

'Come up here, then,' Solly said with a smile. 'It is as private as you could wish for, my friend. Say a little after four o'clock? Gives me time to shoo any earnest young things out of my office.'

LORIMER STUDIED THE forensic report that ran to several pages. There were plenty of pieces of fibre, hair and other materials that had been taken from Pattison's car, all listed according to their chemistry as well as giving their possible sources. The most interesting ones were the hairs taken from the passenger seat, five different types in all. These could be DNA tested and matched against family members and Pattison himself, just like the fingerprints had been. If there were any rogues among them then that would prove to be very interesting indeed, Lorimer thought. The image of a smart, blonde woman came into Lorimer's head. He would bet a month's salary that Zena Fraser had sat in the Mercedes passenger seat plenty of times and that one of these hair samples belonged to her. Was it worth asking her to give a DNA sample for elimination purposes? She could easily arrange to go along to her local police station and have it done.

The thought was no sooner in his mind than Lorimer was lifting the phone off its cradle and dialling the number at Holyrood that he now knew off by heart.

'Zena Fraser, please,' he asked the voice on the switchboard. 'It's Detective Superintendent Lorimer calling.'

BY THE TIME Lorimer arrived in the west end of the city, darkness had begun to cover the skyline with leaden clouds and a light rain was falling. Parking the Lexus was not a problem, for once, as there were now several empty bays along the avenue, most lectures being over for the day. Pulling up his coat collar, the detective hurried across the road and looked up at the double windows on the first floor where Solly had his domain. Since becoming a professor, the psychologist had enjoyed the luxury of one of the university's most coveted rooms. Several departments were housed in this terrace that hugged the avenue, curving around a row of trees between the library block and the Students' Union.

Solly was standing with his hands clasped behind his back gazing out of the window when Lorimer walked into the room and for a moment the detective had a rare glimpse of the professor of psychology in contemplative pose. Just what went on in that brain of his? And how could a man who was utterly squeamish about the carnage at a crime scene begin to fathom what went on in the depraved mind of a criminal? He cast his mind back to the time when he had mistrusted this man and all that he had been prepared to offer. He'd learned a lot since those days, however, and now Solly was one of the first he turned to for advice. Forensic profiling had enjoyed a mixed reception from the public but it was still a tool that many forces throughout the UK used when faced with difficult cases.

'Lorimer, hello.' Solly had turned back into the room and the smile lit up his face when he saw his friend. 'I was just thinking about . . .' He paused and shook his head as though his thoughts were irrelevant to this visit. 'Cup of tea? And there might still be some scones in that paper bag over there,' he murmured as he walked the length of the room to the table that housed a kettle and an assortment of mugs. He picked one up and frowned. 'Hmm, must get them washed. No worries, here's a couple of clean ones,' he added cheerfully, selecting a Celtic Football Club mug with its green shamrock logo and a pretty porcelain one with flowers that had been overlooked by the last lot of students who had been treated to afternoon tea with the prof.

'Aye, tea's fine, so long as it isn't any of your herbal stuff,' Lorimer said, taking off his coat and hanging it on the old-fashioned coat stand that stood in a corner of the room.

He sat on a chair next to the window, sinking gratefully into its cracked brown leather and stretching his long legs in front of him. It was, he thought, the sort of room where he could easily relax, so unlike the office he had been given at Pitt Street. There were books everywhere, of course, not only in the floor-to-ceiling bookcases but scattered across the immense table that dominated the room and in small piles against chair legs and corners as if Solly had been looking for material on a variety of topics throughout the day.

'You've got new information?' Solly asked, pulling out a small side table and setting down the mugs of tea. The promised scones were now on a clean plate, buttered and cut in half. Lorimer picked one up, his fingers becoming satisfyingly floury, realising that he had in fact missed lunch and was suddenly quite hungry.

'Yes,' he replied, taking a bite of the scone.

Solly waited patiently, watching as the policeman wolfed down the food.

'I had a thought about Pattison,' Lorimer said at last. 'Why did he take a car to Glasgow that night when it would have been much easier to travel by train? I asked myself. Then I remembered what you had said about a woman.'

'Go on,' Solly nodded.

'CCTV footage has caught him in the car, probably picking up a prostitute in Blythswood Square,' Lorimer told him, watching for the psychologist's reaction. There was only a nod of that dark head and a thoughtful look in those fathomless brown eyes. Had Solomon Brightman got there before him? Lorimer wondered.

'I think,' said Solly slowly, 'that it might be helpful to look into the background of the first two murdered men to see if they were in the habit of soliciting prostitutes back in their own home towns.'

'What about a possible link between the murdered women and those three men?'

Again that sage nod from the psychologist. 'Perhaps,' he began. 'But is there anything to suggest that there is a killer out there targeting both sets of people? Professional men and street women?'

Lorimer frowned. 'Go on,' he said.

Solly raised his eyebrows in an expression of incredulity. 'I really do not believe that the person who pulled a gun and killed those men is the same one who butchered these girls. Look,' he continued, leaning forward to emphasise his point. 'These men were killed at point-blank range, execution-style, whereas someone else has killed at least two of the women in a complete frenzy. The others may well have been strangled in a moment of rage. Or even frustration,' he added.

'But you still think there may be some kind of link between the two cases, don't you?' Lorimer's mouth twitched at the corners as he regarded the psychologist. He knew this man so well now and could sense that there was more to come.

'Murdering three men who have nothing in common, apart from the make of cars they drive, simply for soliciting girls in a city centre area would be a little extreme, don't you think?' Solly asked. 'And the last known movements of Mr Wardlaw and Mr Littlejohn might well suggest that was what they were doing out so late at night. Hmm,' he said, stroking his beard as though that helped him to process his thoughts. 'And I would want to look for a much more serious motive, wouldn't you?' He looked into Lorimer's steely blue gaze without flinching.

LORIMER KNEW HIS next step would mean an even greater workload for his growing team of officers but at least they would have some help from the forces down south where Matthew Wardlaw and Thomas Littlejohn had originated. Their cars were already being taken apart to see if any of the forensic material was a match for Edward Pattison's white Mercedes; now it remained to be seen if the police could come up with proof that each of the English businessmen were regular clients of the women in their own cities.

Meanwhile it seemed as though he and Professor Brightman might have to spend a bit of time moonlighting on their own before he could dole out actions to his crew that involved trawling through the lives of the women who patrolled the drag night after night. He would create a file on his computer to show all of his movements and give an explanation for them, of course. A detective superintendent out in the drag might raise a few eyebrows, or even jeopardise his career, if it was to be taken the wrong way. Especially if the press were to get wind of his private investigations.

Chapter Twenty-four

HE REACHED OUT his hand to feel the cold surface of the blade shining against its velvet casing on the wall. Where it had come from he did not know but it looked like something from an oriental fairy story, one where heroes fought against dark-skinned warriors, overcoming them despite unequal odds. His lips parted slightly and he ran his tongue across the edge of his teeth, savouring the remembered taste of blood in his mouth. The other weapons shone dimly from their places on this wall, the only illumination coming from a few well-positioned lights set into the ceiling.

The big man turned slightly to glance at the wall next to the half-opened door. These dark wooden cases contained guns, he knew that, but such mechanical weapons would never give him the same thrill as these ceremonial swords. Guns were part of different stories; shoot-outs in the Wild West or duels between foppish men with lace at their wrists and haughty demeanours. But these blades shaped and chased with delicate traceries, some with fine bone handles, created for him a magic all of their own. These were a real man's weapons; scimitars, cutlasses and broadswords that could subdue an enemy or hack to pieces anyone who tried to thwart his desires.

A sound from the next room alerted him to the presence of other people. It was not forbidden, his coming here to stare at the collection arrayed on the walls of this room, but there was a feeling of unease within the big man as he stood there, hands by his side now like a guilty child who fears being caught for a misdeed he had committed only in thought. Taking a step back, he waited for the inevitable entry of the man who was the owner of these wonderful things.

'Oh, it's you,' the man said as he entered the room. 'Thought I'd heard something. Everything all right?'

The big man gave a grunt in reply, nodding his head vigorously.

'Okay, don't be too long in there, will you? There's plenty of work to be done in the morning, remember.'

As the door closed behind the owner of these magical swords, the big man sighed deeply then frowned as he regarded the wall once more. That broadsword hanging up there above the others was not quite flush with the horizontal line of its scabbard so he took a step towards the wall, reached up and removed it from the twin display hooks.

His fist closed around the hilt and he brandished it once, twice, hearing a faint swish as the blade cut through nothing but dusty air. Closing his eyes, the big man imagined the chain mail protecting his body and head, heard the sound of battle cries as his men charged against the foe then raised his arm, ready to enter the fray.

Blinking, he saw that he was still clutching the huge sword aloft but there was no one there in the room but himself. Slowly he lowered it once more and replaced it reverently on the wall hooks, careful to balance it perfectly between them.

Taking a step back, he bowed towards the weapon. Then, as though some sort of ceremony had ended, he stepped towards the door, switching off the lights as he left the armoury behind in its cocoon of darkness.

Chapter Twenty-five

ZENA FRASER SAT obediently, mouth opened wide, while the police doctor ran the swab around the inside of her mouth.

'That's it,' he said, nodding briefly. 'Thanks for your co-operation, ma'am.'

'Not at all,' Zena replied, trying to suppress a shiver of disgust as she rose to leave. In truth she had not wanted to undertake this little visit to her local police office but the fact was that she had to appear as completely apart from the murder investigation as she could. One or two of the tabloids had interviewed her, of course, but her approach to them had been that of a childhood friend grieving for the man who had become no more than a colleague in the Scottish parliament. If anything other than that should leak out then her career could well be finished, Zena thought, her fair brow furrowing in sudden anxiety as she left the building.

ELSEWHERE IN THE capital the business of running the country was continuing as usual, Felicity Stewart's well-oiled machinery of government ensuring that each department had its records up to date for the daily televised appearance within the debating chamber. As ever, questions had been asked about the murder case and, as ever, her answers had been similar to those issued by the police. Enquiries were continuing and evidence being collated but for now, no, there had not been any arrests nor had there been any mention of a particular suspect. And, if the first minister was a little brusque in dismissing any further questions on that subject, she could have been forgiven, since the day's agenda was particularly long.

Frank Hardy listened as the various questions came to the fore, watching Felicity Stewart's face as she parried several points from the Labour benches. She was good, he thought, her replies quick as lightning, some of them witty enough to evoke a ripple of laughter from the entire assemblage. He could see why Ed had jumped ship. Hardy glanced around at his colleagues, many of whom were grey-haired now and aiming to retire at the next election. There was an atmosphere of apathy within his party at times, something that Edward Pattison had had the nous to sense long before anyone else. Still, there were die-hard types like himself who would rally the electorate to their cause, reminding them of the days gone by when men like the red Clydesiders had fought for their rights.

Perhaps that was one of the things that Cathy had found attractive about him; the old dog who still banged on about human rights and the socialist way of life. Opposites attracted, it was said, and there was no greater contrast than between a working-class type such as Frank Hardy and a woman like Catherine Pattison, whose upper-class Edinburgh background had made him believe that she was for ever out of his reach. Lorimer would make the connection eventually, he thought. And what then? Would he become a suspect in the case? Cathy had hinted as much, hadn't she? Well, maybe it was time to cultivate as many alibis as he could. Just in case.

THE FORENSIC REPORTS had helped to show that there had been several women travelling in Edward Pattison's car, two at least easily identified as his wife and his old friend, Zena Fraser. The others remained a mystery for now, but questions were being asked of the Pattison family to see if they might be able to give any clues as to which other ladies could have been passengers in the white Mercedes. Pattison's mother-in-law, Mrs Cadell, was one probability, of course, Lorimer thought, reading the forensic chemist's report carefully once again. The chemist and biologist had been liaising on this one, careful to give cognisance to each other's particular skills. He read on, wondering. To whom did that strand of long dark hair belong? There were no traces of narcotics so it had probably not come from a street woman after all. Would its DNA be found anywhere on their massive database? If so, then the hunt for a possible witness or even a possible killer might be nearing its end.

But why would a girl who stood around on street corners plan the deaths of three men whose only crime appeared to be that of driving a flashy big car? Most of the poor souls were totally out of it by the time they picked up their punters, something every police officer knew well, especially if they'd worked the drag at any time in their careers. The girls were usually off their heads on something to help ease the experience of having sex with some stranger or other. Still, it was going to be his mission to talk to as many of them as he could manage. At least once he had the blessing of DCI James.

IT WAS NOT a good time to be seen around the city, she thought, skimming through the garments on the sale rail in John Lewis. Some of these might come in useful, the dark-haired woman thought, lifting a gauzy blouse and holding it against her body. Every officer on this case would be on the lookout for the woman who had entered Pattison's car, Barbara had told her, another snippet that the detective constable had let slip as she had forced herself to fondle the woman's large breasts. But the woman who was currently rummaging on the sale rail would never be mistaken for a street girl, would she? A swift glance in a nearby mirror confirmed what she had supposed: an attractive, businesslike lady smiled back at her knowingly. She might well be taken for one of those well-kept housewives whose husbands worked in the city, idling her time away. Or some career woman, like a lawyer or an accountant, an image that had fooled the policewoman from that first sighting on the train. At least that was a good cover for what the so-called journalist was doing in her spare time.

The woman who had called herself Diana amused herself as she contemplated what the neighbours would make of her. *Nice lady,* they'd say. (And, yes, wouldn't they just call her a lady?) *Kept herself to herself, never one to make a fuss about the children playing outside her garden.* And that was true. Children had never felt afraid of her, had they? Barbara Knox had hinted that she detested children, as if that was something Diana ought to know. Was the woman trying to hint that they should get together? She had already tried to prise her address out of her and Diana had had to resort to taking a circuitous route home just in case the policewoman did anything stupid like following her like a love-crazed spaniel. Her eyes flashed in a moment of anger. There were no more cosy train journeys; that was something she simply couldn't afford to risk.

She slid the garment back on to its rail and marched out of the store into the maelstrom of people in Buchanan galleries and the pedestrian precinct that was crowded with shoppers eager to claim a late bargain, no doubt thwarted by the bad weather earlier in the month. And, as she made her way through the crowded streets, she felt a sudden panic. Time was slipping by and still she was no further forward. But there was one thing she had in her favour, if Knox was to be believed: Detective Superintendent Lorimer had been ordered to shelve that case and so now she had free rein to find Carol Kilpatrick's killer.

'THERE'S A MATCH,' he stated aloud, though at that particular moment there was nobody around to hear the words uttered by the forensic scientist. It might be a small statement, but it was one that would, perhaps, help to bring a satisfactory conclusion to at least one of Strathclyde Police's ongoing cases.

The white-coated scientist grinned in a moment of quiet triumph: there was now a massive link between two of these murders, since he had been able to match DNA from particles found in the Tracey-Anne Geddes case with traces from the crime scene productions concerning Jenny Haslet. The traces picked up from the more recent victim might be minute but they were sufficient for this particular forensic biologist to be confident that he could stand up in a court of Scottish law and state that there was a strong probability that whoever had murdered Jenny Haslet had also killed the prostitute who had been working the drag. The scientist shifted his spectacles from the bridge of his nose and smiled again as he rubbed his eyes. He knew at least one police officer who was going to like this.

'YOU BEAUTY!' DETECTIVE Superintendent Lorimer whispered under his breath as the voice on the telephone outlined the latest forensic discovery. It was usual for forensic reports to take days, or even weeks, to come through, but the men and women working on these cases were savvy enough to let him have any fresh information as it came in. He might no longer be officially involved but a word here and there had let his friends in the forensic sciences know he wanted to be kept in the loop.

'Thanks, thanks a lot,' Lorimer said warmly. 'I owe you big time for this one, believe me.'

It took only a matter of seconds to forward the email report to Solly and Helen James. Lorimer's smile faded as he thought of the case that he had been ordered to shelve; there was something about these street women murders that needed more attention, not less. Failure to make any headway could see another bloody corpse flung into the dark corner of a pend. Well, if Maggie could endure his absence for a few nights, then he'd be rooting about in the city, seeing what he could find by himself.

Meantime he had instructed the Lothian and Borders officers to keep a sharp watch on Catherine Pattison, not merely for her own protection from the press pack, but because, as he had warned his counterpart on the Edinburgh force, he suspected that she might be impeding her husband's case by deliberate time wasting. The three supposed suspects she had named had been passed over to Lothian and Borders now and there was a general feeling that both Zena Fraser and James Raeburn had nothing whatsoever to do with their colleague's murder. It was partly a matter of eliminating them from the scene of crime, Lorimer had assured them. Frank Hardy, though, posed a different sort of problem. Living so close to the murder scene meant that Hardy's movements on the night of the murder would have to be examined in greater detail.

Lorimer drummed his fingers on the edge of his desk, trying to recall the tone of voice the MSP had used when he had mentioned Catherine Pattison. *Cathy*, he'd called her. And had there been a slight wistfulness there or had Lorimer imagined it? Perhaps the enmity that had existed between the two men had its origins in something much more basic than politics. He sat back for a moment, wondering. If Hardy and Catherine Pattison had been having an affair then that would have given one or both of them a reason to want Edward Pattison out of the way. There had been no love lost between man and wife, if the woman's reaction to his death was anything to go by. A serial philanderer, Pattison was not going to be mourned greatly by that dark-haired beauty in her Murrayfield mansion. Lorimer thought back to Solly's enigmatic text: *Cherchez la femme*, he'd written. Well, that could mean one of two things, couldn't it? *Femme* in French did not only mean a woman – it could also refer to a wife.

THE ROAD WAS endless as is the way in dreams. A shroud of mist seemed to surround him, giving no hint as to what lay ahead as he walked along the wet pavement. His feet, he noticed, made no sound and there was an unnatural quietness in what he knew to be a busy city. Just a little ahead was a street lamp and under it, a woman who smiled at him as he passed it by, her fair hair tied back in a thin black ribbon. As he passed she opened her mouth as if to laugh and he saw her tongue emerge like a snake's, thin, forked and red as though to strike. But when he looked again, sweating and fearful, she was only a little girl swinging on the lamp post and singing some foolish song. The sudden sound made him start as though he would awaken from the vision that held him but something stronger than fear urged him on.

From behind a stone column another woman emerged, thin and dark, her eyes boring into his. She lifted her hand and beckoned him and it was then that he noticed her fingernails painted scarlet and filed into cruel points. Some force beyond his power compelled him towards her and then she was opening her mouth and swallowing him whole, a throbbing darkness taking him into that confined space that always made him scream in terror.

Lorimer woke up and felt the sweat trickle down his chest. It was all right. Everything here was familiar; Maggie's sleeping form a source of comfort in the darkened room. He took several deep breaths, trying to stifle the remnants of the images that had disturbed his sleep. Then, blinking hard, he stopped. He had seen that woman's face before, the dark-haired female who was, in this dream, also the blonde who had appeared before her. There was something, something that he could not remember from the past. A case, perhaps?

Frowning, Lorimer looked at the luminous digits on his bedside clock. It was past two a.m., a time when a different sort of life was happening in the city. Clubs could be emptying by now, hotels disgorging the last guests from late-night revelries. Maybe the dream was a way of telling him to get out there and see for himself just what was happening in the heart of Glasgow? Being there, maybe asking some of the street girls questions about Tracey-Anne, would bring him back to the reality of the case.

Yet, as he dressed, Lorimer could not rid himself of the image of that woman's face and her eyes as she lunged towards him.

THE DRAG WAS quiet tonight, Lorimer thought as he left the warmth of the Lexus. He had decided to park outside the Blythswood Hotel close enough for any CCTV cameras to note his presence. It was, he felt, important not to be seen skulking around but making his presence felt as openly as possible lest anyone misinterpret his motives. The file he had created was in the possession of both Helen James and Professor Brightman and so he felt reasonably assured about his movements should he ever be asked to account for them. He had his warrant card in his pocket so any questions he might ask the girls tonight would be official enough, he supposed. Combining both of these cases would be frowned upon by the top brass, he knew. Still, it was worth it to see what he could make of Pattison's relationships with the Glasgow street girls, other than his public involvement with the Big Blue Bus project.

His initial impression of quietness was broken by shouts coming from across the square soon followed by a group of men and women laughing and screeching as they rounded the corner from West George Street. It didn't take a detective's skills to realise where that lot had been, he thought, seeing the men's kilts and the women dressed up to the nines; Burns Suppers tended to be pretty flexible, stretching both sides of the bard's birthday on January 25th and on into February. This group were singing and making what looked like an attempt at a sort of reel along the pavement and, as they approached, Lorimer noticed one man in particular detach himself from the group and stare at him for a moment. His red hair shone like a beacon under the street lamp and Lorimer groaned inwardly as he recognised DI Sutherland.

'Out on the batter, eh, Lorimer?' the man said as he approached. 'Good night for it, an' all,' he remarked, looking his boss up and down as if to remark on the lack of dress clothes appropriate for the occasion. 'Or maybe ye're after somethin' wi' a bit mair flesh on its bones, eh?' He hiccupped as he lunged forwards drunkenly, taking Lorimer by the arm.

'Hey lads, here's ma boss, Detective Super-intendent Lorrr-imer!' Sutherland roared out, pulling a reluctant Lorimer towards the others in his group. 'What d'ye say we buy the man a drink?'

'Thanks, Sutherland,' Lorimer murmured, pulling his sleeve out of the other man's grasp. 'Got some business to attend to. *Official* business,' he said sternly, hoping that his words would not rebound on him once Sutherland had gossiped about meeting him outside the Blythswood.

'Oops, sorry, boss,' Sutherland grinned at him then laughed and winked as though he knew exactly what sort of business a man got up to at this time of the morning in this part of the city. Waving, the DI rejoined his pals and Lorimer watched them disappear over the brow of the hill and on down towards Sauchiehall Street.

Cursing under his breath, Lorimer made his way across the now empty square and down towards Pitt Street. There was no sign of any woman waiting for custom tonight so he pulled up his coat collar against a sharp wind that had begun to knife his face and started to trace a circuit around the square. Shadows from the darkened streets fell across his path and, looking up at the street lamps ahead, Lorimer could almost imagine the female figures from his earlier dream. But there was no flesh and blood female here tonight to take the place of these spectral figures. Sighing, he decided to take a stroll downhill just in case he ran into any of the regular girls before turning back for his car.

Lorimer was almost level with the entrance to police head-quarters when he slowed down to look up at the building. The street might be deserted but lights from one of the offices above shining into the night showed traces of a human presence. Some-one was doing a spot of overtime. His eyes followed the levels back down to the reception area and the darkened stairwell that led to the main hall where he had addressed the men and women from the press.

Suddenly his feet came to a halt. He had seen that woman in his dream before. And it was inside this very building. She was the stranger amongst the regular journalists who came daily, gath-ering for titbits like the rude starlings clustered around his bird table.

Lorimer frowned, making twin creases between his dark brows. Something wasn't right, though. He was now certain that he had seen her in a different context, though where and when was a mystery. And, for some reason that he could not explain, it was the image of the first woman wrapped around that street lamp, her blonde hair tied back, that kept coming into his mind.

MAGGIE LORIMER GROANED in her sleep as her husband slipped back into bed. Pulling the sheets over his body, Lorimer wished he could cuddle in to her warmth, but that would mean waking her up and he didn't want to be so selfish. Tomorrow was not just a working day for them both: Maggie had all the preparation and work for her school's Burns Supper. She'd mentioned that new woman, Lena or something her name was, trying to muscle in on what was for Maggie a pleasurable activity. She'd not been too happy about the supply teacher staying on, had she? Well, you couldn't always choose your colleagues, he thought, remembering the drunken DI grabbing his arm in the street. Sutherland would have a whopper of a hangover in the morning and with a little luck would have forgotten all about seeing his boss in the passing.

Chapter Twenty-six

'BEST IDEA IS to speak to the warden at Robertson Street,' Helen James told him. 'Mattie Watson. Want me to square it with her?'

'That's probably a good idea,' Lorimer replied. The warden was known to keep her charges under her wing like some sort of mother hen and Helen James had spent months cultivating a friendship with the woman.

'Do you feel well enough to come along with me if she okays it?' he added suddenly.

'I don't think so,' the DCI replied. 'The girls can be a tad unpredictable and I don't feel strong enough to cope if any of them become nasty.'

'Oh?'

'Well,' James continued, 'not all of them look kindly towards the police. See us as out to get them, if you know what I mean.'

'But you've done such a lot to help them,' Lorimer insisted.

'Aye, well, not all of them know that, do they? And there are girls coming on to the scene all the time who don't know me from Adam. Look, why don't I ring you back once I've spoken to the warden? Then you can talk to her yourself. See if you can use some of your legendary charm.'

She chuckled as she put down the telephone, wondering if the man who had been chosen to head up the Serious Crimes Squad had any notion of how his presence might go down at the drop-in centre. Who wouldn't be charmed by a big, bonny lad like Lorimer, she thought dreamily, thinking of the missed chances she had had in her own love life. Ach, it's all this stuff you've been reading, woman! Helen told herself, flinging down her magazine with its pages devoted to romance. Fair addled your brain! Time you were back at work, your mind on real life not stories. She flicked the 'on' button for the television and surfed between the channels. The velvet tones of the actor, John Cairney, made her pause and listen as he recited one of the more amorous poems of Robert Burns. Smiling despite herself, Helen James settled down to enjoy the programme. It was Burns day after all, she told herself, then wondered idly what sort of reception the bard would have got from the girls who frequented the drop-in centre.

'Bet you never paid for it in your life, Rabbie,' she said aloud, then stopped. Was that behind all of those brutal killings? Had some man refused to pay a woman's price? Out of . . . what? Some warped sense of pride? Or some notion that he was above that sordid sort of transaction? Helen blinked, trying to imagine such a scenario, the words of poetry lost to her now as she gazed past the television screen. She rose, pressed the mute button to banish the actor's lovely voice and lifted the telephone once more. Sooner Lorimer got over there and did some digging the better.

'Mattie? It's me, Helen James. Yes, okay, DCI James. Listen, I wonder if you could do me a favour?'

THE WARDEN IN the Robertson Street drop-in centre looked at the
tall policeman from narrowed eyes. They were sitting in a back
room that served as an office away from the main area frequented
by the street women.

'You don't like me being here, do you?' Lorimer asked candidly,
his smile crinkling the corners of his piercing blue eyes.

'The girls are happier with women around,' Mattie Watson
retorted.

'Less of a threat to them?' he suggested.

'Something like that,' she replied grudgingly. 'You know many
of them prefer to live with women, don't you?'

Lorimer nodded. It was hardly surprising, given the way that
so many of Glasgow's prostitutes had been treated, that they had
become lesbians. One familiar pattern was of early abuse at the
hands of a father or father figure, then a decision to go on the
game and earn money for the sexual favours that had already been
stolen from them for nothing.

'Men, for some of them, are merely the means to an end,' Mattie said, breaking into his thoughts.

'A punter for a hit,' he mused.

'Exactly. So, given that we can't do as much as we want about
getting them clean and off the game, we have to have a place where
they can at least get some practical help.'

Lorimer nodded. Beside Mattie Watson's desk were stacked
boxes of leaflets that he knew would contain information about
sexual health and advice on housing; probably the same as the
posters fixed on the walls in this very office.

'Do you encourage them to go on the Big Blue Bus?' he asked.
'They hand out stuff like that, don't they?' He pointed to the flyers
displayed on the walls behind the warden.

'Oh we are all in it together,' she agreed, 'even those do-gooder types,' she added, though there was something in her voice that sounded a tad cynical, Lorimer thought.

'Yes?' Lorimer raised his eyebrows encouragingly.

'Och, you get a few religious nuts who only want to save their souls. But there are other ones who know the score. Like that minister, Mr Allan, he goes around helping the girls, you know,' she added.

'Did you ever meet with Edward Pattison?'

For the first time since his arrival at the drop-in centre Mattie Watson gave a smile. 'Such a lovely man,' she said, dropping her gaze for a moment.

'He came here?'

'Oh, no,' Mattie replied in shocked tones. 'We met at a reception given by the SNP. That was before he made his visit to the Big Blue Bus,' she added.

'Nice man, then?' Lorimer asked casually. 'Never met him myself.'

'Oh, yes. Such perfect manners. He listened to everything I told him about the centre. Promised he'd bring up the subject of funding at government level, you know.'

Lorimer raised his eyebrows, questioningly.

'Well, didn't get the chance to, did he, poor man,' she said brusquely. 'That awful serial killer . . .' She broke off then glared at Lorimer. 'Shouldn't you be out there finding out who killed him?'

'Actually,' Lorimer said gently. 'That's why I'm here. I hoped you might be able to help.'

MATTIE WATSON LISTENED to the door closing behind the tall policeman then headed to the ladies' toilets. A glance in the mirror was enough to show that the warden was badly shaken. It took quite a lot to disturb Mattie Watson's composure but what Lorimer had told her had drained her face of colour. The possibility that Mr Pattison had been consorting with some of the girls had never occurred to her till now. But those CCTV images did not tell a lie, did they? Mattie's mouth pursed: it was just as she had often heard the girls say about men; when it came down to it, weren't they all exactly the same?

'Andie's?' The woman cocked her head to one side, mobile phone pressed close to her ear, making the silver hooped earrings jangle against her dark hair. 'Don't mind if I do.'

She pulled her raincoat closer to her body as though to hide anything that might reveal who or what she was, a raddled street woman who was fighting for her place amongst a lot of younger and more attractive girls. Doreen Gallagher blew out a line of smoke as she listened to the voice on the other end of the line. The money sounded okay and it would be great to be off the streets and into a nice warm place like the sauna. 'How'd you get my name?' she asked suddenly but the pause that returned her question lengthened, then all she heard was a click.

Doreen raised her eyebrows. Cheeky beggar. Wouldn't've hurt tae give her an answer now, would it? Still, she was to present herself at the Govan shop tomorrow afternoon for an interview with the manager. Dropping her cigarette, Doreen ground it under the toe of her patent leather boot then stepped off the pavement to cross the road without a backward glance at the drop-in centre behind her. Mattie had hauled her into the office to quiz her about that bloke who'd got killed, the one from the Scottish parliament whose face had been plastered all across the papers. Aye, she'd seen him around a few times, no' very often, mind, but she'd remembered seeing him leering out of that big white car of his.

The memory had stung the woman. He'd never given *her* the time of day, had he? Taken one o' the younger lassies instead. Naw, she couldnae mind which wan, she'd told Mattie. Anywise, stuff like that wouldn't bother her if she were taken on at the Govan place, would it? She had told that wumman, thon journalist, though, hadn't she? Been paid no' bad an' all. Cash in her hand and no questions asked. No' like the polis. Naw, Doreen told herself, she wasnae goin' tae get messed up wi' speaking tae ony polis. Mattie had been given the information she had wanted and that wis that. Mattie wis owed. She wis a' right was Mattie Watson. Butch as they came but wi' a hert of gold. Such were the thoughts of Doreen Gallagher as she made her way to the subway station in town, her heels click-clacking against the frozen pavements.

'DOREEN? OCH AYE, I know her fine,' Helen James said as she heard Lorimer's voice on the telephone. The DCI listened carefully as Lorimer outlined the morning's events. Mattie had turned up trumps with Doreen Gallagher, letting Lorimer know later that, yes, Pattison was one of the punters who turned up occasionally on the drag. No, she hadn't managed to find a girl who had actually been with him, but she was working on it. Things like that took time, were a bit delicate to handle.

'What's she like? Is she reliable?' Lorimer wanted to know.

'Doreen? Well, hard as nails like so many of them. Have to be in their profession,' Helen reminded him. 'Been on the game as long as I've been in the force, I expect. She'll know all the girls, believe me.'

'Would she be able to make a statement to the effect that Pattison picked up prostitutes?' he asked baldly.

'She'd be able but I doubt she'd be willing. Had too many run-ins with our boys in blue.'

'What if it was to help find Tracey-Anne's killer?'

There was a pause as Helen James digested the detective superintendent's words. She'd been pleased at first that Lorimer was still keen to give some of his time to the case he'd had to abandon, but now she wondered if he was overstepping the mark.

'Does anybody else know what you're up to?' she asked softly.

The answering silence was enough.

'And what if the top brass find out you're moonlighting on a job you were supposed to drop?'

'They won't,' he assured her, but a seasoned cop like Helen James could pick a certain amount of doubt in his voice.

'Be careful, Lorimer,' she told him, suddenly serious. 'It's not just your neck that's on the line, remember.'

Chapter Twenty-seven

THE WHITE MERCEDES rounded the corner of the street and disappeared, leaving him feeling slightly bereft. It had been fun driving it around, the tall man thought, turning back to the concrete walls and metal doors that comprised the garage space where Vladimir kept his fleet of luxury vehicles. Still, there was a need to have a few other classic cars in virgin white, wasn't there? He grinned for a moment, doubting whether any of the brides in their frothy dresses whom he had driven to churches or hotels had actually been virgins on the day of their weddings. They were all the same, he told himself, tossing a grubby rag into the air and catching it again. When it came down to it all women were the same. And he should know better than most, shouldn't he? The massive metal doors shut behind him with an echoing clang and he twisted the lever to lock the premises from the inside. Vlad was taking the car to trade it in, returning later with something that he had promised would make his eyes water. Well, maybe it would, the tall man thought, scrunching the rag into a ball and chucking it so that it fell neatly into an empty waste bin.

He pulled off the dungarees and slid them down over his thighs, feeling the cool air rush at his midriff as he bent over to release the garment now at his ankles. Maybe he would go into town, see what he could pick up in the sales. It was his birthday soon and he deserved a treat. A new Armani suit, perhaps? Something sharp and sleek to make these Glasgow people look at him with appreciation in their eyes. There was no shortage of money, after all. Vlad saw to that, didn't he? A crafty look came into the man's face as he ascended the stairs, the dungarees slung across his shoulders. He had plenty saved up now, easily enough for a holiday in Bucharest if he felt like it. Though whether it would be possible to enter his home country again was a problem that even money might not be able to solve. There were people who could sell you different passports, however. Clever people whose skills in fakery made their prices fairly steep. Could he go along that route? the tall man wondered. Perhaps it was time for a new name and a new identity. Sacha, his uncle still called him, a silly little name for a silly little boy. *Alexander* had always suited him so much better. It was a warrior's name, after all; a name for heroes.

He was still smiling as he crossed the reception area, quite oblivious to the eyes that followed him from behind the desk or to the involuntary shudder the receptionist gave as she watched the handsome mechanic open the rest-room door and close it behind him again.

ANDIE'S SAUNA WAS smaller than she thought it would be, Doreen Gallagher decided, shuffling her bottom further to one side to accommodate the two young girls who were sitting next to her. One of them was vaguely familiar, a pale faced wee thing who kept turning to look out of the window as if she were expecting somebody to arrive at any minute. The manager, or at least that was what she had called herself, had already interviewed the girl's pal who was now flicking over the pages of a much-thumbed copy of *Now* magazine while masticating a wad of gum. Doreen frowned as the pale girl twitched her body around again. *Here, sit at peace*, she wanted to growl at her as if she were the lassie's mammy. But the very knowledge that this was what she would sound like prevented her from opening her mouth.

'Mrs Gallagher?' A middle-aged woman wearing a smart white coat stood there, one hand on the door of the next room. A clipboard in her other hand was meant to give a businesslike impression, Doreen imagined, but she couldn't see anything written on the pages held in place by a metal clip.

'It's Ms,' Doreen corrected the woman, straightening her skirt as she stood up. Head held high, Doreen followed her into the room. Best to get things right from the off, she thought, taking in the peeling paint around the skirting boards and the faded screen over in the corner that had once been decorated with a delicate chinoiserie but was now dull and broken at its hinges.

'Take off your clothes behind the screen. Okay? Then come out with just your knickers on,' the woman said in a bored tone that reminded Doreen of a visit to the VD clinic.

Doreen's heart sank as she removed her black tights. The ravages of years of drug abuse could clearly be seen in these patches of discoloured flesh. Would that matter, though? Nearly every pro she knew was a user after all, and this place was hardly a palace, was it?

Doreen tried not to shiver as she left the confines of the rickety screen and stood expectantly in front of the sauna manager.

What did she see? A forty-something-year-old prostitute whose slender body and well made-up face were perhaps her only assets. Maybe. Or did she look beyond that and see eyes that were glazed against hurting too much, hair that had been dyed repeatedly, taking any sign of its natural colour away, and a shivering woman whose need for another fix was becoming all too apparent.

'Aye, you'll do,' the woman said after a few moments of wordless scrutiny. 'Get dressed and I'll tell you what your shifts'll be, okay?'

LILY SAT ALONE now in the waiting room, alternately eyeing the door where they'd gone and watching the street just in case anyone should see her here. At last the dark-haired woman emerged, a half-smile on her face that told Lily she'd been successful in getting the job.

She rose to take her turn but the white-coated woman raised a hand to stop her.

'Naw, hen, sorry. Ye're too young for us. Come back when you've got a couple mair years under yer belt, eh?' The snigger that accompanied these words made Lily blush and she practically ran out of the shop, colliding with the woman in the raincoat, the one who had been sitting beside her for so long.

'Hey, watch where ye're goin',' Doreen yelled, then seeing the girl's stricken face held out a hand. 'Aw, it's you, hen. Here, did they no' take ye on, then?'

Lily bit her lip in an attempt to stop the tears coming but one slid down her face anyway.

'Och, come on, wee hen, dinna start that. Look, d'ye fancy a cuppa something? I'm Doreen, by the way,' she added, her arm now around the younger girl's shoulders.

'Aye,' she whispered. 'Aye, I'd like that fine thanks, missus.'

Doreen Gallagher fished out the packet of cigarettes and handed one to the girl who shook her head.

'Naw, thanks all the same. Don't do ciggies,' she smiled at Doreen who returned the smile with a short laugh. It was a joke that needed no elaboration. They were both street women whose drug habits were far more harmful than anything tobacco could do to them.

Soon Doreen Gallagher was sitting in a run-down cafe opposite the young girl who had now introduced herself as Lily. The older woman's face grew thoughtful as they sipped their tea. It was the image of a pile of folded notes in her hand that made her smile suddenly. The woman, that journalist, she paid for information, didn't she? Wee Lily might be a bit of a rookie when it came to being on the game but perhaps that was all to the good. If she had someone keeping an eye open for things on the street . . .?

'Hey, wee yin,' Doreen said suddenly. 'How'd you like to make some easy cash?'

'DETECTIVE SUPERINTENDENT LORIMER?' a well-educated voice asked.

'Speaking.'

'Sir, this is DS Jackson, Lothian and Borders. It's about Mrs Pattison.'

Lorimer's eyes grew dark as he listened to the detective sergeant. Why on earth had nobody checked up on this before? Had he been too caught up in the politics of the case to think of this, perhaps? As the story unfolded it became clear that Catherine Pattison had told him a barefaced lie when she had claimed to have been at home the night of her husband's death. All three of her children, the Edinburgh cop went on, had been at their grandmother's home in Barnton. A chance remark by one of the kids to the family liaison officer had opened up a whole new can of worms. Plus nobody had logged the fact that the initial call to Mrs Pattison was to her mobile. In all the excitement of finding the deputy first minister murdered it had slipped the notice of someone in Lothian and Borders that no one had answered the Pattisons' landline number. Lorimer ground his teeth in a moment of frustrated anger. Things like that were elementary and should never have been overlooked. But there was no time for recriminations as he listened to what the officer from Edinburgh was telling him.

'So far the wife is saying absolutely nothing. She's been instructed by her lawyer, of course,' the DS told him. 'What do you want to do?'

What Lorimer wanted to do right now was to hop on a train back to Edinburgh and wring the bloody woman's neck! He knew she'd been wasting their time, but hadn't ever thought that the reason she'd sent them on wild goose chases was to cover up lies about her own whereabouts that particular night.

A quick glance at the clock on the office wall told him he'd be in time to catch an express train if he hurried. The alternative at this time in the afternoon was a lengthy queue of traffic all along the motorway. He could pick up a squad car at Haymarket and be at the Murrayfield house in just over an hour's time. There were meetings scheduled from now till after seven o'clock but he supposed Rita Livingstone could cover them just this once.

'I'm coming across,' Lorimer said at last. 'Tell them I want her to remain in the house. And keep the kids and the granny there too, understand?'

MRS CADELL SCRUBBED at the copper pot with a vigour that surprised her. Though well into her seventies, the old lady could still muster up a cold fury that translated itself into such small actions. Stupid girl, she thought, Stupid, stupid girl! It could all have been so easy if only that Glasgow man had left Catherine in peace. Edward was what people used to call a cad. A love rat, these awful soaps called them nowadays. The old lady's mouth twisted in a moue of distaste. This horrible business was becoming just like an episode from one of these ghastly programmes.

'Gran.' A small voice made her turn to see a pretty child with blonde curls framing her pale face. It was Kim, her youngest granddaughter standing at the kitchen doorway, a favourite raggy doll clutched to her chest.

'Oh, my darling!' she sighed, swooping down and taking the child into her arms as she stepped towards her. The warmth from the child's body coursed through her, bringing an unexpected comfort. It took a huge effort to keep her own tears from falling onto the child's shoulders. She might be old but she had to be strong.

Then that same small voice piped up, crushing her resolve.

'Why is Daddy not coming home?'

LORIMER'S PRESENCE WAS a dark shadow against the glass door, something that a child might tremble to see. Sarah Cadell had made sure, however, that none of the children were downstairs to await the detective's arrival. The television in their parents' bedroom was currently showing one of their many Christmas DVDs and for once Sarah was glad of the space that watching cartoons afforded them all. It had been that police liaison officer's idea. She was a mother herself, knew how to keep her own brood amused, she'd said, as she'd asked if there was another television anywhere in the house.

'Can I stay when the Detective Superintendent arrives?' Sarah had asked, but Catherine had shaken her head then glared a warning at her. There was a back room that served as the children's playroom. A family room, Catherine called it, though God alone knew when they had last all sat there as a family. Sarah slipped into it, knowing she was close enough at hand should the tall policeman demand to see her. She was also in earshot of anything that might be said in the drawing room should she be able to keep both doors slightly open.

Sarah Cadell heard the door opening and then one of the uniformed officers was speaking to the man from Glasgow.

'The children are upstairs, sir. Family liaison officer will keep them there until you need to speak to them.'

'They will need to be with their mother or another adult relation,' Lorimer was saying when Sarah stepped hurriedly out of the playroom and approached the tall man whose long shadow seemed to stretch out unnaturally along the corridor.

'I can stay with the children,' she said quickly. 'I'm Mrs Cadell, Mrs Pattison's mother.'

'Yes,' Lorimer said, taking off his gloves and clasping her hand. 'We met before,' he added.

Sarah Cadell took in a sudden breath. It was not just the strength of that warm hand closing on her own, but the directness of his gaze and those blue eyes . . . lovely eyes, she thought, eyes that should be painted by a master, but eyes that would surely follow you around any room looking down from their face in a portrait.

'You will be kind . . .?' she asked falteringly as he released her hand.

But all she received by way of an answer was a tired sort of smile and a nod of the head. Sarah stood, helplessly, unable to decide whether to go back to the room next door or creep upstairs and join the children.

She watched as they moved into the drawing room then sighed as Lorimer closed the door firmly behind them.

CATHERINE PATTISON DID not rise as the men entered the room. Instead she merely turned her head and stared, an expression of defiance etched on her handsome features.

'Mrs Pattison,' Lorimer said, then turned his attention to a slim blonde who had risen to her feet, hand outstretched.

'Belinda Joseph. Joseph, Connery and partners,' the woman told him. 'I'm Mrs Pattison's solicitor,' she added in a slightly patronising tone as though it were necessary to spell things out in plain English for this man from Glasgow.

'Detective Superintendent Lorimer,' he replied briefly. 'Now,' he said, turning to gaze at Catherine Pattison. 'Would you like to tell me why you've been wasting so much police time, Mrs Pattison?'

'I've instructed my client to say nothing,' Belinda Joseph stated with a toss of her head that made her blonde ponytail swish. For an absurd moment she reminded Lorimer of a well-bred race-horse, nervy and highly strung.

'Well, if that's the case perhaps I should ask Mrs Pattison to accompany us to Glasgow,' he began, watching the reaction in the two women's faces.

Catherine Pattison opened her mouth to speak, her cheeks suddenly turning white but the solicitor raised a hand to stop her, eyes flashing angrily.

'Are you threatening my client?' she asked, hands on her hips. 'If so, I can report you—'

'Let's get one thing absolutely clear,' Lorimer stormed, cutting across the woman before she could utter another word. 'This is a serious murder case and Mrs Pattison has already lied to me about her alibi for the night on which her husband was killed. I want to know why. And if I don't get the answers here I can try to get them back at police headquarters.' He turned to Catherine Pattison, fixing her with his blue gaze, adding sternly, 'Even if I have to arrest you on suspicion of murdering your husband!'

The gasp from the doorway made them all turn to see Mrs Cadell who was standing, hands by the sides of her face.

'No!' she said. 'You can't do that! It wasn't what you think . . .'

'Mother!' Catherine Pattison was on her feet now, her face a mask of terror. 'Don't!'

'I have to,' the old lady said, stumbling forward and catching hold of the back of a chair. 'It's no use, Catherine, they have to know the truth.'

'Mrs Cadell.' The solicitor stepped forward and made as if to take the old lady's hand but Sarah Cadell shook her off.

'No, the detective superintendent needs to know what's been going on here. There have been too many lies told already,' she said.

'Mrs Pattison?' Lorimer murmured quietly, moving around the room so that Catherine Pattison could not avoid looking up at him. 'Perhaps *you* would prefer to tell me what this is all about?'

Catherine Pattison shot an anguished glance at the solicitor who merely shrugged then looked at Sarah Cadell who was clutching the back of the chair to steady herself.

'Come and sit down, Mother,' she said softly. 'I'm sorry. It's been such a strain for us all.'

Lorimer rose to assist the old lady into a vacant chair so that the three women were sitting side by side. He remained standing, hands behind his back, deliberately towering over them as though to symbolise the presence of law and order.

Catherine Pattison sat up a little straighter then cleared her throat. 'My husband was not a faithful man,' she began. There was a pause as she bit her lip before continuing. 'But then, I was not a faithful wife.' She had clasped her hands now and Lorimer watched as she wrung them together, in an unconscious gesture of despair.

'Frank Hardy?' Lorimer asked quietly.

Catherine Pattison opened her mouth in an O of astonishment. 'You *knew*?' she said, frowning as though she had suddenly been tricked.

'No,' Lorimer replied. 'But I did make an educated guess.'

'Oh,' the woman replied, suddenly at a loss for words.

'And were you with Hardy on the night of your husband's death?'

She had dropped her gaze now and was sitting, head bowed so that her nod was barely imperceptible.

'So why did you tell me that he might be a candidate for killing your husband? I don't quite understand,' Lorimer continued.

'We thought . . .' Catherine tailed off, sniffing into a handkerchief that she had found behind a cushion.

'Mrs Pattison thought that if you knew about her affair with Mr Hardy then that might constitute a motive for murder,' Belinda Joseph told him.

'And it might still,' Lorimer replied.

'You see, giving you Frank's name was Catherine's way of distancing herself from him,' the solicitor continued, but Lorimer hardly acknowledged her breathless interruption. He'd already come to that conclusion anyway and didn't need anyone else to spell it out for him. Instead he hunkered down in front of Catherine Pattison, forcing her to look him in the eye.

'What we need to know, Mrs Pattison, is where exactly you were with Hardy on the night Edward was killed and if you can provide alibis that place you both firmly elsewhere than Erskine woods.'

'I . . .' The woman seemed caught in his gaze but she nodded her understanding. 'We were together all night. Frank has a flat here in the city.' She bit her lip once again. 'I don't think anyone knew we were there that night, though. You see, we try to be as discreet about going there as we can,' she added, her face reddening.

'Still, someone may have seen you?' he offered.

'I don't know,' she said sadly. 'I always wear a scarf over my hair, pull my collar up, that sort of thing, you know?'

Lorimer gave her a nod. It didn't take much imagination to see how they had conducted their clandestine affair here in this city with its watchful eyes everywhere.

'One wrong move and the press would have had a field day,' Catherine muttered.

SARAH CADELL SWITCHED out the light but left Kim's bedroom door half-open. The child was having night terrors as it was. Waking up to find her mother gone was not going to be easy. The old woman gave a sigh as she stood in the corridor, one hand against the wall as though for support. Would she be charged? That tall policeman had hinted that wasting police time was a serious offence. It had taken quite a long time for Catherine to untangle the web of deceit she had spun for herself. And, even now, Sarah Cadell was not completely sure if what she had heard earlier this evening had been the entire truth. Glancing at her daughter's profile, Sarah had felt a frisson of fear. Was that lovely face hiding some darker, deeper secret? She'd been with the man, Hardy, Catherine had told them eventually. That much she had guessed already. Yet hearing her daughter's words come tumbling out, Sarah Cadell had been amazed but not shocked. Little about human nature could shock her these days. And infidelity was so utterly commonplace nowadays, wasn't it? she thought, a spasm of contempt crossing her fine features. Besides, she had known pretty much what Catherine had been up to, hadn't she? Edward may have been a fool, but Sarah Cadell knew the sort of woman Catherine was much better than the man who had taken her daughter for better or for worse.

Chapter Twenty-eight

'ARE YOU COMING up to Blythswood Square?'

Barbara Knox spun round to see two of the detectives standing behind her desk.

'Everyone's going up. It's the rally.'

'What rally?' Barbara asked, puzzled, then frowned as one of them gave her a pitying look.

'Only the start of the Monte Carlo rally, love,' he said. 'History in the making. Thought you were a car buff? Or is it just Mercs that turn you on?' he laughed.

'Oh, is it today? I'd totally forgotten,' she said, grabbing her jacket and following the two men as they left the room.

The day was darkening as they walked briskly up away from HQ and Barbara could hear the crowds before she saw them. Already the pavements were three deep on each side of the square and she had to strain to see the rally cars all lined up along the perimeter. It was, as her colleague had pointed out, a little bit of history. Decades before, amateur rally drivers had left the front of the stately building that was now the Blythswood Square Hotel to make the journey through Britain and France; something that had captured the imagination of the entire country. In those days the hotel had been the premises of the Royal Automobile Club.

Diana had told her that there were certain bits of memorabilia still in the place, though Barbara had never been over its threshold in her life. A spurt of envy surged through her as she looked at the steps leading up to the entrance, a commissionaire in top hat and tails standing looking down on them. *She*'d never get to stay in a classy place like that on her salary, would she? Yet Diana had been there. Och well, she was here to see the cars, not to hang out with the clientele over there. And so it was to the cars she turned her attention as one of the men nudged her arm.

'Hey, check out that one, Knox!'

Barbara blinked in the gathering twilight, following his finger towards a chocolate-coloured Porsche.

'Cool, eh?'

She smiled and nodded then her eyes widened as she saw a blue Morgan gleaming under the lamplight, its running board a graceful curve along the length of the car. The policewoman took in every detail of the bodywork, sighing over its curved chrome radiator and frog-eyed headlamps. Next to it was a black Lancia, covered in signs that showed it to be a veteran of this *rallye classique* as one metal plaque proclaimed. Barbara moved a little to see the car behind, a red sports car with the familiar silver wings that were, she knew, etched with the Austin Healey name. She'd been a car nut since childhood, much to the despair of parents who had once hoped to encourage her towards more gender-appropriate interests. Somehow the boys at Pitt Street must have sussed this out, she mused, wandering further along to admire the classic cars with their drivers all ready to set off on this historic rally.

Tag Heuer signs were plastered everywhere, reminders that this was big business and only the few wealthy or well sponsored owners of these fabulous cars could take part in something as prestigious as this. Nevertheless there was an atmosphere around the square that Barbara felt: this was Glasgow and these were Scottish drivers. National pride hung in the air, evident without anyone needing to say a word.

A disembodied voice from a loudspeaker was telling them all about the cars, their drivers and co-drivers, but Barbara's attention was suddenly taken by a tall figure moving along the path inside the private park.

Pushing her way out of the crowd gathered by this side of the square was no easy matter but her bulk and her stern look made a few of them move as she tried to cross the road.

'Sorry, miss, no one's allowed to get closer than this,' a man with a steward's armband informed her, lifting his hands and directing her back.

For a moment Barbara was tempted to whip out her warrant card and say she was on official business but her colleagues might notice and, besides, it was bad form to use it like that. Instead she made her way back, pushing through the press of people, one eye on the corner of the square where she thought that Diana might emerge.

The dark silhouette flitted across the road away from the square and, just as Barbara opened her mouth to call her name, a roar went up as the first car set off, preventing any thought of following her friend.

It was no use, Barbara fumed. She was going nowhere fast and would just have to wait until all the cars had left the square. A sense of disappointment filled her and with it an unnatural disquiet.

Hadn't Diana said she was going to be out of the city tonight? But then, a small voice suggested, had it really been Diana after all? Perhaps she was becoming so besotted with the woman that she had begun to imagine seeing her wherever she went?

As she watched the line of cars drive off amid cheers to the south of France, Barbara Knox reflected gloomily that she wasn't going anywhere glamorous any time soon. These lucky beggars would be sunning themselves in Monte Carlo while ordinary folk like her stayed home in cold, rainy Scotland. Even Diana's hints about a holiday abroad had ceased to charm her. What she really needed was a tangible sign of the woman's intentions when all she had to look forward to was yet another night in her lonely bed.

'COMING TO BED?' Maggie Lorimer stood in the doorway, feeling the chill from the room swirl around her ankles. She smiled ruefully, glancing down at her new silk negligee, a Christmas present from Bill. He'd been so tired lately, and now this idea of pacing the streets on a cold January night was just too much to bear. Could she tempt him into staying home with her?

'Aye, why not.' His eyes flicked over her from head to toe with that lazy smile that made her stomach flip in anticipation.

'And,' she paused for a second, 'will you stay there afterwards?'

He shook his head but the smile did not falter. 'Go on, I'll be right up.'

The room was not completely dark, a flickering light from the street lamp outside shining through the window where Maggie had left the curtains still tied back. It was a wild night, wind whistling through the trees and rain lashing against the window, rattling the panes. Maggie smiled, remembering the lines from a poem that one of her third years had recited yesterday at the school's Burns Supper. The Bard's entrance to the world had been heralded by '. . . a blast o' Janwar Win'.

Her smile faded as a different thought came into Maggie's head. Somewhere out in that storm there were women plying their ancient trade, fighting not just against the elements but against the pull of the drug that forced them into the streets night after lonely night. Bill's determination to seek them out and ask questions was typical of the kind of man her husband was. He'd worry away at a problem until something yielded. There had not been much said about the Pattison case, only that Mrs Pattison was now helping with their enquiries. Maggie's raised eyebrow had given her husband a chance to tell her more but he'd not chosen to go into any further details.

'Hope you're not sleeping, Mrs Lorimer,' he said softly, slipping into bed beside her. Then, as his arms encircled her, Maggie's thoughts about what her husband might find out later during the wee small hours vanished as her body responded to his.

LILY CRIED OUT as the man slammed her against the wall but her protest only served to make the punter more excited as he pushed himself into her, forcing her head back as his grunts became louder and louder.

It was soon over and she breathed a silent prayer of gratitude as he released her from his grip.

There was no word of thanks, no word at all, as he tucked his shirt back into his trousers and headed back down the cobbled lane leaving Lily shivering with a mixture of fear and disgust. The rain that had made puddles all along the rutted lane had become a thin drizzle, soaking through her clothes and making rats' tails of her hair. She should do something with it, tie it into a band or something; tidy herself up in case another punter came her way. But that last encounter seemed to have leached every last drop of the girl's energy and she stood there wanting only to add her tears to the water running down her face.

Some of the other girls had mentioned you might get ones like this; brutes who only wanted a quick shag and could be rough about it. You were a body for sale, that was all, Doreen had told her with a laugh as though it were a matter of no significance at all.

Well, maybe it wasn't such a big deal, Lily thought, gathering up her bag and straightening her skirt. *The oldest profession*, one of the women at the drop-in centre had called it, though Lily hadn't been sure if the words had been spoken with pride or sarcasm.

She heard his footsteps before she saw him. Bracing herself for the approach of another punter so soon after the one that had left her, Lily leaned back against the wall, tugging her coat more closely around her. The man who was walking towards her was tall and strong-looking, but something about the way he walked on the other side of the lane, dodging the puddles, made Lily feel a little less anxious.

He regarded her with interest as he approached, then, just as Lily had decided he was definitely a potential customer, he pulled out a card with a familiar badge.

'Hello,' he said, 'I'm Detective Superintendent Lorimer.'

Lily blinked as the tall man gazed down at her. 'Are you wanting . . .?'

He shook his head and smiled. 'Sorry to intrude on your working hours, but, no, all I want from you is some information.'

'Oh,' Lily said and for a moment she felt a stab of disappointment. Being taken by this man would have made up for the hurt she'd just had, she felt sure of it.

'Are you married?' she asked suddenly.

'Yes. Very happily,' the tall man replied. And there was something sincere in his tone that made Lily glad. Not all men were brutes, then, were they? Some of them didn't need to come out in the dark and wet looking for the likes of her to answer their needs.

'What's your name?' Lorimer asked.

'Lily.'

'Well, Lily, I'm hoping some of you street girls can assist me with a case.' He paused then fished into an inside pocket of his coat bringing out a folded sheet of paper that had been coated in some shiny plastic stuff. Lily stepped forward as he unfolded the paper, revealing photographs of four different women.

'Did you ever know any of them?'

Lily put a wet finger on to the laminated sheet as she peered at the pictures.

'Sorry, no. Don't know any of them. Who are they?' she asked.

The tall man's face grew grim as he refolded the paper and put it into his pocket. 'Who *were* they, you might have asked. They're all dead, Lily.'

'Oh.' The girl bit her lip wondering if she'd said something wrong.

'They were all street lasses, like you, Lily. But someone took their lives from them. And it's our job – the police's job – to find out who that was before he can harm any other wee lassie.'

'Is that why you're out on a night like this?' Lily asked as a gutter beside them began to overflow and splash onto the cobbles. She moved out of the way, coming closer to the policeman who had shifted into a doorway opposite.

'Aye, it is,' Lorimer replied. 'And how about you?'

Lily gave a shrug but said nothing. He knew fine why she was out here, why they were all out here. The need for money. The need for a fix.

'There's something else, Lily, something you may have heard about in the news. A man called Edward Pattison was killed recently.'

'Oh, him? The one in the parliament?'

'That's right. What I want to know, Lily, is if you ever saw him around this area.'

'In the drag, you mean? No.' She bit her lip and looked away, suddenly ashamed that there was nothing she could offer this nice big man. 'I haven't been doing this for very long,' she admitted, her eyes cast down so she did not need to look him straight in the face.

'Listen, lass, it's not too late for you to get help. This doesn't have to be the way things are, you know,' Lorimer told her gently. 'There are places that can help you to get clean.'

Lily's eyes did not change their focus and the cobbles at her feet seemed to hold a greater fascination for her than the man whose words were making her feel so uncomfortable.

'Here's my card,' Lorimer said. 'If you hear anything about Mr Pattison, or anyone who saw him, can you let me know?'

Lily nodded silently, her head still bent.

'And if you ever just want to talk you only have to ring my number. Okay?'

As he walked away Lily wanted to run after him, catch the sleeve of his dark coat, beg him to take her away from this dreary lane, this empty life. But how could he? She swallowed down the tears as his figure disappeared around a corner. There hadn't even been any mention of paying her for information, had there? she thought bitterly. And money was what she needed most right now.

Doreen had talked about easy money, hadn't she? Money that didn't come from the police. Should she have told him about Doreen? No, she decided. She'd be Doreen's eyes and ears, maybe pick up something for her efforts.

But as Lily stood there in the misty night something stirred within her, something that she vaguely recognised as regret.

THE YOUNG GIRL was the only person he had managed to see in his walk around the drag and Lorimer felt a keen pity for the lassie standing at the entrance to that lane, waiting for her next customer. She had looked not much older than one of Maggie's senior pupils, sixteen maybe. Far too young to have her life wasted like this, he raged, as he opened the door of the Lexus and climbed in. For a moment he understood the crusade that DCI Helen James had been waging in the war against prostitution. But was this night-time wandering helping to find the girls' killer?

The road back home was a dark grey ribbon, its surface glossy with rain. An orange pall hung over the city behind him, reflected in the rear-view mirror with only blackness ahead as he drove south. Yet he was part of this great city with its beating heart, even though he and Maggie had chosen to live in the suburbs. Glasgow was still a special place to him despite all its broken dreams and those girls who wandered its streets looking for someone who would buy their flesh.

As he turned into the drive Lorimer looked up at the bedroom window. The curtains were now closed against the night but Maggie would be there, waiting for him. Who, if anyone, might be waiting up for the girl called Lily?

ALEXANDER TURNED IN his sleep, pulling the corner of the blanket over his shoulder and dislodging one of his pillows so that it tumbled silently to the floor. The sleeping man was quite oblivious to the figure standing in the darkness looking down at him, who saw Alexander's expression in repose as childlike, innocent even. Vladimir stood still, his back to the window, his jaw hardening as he gazed. Looking at that figure slumbering so peacefully it was hard to imagine the heartache he had brought into everybody's lives. Vladimir had made a promise, though, and it was a promise that he intended to keep. Yet his fingers twitched by his side even as he imagined picking up that discarded pillow and pressing it down on that handsome face.

PERHAPS IT WAS the lack of sleep but as Detective Superintendent Lorimer sat at his desk next morning his head seemed to swirl with all the disjointed pieces of information that simply refused to make anything like a whole picture. It was, he thought gloomily, as if he had lost his usual ability to see things objectively. Images of that wee lassie, Lily, her hair slicked against her head with the rain, kept coming back to haunt him. He pushed the thought aside, wearily regarding the piles of officer appraisals he was meant to be reading. He hardly knew any of the officers in this unit, yet somehow he must put words on paper so that when the time came they would have a decent billet to go on to. Joyce Rogers had given him fair warning that the Serious Crimes Squad was winding down and it was only a matter of time before he'd be making decisions about the futures of some of the men and women in Pitt Street.

The rain had stopped some time during the night and now a freshening breeze had brought some hazy blue to the skies above the city. The sight of it from his window ought to have lifted his spirits, reminding him that January was drawing to a close and lighter days lay ahead, but it was as though the dark storm clouds still held him in their grip as he sat, pondering where his next step should take him. All the officers were out on actions relating to the Pattison case, he thought. Perhaps nobody would notice if he were to absent himself for a little while.

Picking up the telephone, Lorimer dialled a number he knew off by heart. A small smile of pleasure softened his features as he heard the man's voice.

'Solly? Any chance you'd have time to see me right now?'

'I JUST CAN'T make head nor tail of it any more, Solly,' Lorimer said as they walked through the university grounds. 'Mrs Pattison swears now that she was with Hardy in his Edinburgh place. And of course that puts paid to Hardy's earlier claim that he was with his wife all night in Erskine. One of them's lying and I think it's probably him.'

'Do you really think there is enough evidence to build a case against them?' Solly asked quietly as they passed through the ancient arches of the quadrangle.

Lorimer shrugged wearily in reply.

'Let's take it step by step,' the psychologist suggested. 'What you want to know is the identity of the person who shot three men in their white Mercedes cars.'

'Person or persons,' Lorimer replied glumly.

Solly shook his head. 'No, you're looking for one person, Lorimer,' he said firmly. 'And to find that person you should be asking yourself why anyone would want to kill these men in the first place.'

'You make it sound very simple,' Lorimer sighed.

'Let's look at what you have on the Pattison case. The man has been caught on CCTV camera leaving Blythswood Square in the company of a person we think may be a prostitute. With me so far?'

Lorimer nodded, trying to suppress a yawn. He'd been over and over this territory till his head swam.

'Why would a street girl want to kill men who came to them for sex?' Solly asked.

Lorimer frowned. 'D'you really want an answer to that?'

'Yes. Give me any reason why someone kills another person.'

'Money, drugs, falling out, spite . . .' He yawned for real now.

'Or, perhaps, some notion of revenge?'

'What are you cooking up in that brainy head of yours, pal?' Lorimer smiled despite himself as they headed around the corner towards the university chapel.

'It's not that difficult, really,' Solly replied with his customary modesty. 'A woman with a gun who targets specific victims has an agenda. Agreed?'

'Agreed,' Lorimer said, 'though we don't know if the perpetrator was a woman.'

'Let's say it was,' Solly came back firmly. 'The last known person with Mr Pattison was a woman, from the image of her on that CCTV footage. Now, if a woman sets out to kill men who pick up prostitutes, there has to be a reason for it, doesn't there?'

'What on earth are you suggesting?' Lorimer asked, frowning.

Solly stopped at the foot of the steps leading up to the chapel and turned to his friend, his hands spread out as he began to explain.

'If a woman wants to kill someone over and over again like that she must be under some kind of compulsion. Not necessarily one that afflicts her mental state.' He paused for a moment as though searching for the right words. 'I think you should be looking for someone who has a deep-seated grudge against someone she doesn't even know.'

'What?'

'Doesn't it stand to reason?' Solly asked. 'All she knows is that her intended victim picks up prostitutes in a particular type of white car. She can't possibly know his identity or else she wouldn't have killed three times already.'

'Unless she's a prize nutter,' Lorimer put it, glad to see the psychologist wince at his political incorrectness. The two men climbed the stone steps and entered the chapel. Rays of sunlight from the stained glass windows made shapes of colour dance across the ancient flagstones. All was quiet within, save for the sound of their echoing footsteps.

'Let's say that she is not,' Solly continued, sitting down in a row of wooden seats that faced the main altar. 'The killings are planned and show an orderly sort of mind. Now,' he went on, wagging a professorial finger, 'most of these women are in thrall to drugs and often not capable of doing anything at all like this, agreed?'

'Ye-es,' Lorimer said slowly, flicking the tails of his coat as he sat down beside the psychologist.

'Don't you see?' Solly smiled suddenly. 'If this killer *is* a woman from the streets she is unlikely to be an addict. The unidentified hair sample suggests as much. *Plus*,' he went on, 'she must have obtained the gun from somewhere and knows how to use it.'

'And she's forensically aware,' Lorimer pondered, following Solly's line of thought now.

'There's something else,' Solly went on then paused as though to gather his thoughts or, Lorimer suspected, to choose his words carefully. The policeman glanced sharply at his companion; he had a feeling that whatever Solly was going to tell him was not something he wanted to hear.

'I've been going over this from different angles,' he began. 'Thinking out of the box, you might say,' he added. 'What have the three men in common apart from their cars and the way they were killed?' he asked quietly.

Lorimer's frown deepened. This was something he'd been over and over with other officers. 'Nothing, so far as we know,' he muttered.

'Let's say that the woman who picked Pattison up was a Glasgow prostitute. Just for argument's sake,' Solly said.

'Okay.'

'She gets into the cars after making some sort of proposition to each of these men, shall we say?'

'Go on,' Lorimer said, wondering where this was leading.

'Well,' Solly said, 'think about it. There has to be a verbal exchange of some sort. She doesn't get into the car until she has spoken to them and they with her. Don't you see? She's looking for a particular person, but since none of these three men had any visible resemblance to one another that just leaves one thing, doesn't it?'

'You mean . . .?'

'Their voices,' Solly said firmly. 'Each of these men came from a place outside Glasgow. Two of them had English accents and Pattison had a cultured, Edinburgh accent, something that Glaswegians sometimes associate with an anglicised accent. There have been studies into this, by the way,' he added as though to reassure the detective.

'I can see what you're saying and it does make a sort of sense,' Lorimer admitted. 'She's looking for somebody who drives a type of car like that, a man from outside Glasgow who picks up prostitutes.' He shook his head as though he were failing to convince himself. 'But why?'

'Ah.' Solly wagged his finger in the air once more. 'That's my point exactly. *Why* is this mystery woman seeking to kill the man in the white Mercedes?'

'So, let me get this straight. You think that these three men may have been killed by mistake?' He shook his head at the idea of such callousness, then paused. 'Well, doesn't that mean that she is still looking?'

Solly nodded. 'It's possible. There may be a target that fits all of the killer's criteria but her knowledge of him is so scanty that she is taking a chance on anyone who ticks these particular boxes.'

'We've been looking for all the owners of white Mercs,' Lorimer said slowly. 'But not with this in mind. We just wanted to see if there was any sort of pattern we could establish that might help find the killer.'

'I did wonder . . .' Solly began and looked into the distance as though he were too shy to look his friend in the eye.

'What?'

'Well, this mystery woman. Is she really a prostitute?'

'We've got information about the first two victims. They did use street girls. And so did Pattison,' Lorimer began slowly. 'But I can see what you're saying. This woman has to have had a clear head for what she did. And we know most of our poor lassies are usually doped to the eyeballs when they're out on the game.'

Solly smiled sadly. 'I have given this a lot of thought,' he said. 'And the more I consider it as a possible theory the more it seems to make sense.'

Lorimer nodded but said nothing. He had sought help from this man to clear his head, make things a little more objective. But all the while Professor Brightman had been creating a profile for the killer they sought and now he had begun to share it with him. It might be true, or at least have some grains of truth in it. Solly's previous profiling had been invaluable and Lorimer had learned to listen without prejudice. But would the rest of his team take this idea on board? And how would they set about finding this mystery woman?

'You're not being permitted to charge her,' the deputy chief constable told Lorimer.

'And what would we charge her with anyway? Wasting police time? I see that might not be in our interest right now,' Lorimer replied, unable to keep the cynicism out of his voice.

'Probably not,' Joyce Rogers agreed. 'The newspapers would have our guts for garters. Poor widow being hounded by police when they should be finding her husband's killer etc., etc. Aye, I know what you're thinking and believe me it sticks in my craw as well that so many man hours have been wasted. Our budget's shot to buggery as it is,' she added gloomily.

'There is one thing that has come up,' Lorimer began.

'Oh?' Joyce Rogers raised her eyebrows as she heard the tentative tone in her senior officer's voice. 'Am I going to like it?'

'Oh, maybe not,' Lorimer said with a long sigh. 'It's something Professor Brightman suggested.'

The deputy chief constable listened to Solly's theory, not interrupting once, though her eyes grew wider as Lorimer went on.

'So, if it is true that there is a woman behind all of this, we need to decide on our next plan of action.'

'This isn't just one of his latest hobby horses, is it? I know the professor was writing a book about women serial killers,' Joyce asked.

Lorimer shook his head. 'I don't think so. He's quite correct about the killer being organised and although we've seen psychopaths committing crimes that show a degree of organisation, Professor Brightman doesn't think this protagonist fits into that sort of category.' Lorimer bit his tongue. The profile that was emerging was one that might well fit an experienced police officer; a woman who was not only adept with firearms but was forensically aware. He was certain Solly was thinking along the same lines though as yet neither of the men had voiced this particular theory.

'Does he not, indeed?' Joyce replied tartly. 'Well, that remains to be seen once you've caught her. If it is a *her*,' she added darkly. 'Meantime, what is this I've been hearing about you wandering around the drag during the wee small hours?'

Lorimer bit his lip. Curse the man! Sutherland's tongue must have been wagging, he thought. 'Well . . .'

'Moonlighting, are you? Hoping to combine this with Helen James's cases?' She looked keenly at him and nodded. 'Well, for God's sake don't let the chief know about it. I can only keep a lid on this for so long. He'd have something to say if he thought you'd deliberately crossed him, Lorimer.'

'It's not quite like that, ma'am,' Lorimer protested. 'Okay, I'd love to find out who killed Tracey-Anne Geddes, but it's more than that. With the CCTV footage of Pattison there's every chance that the two cases might be linked.'

'Because a girl got into his car in Blythswood Square?' Joyce Rogers asked. 'That's pretty flimsy linkage if you ask me, Lorimer.'

'Frank Hardy told me that Edward Pattison used prostitutes in Glasgow,' Lorimer went on. 'And we know that Littlejohn and Wardlaw also used girls from their own neck of the woods so there's reason to suppose they might have tried it out here too.'

'And their deaths happened not long after Carol Kilpatrick was killed and just before the attack on Tracey-Anne,' she said slowly. 'You really think there's something behind these poor lassies' deaths to do with the car killings?'

Lorimer nodded. 'With your permission, ma'am, I'd like to continue my own investigation into this. I'd thought I might take a trip on the Big Blue Bus, ask some of the girls there if they know anything about Pattison or the other men.'

Joyce Rogers smiled. 'I can't stop you, of course, but see if you can confine your nocturnal wanderings a little, hmm? Otherwise tongues will wag and I'd hate to see you castigated for something as stupid as this.'

THE MEETING WITH the deputy chief constable was a lot easier, Lorimer decided later, than the one with his squad of hand-picked detectives, who were not afraid to criticise Solly's theory. However, with the exception of Duncan Sutherland who had stood with a leering grin on his face throughout, all hands had been raised when Lorimer had asked for their support in tackling the case from a different angle. Barbara Knox, in particular, had shown her enthusiasm, her hand shooting straight up in a manner that made Lorimer fear the big woman actually had a crush on him. Some of the actions would be going over old ground, like visiting the owners of several white Mercedes cars.

Solly had not voiced any explanation about why such a person might have sparked off a killer's intent, but it was there all the same: somebody had deserved to die. That was the thinking of this mystery killer, wasn't it? And from there the next logical step was to ask what it was they had done to provoke such a desperate chain of events.

Chapter Twenty-nine

SHE WOKE WITH a cry, sitting up in bed, staring into the empty darkness. Carol's face had come floating towards her, hair lapping on the endless waves as though they were both deep underwater, drowning together, helpless as each sought to clutch the other's hand. Then, that noiseless cry as she felt the tug of the current pulling her under.

It was only a dream, a fantasy bred in the subconscious mind. Everyone had dreams that impinged on their waking thoughts, didn't they? But it had been Miriam, not Carol, whose body had been washed up from the river. Dreams, like newspaper reports, they always got things a bit muddled, she told herself, rolling onto her side and tucking the duvet around her shivering body. Reality, now that was a different thing altogether. In real life she was capable of shooting her gun and killing a man. But this time she would find the right target, thanks to dear little Barbara.

The woman's smile faded as she thought of the lesbian officer. It was as if she had prostituted herself with the girl. But then, perhaps she now had an inkling of what it had been like for Carol, having to give her body in return for something she wanted.

The cold, long month of January was drawing to its close, she thought, clenching her fists and drumming them together in a determined beat. And soon there would be a new month and a new opportunity to seek out and destroy the man who had robbed her of everything she had held most dear in this sorry world.

BARBARA KNOX GRINNED at her reflection in the bathroom mirror. The cost of that stylist had made a pretty big hole in her budget but the result was well worth it, she told herself, turning her head this way and that to admire the sharp cut and flecks of deep red that tipped each spiky lock. A quick dab of gel and fingers raking through was all that was required now to make her look the part. Her smile faded as she moved away from the mirror; that ever-present muffin top revealed above the elastic of her pyjama trousers. Scowling now, Barbara turned from the glaring truth of her image and began to pull her clothes out of the walk-in cupboard that served as a makeshift dressing room. Okay, so she was fat. All the women in her family had been the same. It was a hereditary thing. Something she simply couldn't help. But some folk liked a bit to cuddle, didn't they? And Diana didn't seem to mind.

Cheered by that thought, Barbara began to hum tunelessly to the music on her radio. Today might be just another working day for most folk but for Barbara Knox it was something much more exciting. Being part of the Serious Crimes Unit, however temporary that might prove, was a hell of a lot better than being dogsbody to Mumby, wasn't it? Now that the case had taken this strange twist there might well be an end in sight. Detective Superintendent Lorimer had spoken with such conviction yesterday, though the line of enquiry was pretty surprising. He'd been fairly impassioned and DC Knox had listened to all that he'd said, nodding her approval even though that tosser, Sutherland, had had a face on him like a fried egg. They'd all discussed it afterwards, of course, and Barbara had been gratified to hear that most of them had taken Lorimer's side.

Her work on the cars had come in for a wee mention too, Barbara remembered, smiling in satisfaction as she recalled the titbit of praise the boss had handed out. He was fair minded, that man, but oh how driven! Sutherland had been passing round rumours that Lorimer had been mooching around the drag, but that one had been nipped in the bud by the man himself when he revealed that he had spent time talking to the street women on his own. *Crazy!* some of them had said, *Imagine getting up in the middle of a bleak January night.* But it was his devotion to duty that had prompted him, though Lorimer hadn't said that himself. He didn't need to, Barbara thought as she pulled on her trousers. It was there for anyone to see and if Duncan Sutherland thought he could sully that good man's reputation, well, he'd have the entire squad down on him like a ton of bricks. The actions had been given out and Barbara had not been at all surprised to learn that she had more stuff to do with contacting the owners of these white Mercs once again.

A name flashed into her mind as she switched off the bedroom light and made her way into the kitchen. Vladimir Badica. A Romanian garage dealer. 'Bad Vlad,' she said aloud then raised her eyebrows thoughtfully. Would Diana be interested in this new line of enquiry? Or had she chanced her arm enough for the dark-haired woman, the very thought of whom made her pulse beat faster?

FRANK HARDY SAT quite still, watching the woman opposite weep silently into her hands. It was odd this sudden urge to take her into his arms, comfort her, tell her it had all been a terrible mistake. He had expected screams of recrimination, Jill throwing things at him, crashing plates off the wall; all the classic stuff he'd seen in films. But Frank Hardy had not been prepared for this display of genuine grief. Had Jill had no inkling at all of his infidelity, then? Even when he'd asked her to lie to the police, hadn't she suspected a thing? And now, seeing her so broken, it was not just guilt that Hardy felt but a stronger emotion, something that he might once have called love.

'Jilly,' he began, 'I'm so sorry, truly I am.' Then, when she made no reply, Frank Hardy drew his wife's hand away from her face and held it in his own. Jill's shoulders heaved but she did not attempt to pull her hand out of his grasp as he had expected. Instead she raised her tear-filled eyes to his and spoke just one word.

'Why?'

The lump in his throat made speech suddenly impossible and he leaned towards her, arms around her shoulders, holding her close and patting her back gently the way he had when her mother had died. Why had he let himself be beguiled by Cathy Pattison? Had her allure been something to do with a subconscious desire to cuckold a man he despised? Or had it been nothing more than an episode of male lust? In the cold light of dawn Frank Hardy saw his affair now for what it was. A stupid act of bravado. Stupid and thoughtless, he reminded himself, stroking Jill's back. Had he ever really given his wife a second thought? Well, he would have to do that now, wouldn't he? The whole sordid affair would come out as part of the investigation into Ed Pattison's murder.

IT WAS ONLY a week until her husband's birthday, Maggie realised with a slight sensation of alarm. One week to finalise all the arrangements. Mentally she ticked off what had already been done. The cake had been ordered from the Malmaison Hotel and they were also providing champagne for a toast before the meal. All the invitations had gone out by email from her school address so that there could be no reply coming to the house. That had been underlined with SURPRISE PARTY put into bold lettering. Solly's mother was due to arrive this coming weekend and Ma Brightman would be looking after baby Abigail while Solly and Rosie attended the celebrations. Maggie smiled to herself as she remembered Rosie's words on the telephone.

'What on earth am I going to wear? My boobs are still enormous from feeding her ladyship and my pre-baby clothes are way too tight,' she'd cried.

'Sounds like an excuse to go shopping,' Maggie had suggested with a laugh. And Rosie had cheered up almost immediately.

Her own outfit was not such a problem. After all, she was supposed to be taking her husband out for a posh meal for his fortieth birthday so a new dress would not arouse any suspicions on Bill's part. In fact Maggie had splashed out on a red and black two-piece, the silky pencil skirt hugging her figure in all the right places, the top belted in matching fabric to show off her tiny waist. She'd even purchased some nice costume jewellery from a case at the counter, no doubt positioned to tempt customers into a spur-of-the-moment decision to complete their outfit. There was something a little naughty about the feeling of spending so much money in that exclusive west end boutique, watching the garments being folded carefully between layers of tissue, brazenly adding the jewellery to her credit card as if money was no object. And the shop assistant calling her Madam all the time! Such deferential attention was so at odds with how Maggie Lorimer was normally treated. *Miss* or *Missus Lorimer*, the kids called her, sometimes even *Mum* by a new first-year pupil in a moment of unself-conscious affection before the hoots of fellow classmates made him redden and correct himself. (It was always a wee boy who made that mistake, Maggie reminded herself. The girls were far too streetwise for any of that.)

Maggie put all thoughts of the impending party aside as she drew a new pile of marking towards her. Fifth-year prelims required to be marked and handed back by the end of this week so she'd have her work cut out to finish them in time. Sometimes it was good having a policeman husband who worked late hours. And, with no family demanding she be home at a certain time, Maggie could stay behind and do her marking and preparation hours after many of her colleagues had gone home.

BARBARA KNOX FROWNED as she logged into SID, the Scottish Intelligence Database. Access to this was given to police officers wishing to know secrets about investigations across the country. Every enquiry was electronically tagged so her efforts to find information were like sitting naked in a glass box for all to see. But there would be nobody to see her passing on bits of news to Diana when they were alone together, would there? Her face darkened as she saw that there was absolutely nothing on Vladimir Badica. She'd been so sure that the Romanian had to be shady, somehow, a xenophobic prejudice that was, she realised, unworthy of her. Some folk were still bolshy about gays, after all. She shouldn't be so quick to judge another sort of minority within Scottish society. But it was her police training that made her perennially suspicious,

Barbara told herself; that and the staffroom gossip. Older officers were forever making cynical remarks about suspects who came within their orbit and the new wave of immigrant businessmen was fair game for their comments.

Anyway Bad Vlad, as she had termed him, appeared to be as pure as the driven snow. Or else he just hadn't been caught yet, she grumbled to herself, still wishing that some dirt had attached itself to the wealthy Romanian. All of the garage franchises south of the border had been checked out once and now it seemed they had to be checked out again in case a car had been shipped up here to Scotland. Someone was the target for these three killings, someone, Lorimer had insisted, who was still at large. But would they still have their white Merc? one of the officers had asked, a fair question after all. And so the movement of all these models within the last eighteen months had to be carefully checked and rechecked, a task that had fallen to DC Knox. She was only a third of the way through the list of Mercedes dealers to see if there were any cars for sale but at least the guy she'd spoken to at the vehicle licensing office was doing plenty on her behalf.

'Hey, nice hair,' a voice behind her remarked and Barbara swung round to see DI Monica Proctor smiling at her.

'Thanks,' Barbara replied, reddening slightly as the DI passed through the office, then she looked back once more at the computer screen. Barbara Knox gave a sigh. Oh, to be a DI like Monica, always out and about! She loved her job but sometimes the public simply didn't understand all the work that went on behind the scenes, some of it frankly tedious. Not their fault. It was all action man stuff to them, wasn't it, like the cop shows on the telly.

Diana understood, though, and that was one big consolation in the detective constable's life right now. She passed her fingers through the spiky haircut. Would the journalist like it? she wondered anxiously. Well, they had a date tomorrow night so she'd find out then. And if she could offer her friend something a bit more concrete to help her research then all to the good.

THERE WAS, SHE thought to herself, no need to carry on. She could quit right now, leave the country even, forget all about the killings and start a new life for herself where nobody knew who she was or what she had done. There was plenty of money in her bank account after all. The insurance claim and a keen-eyed lawyer had seen to that. Besides, she was tired of waiting for one of these street women to tell her if another white car had been seen around the drag. Often as not it was a Skoda, since a private taxi firm in the area seemed to have loads of them cruising around at night. Some nights she'd prepared for hours in the hotel room then emerged into the street, dressed to kill. And, if the punters thought it strange that a hooker was ignoring their overtures, well, that was just too bad for them. The other women didn't seem to notice, probably glad to get the custom that came their way.

Yet there was something that would not let her go. A memory of Carol, perhaps, laughing as they'd run along that beach in Cyprus. Or the night she'd died, hearing her described by that uniformed officer as though she was less than human, just a bit of society's flotsam washed up on the shore of the city's streets. Whatever it was, she could not leave this task unfinished. Soon, surely it would be soon, she would find the man who had murdered Carol and bring him to justice.

She looked at the date on the digital clock by her bed. Tomorrow was the first of February. She would be meeting Barbara after the girl had finished work. But would the policewoman have anything worthwhile to tell her? She had kept one step ahead of Detective Superintendent Lorimer, thanks to her inside information, but she needed more than that. Perhaps it might be worth seeing if that woman called Doreen was around today? A couple of folded twenties could do wonders if you knew the right questions to ask. She keyed in the woman's number and waited but there was no answer, just the usual recorded message.

'Hey. It's your friend here,' she said as Doreen's answering machine kicked in. 'Can you text me if there's anything interesting going on?'

She flipped the mobile phone shut. Maybe the woman was busy right now. Too early for trade. Then, just as she was about to put the mobile back into her handbag the vibration that signalled an incoming text made her take it out again.

MT U ON BIG BLU BUS 2NT

The woman who had befriended the prostitute looked at the message intently. Doreen was obviously in a situation where she couldn't talk. But she'd picked up her voicemail nonetheless. The Big Blue Bus left the centre of town at midnight. If Doreen really had something to tell her then it might be worth her while making that particular trip.

'WHAT ABOUT THE Big Blue Bus?' Helen James asked. 'You might want to talk to some of the volunteers. Probably not worth your while trying to ask the girls anything. They're either out their heids or too pissed off with us coppers to gain anything at that time of night.'

Lorimer grimaced as he listened to the DCI's advice. She was right, of course, and it was very much DCI James's territory, after all. And he was tired, he had to admit that too. Another night spent away from home was not what he had had in mind. Still, now that James had suggested it . . .

'Okay, I'll ring up the contact you've given me, see if I can meet them in George Square tonight.'

Lorimer put down the phone with a sigh. He'd go home, have dinner with Maggie and then change into different clothes, things like his old donkey jacket and jeans that wouldn't intimidate the street women. The Big Blue Bus only went around the city on certain nights and this Tuesday was one of them. So, if he wanted to push this line of enquiry on he had to take the opportunities as they arose.

Chapter Thirty

RED SQUARE, SOME local folk had dubbed it, due to the red asphalt surface that had replaced the former tarmacadam and flower beds of the city's central square. The city fathers had deemed it an improvement but Lorimer was one of many who dismissed that notion, remembering springtime outings as a boy when he had crossed the square and his senses had been assaulted by masses of pink, white and blue hyacinths wafting their heady perfume from the many raised flower beds dotted around the place. There was no such olfactory welcome tonight, just the leftover smell of home-made soup from the all-night van that served the down-and-outs who came shuffling along for what might be their only decent meal of the day. Glasgow might have its fair share of social problems like homelessness and prostitution, Lorimer thought as he parked his car at the edge of the square, but at least there were those good folk who were willing to give up their time to help them. The thought made him feel at once guilty when he remembered his unwillingness to leave the warmth of his own home and somehow glad that he had come.

The street lights illumined the grand buildings on all four sides: the old Post Office that was still under renovation, the Millennium Hotel opposite, the Merchant's House and of course the graceful Victorian façade of the City Chambers that dominated the whole square. Lorimer walked past the recumbent stone lions guarding the cenotaph and headed towards the Big Blue Bus whose interior lights showed that it was ready and waiting for its nightly passengers.

'Superintendent Lorimer? Richard Allan. Pleased to meet you.' The man with the beaming smile and outstretched hand was suddenly there as Lorimer approached the double decker bus sitting right outside the City Chambers. The Reverend Richard Allan was, like Lorimer himself, devoid of the usual signs of rank or status. No dog collar peeped from under that stripy scarf, nor, at first glance, was there anything other than the man's bright countenance to show his Christian affiliation. However, Lorimer did notice the tiny silver lapel badge in the shape of a dove – a visible reminder of the man's faith. Allan, like so many other men of the cloth, had put his burning desire to do something for the poorer elements of society into practice. Lorimer remembered reading an article about the pastor when the project had taken off; how he had pestered the owners of bus companies into letting his organisation have the vehicle they needed and how the women had gradually responded to the facilities offered aboard the bus. Not only that, but there was something else, something Lorimer wanted to ask the man right away.

'Didn't I read that you'd had some success in helping the girls to come off drugs?' he asked as Allan ushered him on board.

'That's quite correct,' the pastor replied. 'There have been a few, sadly just a very few, who have managed to kick their habits, both drugs and prostitution. Still, one lost lamb and all that. The volunteers here do a marvellous job, though. There's always someone to listen to the women and give them advice about anything at all. Quite a number of them have served prison sentences and that can have a terrible effect on their self-esteem. That's one of our biggest challenges, you know,' he continued. 'Trying to let them know that nobody is worthless.'

Lorimer made a non-committal noise in reply. He'd like to have told this kindly soul just how bad it really was when even some of Strathclyde's finest regarded these women as less than human and undeserving of police time.

'DCI James,' he began.

'Ah, Helen, she's a wonderful lady,' Allan enthused. 'Knows just how to speak to the women. They like her, you know. Trust her, too. So, when I introduce you to them I'll say that you're a friend of hers, shall I?'

'That's a good idea, but I will probably have to tell them the reason I'm here,' Lorimer reminded him.

'Ah, yes.' Allan frowned suddenly, his face clouding for a moment. 'Of course. Terrible business. We used to see Tracey-Anne on a regular basis. Poor little thing.' He shook his head sadly. 'Doesn't bear thinking about.'

'Reverend—'

'Richard, please,' the pastor interrupted with a smile.

'Richard, one of the things I want to ask the women who board the bus is if they have ever seen a white Mercedes sports car cruising around the drag.'

'Ah,' Allan replied. 'I read about that. Edward Pattison and these other men.' He looked intently at Lorimer. 'Do you have suspicions that they had been consorting with the Glasgow women, then?'

Lorimer nodded and was met with an understanding look. The Revd Richard Allan could be trusted with this intelligence. For all his spirituality there was something to this man that Lorimer liked; a sense that he was with a man whose keen intellect was matched by a burning zeal to use his time and talents to make the lives of other folk a little better. And right now that included helping Strathclyde Police with their investigations.

'Oh, here's Doreen,' Allan said suddenly, looking across the square at a couple of women who were approaching the bus.

Lorimer followed his gaze toward the two figures. Despite the chilly night, one of them wore a short red coat and was teetering along on high-heeled boots. The other, dressed in a long black coat, a camel scarf covering her hair, was looking around her as though this was something of a novelty. Lorimer was standing a little behind Richard Allan who waved them on board with a welcome, so it was not until he was on the bus that he saw the taller of the women had turned back and was now disappearing across the square. He frowned. Hadn't he seen her somewhere before?

'Have you ever had members of the press coming on board?' Lorimer murmured to the minister.

Allan's bushy eyebrows shot up in surprise. 'That lady who was with Doreen . . .?'

Lorimer nodded. 'I think so,' he said slowly. 'But it seems she's changed her mind.'

'Well.' The minister puffed out his cheeks. 'Perhaps she only wants to see us from the outside,' he said.

'Do you think she might be a friend of Doreen's?'

'Could be,' Allan replied doubtfully. 'I haven't seen her here before,' he added, peering into the blackness. 'But I do worry about certain of the newspapers, you know, Lorimer. Always looking for a negative, sensational sort of story to print. Stuff that doesn't do us any good at all.'

'Want me to have a quiet word if she attends any of my press conferences again?'

'Would you, Lorimer? Thanks, that is kind of you.' Allan beamed once again as though his world had tilted back on course.

The woman called Doreen had walked right up to the front of the lower deck and was sitting next to a display of leaflets. She had begun to pick out one or two and was examining them as Lorimer approached.

'May I?' he said, taking a seat next to her across the aisle.

The woman jumped and gasped.

'God!' she exclaimed. 'You gied us a fright!'

Lorimer began to smile an apology; the woman's face had turned such a sickly white.

'We haven't met before,' he said, putting out a tentative hand. 'I'm Detective Superintendent Lorimer.'

Doreen's face changed so immediately that the detective superintendent wondered if his initial impression of shocked disbelief had been wrong. Just a trick of the light, perhaps?

'Aye,' she replied shortly, not reaching over to shake the policeman's hand. The street woman's dark eyes narrowed, however, as she scowled at Lorimer.

'You came with another lady tonight, but she seemed to have changed her mind about getting on the bus,' Lorimer began.

'Naw, I dinna think so,' Doreen said sourly.

'Isn't she a journalist, then?' Lorimer persisted.

'Don't know whit ye're on aboot,' Doreen said sharply.

Lorimer nodded. The woman's riposte had been a touch too acerbic. There was something she didn't want the policeman to know and he was certain it had to do with the woman who had disappeared across George Square.

'I think she's writing about the death of the deputy first minister,' he ventured.

The street woman turned on him, eyes flashing.

'She's writing about us,' Doreen broke in, 'no' that it's ony o' your business.'

'Ah, but that's where you're wrong,' Lorimer replied. 'You ladies are very much my business, I'm afraid.' And before Doreen's scowl could deepen any further he went on. 'I'm here concerning the death of Tracey-Anne Geddes. I hoped that talking to some of the ladies who knew her might help,' he said.

'Oh. Well, in that case . . .' Doreen replied, her mouth open in surprise. 'See, I thought . . .' The woman bit her lip suddenly.

'You thought I was working on the Pattison case,' Lorimer finished for her. 'And of course I am. But the other case is still something I take an interest in,' he said blandly.

'Tracey-Anne didnae deserve tae die like that. Some fu— some animal did that tae her!' Doreen exclaimed, tempering her language as she remembered who she was talking to.

'I know,' Lorimer said gently. 'But there is something I wanted to ask, Doreen. Something I'll be asking all the girls tonight,' he added, turning slightly as voices behind them showed that more passengers were now boarding the bus. 'Did you ever see a man in a white sports car, a Mercedes, kerb crawling around the drag, looking for custom?'

'Well maybe I did and maybe I didnae,' Doreen said slyly. 'Not always easy to make out whit types o' car the punters are in. And ah'm not always quite masel, know whit ah mean,' she shrugged.

'Can I trust you to keep all of this completely confidential?' he asked.

The woman nodded, her earrings jangling softly as she looked at him.

'Anythin' in it fur me?' she asked, then licking her lips mendaciously.

'Possibly,' he replied, his answer deliberately non-committal. 'And I'd be grateful if you didn't talk to anyone from the newspapers, okay?'

'Aye, fair 'nuff,' Doreen agreed.

Lorimer gave a small sigh of relief. There was so much to think about and sudden interference from the press was something he could well do without. He was taking a risk in talking to the street women too, though. They might well sell a story about a policeman who asked them questions relating to the death of the deputy first minister of Scotland, even if those questions were couched solely in references to the white cars.

As he moved away, Lorimer recalled what Solly had told him about the two girls from the sauna. Miriam and Jenny had frequented the Big Blue Bus, hadn't they? He turned back again for a moment.

'Do you know a place called Andie's Sauna?' he asked.

Doreen shifted uneasily in her seat. 'Whit's that tae youse?' she muttered.

'Two young women who worked there ended up dead,' Lorimer said softly. 'And we're investigating all the places they worked prior to that.'

'Ah'm in Andie's noo,' Doreen told him. 'An' I ken who ye mean. Thon posh lassie Miriam, and wee Jenny Haslet, in't it?'

Lorimer nodded. 'Jenny came here and was given help,' he said, nodding towards the rack of leaflets. 'And that's something Strathclyde Police want as well. Folk like my colleague, Helen James, believe that there should be no women out on the streets endangering their lives.'

'Ye ken there's two o' them? No' jist the wan in Govan where ah work,' Doreen told him. 'They've got wan ower in Partick an a'.'

Lorimer nodded. Places like that were never listed in any telephone directory but sometimes business cards would be stuck to the insides of telephone boxes, in toilets or on the walls of the underground railway. Solly had visited the one in Govan but he had not given the policeman any new information about that. Perhaps he could see if his friend would take time to explore this further.

'Thanks, Doreen. Nice to talk to you,' he added, nodding politely as he got up to leave. The bus had started up and was now lumbering around a corner of the square so it was time to sit with the other ladies of the night and see what they could offer in the way of information.

As he held on to the back of a seat to steady himself, Lorimer glanced behind him. Doreen Gallagher looked away swiftly, but not before he had seen an expression cross her face: one that he recognised as sheer relief.

THE REST OF the night passed calmly enough, the street women proving to be every bit as wary as Lorimer had expected, but his polite and quiet manner did coax a few of them into sharing some of their stories with him. So it was that he heard tales of juvenile rape and incest, stuff that was shrugged off by some of them as though these things were ordinary life experiences. What did amaze the policeman was the women's resilience in the face of so much hardship and squalor. Early death was taken for granted, stories of girls coming out of prison to meet with their drug dealers and overdosing on the way home were not unknown. One other thing he had learned was that the Revd Richard Allan ran a centre for women up in Stirlingshire, near the village of Arnprior. It was a place of hope, the man had told him, the converted farm catering for women who had lost their way, often through drugs. Fortunately the charities and trusts that funded it had not been hit during the recession and they could continue their good work.

It was a chastened Lorimer who reached home as the birds began the dawn chorus, grateful that fate had dealt him such a good hand. *There but for the grace of God . . .* Richard Allan had murmured. And it was true. He looked at the front of his home with a sudden spurt of joy. They had this lovely house, he and his darling Maggie who was asleep upstairs. He had a job that he loved and good health to enjoy so much of life. As he stood there on his doorstep a blackbird suddenly opened its throat and filled the cold morning air with liquid notes that thrilled him through and through. He inhaled deeply then sighed, his breath making a small white cloud. Life, in all its vagaries, could still have moments of glory, he thought, turning the key in the lock and pushing open the door to his home.

Chapter Thirty-one

'WHY DO PEOPLE do these terrible things?' the girl asked him.

Professor Solomon Brightman smiled sadly. Today he had been presenting a seminar on intention, the discussion drifting, as it often did, into the mentality behind criminal behaviour. He looked at the girl, feeling a pang of despair. This fresh-faced second-year student showed a lot of academic promise in her subject, yet Solly felt that she had been sheltered from the reality of life in many ways and suspected that her education at a private school down south had failed to give her any insight into the sort of world that many of these case studies inhabited.

'Well,' Solly began. 'There is no easy answer to that question, I'm afraid.' The discussion had ended with a debate about the link between sex and violence, the outcome of which had been terminated by the clock, but this particular student had lingered, wanting more.

'Recent research has come up with a model that shifts our perception of mental illnesses that present aggressive behaviour and sexual arousal,' he told her. 'Psychiatrists thought at one time that such illnesses might be caused by chemical imbalances, but the most recent thinking is that neural circuits in the brain might actually be overlapping.'

The girl frowned, concentrating on her professor's words.

'What I mean is this,' he went on. 'There are two sets of neurons that control sex and violence and in most people these are mutually exclusive. So, while these two circuits overlap physically, there is a sort of switch that keeps them apart. Follow me?'

She nodded.

'Then if a scenario arises whereby there are too many or too few connections between brain cells, those two behaviours cease to be mutually exclusive.'

'Oh,' she said, 'so it's not their fault if they become violent when they're having sex?'

'A pathology might well occur from such a physical situation,' Solly admitted. 'But it would be very difficult to say just how far a person was capable of controlling his or her violent behaviour.'

'But they might not be able to control it at all,' his student insisted.

'There might indeed be a predisposition for sexual violence in an individual whose neural pathways were intermingled in such a way as to . . .'

'Make them killers?' the girl finished off with a gleam of triumph in her eyes. 'Thanks, professor, that's much clearer now,' she said cheerfully, swinging her bag onto her shoulder and smiling at him as she left his room.

Solly closed his door with a sigh. It was true that much research was ongoing into the behaviour of sexual offenders and perhaps in time better treatments might be offered to them. The theory was absorbing for so many of his students. But the sigh he had given expressed the dichotomy between this girl's academic approach and the reality of his own preoccupation with the case that Lorimer had given him. At least two of the dead street girls had been brutally murdered by someone who could well fit the profile of a sex offender that he had just outlined to his student.

Violent sexual behaviour might be tolerated by some for the simple reason that, were the women who suffered to complain, it would lose them money. Solly's mind turned once more to the sauna in Govan. There was another place down in Partick, Lorimer had told him, also called Andie's. Who, he frowned, was this Andie person? With a twinge of guilt, the psychologist realised that he had done nothing yet to follow up this particular line of enquiry. It was, he consoled himself, something that he normally left to the police. But with the Pattison case absorbing so much of their manpower, there was little left over for a search into the two saunas. A quick look at his watch told Solly that if he was to forego his lunch then he could spare two hours until his next class. A walk to Partick would do him good, too. It was a cold February morning but the skies were clear and a weak sun was making its hazy presence felt through thin wisps of milky cloud.

Solly turned up his collar against the breeze as he crossed Byres Road and headed left. Once sheltered from the wind that blew down University Avenue the psychologist's mouth turned up in a smile. Being out on the streets was something he always enjoyed; taking in snatches of conversation as people passed him by, watching the way everyone went about their business, catching glimpses of human behaviour in the raw. It was an absorbing walk down to the corner where the classy shops and cafes gave way to a more homely type of area altogether in Dumbarton Road. Native Glaswegians had informed the professor that Partick had been a village at one time in the city's history and today Solly caught an inkling of what that still meant.

Andie's Sauna was a fair step along the road, past Partick Library and down a small side lane that led away from the busy main road. Like the one in Govan, this place was fronted by a large window, but here the difference was that a dusty Venetian blind had been pulled down to give some notion of privacy.

Solly pushed open the door and entered. There was a reception desk straight ahead and a row of bentwood chairs placed along one side, a pile of well-thumbed magazines laid on top of the one nearest to the door. Nobody was there but he could hear the sound of a vacuum cleaner somewhere beyond the door behind the reception area. Perhaps Joe Public was not expected at this time of day, Solly mused. There was no sign of a bell on the counter so he walked up and down, hands behind his back, taking in the state of the place. Lorimer, he knew, was fond of telling his younger officers how much one could learn about a person from the house that he inhabited. What, Solly wondered, could he find out about this establishment from this front-of-house area?

It needed a good clean, he told himself, looking at the dusty sills and fly-blown window panes, and there had been little attempt to make the place attractive. No vase of flowers graced the reception desk and, as Solly peeped over its edge, all he could see was a telephone, a thick ledger and an open laptop with several unopened letters laid to one side. There was an ancient swivel chair behind the desk, some of its seat padding ripped and worn; Solly nodded to himself, concluding that there was probably only a single member of staff who fronted the sauna. The same person who was now behind the vacuum cleaner, perhaps? As he paced back and forth, Solly became aware that the flooring beneath his feet was slightly uneven; whoever had laid the thick blue linoleum had not bothered to put down any underlay. At each step, the professor could hear the squeak of floorboards and he was so fascinated by this, looking down at his shoes, that he failed to notice a door opening to his left.

'Who are *you*?' a man's voice demanded.

A short, thin fellow in blue jeans and a checked shirt, its sleeves rolled up past his elbows, stood before him, one hand on the hose of the vacuum cleaner.

Solly gave a start then turned and gave the man a smile, holding out his hand. 'Professor Brightman, University of Glasgow,' he said.

'We're no' open yet,' the man said shortly, scowling suspiciously at Solly. 'And I don't remember any Brightman in our appointment book,' he went on, confirming Solly's first impression that this was a one-man business.

'Are you Andie?'

The man's face changed immediately as he hooted with laughter.

'Me? Naw, son, ah'm no' Andie. Why? Is that who ye're looking fur?'

'Actually,' Solly stepped forward, nodding in a confidential manner, 'I'm here on behalf of Strathclyde Police. It's to do with the murders of some of the Glasgow street girls,' he went on. 'I'm a professor of psychology, you see, and sometimes I help the police to establish things like criminal profiles.'

''S'at so?' the man replied, clearly unimpressed. 'Well, how did ye come in here, then?'

'Andie's Saunas was the place of work for two of these women,' Solly explained. 'Miriam Lyons and Jenny Haslet.'

'Never heard of them, pal,' the man said quickly. Too quickly, Solly decided, and he was forced to take a step backwards as the man bore down on him.

'I was hoping to make contact with the owner,' Solly went on, feeling just a shade intimidated: despite the fact that the man was older and shorter in stature there was something menacing about him that put Solly on his guard.

'Well, now, maybe you should write a letter,' the man sneered.

Solly nodded. 'Yes, a letter. Well to whom would I write?' he asked. 'And does this Andie have an email address by any chance?'

The man stopped and blinked. Then, to Solly's surprise, he let go of the vacuum cleaner and went around to the other side of the desk. Picking up the telephone, he dialled a number and waited, all the while staring hard at the psychologist.

'Boss,' the man said. 'There's a fella here tae see you. Name of Brightman.'

Solly waited, wondering if he was going to be handed the telephone and allowed to speak to the person on the other end of the line.

'Oh, aye, 's'at right?' The man's eyes flicked across to Solly with an expression of distaste. 'Aye, aye . . . okay,' he continued, nodding as he listened but continuing to regard Solly with what the psychologist recognised as suspicion.

Then, to his disappointment the telephone was replaced and the man jerked his thumb towards the door.

'See if the polis want tae speak tae ma boss, they've tae come ower theirselves. Get it? Now beat it, pal. Ah've got work tae dae afore we open up.'

The man came around the reception area, fists clenched, and Solly backed away, fumbling for the door handle and opening it swiftly.

He stumbled back along the lane, only glancing once behind him to see the man standing, arms crossed, watching him leave, a sneering smile on his face that made Solly shiver.

As he crossed back over Dumbarton Road Solly reflected that it might have been wiser to have sought out the company of a uniformed officer. But sparing such a person was hard since every single man and woman in the force had to account for how they spent their time. Babysitting the criminal psychologist was not part of their remit, he told himself, heart thumping. But, if he had not gleaned any information about the owner of these saunas, he had learned quite a lot nonetheless.

THE MAN IN the checked shirt looked to his left and right as he turned the key in the lock. Andie had not been best pleased at the news of such an unexpected visitor. Coming to the sauna as a punter was one thing but nosing around out of hours only meant trouble.

Micky Devlin pulled his coat around him, buttoning it hastily as he walked along the lane. He could still see the retreating back of the bearded professor as he walked along Dumbarton Road. The psychologist had no inkling whatsoever that he was being followed and that, just as he often watched other people, the man from the sauna was observing his every step.

Devlin's eyes bore into the back of the professor's skull, waiting for him to whip out a mobile and call the police. But nothing like that occurred all the way back to Byres Road and up as far as the university. Dodging nimbly between pedestrians, Devlin managed to keep Solly in his sight without the psychologist once noticing his presence. At last he stood, almost disappointed, opposite the main door to the department of psychology, watching as Brightman disappeared inside.

Leaning against the fence that ran along the avenue, Devlin keyed a number into his mobile.

'Think he is who he says he is,' he said then waited as the voice on the other end of the line told him exactly what to do.

'Aye, okay,' he grinned, and, snapping the phone shut, he pocketed it and walked smartly back the way he had come, whistling softly through nicotine-stained teeth. It didn't pay to take too many chances in this game and Andie had been dead right to send him after the man with the thick black beard.

Chapter Thirty-two

THE SONG PLAYED on the radio was an old one, long before his time, some soft crooning designed to lull the listener into a romantic frame of mind. But it was not the tune that lingered in his brain, but the images dredged up by the words. A full moon was glinting on the water and a dream maker playing with his mind, coaxing him into that place where the heat from his skin made his blood thick and strong.

The image persisted long after the song had ended, the reflected moonlight shuddering in ripples against the dark water.

LILY STOOD ON the corner of the street, her only shelter the dark forbidding walls of the office block behind her. The night had turned colder, and as she looked up at the skies she could make out a few stars struggling to be seen against the light pollution from the city. Up there, Lily thought, was there any form of life like hers? And if there was, did they have to stand waiting for punters? Her mind drifted as the thought took hold: was anywhere better than here where corruption and greed killed thousands of innocent victims across the globe? There had to be a better place, Lily decided, a corner of her mind holding on to a glimmer of hope; even on this godforsaken planet. That tall policeman, he had a wife that he loved; she had seen that in his eyes. And, when he'd left on that wild night, hadn't he been going back to a place where life was good and nice and warm?

The girl swayed back and forth, humming a tune to herself as her thoughts turned to images that might comfort her. She remembered the fire in the woods where she'd sat with pals from school, its flickering flames illuminating all their faces, the crackling hissing sounds made by damp pine cones they'd tossed in. If she thought hard enough, she might even recapture that bit of warmth.

The sound of a car engine approaching made the girl stand back from the edge of the kerb. A large white car turned the corner from Sauchiehall Street into Blythswood Street and approached the place where Lily stood, the lamplight above her reflected in the puddles. She watched it intently. At first she thought he was going to stop, ask her for a price, but as the car slowed down, Lily saw the driver simply looking at her, his mouth partly open, revealing his teeth.

Lily shivered, all imaginary fires suddenly spent.

His eyes were upon her, dark and menacing, as though she had made him angry, and Lily took another step back, waiting and wondering. Was he playing some sort of sex game, perhaps? The other girls had told her so many lurid stories of punters' bizarre sexual tastes that she was prepared for anything.

But then the car moved away and disappeared along a lane that ran between the backs of the office blocks. Lily watched the red tail lights as it travelled the length of the lane. So, no takers for

Lily this time, she thought, turning away and shrugging off a dull disappointment.

She did not hear the car door close nor see the man emerge from the car at the far end of the lane, but some sixth sense made her look towards the darkened place behind her.

The man was coming back again and she could see his huge form like a dark shadow as he approached her, fists bunched against that massive body as though he were coming to pick her up and carry her off like some fairy tale ogre.

Lily shivered suddenly but waited nonetheless, watching the man coming nearer and nearer, transfixed by the very sight of him.

He was almost upon her when Lily noticed the fabric twisting between his hands and that look of utter malevolence in his eyes.

In a split second of understanding the girl knew just what he intended.

As the sound of a heavy vehicle approached them Lily turned and ran.

Chapter Thirty-three

It was the first morning that Professor Brightman had felt any warmth from the morning sun as he crossed Kelvingrove Park and headed towards the university. Tilting his head upwards, Solly enjoyed the brightness and his heart lifted as he paused. Smiling to himself, he walked on, glancing at the base of the trees. His smile broadened as he caught sight of clumps of snowdrops and the first tentative buds of yellow crocuses. He might still have to wrap his long striped scarf around his neck, but these first signs of spring meant that the long nights of winter were nearing their end.

His smile faded as though a dark cloud had blotted out the sun when he thought of the cases that Lorimer had entrusted to his care. Would that they were also at an end, he thought. Much still needed to be done to create a proper profile of each of the killers; a woman, he believed, who had shot dead three men and some psychotic person, almost certainly male, who had dispatched these street women to their deaths. His disquiet following that visit to the west end sauna had continued late into the night; the fear those two women in Govan had revealed and the angry dismissal he had received yesterday spoke volumes about the person or persons behind that organisation. It was well known, of course, that saunas tended to be fronts for nothing more than brothels and the police had little time to make raids on such establishments unless there was something seriously criminal going on behind the scenes. Helen James had spoken about the saunas as though they were places of safety for her street women and so they probably were, but there was something wrong with those two particular establishments.

The psychology professor had tried Googling the name, Andie's, but had come up with nothing more than a list of retail outlets and restaurants. It was, he felt, time to hand over the investigation to police officers who could make searches into companies and the like. Besides, hadn't he been smartly warned off? Told that if the police wanted to see the owner they would have to come in person? Solly gave a sigh. Lorimer had plenty on his plate right now and an additional detail like the psychologist's unease might prove quite unwelcome. Yet something, perhaps his own fright at the treatment he had received yesterday, made Solly decide to contact his friend at Pitt Street.

'I NEED TO speak to Mr Lorimer, please.'

'Lorimer speaking.'

'You said to call if I needed . . .'

Lorimer sat up immediately. 'Is that you, Lily?' he asked, his voice suddenly more gentle.

'Mr Lorimer. Something bad happened last night. The gritter man said I had to tell you about it. A man . . .' The girl's voice cracked and Lorimer caught the sound of a muffled sob. 'He came at me. He was, he was goin' to kill me,' she whispered.

'Where are you now, Lily?'

'At a flat. I sleep over here with some other girls. You can't come here, though!' The girl's voice rose in alarm.

'I would like to see you, though, Lily. Can you come into town? Meet me at the drop-in centre in Robertson Street, perhaps?'

'Well . . .'

Lorimer heard the doubt in her tone. Had that been a bad idea?

'Could I meet you in the bookshop?' she asked.

'Waterstone's? Sauchiehall Street? The one opposite Marks and Spencer?'

'Uh-huh. I can be there in about a quarter of an hour. Downstairs in the coffee bit,' she added.

Lorimer looked at the clock on the wall. He could be there and back within the hour, he supposed; time enough to see the girl before his daily meeting with the press.

'I'M SORRY HE's not available at the moment, may I take a message?' the woman asked.

Solly paused, wondering. Then, 'To whom am I speaking?' he asked.

'It's DC Knox,' the voice replied.

'Ah,' Solly nodded to himself. He remembered this enthusiastic member of Lorimer's team. And surely he could entrust a little thing like this to her?

'Well,' he continued. 'It's like this.' And the professor told Barbara Knox all about his two visits to Andie's Saunas and his unsatisfactory results.

'Want me to check up on them for you?' she offered.

Solly beamed, though there was nobody to see his sudden relief. 'Would you? That would be a load off my mind, DC Knox. Don't really want to bother your boss, you know.'

The psychologist put the telephone down and immediately turned his mind to his next tutorial session. The subject of dreams had come around once more, he realised with a sigh, remembering a similar session the previous year that had resulted in the strangest and saddest of consequences. A student with red hair, a hit man on the loose and a throwaway remark had all combined to form one of Lorimer's more notable cases.

Solly raised his glasses on to the top of his dark curls and rubbed his eyes as though to erase the memory. These were different students and he owed it to them to be as objective about the subject as possible.

BARBARA KNOX SAT quietly, thinking about the task she had offered to undertake. The professor had sounded a little uncertain. It was strange how you could always tell how a person was feeling from their voice. A psychologist, especially, would agree with that. She really ought to have permission to tackle this, but, what the hell! Barbara grinned to herself. She was good at showing initiative and besides, if what she had heard about the demise of this unit was true then she needed all the brownie points she could get for her career to maintain its upward trajectory. It would be easy enough to find out what the professor wanted to know and then to dig a little deeper.

LORIMER COULD HEAR the hiss of the coffee machine and the undercurrent of chatter as he rounded the balcony. His eyes roved across the customers seated down below until they lighted on the girl. She was sitting hunched up on one of the deep leather armchairs, her head turning this way and that, obviously searching to see if he would come. Lorimer stepped swiftly down the main staircase and strode over to where she was sitting.

'Oh,' she said, clutching the arms of the chair with her tiny white hands. 'You're here!'

'Of course,' Lorimer replied lightly. 'What can I get you? Coffee?' He looked more closely at the girl, noting her thin, pale face. Had she even eaten today?

'Or,' he continued, smiling his best avuncular smile, 'how about breakfast?'

He nodded as her eyes lit up. 'Right, breakfast it is.'

LORIMER SIPPED HIS black coffee watching the girl as she wolfed down her food. He'd spent a few quid, wouldn't miss it at all, but he guessed that for Lily this was a feast. Fresh orange, a large cappuccino and a plate full of pastries disappeared in minutes, the girl's attention totally taken with assuaging her desperate hunger.

'Better?'

She nodded, eyes on him now, wiping a few flakes of croissant from her lips. 'Thanks, Mr Lorimer.'

The detective shrugged. 'That's okay, Lily. Now. You wanted to tell me all about this man?'

She nodded, hunching over once again as though to protect something painful deep within her body. Lorimer read the signs, knowing that whatever hurt this girl was more mental than physical.

'I was out on the drag last night,' she began.

Slowly the story unfolded: the waiting by the kerb; the white car crawling along; the strange-looking man and then his attempt to catch her. Lorimer listened without interrupting, taking in each shudder as Lily recounted her experience. A look of pained relief crossed her face as she told how the gritter lorry had stopped and the driver had jumped down from his cab, catching her in his arms as she fled. The big man with the scarf had turned and disappeared back down the lane, but the lorry driver told her afterwards that he had got a good look at his face.

'And you've got the driver's name and other details?'

Lily nodded. 'He said I was to go straight to the police but when I told him about you he said that sounded all right. Didn't want to call you in the middle of the night,' she added, shame-faced as though the incident were her fault.

'The white car,' he began at last. 'Did you notice what type of car it was?'

Lily's face grew doubtful. 'Sorry,' she said. 'I'm not very good at cars. It was really big, though.'

Lorimer nodded then took out his pen and doodled on a napkin. 'See this?' he said, turning the paper towards her. 'Did the car have something like that on it?'

Lily squinted at the circle he had drawn, the lines creating the three segments of the Mercedes-Benz logo, then looked up at him and nodded. 'I think so,' she said at last.

'Can you describe the man, Lily?'

The girl bit her lip, looking uncertain for a moment.

'He was very tall. Bigger even than you,' she began. 'And he looked different. He was kind of good-looking,' she stopped then blushed, realising her gaffe. 'I-I didn't mean that,' she stammered. 'I mean you look nice and . . .'

'Lily,' Lorimer said gently. 'Let's concentrate on trying to picture exactly what he looked like, eh? Colour of hair, shape of face, that sort of thing.'

The girl nodded again. 'Sorry. He frightened me. Like one of those vampires you see on TV. They're dead handsome as well, aren't they?' Her blush deepened as she tried to extricate herself from the unintended insult.

'Take your time, now. Remember we can always get one of our clever folk back at headquarters to create an e-fit image from anything you and the lorry driver tell us.'

'Would I have to go there?' A worried expression crossed her face.

'Not if you don't want to,' Lorimer shrugged. 'But it might help us to trace this man.'

Lily looked into his eyes as though she were making a momentous decision.

'There's this woman called Doreen,' she began. 'She said I'd get money if I told her things.'

THE MORNING SIMPLY flew past as DC Knox tapped away at her computer keyboard, her eyes gleaming. Andie's Saunas were owned by a company purporting to be part of a health organisation, according to what she had found. Barbara had snickered at the blurb, wondering how healthy the punters felt after a quick shag. It was a registered company all right, but then any company that was trading had to give some account of itself for legal purposes. And the police were able to access such classified information pretty speedily if they wanted. Barbara scrolled down, wanting to see the names of the directors. She sat upright, suddenly, her lips parting in astonishment as she read the three names.

Vladimir Badica and Alexander Badica sprang out at her as though their names had been illuminated. 'Bad Vlad!' she exclaimed in a whisper. Then she nodded in sudden understanding as she read the first name on the list: *Andrea Badica, owner.*

'Andrea. *Andie's!*' Barbara sighed. It was one of the oldest tricks in the book. Put a company into the wife's name and if anything goes pear-shaped then the real owner gets off scot free. Or, she mused, maybe Bad Vlad had put it into this woman's name for tax purposes. But who was Alexander? The son, most probably, Barbara decided.

The owners didn't want poor Professor Brightman snooping around. Wonder what they've got to hide? Barbara asked herself, grabbing her jacket from the back of her chair. The woman's large face split into a grin.

A bit of nosing around the Badica place might just be in order.

LILY WAITED WHILE the tall man opposite finished his telephone call. There was a way out for her, he had explained, after Lily had admitted her age.

'They'll put me into one of these homes,' she'd cried. 'And I know what happens in these places,' she'd insisted, her eyes pleading with Lorimer. The policeman's face had remained impassive. Then he'd made that suggestion, told Lily about a kind man, a minister, who helped girls like her.

'If you wait here, I can ask Richard Allan to come and fetch you. He runs a place out in the country, near Stirling,' Lorimer told her. 'It's on a farm and there are other girls and women there too.'

'Is it a refuge?' Lily asked.

Lorimer nodded. 'It's a special sort of refuge,' he told her. 'Girls go there voluntarily to get over their problems.'

'You mean they get them to come off the drugs?' Lily's fifteen-year-old face was suddenly older and wiser in a way that Lorimer found disquieting.

'Yes, that can happen,' Lorimer said. 'They do all sorts of things to help,' he continued, trying hard not to look at his watch. It had taken a little while to establish trust with this girl and he was reluctant to leave her on her own now but the press pack would be assembling in Pitt Street and he needed to return there now.

'Okay,' Lorimer said, nodding briefly as he listened to the person on the other end of the line. 'I'll ask her.' Cupping his hand over the end of his mobile, Lorimer looked at Lily.

'Someone can be here in about an hour's time,' he told her. 'Will you wait here for them?'

The girl's face clouded. 'Can't you stay here with me?' she asked in a small voice.

Lorimer bit his lip. If he were to miss the daily meeting there would be hell to pay. But, on the other hand, if Lily wouldn't wait for Richard Allan or one of his team to arrive, then what would become of her? She was obviously still traumatised by the man twisting that scarf in his hands. Lorimer's mind flew back to the other two street women who had been strangled. If what he thought was correct, then Lily had had a lucky escape.

There would be a crowd of reporters gathering at HQ and here he was with one young girl, dithering about what he should do.

Words came to him, then. Something Richard Allan had said. Words that echoed lessons from his past when he had been too young to rebel against being sent to Sunday School. Hadn't the shepherd left all his flock to go and rescue one lost sheep?

He looked at the girl, her face turned up to his, and made his decision. Duncan Sutherland would just love to take the press conference, wouldn't he? And, besides, it might help to build bridges between them if he relinquished some of his responsibility to the red-haired officer.

'Okay, Lily. Just let me make another call, will you?'

The girl brightened immediately. 'And maybe we could go and see about that thingummy, the photo stuff you said . . .'

JIM BLACKBURN HAD made a careful study of page after page of faces in a pile of folders as well as looking at the database on a computer screen. As each image appeared, Jim had shaken his head.

'That's them all, Mr Blackburn.'

'You mean he's not in any of your files, then?' Jim said, a sense of desolation sweeping over him.

The officer's face remained impassive. 'If he has no record then your description is all the more important for us to find him, sir.'

Jim brightened at that. The last couple of hours had seemed interminable, his head swimming with the images, all the while trying so hard to keep the picture of that brute in his mind. 'So I can still help you, then?'

'Oh, yes, sir. Now let me explain how this works.'

'I HATE TO raise any hopes and call this a breakthrough,' Lorimer began. 'But I'm not one for believing in coincidences. Lily Winters was almost attacked by a man wielding a scarf, perhaps the same person who attacked and killed Miriam Lyons and Jenny Haslet. Of course, unless we find and apprehend this man we have no way of matching his DNA on our current database. But it is surely not a coincidence that he was at the end of the same lane where Carol Kirkpatrick and Tracey-Anne Geddes were both attacked. *And* he was driving a white Merc when he went after Lily Winters.'

'What's with the Mercedes?' a voice asked. 'Surely we're not looking for another link to the Pattison case?'

Lorimer stifled a sigh. Duncan Sutherland was always going to play devil's advocate, wasn't he?

'We could be doing just that, Duncan,' Lorimer admitted. 'If what Dr Brightman thinks is correct, then we have a scenario where a female perpetrator is picking off punters in a white Merc in revenge for the prostitute killings.'

'A prossie shooting three innocent men?' Sutherland's tone was full of derision.

'Perhaps not a street woman, but someone close to them,' Lorimer replied evenly. 'As we have seen, this series of murders has required an organised mind and a lucidity that would probably not be found in most of these women.'

'Too doped-up to see straight, never mind hit their target,' someone else added.

'Right,' Lorimer agreed. 'So we have two concurrent cases.' He curled his fist, sticking up his thumb. 'One, we see four prostitutes murdered in our city over a period of less than two years, all of them known to have worked the drag. Two,' he lifted his index finger, 'during that same period three men are killed in their Mercedes cars, one of them our deputy first minister.' Lorimer swept his gaze over the room of officers, each one focused on his words.

'Now for the third part of this series of coincidences,' he said quietly, raising a third finger. 'It had initially escaped our notice, but each of the women just happened to have been murdered on the night of a full moon.'

There was a rustling of diaries as some of the officers checked the date.

'Last night wasn't a full moon, sir,' Rita Livingstone said at last.

'No, it wasn't,' Lorimer said. 'But Lily wasn't murdered, was she?'

'Are you seriously wanting us to believe that some head case is out there baying to the moon?' Sutherland asked.

'It has been documented that patients suffering some types of mental disorder can be more seriously disturbed on the nights of a full moon.'

'Looks like we need to be careful next week, then,' another voice chimed in. 'Tuesday the seventh is the next one.'

Lorimer gave a start. That was the date of his fortieth birthday, an evening he had promised to keep free to spend with Maggie for the celebration dinner she'd arranged.

'Once we have circulated a photofit of this man,' he pointed to the picture behind him on the screen, 'there might not be any need for extra vigilance on that particular date. Maybe we'll have caught him by then,' he said grimly.

All eyes turned to the black and white image behind the detective superintendent. A man with dark hair and high Slavonic cheekbones stared back at them. It was not the picture of a monster some of them might have expected to see; in fact the technician responsible for creating the e-fit had shown the suspect's features to have a certain boyish charm. That, thought Lorimer, was one of the enduring things about chasing criminals: *many of them look just like you or me*, he continued to tell his junior officers. And this lot here knew that full well, even hardened cynics like Sutherland who saw junked-up street women as simply worthless and killers as evil monsters. The truth was usually far more subtle than that.

'What are you going to tell the press?' a voice asked and Lorimer turned to see DC Barbara Knox, her eyes bright and eager as though this was something that concerned her.

'I think we have to tread warily,' Lorimer answered. 'If we give them this photofit then that could drive the man underground.'

He turned back to point at the image. 'I think you'll agree that there is a slight hint of Eastern European about him. And we don't want him to head for those particular hills. So,' he went on, 'officers at all airports and seaports will be given this picture and a briefing, but the press will be kept out of it for now. If we fail to make any real headway, it might mean a nationwide alert, though. So, it's back to some of our original ground. If we are right, and this man was responsible for attacking Carol Kirkpatrick and Tracey-Anne Geddes, then someone in the city may have supplied him with the weapon he used. So, let's see if this picture can jog a memory or two.'

As LORIMER ENTERED his room he could hear a 'woooooo!' coming from the far end of the corridor, no doubt some clown (Sutherland?) mimicking a wolf howling at the moon.

He scratched his cheek thoughtfully. The Malmaison Hotel where he was to dine with Maggie wasn't too far away from headquarters. If he had a surveillance team organised for that night, would the man in the white Mercedes make an appearance? Or would it be better to have special officers focused on the CCTV cameras around the drag? Perhaps undercover police officers might be required to take the places of the Glasgow street women that night? These and other questions filled the detective superintendent's mind as he considered his strategy.

Chapter Thirty-four

'I NEED TO see you,' Barbara whispered into her mobile. 'Things have started to hot up at this end.'

'Meet you at our usual place. Seven o'clock?'

'I'll be there,' Barbara replied, breathing hard. The Starbucks cafe on Bothwell Street had become something of a howff for the two women; Barbara preferred to see it as a romantic location, since it had been the scene of their initial getting together, rather than a convenient stopping point between Pitt Street and Central Station.

She glanced at the clock on the office wall, calculating how long it would be before she saw Diana Yeats again, then sighing at the long hours between. Still, if she could finish all this stuff about Andie's Saunas and get on with the meatier details of the new lead, the time should fly by. It was strange, Barbara thought to herself, how this case had revolved around one man, Edward Pattison, but that now it had turned and twisted in ways she could never have envisaged. That, Barbara, is why you joined up, the detective constable reminded herself with a grin.

THE TALL DARK-HAIRED woman glided into a booth near the back of the crowded cafe, placing her satchel on a seat beside her. The place was busy enough to preclude any intimacy and noisy enough to drown out whatever it was the policewoman wanted to tell her.

Diana Yeats swallowed a mouthful of coffee and set down her espresso cup. The night when she had almost got on the Big Blue Bus had given her plenty to think about, not least a persistent image of that tall man with the piercing blue eyes. Diana shivered. She had come so close to the very man who wanted to hunt her down. Yet perhaps it was the killer of the street women who had haunted his thoughts too, not just the person who had shot dead three punters in their fancy white cars.

She saw Barbara through the plate glass window, hurrying along to the entrance, her coat flapping untidily around her, revealing her flabby figure. The new hairstyle had only served to emphasise those chubby cheeks and layers of flesh beneath her chin and to Diana it only underlined the girl's desire to make an impression. That was all to the good, she thought. She'd caught her now, like a greedy fish mouthing its way towards a tasty fly and DC Knox was being slowly but surely reeled in.

'Hi.' Barbara sat down beside her on the leather banquette, plonking a chaste kiss on Diana's cheek.

Resisting the urge to rub it off, Diana turned to her and smiled. 'Lovely to see you, darling. Had a good day?'

Barbara felt a rush of pleasure at those words. 'Wait till I tell you . . .' she began.

Diana placed one finger to her lips then glanced around as though to check if anyone was listening to their conversation, a simple enough ruse to heighten the cloak-and-dagger atmosphere that this policewoman loved.

Giving the girl a nod, Diana smiled reassuringly. 'Right, what is it you want to tell me?'

BARBARA KNOX SLAMMED the door of the flat behind her. Why was it that Diana could make her feel as though something nice was about to happen and then just as quickly let her down? A creeping suspicion entered the woman's mind as she tore off her coat and flung it at the hall stand, missing completely. Leaving it where it lay in a crumpled heap, Barbara stomped into her tiny kitchen and opened a cupboard on the wall. She'd bought the bottle of red in the hope of entertaining Diana here again one night, but since that first time it simply hadn't happened. Was Diana Yeats (or whatever her real name was) just using her for what she could get?

Barbara wasn't so besotted that she hadn't had some doubts already. Googling the woman's name had resulted in finding just one elderly lady on Britain's south coast, but then, she'd reminded herself, she had never expected to find a website for a freelance reporter who worked undercover.

Uncorking the wine, Barbara poured herself a good measure into one of the crystal glasses she'd bought specially. It was a Friday night and half the city would be out having fun while she was resigned to yet another night of solitude. Even her visit to Badica's car hire place had been a waste of time; it had been all closed up for lunch with nobody in reception.

Twenty minutes later the bottle was more than half empty and Barbara's view of the world was in accord with that. She'd been taken for a mug. She'd given away secret information to a reporter, and with it possibly her entire career. And for what: a few hours of sex and the promise of more? Tears of frustration and rage coursed down her cheeks. She, who had congratulated herself on being such a good judge of character, had been conned good and proper.

Or had she? Barbara swallowed another mouthful of the Merlot. Was Diana perhaps being absolutely straight with her? She shook her head, bitterness showing in lines around her mouth. Why would a classy female like Diana choose to consort with a fat slob like Barbara Knox if it were not for what she could get out of her? Yet hadn't she picked her up in conversation before she had any inkling of Barbara's profession, never mind the link to the Pattison case? As she poured another glass of wine, letting some of it splash onto the carpet beside her, Barbara simply could not make up her mind.

FRIDAY NIGHT IN the city was divided into several stages, depending on age and social status. First, the rush-hour trains would be full of men and women anxious to be free of their working week, some of them ready for a weekend at home, others already working out what to wear before returning to the town for a night out. Later, two different generations would sometimes collide between the railway platforms, middle-aged theatre goers heading for home just as a crowd of young things arrived. The girls were always dressed for a big night in sparkling outfits and impossibly high heels that would have to be carried home later after hours of dancing, bare feet oblivious to the cold pavements at the taxi rank.

This particular Friday the Glasgow pubs were full to overflowing with a raucous clientele, Irish rugby supporters making their presence felt through song and banter before the next day's big event at Murrayfield Stadium. There would be plenty of sore heads by the morning, but these would clear in the cold Edinburgh air as supporters gathered to see the first game of the Six Nations tournament. Lorimer smiled as he listened to the Irish voices declare that this player or that was *really no good, no good at all*, and that *their chances of winning were slim to none*. His own love of the game had lasted long past school days but was confined nowadays to watching these national battles on television, only occasionally allowing himself a day away in the east.

'Don't think they really mean it, do you?' he asked Solly as he lifted the whisky glass to his lips.

'I can see that they would like to beat Scotland,' Solly replied. 'And telling themselves it is impossible will only heighten their pleasure once they do.'

Lorimer nodded. Solly was interested in the human and sociological behaviour of these Irishmen rather than the rugby itself. Still, it was a rare interlude for the two men, meeting for a drink after work even if Solly's tipple was a half pint of cranberry juice with a slice of lime bobbing on its surface.

Don't mention the party! Rosie had warned him before he had left the flat, knowing her husband's tendency to forget such things. And so far he had remembered not to utter a single word about it, careful to avoid any mention of his friend's fortieth birthday. It was the sort of thing that the women were more likely to discuss, Solly had told his wife, and the subject had not come up once during their time in the pub. Instead the psychologist had turned the conversation from rugby and human expectations to the puzzle surrounding his visit to the two saunas.

'If they're hiding something it's a load of girls upstairs,' Lorimer laughed. 'Or maybe you simply frightened the guy in Partick. Maybe he'd never met a real psychologist before,' he joked.

'There's something that still bothers me,' Solly went on. 'If Jenny and Miriam had been given work there one would have assumed that they would have been safe from any predator, yes?'

'Maybe,' Lorimer replied. 'That would depend on the level of care shown to the girls. Helen James reckoned that getting them all off the streets was a good start.'

'Have you told her about the man who tried to attack Lily?'

Lorimer nodded. 'The picture is being circulated amongst the girls out on the drag over this weekend as well as in the Robertson Street drop-in centre. It was a calculated risk,' he added as Solly's bushy eyebrows rose in surprise.

'You don't think any of them will blab to the papers?'

'As I said, it's a risk I was prepared to take. Anyhow, the press have to clear it with us before they print a single word, never mind something as highly sensitive as that.'

'And you're going to set up your officers for Tuesday night?'

Lorimer nodded again. 'Aye,' he gave a rueful grin. 'My big four-o.' He laughed and shook his head. 'Maggie's got me on a date that night and I can't disappoint her.'

Solly ducked his head and rummaged in his coat pocket, bringing out a large white handkerchief to blow his nose. It was a simple enough ruse to cover up any hint that he knew what Maggie Lorimer was really up to. The policeman was good at reading anybody's body language and Solly knew he had to keep one step ahead if he was to avoid giving the game away.

'Coming down with a cold?'

'No, probably just all the dust in here,' Solly answered, shrugging his shoulders.

The pub suddenly erupted as one voice raised in a chorus of 'The Irish Rover' was joined by several others and Solly smiled to see Lorimer beginning to mouth the words, his head turned away to look at the crowd of singers. As a Londoner he should feel like an outsider but years of living in Glasgow had given Solly a feeling of kinship with these people, gathered together; Celts united in song who would only be divided by eighty minutes on the rugby field before heading for the pubs once more, the afterglow of success or failure bringing the supporters together again. Tonight was all about the thrill of anticipation, tomorrow the tone would be one of telling over and over what had taken place at Murrayfield and putting to rights any poor play shown as though each and every one of the men talking was a seasoned rugby coach.

Was that how the undercover officers felt as they waited for the next full moon to rise over the Glasgow rooftops? Solly wondered. Was there a sense of camaraderie, all of them hoping fervently to trap this man who had wreaked such havoc in their city? He had worked on several cases now with Lorimer but this was the first time he had felt a bit adrift, not really a part of the whole set-up. Yes, he had been trying to create a profile of a killer, yes he had come up with some suggestions that were even now being acted upon, but there was not the same sense of being part of a team at Pitt Street as there had been in Lorimer's previous division. And he was certain that the detective superintendent felt it too.

'What will happen to you when they wind up the unit?' he asked, but Lorimer was in full song now and did not hear the psychologist's question.

THE HOTEL WAS eerily quiet tonight, most of the staff having left earlier in the evening, as the woman in the darkened booth sat drinking her second glass of Pinot Grigio. The food had been exquisite, the room where she slept becoming almost like home, but it would soon be time to leave here for good and as she contemplated her uncertain future, the woman who had called herself Diana Yeats wondered just what would happen four nights from now. She would check out on Wednesday morning, she decided, and return home to pack. A new beginning was called for, somewhere far from Scotland, far from all the memories that had haunted her for too long now. She had played with Barbara, hinting at a trip to Mauritius, so perhaps that thought could be translated into a plan of action. Tomorrow, she promised herself, tomorrow she would take her passport and buy tickets, but only for herself. There would be no lady in her company this time, she knew, just the shadow of a girl whose murder she was destined to avenge.

The barman had glanced her way a few times already, waiting to see if she wanted anything else, but Diana had studiously avoided his eye, contenting herself with the dark green bottle that sat at an angle in its ice bucket. If only he knew, the woman smiled to herself. How had she appeared to them? A sophisticated businesswoman, probably? Certainly not a person who posed any sort of threat.

On Tuesday she would dress in her trashy clothes for the very last time, take her silvery-blue pistol, and gun down the monster who had taken away the only love of her life.

She had been surprised and annoyed that it had taken the policewoman to point out the dates of the women's deaths to her: four full moons suggesting some maddened creature fulfilling his bloodlust in the dark. How could she, who was so meticulous in other ways, have failed to notice that piece of information? How could *they* have failed to see that until now? Her grip tightened on the stem of her wine glass as she cursed the police and their ineptitude. Well, she was forewarned now and had also been given the nod that several of the street women would be officers in disguise. But it was something else that Barbara Knox had told her that made the woman twirl her glass around and around, smiling as though she was still one step ahead of the police. If what she thought was true, then no white Mercedes would circle the drag on the next full moon. Its driver would have no need to drive round and round the square when she would be ready and waiting for him.

Chapter Thirty-five

SACHA STOOD IN the doorway, listening hard. The house seemed to be listening back, waiting for him to make the slightest sound. His uncle and aunt had gone to bed hours ago and Sacha had heard them snoring as he'd passed their room. Light from the moon shone down through the landing window, a cold brightness that flooded across the stair carpet, silvering the metal stair rods as he crept down to the hall.

They had no idea about his nocturnal wanderings, though he knew that his uncle Vladimir had kept a watchful eye on him for the first few weeks after his arrival in the city. That was more than two years ago and Sacha was one of the family now, though sometimes he felt that they treated him more like a family pet that had a wayward disposition and had to be guarded with care.

The big man padded across the remaining length of hallway and pushed open the door of the lounge. The armoury was located through a panelled archway at the far end of the room and through another door, but first he had to make his way across this place without knocking into any of the furniture or sending one of Andrea's precious ornaments tumbling to the floor. One small sound and his aunt might come pattering down the stairs, her fear of burglars no doubt fuelled by his uncle's refusal to insure all her stupid china figurines. Once he had asked about the antique weapons: did Uncle Vlad have any idea of their worth? But Vladimir Badica had shaken his head as if such a question was not to be asked. They were, he told Sacha coldly, of *historic* value, as though any mention of a price tag on his collection was somehow vulgar.

To Sacha, the weapons meant more than money or history. As he stood before the glass case he peered through the gloom to make out each and every different sword and scimitar: each piece was endowed with a magic that only one who had held and wielded the weapon could understand. After each of the executions, he had wiped the blades clean, careful to ensure that there was not a single mark left on blade or heft, before returning them to the display case. It was almost time to choose again, he thought, reaching up to unfasten the catch that held them behind the glass. It would be the third time he had chosen one of these special instruments of death. Three was a significant number, he knew, though what it truly meant was hidden somewhere beyond his understanding. And if he succeeded in vanquishing another of these females, then his blood count would have risen to ten, a number that made him tingle with apprehension and delight.

They were easy prey, these feeble creatures waiting for him in the darkness, standing on the edge of pavements, teetering in their thin-heeled shoes. He remembered how their heads would bend forwards like anxious birds to peer into his wonderful car, willing him to stop for them and barter their stricken bodies for his hard-earned cash.

It gleamed out at him as the case door swung open, a blade so magnificent that for a moment Sacha wondered why he had not chosen it before. As his fingers closed over the hilt, he realised that it was something he had not seen before. Uncle Vlad must have made a recent purchase, possibly in the wake of trading in the one that had been his very favourite of all the white sports cars. The sabre was heavy as he lifted it from its place against the velvet back cloth and he weighed it carefully in both hands. A cavalry sword, he decided, a Hungarian *szablya*, perhaps, gazing at all that intricate tooling on its heft. The curved blade had a single cutting edge, designed to cut a swathe through the enemy as the weapon was raised above the head of a galloping horse. Sacha could hear the screams of his adversaries as he sliced through them, the whinnying of his steed as he surged against the tide of bodies coming at him.

Then the moment passed and he was stood there in the darkness, the sabre in his right hand, no sounds but his own breath and the blood ringing in his ears.

Carefully, reverently, he replaced the weapon and nodded his approbation. His choice was made. Now all he needed was a new victim.

Chapter Thirty-six

IT MIGHT BE her day off, but Barbara Knox was up bright and early, slicking fingers through her gelled hair after a quick shower. The radio was playing some old cheesy pop tune and Barbara found herself singing along, her mood lighter now that her decision had been made. She'd checked and Sundays were days when the car hire place would be open to the public. And why not pay it a little visit, just on the off-chance that she might stumble across some new information. Her smile broadened as she imagined Lorimer's face when she presented him with the facts and figures on Monday morning. Wouldn't that just make Sutherland's eyes water! She'd sensed from the off that the DI had her down as no more than a filing clerk. Now she'd show him and all the rest that DC Knox was a force to be reckoned with.

Barbara's smile dropped a little as she checked her mobile for any text messages but there were none. She flipped the phone shut and made a mental note to delete Diana's number. Perhaps it was time to admit that she was finished with playing the woman's games. In the clear light of day it was easier to see how she had allowed her judgement to be clouded by a collision of fantasy and reality. Today she would begin afresh, putting the job first.

Her hand reached out to switch off the radio and the abrupt cessation of noise left the flat empty and suddenly cold. Barbara blinked once, listening to the distant sounds of traffic that emphasised just how quiet it was in the flat. It was *peaceful*, she persuaded herself. She had space to do her own thing, didn't she? But it's *lonely*, a small voice answered her back from deep inside. Ignoring the voice, Barbara picked up her overcoat from where it had fallen two nights ago, gave it a quick brush and pulled it on.

Outside a hard frost had formed and Barbara took extra care stepping down the last few steps from the entrance to the block of flats where she lived. There was no direct route to Badica's car hire premises and so she would have to take a train and a bus to get there, more than an hour's journey on this freezing morning. Should she have called for a taxi, she wondered, shivering as her breath made puffy clouds like a cartoon dragon's smoke in front of her face.

As though in answer to her thoughts she caught sight of a local cab coming to a halt across the busy main road, its passenger pausing to pay the driver.

Barbara reached the opposite kerb just as the Skoda began to move off but then the driver clocked her waving hand in his rearview mirror and stopped once more.

'Glasgow, please,' she gasped, her chest hurting from the dash to reach the cab. 'Badica's car hire, Argyll Street. Do you know it?'

'Naw, whit end's it at?' the driver asked and Barbara told him, settling back against the back passenger seat, rummaging under her left side for the safety belt.

THE CAR HIRE was situated on a corner of Argyll Street behind Dumbarton Road, not far from the Kelvingrove Art Galleries and Museum where Barbara had been taken as a kid on several school trips. The museum had been closed for renovation some years back and Barbara had always meant to see the new layout that had been so widely publicised. Maybe she could go there afterwards, get a bite to eat in the wee snack bar on the ground floor, if it was still there. The very thought of a hot cup of coffee and a sticky bun cheered her as she stepped out of the cab and stood in front of the white painted building.

There was no name above the main door, simply a neon sign that read LUXURY CARS FOR HIRE. The premises extended out on two sides; one was a glass-fronted showroom with just a few cars to be seen, the other held a blank wall with a metal-shuttered door and Barbara guessed that the messy business of servicing and maintaining the cars went on behind this area, out of the public's sight.

Barbara strolled past the window, taking note of the cars gleaming in a morning sun that held more brightness than warmth. There was a lovely dove-grey Mercedes and, had Barbara been a genuine customer, this was the car she'd have hired for herself, its sleek lines making her sigh with sheer pleasure. The others were classy enough, she supposed; another Merc, the sort of colour the manufacturer probably termed as gold, and a neat little Audi cabriolet in a dishy shade of ice blue. Further back were a couple of Mercedes Sports, neither of which was white, Barbara noticed, and a graphite-coloured Porsche.

Pushing open the main door, Barbara saw that while the door into the showroom was made of glass, all the rest of the offices were rather old-fashioned, solid doors and dark wood panelling giving the place a rather shabby appearance, as though this part of the business didn't really matter. The cars spoke for themselves, Barbara supposed, and it wasn't as though they were trying to sell them, after all. Anyone patronising this place would have already decided they wanted a hire car. Probably didn't even come themselves, just sent their office minions to collect one for them.

'Can I help you?' A young girl with curly blonde hair wrapped up in a bandeau was sitting behind the desk, a copy of *OK* magazine propped in front of her.

'I was wondering about car hire,' Barbara began.

'Well, you've come to the right place,' the girl replied dryly and gave her a smile. 'Is it for a wedding?'

Barbara thought quickly. A wedding would require a white car, wouldn't it?

'Yes,' she said. 'Can you show me anything?'

'Here's our brochure, and this is the current price list,' the girl said, picking up a couple of leaflets from a stand on her desk that Barbara had already noticed.

'Oh.' Barbara took them in her podgy hand, then flicked through the glossy leaflet until she came to a page where bridal couples posed in front of a selection of cars. 'Can I actually get to see one like that?' she asked, pointing to a white Mercedes.

'If you like,' the girl replied brightly. 'Just let me put a call through to the garage and I'll have somebody show you round.'

She picked up the telephone and pressed a number. 'Sacha, there's a customer here to see wedding cars. Can she come down to the garage? Okay. Fine. I'll let her know.'

The girl put down the phone and smiled again at Barbara. 'He won't be long. Just take a seat over there and the mechanic will be with you in about ten minutes. Would you like a coffee?' she added, nodding at a machine beside a long table. 'It's not bad stuff. I brought it in myself yesterday morning, I only work weekends here,' she rattled on, already moving towards the coffee machine and pulling a cup and saucer from a rack above the table.

'Thanks,' Barbara replied, her mind working swiftly. If this girl was only a weekend worker, then did she know much about the entire business? Maybe it was time to be a nosey parker, before the man downstairs took her to see the cars.

'Who owns this place?' she asked, stirring a sachet of brown sugar into her coffee.

'Oh, it's a family-run place,' the girl answered. 'Mr Badica and his family own it. He's Romanian, you know. Has a big house over in Bearsden, apparently. Dead rich,' her voice fell to a whisper as the girl shared the gossip. 'Seems he's got quite a few business interests around the city,' she told Barbara, who nodded, wide eyed, pretending to be impressed.

'When's your wedding?' the girl went on and Barbara spluttered as she sipped the hot coffee.

'Oh,' she improvised, 'I'm just the bridesmaid.'

'I thought it was the groom who traditionally looked after the cars side of things,' the girl went on.

'I'm his sister,' Barbara continued, making it all up as she went along. 'He's in the Forces.'

'Oh, right. So do you all have a date?'

'September twenty-ninth,' Barbara said, remembering her own birthday was to fall on a Saturday this year.

'Did you see that wedding last week . . .?' The girl drifted back to the desk then returned with the magazine open at the centre page. 'Here, aren't they lovely!'

Barbara peered at the froth and frilliness of a pop star's over-the-top nuptial celebrations, trying to conceal her disgust.

'Oh, lovely,' she lied, then, as a door opened beside her, she dropped the magazine into the girl's hands, her mouth open in a moment of unconcealed astonishment.

There, wiping his hands on a piece of rag, stood a huge man in ochre-coloured overalls.

Barbara looked up, her eyes travelling to his face, noting the triangular shaped cheekbones and the jaw that tapered sharply to a small, firm chin. It was the same face that had been so recently thrown up on a screen back at police headquarters. For a moment he met her gaze.

'Gorgeous, isn't he?' the girl whispered behind her hand as she retrieved the magazine, then took her place behind the desk once more as Barbara, her heart beating hard in her chest, followed the man dumbly down a flight of steps that led to a cavernous base-ment garage.

Chapter Thirty-seven

SUNDAY AFTERNOONS IN Kelvingrove Park were becoming something of a regular event, Solly thought, pushing the pram along the path, Rosie walking quietly by his side. Abigail was sleeping now, the motion from the pram having soothed her at last, and the two parents were enjoying a little respite from the baby's crying. It had not been a good Saturday night. Abby had woken them both around midnight and, despite feeds and changes of nappies, she had wailed incessantly for hours, Solly and Rosie taking turns to walk her up and down, wearied and anxious, looking for any signs that would explain the child's malaise. One little red cheek had Rosie suggesting that the baby might have begun teething, but since it was impossible to ask Abigail herself, Solly had simply nodded, letting his wife rub some gel on the little one's gums.

Now they were walking side by side and it was a considerable relief to them both that the baby was sleeping soundly.

'Remember when we used to go over there for breakfast?' Rosie murmured, pointing at a riverside cafe.

Solly nodded. The carefree days when they had risen late at weekends and made the day their own seemed like another life altogether. Rosie's tone was wistful and he knew that, just for a moment, she longed for that freedom again.

'We can all go when she's a bit older,' he suggested gently, taking one hand off the handle of the pram to reach out and squeeze his wife's gloved hand.

Rosie smiled and nodded. 'Aye, if she *gets* to be a bit older,' she threatened, jokingly. Then her face took on a tenderness that never failed to touch Solly's heart. 'Poor wee mite,' she whispered, 'no wonder she's so sound; must be as tired as we are by now.'

They continued to walk along the path, heading in their usual direction towards the pond where a resident grey heron could usually be found.

'Look,' Rosie said. 'The bird man. He's got a load of people with him today.'

As they drew nearer, they could see the tall, slim figure of a man surrounded by a couple of families, all looking up as he spoke to them about the different birds in the park. As Solly and Rosie slowed down, the bird man took out a tin of seed then placed a little into the hands of each of the children. They watched and waited as the children stretched out their palms, standing stock still offering the seed to any little birds that might be brave enough to venture from their perches in the bushes and trees that surrounded the pond.

Sure enough, a great tit appeared, landed on one of the girls' hands, pecked then flew off again. A low murmur of pleasure came from the families and Solly and Rosie exchanged glances.

'That'll be us one of these days,' Solly murmured, moving past the little group. Rosie caught his arm and gave him a hug. Things might have changed for ever with the arrival of their daughter in their lives but there was so much to look forward to and Abby wouldn't always be a little baby whose every need seemed a mystery to him. As he glanced back at the families, Solly saw the little girl who had fed the bird taking her father's hand and smiling up at him. That would be him, one day, he thought again. And the child's innocence gladdened his heart.

Smiling still as they made their way along the narrow path, Solly's mind was blissfully free from any thought of the police cases that had commanded so much of his time and energy.

There was no premonition of danger, no hint on this peaceful Sunday afternoon that the man whose profile he had helped develop was at this very moment threatening the life of another young woman.

BARBARA WOKE, WONDERING why she felt so thirsty and why everything hurt so much. Just as the darkness refused to turn to light, Barbara remembered where she was. It was at that same moment her bladder decided to release its contents, warmth flooding her trousers and with it came a sense of helplessness that made her weep. Then the events of the Sunday afternoon began to come back to her.

Stepping down into the chilled interior of that garage space, everything in the detective constable's head had screamed out that she should turn around, call this in at once and wait for backup. She had been trained to follow certain procedures when facing a potentially dangerous situation. Hadn't she? So why had she meekly followed the suspect down to the basement? Why had she asked such obviously pointed questions?

He'd sussed her pretty quickly for a cop, hadn't he? Yet there were some moments that Barbara simply could not remember, like that blow to her head as she'd turned away, still pretending to examine the white Mercedes car. Now she was closer to that vehicle than she had ever wanted to be, her body crushed into its boot, legs and arms fastened tightly, duct tape preventing her from crying out. Barbara's head throbbed as she tried to make out any sounds that could give her a clue as to where she was being held captive, but there were none.

The cold was intense and her body, already rigid from its enforced position in the car boot, was probably suffering from a mild case of hypothermia. Wetting herself wouldn't help any, either, she thought gloomily. Was she still in the garage then? Not knowing how long she had lain unconscious in the dark made Barbara unsure whether it was still Sunday or not. The lack of any noise from the premises upstairs suggested it could be night-time. She tried to remember if the opening times had been listed anywhere on the front door but thinking only made her head ache and she gave up, concentrating instead on her imme-diate needs. She wanted desperately to get out of her enforced imprisonment. And her throat ached with thirst. How long ago had she drunk that coffee in the reception area? It was impossible to tell.

For a moment Barbara considered her situation.

Why was she still alive, trussed up like a big fat turkey? The mechanic had bumped off several women with impunity, hadn't he? So why spare a single policewoman, especially when Barbara had posed a threat to him? Did he imagine that one more corpse would change his life sentence? Perhaps, she thought. Maybe he reckoned that killing a cop would bring down the whole weight of the law upon him.

Cling to that thought, she told herself, blinking away the tears beginning to form in the corners of her eyes. *Don't give in to despair.*

She recalled the intensity of those dark eyes boring into her own. He had known in an instant that the policewoman had identified him.

Would he already have fled the country? she wondered. Or, a more hideous thought, was he going to come back for her?

Chapter Thirty-eight

THE SCHOOL BELL rang out and several hundred pairs of feet clattered up stairs and through corridors, filling the classrooms with a more subdued chatter now that they were in the presence of their form teachers. Maggie Lorimer looked up and smiled as her sixth years trooped in, some of them yawning as they slumped into their places. There was only one week left until half term and this lot looked as though they needed the break. There was going to be a Valentine's disco for the junior school, something that had elicited a lot of excitement from her first years, but this lot were much too sophisticated for that sort of thing, she thought with a pang as she ticked off their names on her register.

Looking around the room, Maggie saw young men and women, poised to fly off to new beginnings in just a few short months. She'd known most of them as eager twelve-year-olds, kids who had shared so much of their lives with their form teacher, some of them treating her almost as a surrogate mum. Would any of the girls come back to visit once their school days were over? Or would they forget all about Mrs Lorimer and the secrets they had told her, the boys they'd cried over? She didn't expect the boys to keep in touch. Boys usually didn't and that was the way it was.

As the bell rang once again for the start of the first lesson, Maggie's sixth years left the room, some giving her a tired smile and a nod, acknowledging the beginning of another school week. Maggie brightened and smiled back. It was as though they were suddenly aware of her as a person rather than as a teacher. Well, that was life, wasn't it? The kids came and went, hopefully better equipped to face the big, bad world, and then a new lot would arrive after the summer, kids who were at present the big boys and girls of primary seven but who would be small fry all over again once they'd entered the gates of Muirpark Secondary.

Maggie's smile deepened. Life wasn't too bad, was it? Tomorrow she would have the pleasure of surprising her husband for his birthday. Wednesday might see her far more tired and jaded than her sixth years on a Monday morning but it was going to be well worth it to see Bill's face when the lights went up and he saw all his friends there in the restaurant. She shivered suddenly. He would like it, wouldn't he? And surely nothing would happen to spoil the evening?

THE SOUND OF the boot opening woke Barbara from a confused dream where she was being held underwater. Her eyes flew open, blinking against the artificial light but just at that moment the boot slammed shut and she was confined to darkness once more.

As the noise of the engine began Barbara could hear another sound, a grating metallic hum that could only be the garage shutters sliding upwards. Then her whole body was jolted sideways as the car turned and moved off.

Heart thumping, Barbara struggled against her bonds once again, panic lending her renewed strength. If she could only get her hands free, reach the mobile phone that was zipped inside her man-sized coat pocket then maybe someone would come to her rescue.

The big man had secured her wrists with plastic binding tapes, the sort that were used for packing newspapers or by thieves getting into cars, and the more Barbara had struggled against them the deeper they had cut into her flesh. Now she could feel the slipperiness of blood making further struggle useless. Tears began to roll down the policewoman's face. If she wasn't so bloody fat, then perhaps she'd have been able to slither out of her bonds. A fleeting memory of Diana's slim fingers came to her mind and the tears fell hotly against her cheeks. Where was the woman now? Had she been missed over the weekend or had Diana Yeats consigned Barbara to the past as they all did eventually?

'Tom, where's Knox?'

'Don't know. Haven't seen her this morning.'

'But she's always in early.'

'Well, you know the drill. Give her a call on her home number,' Tom Armstrong replied.

'Right.'

DI Monica Proctor riffled through the pages of personnel files until she came to a small section under K. Picking up the nearest telephone, the DI dialled her colleague's home number. She listened to the ringtone for a few moments then an automated voice invited her to leave a message.

'Barbara, DI Proctor here. Are you okay? Call in and let us know if you're sick, will you? Thanks.'

Monica Proctor put the phone back down, frowning. DC Knox was punctilious about being at her desk before anyone else. Annoying as her over-efficiency could sometimes be, the fact remained that it was quite out of character for the girl not to let her workplace know if she was unwell. Monica studied the paper again. She'd try Barbara's mobile, just in case there had been some major hold up en route to work. But here again there was no answer and the DI felt a sudden sense of disquiet.

'Tom, there's no reply from either her landline or her mobile. I don't like it,' Monica said slowly, making DI Armstrong turn in his chair and stare at her.

'D'you want me to make calls round the local hospitals? She lived alone, didn't she?'

Monica shrugged. 'Don't know. She was one of Mumby's lot. Don't know much about her at all.'

'She's a car nut,' DS Martin Gray offered. 'We went up to see the start of the rally a wee while ago. Don't know much else about her, except . . .' He bit his lip as he let the rest of his words tail off. Barbara's sexuality wasn't a matter for discussion but they had all guessed that the detective constable had no interest in men.

'Any family or girlfriend we should know about?' DI Proctor asked briskly.

'Sorry, can't help you there. She's a very private sort of person,' he added thoughtfully. 'Takes her work terribly seriously. Don't know if she ever has much time for any fun.'

'Well, I think we should ring round the hospitals. See if she's been admitted anywhere in the Glasgow area, maybe start with the Royal Alexandra. That's the nearest to where she lives, isn't it?'

As Detective Superintendent Lorimer scrutinised the latest memo from the deputy chief constable he shook his head, wondering at the way a simple decision could affect so many people's lives. Politics had never been his strong suit and he had expected his position of greater authority to carry some sort of weight when it came to deciding the future of his officers. But now that he had been in this job a few weeks, Lorimer could see that he was entirely wrong about that.

What was it that 'Desiderata' said? Something about there always being greater and lesser peoples than yourself? He still hadn't had time to fix his pictures to the wall and the framed prayer sat with all the rest of his stuff in a box behind the office door. He wasn't a conventionally religious man, Lorimer would admit to anyone who asked, but 'Desiderata' had the sort of wisdom that spoke to any sort of heart.

He sighed, wondering when he ought to call a staff meeting. They were all up to high doh right now, preparing for the surveillance operation tomorrow night. It wasn't the time to drop a bombshell like this in their midst, was it? In less than two months all of them would be deployed into different divisions throughout Strathclyde, with the options of selecting a post in another force if it could be managed. Joyce Rogers had warned him that the squad might be disbanded within the year but even she had admitted a degree of surprise at the news when he'd called her this morning.

It's been taken out of our hands, Lorimer, she'd told him. *All to do with streamlining. It's the in word, apparently.* Lorimer had been only slightly mollified to hear the disgust in her voice.

So, here he was on this Monday morning, with the notification that the officers who had worked their butts off in recent weeks were to come off whatever case they were working on and leave Pitt Street in a measly eight weeks' time. Only Rita Livingstone would be kept here, intelligence being an integral part of the set-up at headquarters.

And he hadn't come anywhere near solving this damned case, he thought, clenching his teeth together.

'Sir?'

Lorimer turned as the door was knocked and as he caught sight of DI Proctor, his hand slipped the memo under another set of papers.

'It's about DC Knox, sir,' his DI began.

BARBARA LAY AS still as the motion from the car allowed, her teeth gnawing against the duct tape. Breathing was becoming more difficult, especially as the smell of exhaust fumes mingled with the stink from her own urine was beginning to make her feel nauseous. She had managed to grip a bit of the tape between her teeth and could feel an edge of something as she chewed. Her tongue probed, examining, and then she experienced a small moment of triumph as it penetrated the tape completely.

Blowing her breath out through the tiny hole felt like a major achievement. But there was still so much to do, she thought, moving her wrists feebly against their bonds. Her head ached and Barbara knew she must be dehydrated by now. How long was it a human could carry on without water? She cursed softly, thinking of the last drink she'd had back at the garage.

It was only a matter of time before her various organs began to shut down, the policewoman knew. But the car was still on the move, Badica at its wheel, so perhaps her fate was to be decided sooner than that.

The sound of her mobile ringing in the inside pocket of her coat made Barbara freeze for an instant. Would he hear the ringtone? Guess that someone was trying to locate her? She held her breath as the noise of the engine and the rattle as the car passed over yet another pothole drowned out the sound of her phone. For a moment her thoughts raced. If this was Monday morning then perhaps she had already been missed? Maybe at this very moment officers were out combing the countryside for her.

As the car turned a sharp bend Barbara sensed that they were climbing upwards into hill country, her body rolling back against the edge of the boot. She had tried to make out whereabouts they were going after the car had left the confines of the garage but it had been hopeless. Stops and starts that might have signalled traffic lights, the thunderous noise of lorries (on a motorway?) and the whine of vehicles passing them by had given way to the sound of the Mercedes' engine note alone and Barbara guessed that they had left the city behind.

When the car stopped abruptly, she felt her whole body being jolted against the sides of the boot. Then she heard the sound of footsteps on gravel and at last the boot door was raised and a sudden light flooded onto her face.

Barbara squeezed her eyes shut, too terrified to look at the man who bent over her.

With an exclamation of disgust he pulled her roughly from the boot, hauling her by the binding tapes so that she cried out as they bit further into the flesh around her wrists.

Then her feet were being dragged along the ground and Barbara felt the freezing air around her and heard the incongruous note of a robin shrilling nearby.

As her head hit the frozen ground Barbara thought for a moment that he was going to leave her there. But the thought was short-lived as blow after blow rained down on her unresisting body.

She heard the sickening crunch of metal on bone as something struck her bare wrists but the gasping moan was drowned out by her attacker's sudden yell.

She couldn't understand the language but there was no mistaking the tone of venom.

The words were scarcely out of his mouth when the man's boot made contact with her back and then she was rolling down and down, pain coursing through every bit of her body as she thudded over tussocks of frosty grass and sharp stones that bruised her face and hands.

The thorn tree that broke her fall was halfway down a steep gully so full of litter that the policewoman's body would look like just more rubbish left by fly-tippers.

Her head pounding, Barbara heard the car door slam somewhere in the distance then the noise of the Mercedes' engine became quieter and quieter until it disappeared completely. As she lay there, pinned against the trunk of the tree, her eyes closed against the cold skies.

The vagrant robin called fretfully from a neighbouring bush but there was no listening ear to hear his song.

'WHERE THE HELL is she?' DI Proctor cursed under her breath. The telephone call to Mr and Mrs Knox had not helped in the slightest and had only caused Barbara's mother to become alarmed for her daughter's safety.

'Any luck?' Tom Armstrong leaned against the door jamb, his brow furrowed in concern.

'Nope. And still no reply from her landline or her mobile. Think we'll have to put her door in by the looks of it. Her folks don't have a spare key and didn't know of any neighbour who would have one.'

'Want me to call Mill Street, see if they can spare a couple of their heavies?'

Monica shook her head. 'No. Lorimer wants this kept in-house for now. Besides, I'd like to go over there myself. See if she's okay.'

'Right. Give me a minute to see if Duncan's around. Between the pair of us we'll break the door down, no bother,' Armstrong assured her.

A SMALL WOMAN carrying heavy shopping bags and coughing badly was trudging up the flight of stairs in front of the three officers as they entered the block of flats where Barbara lived. Monica looked questioningly at the men. Should they ask the wee wifie if she knew DC Knox? Armstrong caught her look but shook his head and they fell back a little against the first turn of the stairs to let the woman get ahead of them and into her own flat. Monica sighed. This was a delicate affair: if Barbara was unwell and inside her flat she'd be affronted if they caused a fuss. The noise of a door being put in would echo loudly in the frosty air and no doubt bring neighbours running.

'Okay,' Sutherland whispered. 'Next floor up and to the right.'

Barbara's door was a plain wooden one with a brass knob, and on the wall to the left was a clear plastic nameplate with KNOX in plain bold lettering just below a doorbell.

Monica put out one gloved hand, pressed the bell and let it ring out. A peremptory rapping on the door itself proved just as fruitless and Armstrong took a couple of steps back, positioning the ramrod for maximum impact.

Whumph!

The sound of splintering wood echoed through the stone landing as the door sagged backwards.

'Good God in Govan! It's like a bit of matchwood,' Armstrong declared, stepping into the hallway and examining the twisted hinges.

Monica pushed her way past him and went from room to room, calling Barbara's name. There was no reply. Monica moved quickly now, her eyes frantically taking in any clue as to where their missing colleague might be.

'Nobody here,' she said at last.

'Come through to the lounge a wee minute,' Sutherland called. See what our pal's been up to.'

Monica walked back into the main room, wondering what mischief Sutherland was intent on. What had he found? Some sex toys, perhaps? It was common knowledge that he had harboured a bit of a grudge against the woman, not least because of her sexuality.

'Here,' he said, waving a sheaf of papers as Monica approached. 'These shouldn't be out of HQ. Not under any circumstances.'

Monica snatched the papers from him and immediately recognised them as printouts from their case. 'Good Lord!' she exclaimed, reading page after page of highly sensitive information. 'What the hell's she been doing?'

Chapter Thirty-nine

THE CLOUDS THAT covered the stars drifted across the heavens, a freshening breeze bringing a hint of moisture in the air. As the first drops fell to earth they splashed against last year's fallen leaves, creating tiny puddles in crevices hollowed out by the roots of the tree.

Barbara opened her eyes, feeling the raindrops on her face. Thrusting out her tongue between the lines of duct tape that she had already chewed away, she held them as they fell, swallowing painfully. She had no idea how long it might have been since he had left her there like a useless piece of garbage, but darkness had already fallen and the cold was making her body stiffen. Was that her fate, then? To die here in this filthy hollow? Was there any point in tasting these precious drops or was her body simply obeying a primitive need?

When the shivering began, Barbara tried to take deep breaths but somehow all she could do was shudder and gasp as the rain drilled against her face. She made to flex her fingers in one last vain attempt to free herself from the bonds but somehow her hands did not obey her brain, numbed as they were, and Barbara gave a huge sigh as the yearning to sleep took over.

She was only dimly aware of the strong scent of musk as the fox came closer, sniffing the ground as it padded around the bole of the tree. Then the sky seemed to splinter into shards of silver light as the world tilted sideways and her body convulsed into spasms of shivering, her teeth chattering inside her head.

TOMMY CARMICHAEL DREW into the lay-by, cutting the white van's engine. Giving a cough, he pulled out a pack of cigarettes from his jacket pocket and put one into his mouth, fishing in the other pocket for his lighter. The snap then flare was followed by a contented sigh as he inhaled and felt the nicotine reach his lungs. The rain had stopped pattering down against the windscreen and the clouds had shifted enough for Tommy to see the hazy outline of the moon. He sat back, smoking contentedly. There was no hurry to shift the mattress in the back and let it fall down into the gully. The man sniffed. Was he starting a cold? He wiped his nose on the back of his hand. Maybe he shouldn't have been so daft taking off his strip and waving it aloft at that last Rangers game. Tommy grinned. Och but he'd been blootered out of his heid, hadnae noticed the cold a bit.

The cigarette finished, Tommy rolled down the window and flicked the stub away, watching the glow describe an arc in the cold night air. Then he stopped. What the hell was that? A faint yet discernible sound that could only be the ring from a mobile phone reached Tommy's ears.

Curious, the man slipped from the cab of the van, his feet touching the gravel with a crunch. The noise was coming from his left, below the edge of the road. As Tommy peered into the darkness, the moon came out from behind its wisp of cloud and shone down, making the dark shapes suddenly brighter.

'Name o' God!' he gasped, his hand across his brow as he saw the figure slumped at the foot of the tree. The ringing stopped and Tommy stood there, biting his lip, unsure of what he wanted to do. A deid body was a deid body, wasn't it? *He* couldnae do onything to help. Could he?

The sudden bark of the unseen fox made him start. Time tae get oot o' here. Yet he hesitated still. That wis somebody's kin doon there. Wouldnae hurt tae make wan call, would it?

Reaching for his own mobile, Tommy dialled 999.

'Ah'm up on the Braes, so ah ah'm,' he explained when he was finally connected to the police. 'Stopped fur a fag at the lay-by up the top. Think there's a deid boady doon in the gully, so ah do.'

But when asked to give his name, Tommy Carmichael shook his head. Enough was enough. Snapping the phone shut he turned and climbed into the van once more. He'd done his duty, hadn't he? Wasn't goin tae be there when the polis rolled up, asking questions and wantin tae see what was in the back o' the van.

'THEY'VE FOUND HER.' Lorimer put down the phone with a sigh, Maggie's anxious face looking up at his.

'Is she . . .?' Maggie left the words unspoken but her husband smiled wearily, shaking his head.

'She's been taken to hospital. Suffering from hypothermia and concussion at the very least, the paramedics reckoned. We'll see,' he added, pulling Maggie into his arms and sending up a fervent prayer that his over-zealous detective constable would survive the next few hours. Proctor and Armstrong had hinted that the DC might have been moonlighting, but it was hard to know just where she had been and who had done this to her.

'Come on, back to bed,' he said softly. 'We'll know more in the morning.'

Maggie yawned suddenly, shivering in her thin nightdress. She had wanted to give him his card first thing, but when that phone call had shattered the night, bringing such awful news, all thoughts of her husband's birthday had been pushed to the back of her mind.

As they slipped under the duvet, Bill's arms encircled her, his hand rubbing her back. Still shivering, Maggie tried not to think too hard about the woman who had been discovered on that lonely spot or how the cold must have gnawed into her very bones.

Chapter Forty

THE TELEPHONE RINGING at 6.30 next morning made Lorimer sit up in bed and snatch it quickly. Maggie sat up sleepily, watching her husband's face for any signs that might tell her what was happening. When it lit up with a smile she let out a sigh of relief, unaware that she had been holding her breath.

'She's going to be all right,' he said as he put down the phone at last. 'Still hasn't regained consciousness and they're taking her in to theatre first thing but she's out of danger, they say.'

Maggie reached out and clung to his arm. 'Happy birthday,' she whispered, finding his cheek and kissing it.

'Good grief! I'd forgotten all about that,' he smiled, turning to her and taking her into his arms. 'Well, that news is the best present I could've had,' he added softly.

Tucked against his chest, Maggie gave a grin that she knew he could not see: there were more surprises in store later on. Just wait and see if this day didn't get better and better, she thought happily.

Rita Livingstone sat nursing her coffee cup as Lorimer outlined the plans for the squad. It had been a long morning so far. The news about Barbara Knox had spread like wildfire throughout the department, speculation running high about who had abducted the police officer and why. It had been a stroke of sheer luck that she had been located way up in Glennifer Braes. Whoever had made that 999 call deserved a medal. Although a cynical part of Rita wondered if the caller might have been instrumental in throwing the woman down that gully in the first place. Some villains simply baulked at the idea of doing in another human being and this was, after all, a police officer. But now there was a different sort of news to consider, something that would affect them all.

'What will you do yourself, sir?' she asked quietly.

'That hasn't been decided yet, Rita,' Lorimer sighed. 'But it was hinted that I might be transferred to a divisional HQ somewhere.'

'In Strathclyde?'

Lorimer's eyebrows rose. 'Better be. My wife works in Muirpark Secondary and I don't think she'd be too happy to have to relocate.'

Rita Livingstone noticed a softness in her superior's eyes at the mention of his wife but she did not change her own expression. There was something there that caused her a sudden pang. This man, childless though he might be, had that rare thing: a loving marriage. It was his fortieth birthday today, Rita knew. She had noticed the date on his personnel file way before Christmas and made a note of it. His wife had sworn her to secrecy about the party this evening and Rita was gratified to have been the only one in the squad to have received an invitation. *He hasn't had much time to get to know his new colleagues*, Maggie Lorimer had told her, *but he speaks so warmly of you that I thought you'd like to come along.*

This afternoon she had planned a wee surprise for the boss: a cake from Asda with the Strathclyde Police logo on top and two chunky wax candles shaped in a 4 and a 0. Not everybody would be able to be there, given the workload, but enough to wish this man well on his special day.

'I've hardly had time to get to know any of you,' Lorimer said, unconsciously echoing his wife's words.

'It happens,' Rita shrugged. 'But we did think the squad might have lasted a good bit longer or been transformed into something else. You know, same thing but under another name.'

Lorimer remained silent. The squad was being streamlined, Joyce Rogers had told him, but there had been a hint that a similar unit might emerge elsewhere, possibly out at Govan. Yet there had been no mention of the Pitt Street officers being deployed there. Had the Pattison case come to a satisfactory conclusion would he be looking forward to commanding a new squad over on the south side of the city? Perhaps. He hadn't asked that particular question, though, preferring to await whatever fate had in store.

AS THE FINAL bell of the day rang out, Maggie packed up the last of her papers into a well-worn satchel and headed out after her class. The day had remained clear and crisp and the sun was still above the rooftops as she left the school, the sky blue beyond the lines of leafless trees that ran along the adjacent cricket grounds. It looked like being a fine night for the party. She had plenty of time to get ready at home, call anyone who might have left messages and leave out packs of food for Chancer. Jean, their wonderful cleaning lady who came in twice a week, had offered to pop in and feed the cat so that they could enjoy their overnight stay in the Malmaison. As she drove home, Maggie found herself humming along to an old Joni Mitchell song that she'd put on the CD player.

There was a DJ coming later on after the meal and there would be dancing till after midnight. She grinned as she remembered being shown that luxurious room and the chequered floor in the en suite bathroom: the bed was easily big enough for a night of fun and games. Then there was the promise of a big breakfast (if they got up in time, she thought wickedly) before a taxi took her back to Muirpark for work. Maggie made a mental note of everybody who was to be there and her grin deepened as she anticipated her husband's delight at seeing so many of his old friends. Och, it was going to be a night to remember! She was certain of that.

THE WOMAN WHO sometimes called herself Diana sat on the edge of the bed, intent on filing her nails into gentle curves. A pot of scarlet polish sat on the bedside table, ready to be applied once she had performed the initial manicure. Tonight was going to be the night when she finally found him. Her face took on a thoughtful cast. Barbara had been able to tell her so much, hadn't she? The surveillance operation was a difficulty she hadn't expected to face, though. The woman smiled, tossing back her mane of dark hair. With any luck they would simply take her for one of the undercover officers. And that shouldn't be something that would present any problems, should it?

She laid down the nail file on the satin bedspread and glanced out of the window. It was to be a full moon tonight and the scraps of cloud lingering above the city were shifting fast, swept along by a chill east wind. Well, neither wind nor weather was going to stop her now: she'd be ready and waiting whenever that white car appeared on the corner.

LORIMER SMILED TO himself as he tucked the birthday card away in his desk drawer. It had been nice of Rita to organise the cake and everything and several of the team had managed to sign his card, some of them adding cheeky comments. Then the smile turned to a sigh. It would remain as a small souvenir of his time with them all in Pitt Street, something to look back on when he was fifty, maybe, and approaching retirement.

He looked at his desk and nodded in satisfaction. All the paperwork was in order, the undercover units organised for tonight so he could slip off with a clear conscience and enjoy his evening with Maggie. A quiet night, just the two of them, was what he wanted and he was glad she hadn't suggested anything more. He glanced at his watch and rose from his chair. It was time to be off, have a quick shower and shave then change into whatever met with his wife's approval for their night out.

As Lorimer walked across the street to where the silver Lexus was parked, he saw its outline glimmering in the moonlight. *Happy birthday to me*, he sang softly. He hoped Maggie wouldn't have spent her hard-earned money on anything else. *It's all I want*, he'd told her simply, when he'd first brought it home. The big car unlocked itself silently and he moved into the driver's seat, shivering suddenly. *Goose walked over your grave?* he asked himself then pushed the heated seat control to its maximum before driving off into the night.

Chapter Forty-one

'HOPE YOU ENJOY the food,' Maggie said as she teetered down the spiral staircase in her high heels.

Were these new shoes to match her classy outfit? Lorimer wondered, catching her arm lest she stumble. It was quite dark down here in what the receptionist had called the brasserie. Too damn dark for anyone to see where they were going properly, he thought, finding the ground floor at last.

'Surprise!!!'

When all the lights went on Lorimer raised a sudden hand to shield his eyes from the dazzle. A chorus of 'Happy Birthday' rang out and he stood, mesmerised, looking at all the familiar faces grinning back at him.

There was Alistair Wilson and his wife, Betty, Niall Cameron, the lanky Lewisman, and even wee Sadie Dunlop from the canteen, dressed up to the nines in a sparkly number.

'Flynn!' he said in surprise as he noticed the lad who he'd taken off the streets and who now made an honest living as a landscape gardener. They were all here, his pals from the old division as well as the familiar faces of neighbours, good Lord even Joyce Rogers! His eyes scanned the crowd, picking out some of his cousins and their wives and, oh there was Rosie looking ultra glamorous, hanging onto Solly's arm.

'Good Lord!' he said at last, turning to Maggie. 'You wee rascal!' he beamed.

'You're not cross?'

'Do I look it? No way,' he whispered, bending to kiss her lips and evoking a cheer from the assembled guests.

Three dark-suited waiters appeared bearing trays of champagne and then, amidst the buzz of talk and glass in hand, Lorimer found himself moving amongst his friends, shaking his head in mock bewilderment, as they all tried to tell him how his face had looked when the lights had gone up.

'Maggie's been really good at keeping it a secret,' Rosie told him.

'And I didn't say a thing,' the deputy chief constable said. Resplendent in a short black number she gave him a toothy grin as she raised her champagne flute in a silent toast. 'Just made sure you weren't on duty, that's all.' She winked conspiratorially.

THE DARK-HAIRED WOMAN regarded herself in the bedroom mirror. Her face was thin and devoid of make-up, her chiselled cheekbones giving her a haunted look. She could easily be taken for a junked-up street woman. Her hand hovered above a mass of brushes and make-up palettes. Was it better to keep to her natural pallor or to go through a routine that would find her looking back at the sort of face that might grace a glamour magazine? She had to tempt him, ensure that he stopped to pick her up, didn't she? Tilting her head upwards so that the light caught all the angles and shadows, she squeezed a blob of foundation onto the back of her hand then dipped her finger into it like an artist beginning a new canvas.

Downstairs there was a birthday party going on. She had heard the noise of celebrations earlier and had seen the pale blue balloons with their ribbons stacked in a corner of the dining room as she had finished her meal. So much better for her: the noise and goings on would keep the staff too busy to notice her leaving and returning late on into the night, especially now that she was familiar with the back stairs that led to the upper floor.

This was her last night here, she told herself. She shivered as though some premonition had caught that thought and held it up for scrutiny, daring fate to meddle in her plans. She was overwrought with nervous excitement; that was all. Her eyes fell to the Starfire pistol lying openly on the counterpane. One swift shot and it would all be over. Then her nights would be free once more, memories of Carol tempered by the knowledge that she had avenged her killing.

A SWATHE OF blood-coloured cloud split the sky above the horizon, its edge like the crest of an endless wave, silvered in the moonlight. Pinpoints of red and amber twinkled and shimmered; the city seeming vibrant and alive those miles away to the east.

He tried not to stare at the moon that was looking down upon him from the upper darkness. Wisps of cloud rolled off the mass like smoke, obscuring the moon, its white gold glow an arc of mysterious light. Then the shreds and scraps of cloud separated, drifting apart to reveal the face that was leering down at him once more.

As though in a dream he picked up the clothes he had left on the chair by his bed and began to dress. It was time. The image of the sabre downstairs came to him as sharply as its cutting edge. The house was in silence, Vlad and Aunt Andrea asleep long since. But they could not awake tonight. This was his time, his destiny. Still, he tiptoed quietly downstairs, despite the certainty that they were colluding in this enchantment that kept all bad things from him.

The sabre flickered in the moonlight as he drew it from the case and he breathed a sigh of gratitude that it had waited for him, for this night.

He had left the car parked near the open gates, facing outwards. Placing the weapon reverently across the back seats, he started the engine and drove slowly onto a road that was a stream of moonlight pulling him back to the city.

THE PARTY HAD been a great success, Maggie knew, looking around at all their friends. The dinner and speech-making now over, dancing had just begun. For a moment or two she had been terrified that he would have hated the whole idea but Lorimer had entered into the spirit of the party almost as soon as the lights had gone up. Now he was walking across to the toilets, having given her a promise of the next dance as soon as he returned.

'Just going up to the room. It's pretty busy in there,' he told her, coming back a few moments later, nuzzling into her neck and making her laugh.

'Okay, see you in a couple of minutes,' she replied, turning back as Flynn grabbed her hands and swung her into a dance.

'C'mon, Mrs L., let's show these oldies a thing or two,' he called out as the tempo of the music quickened.

LORIMER SMILED AS he left their room, heading for the back staircase with its arrangement of gilt mirrors. It had been a great surprise, lovely of Maggie to do all of this, he thought as he began to walk along the narrow corridor.

Just at that moment a door ahead of him opened and a woman slipped out. Lorimer stopped for a moment, observing her with professional interest. She was dressed in a short skirt and fishnet tights, carrying her high-heeled shoes in one hand as though to effect some sort of escape. Had someone in the hotel been enjoying the services of a high-class call girl? Lorimer frowned. There was something familiar about the tall figure, her dark hair swinging loose around her shoulders. He blinked. Too much of the bubbly stuff, he told himself. Yet as he followed her along the carpeted passage he could not rid himself of the feeling that he had seen this woman somewhere before tonight.

The lamps were all lit above the staircase and, as he descended, he caught a glimpse of the woman's reflection as she passed one of the gilded mirrors, the artificial light turning her dark hair to a halo of gold. The image of the woman in his dreams came back to him then, making Lorimer stop where he was.

'Claire,' he said suddenly, the name coming back to him like a dam bursting, bringing with it all those memories of the scandal that had tarnished the good name of Strathclyde Police for a time.

The woman turned and saw him looking at her; red lips parting in horror as she recognised the detective superintendent.

'Claire,' he said again, but she had sped down the remaining steps and was gone even before he reached the reception area.

Heart thumping, Lorimer pushed open the doors, anxiously looking up and down the deserted street. He knew now who she was. And in a moment of revelation he understood exactly why she was here.

Claire Johnson had been entangled in one of Helen James's cases, hadn't she? As he walked uphill towards Blythswood Square, Lorimer remembered the details of the scandal. How the lesbian officer had sued the force for discrimination and won: receiving substantial damages out of court as well, if the rumours were to be believed. But there had been other rumours too, rumours surrounding the Carol Kilpatrick case. DS Claire Johnson had been Helen James's right-hand woman, someone the DCI could trust. Yet it had been pictures of Claire weeping at Carol's funeral, not Helen, he remembered.

Pressing himself against the wall of the office buildings as he rounded the corner, Lorimer looked along the west side of the square. It all made sense now. An intelligent woman, used to firearms. Set on revenge. She couldn't have known many details of the case, Carol had died during that night. But suppose she knew enough to chase after a man with a certain type of white car, a man who came from outside the city, his accent betraying his origins? And she'd been smart enough to infiltrate that press conference at Pitt Street, seeking out just what was happening in Lorimer's cases.

Yet how could she have known about tonight? About the surveillance op? And about the full moon? With a groan, Lorimer remembered what Sutherland had told him about the papers they had found in Barbara Knox's flat. Surely his faithful detective constable hadn't . . . but even as the thought came to him, Lorimer knew with a certainty that Claire Johnson had beguiled his young lesbian officer.

He stood stock still, waiting to see where she had gone. The square was quiet on this side though he could see a few late-night revellers in the distance who were staggering up the steps of the

Blythswood Square Hotel. Some of the undercover team, perhaps? He had been involved to an extent in the planning but had left some of the finer details to these expert officers themselves.

Suddenly he caught sight of her emerging from the deep recess of an office doorway halfway along the square. And at that same moment the white nose of a car emerged from the shadows coming directly towards her.

'Claire!' he shouted, his voice falling like a stone as he began to run.

She did not even turn at the sound of his cry. Instead she tee-tered in her stiletto heels towards the edge of the kerb, one hand raised towards the approaching car.

SACHA SAW THE woman standing in the moonlight, her smile as fixed and red as a gash of blood. His pulse quickened as he thought of the wounds he was going to inflict, the red slashes that would criss-cross these pale arms.

'Get in!' he commanded and she slipped into the car, still smil-ing at him. But then, as he prepared to drive off another figure hurled itself at the car, making him skid a little. He heard the thud as the man hit the pavement then he accelerated, his tyres squeal-ing as they sped off into the night.

Sacha bared his teeth in a snarl: *the woman was his.* Who dared try to steal his prize tonight? The steering wheel slid under his fin-gers as he took the corners recklessly before descending down that steep hill. Under the lamplight he caught a glimpse of her long legs, their white flesh encased in a diamond pattern, her sex barely hidden by that strip of skirt. He had a sudden longing to grasp the weapon that lay along the length of the rear seats, imagining it glittering in the moonlight as he raised it above his head.

'I know a place,' the woman said dreamily and Sacha looked at her in astonishment as she turned the pistol towards him.

LORIMER PICKED HIMSELF up from the ground, oblivious to the tear in his good trousers and the bloodied knee. Limping slightly, he ran after the white Mercedes, cursing as it turned into West George Street. Then he heard its tyres squealing as it took the corner too fast and disappeared over the brow of the hill into Blythswood Street.

His feet thudded as he raced into the middle of the road. They had to slow down on this steep incline . . . . The red tail lights seemed to flicker for a moment as he charged towards them.

CLAIRE SAW THE man's mouth open as though to protest, his eyes bulging in sudden fear. She smiled and nodded.

'Retribution,' she whispered then laughed aloud at his expression of disbelief.

He knew he was about to die. And she wanted him to die in a moment of sudden understanding. She had made no mistake this time. The accent as he had spoken, the glint of metal she had spied behind them . . . everything was clear to her now. Her mouth closed in a grim line as she pressed the trigger.

Then the world tilted sideways as the street seemed to close in and swallow her in its hard embrace.

WHEN THE SHOT rang out it was as if the car had backfired. Lorimer ran on then stopped, watching helplessly as the car jerked against the kerb. For a moment it seemed to take flight, a white bird soaring up through the darkness.

Then an agonising crash as metal hit stone. Followed only by silence.

He ran on, mouth falling open in dismay at the scene. The car had ploughed into the side of a building, its bonnet open and bent. Then the whole place seemed to come alive as police officers appeared from the darkened lanes of the drag, one car sounding its siren.

The driver of the car was slumped sideways, a neat bullet hole in his chest. But the woman had fallen forwards against the windscreen, face smashed against the glass.

Even as he looked at those wide eyes and open mouth, Lorimer could tell that she was dead.

'Sir? Are you all right, sir?' DI Armstrong was suddenly at his side. 'Thought it was your birthday party tonight . . .' His voice trailed off as the DI followed Lorimer's horrified gaze.

'Christ! Looks like we've got her, then, sir,' Armstrong said, putting his radio to his lips.

'We've got them both,' Lorimer said, stepping forwards and pointing at the shining blade that had fallen between the two bodies. 'You'll find that the woman's name is Claire Johnson,' he said, reeling back slightly from the carnage inside the vehicle.

'You okay, sir? Sir?' Armstrong had caught his sleeve before Lorimer stumbled back onto the road. 'And how do you know the woman's name?'

'That's a long story,' he replied. 'But then, I expect this is going to be a long night.'

Chapter Forty-two

MAGGIE LISTENED AS the dawn chorus began. A memorable night, he had said. Well nobody in Strathclyde Police would easily forget the night of Detective Superintendent Lorimer's fortieth, would they? He had called her, of course, let her know why he had failed to return from that trip upstairs. The dancing had continued till well after midnight, Maggie watching the door to see if he would return before the last guests departed. She had made her lonely way to the empty room, taken off her pretty clothes and slipped ruefully into the new nightdress bought specially for the occasion. He had come back when the first stirrings of life had begun in the hotel, taking off his clothes quietly so as not to disturb her. But Maggie had been awake, full of questions, and so he had talked and she had listened, hearing the parts of the story he wanted to share. Tomorrow would bring more answers, he'd promised.

Till then Maggie lay listening to her husband breathing. Two more lives had been snuffed out tonight, one a man whose intentions appeared to be as vicious as the weapon taken from the wrecked car; the other a woman who had hidden her identity behind a façade, seeking to avenge the woman she had loved.

She looked at the sky that was visible above the buildings outside the hotel window. Then, as Maggie watched, the skies began to lighten, the moon unseen now behind a bank of clouds.

Epilogue

Detective Superintendent William Lorimer closed the file on his desk and nodded quietly, though the bearded man gazing out of the window appeared to be unaware of his approval. Solly's profiling of the killers had been frighteningly accurate. The one person who could have committed the crimes against those men had indeed been a person who was forensically aware, experienced in handling firearms and had been passionately motivated, just as the psychologist had suggested. Claire had not been a street woman tarted up to pull in the punters for money but rather she had hidden behind her disguise with murderous intent. It had been a double blow for Helen James. Not only had she been unable to protect all of the girls out on the street but her former colleague, her favoured officer, had become a ruthless killer, lurking in the shadowy world of the Glasgow prostitutes.

He placed the file on top of the one marked BADICA, ALEXANDER and gave a sigh. There would be no trial, no opportunity for a judge to mete out a sentence against the Romanian. Yet, he frowned, would that have actually happened? Would a man like Badica have been fit to plead?

'He'd have gone to Carstairs Mental Hospital, wouldn't he?' he mused aloud, causing Solly to turn from the window.

'I expect so,' the psychologist nodded. 'I imagine she knew there was a strong possibility that a violent killer like the man who had murdered Carol Kilpatrick and the other girls would never stand trial.'

Lorimer thought about the former police officer who had taken the law into her own hands. *Once a cynical cop, always a cynical cop*, Helen James had told him sourly. But this had not been about cynicism, he mused. This had been about love.

And what had Barbara Knox felt for the woman she had known as Diana? Had that been love? Or had she simply been beguiled by Claire at a time when she had desperately needed to prove herself to her superiors? He had written an extensive report stressing the young officer's previous exemplary record, hoping that it might help to offset the damage she had done. There was no date fixed yet for her disciplinary hearing and Lorimer had no way of knowing whether the career of DC Barbara Knox had any chance of survival.

'Sometimes fate takes a hand in the affairs of men,' Solly said quietly, interrupting Lorimer's reverie. 'Though perhaps Claire was careless of her own fate. Finding Badica and ending his life was all she really wanted.'

'You really think she had no plans for her own future?'

Solly shook his head. 'I think the day that Carol Kilpatrick died was the day that Claire's dreams for the future ended. And perhaps there was something fitting about being killed after she shot the man who had robbed her of that.'

He looked into the distance thoughtfully 'What was it that Shakespeare said? *This even-handed justice commends the ingredients of our poison'd chalice to our own lips,*' he quoted.

Lorimer looked at his friend. Perhaps there was some higher authority that decided our fate. Perhaps not. He was just a copper, someone whose job it was to bring criminals to justice. But, God help him, it was a job that he loved.

BARBARA KNOX LAID her small posy on the grave and stood back. There was nobody there to see her action, nobody to condemn. The policewoman had heard all the evidence against Diana, or Claire as the name on her headstone proclaimed. Yet, despite the suspension and the aftermath that had followed her stay in hospital there was still something that she did not regret. Those few happy hours when she had been made to feel special might still come again, if only she met the right person this time. Something in her was glad that her friend had fulfilled her quest to kill Alexander Badica, but Barbara could never bring herself to condone the waste of those three innocent lives.

The Romanian had been wanted for the murder of street women back in his own country and there were still questions being asked of Vladimir concerning just how much he had known and attempted to cover up. The two saunas had been his nephew's initial source of women, but that had apparently failed to satisfy the man with a penchant for cruelty. Whether they could ever lay all the unsolved murders at Alexander Badica's door remained to be seen, but DNA had confirmed his involvement in some of them at least.

A bitter wind sprang up from the east and Barbara wrapped her coat more closely around her, wondering if she would ever be warm again. *April is the cruellest month*, Eliot had written, and so it seemed, with the squad now disbanded and Mumby making noises about not wanting her back in his division.

'Are you okay?' Monica Proctor was waiting for her at the cemetery gates, an anxious expression on her face. Barbara nodded then let herself be led away, her hands empty now but her heart a little lighter as the spring skies opened above her and the sun came out at last.

Acknowledgements

THIS BOOK WOULD not have been possible without help from
many sources. First to former DCI, Nanette Pollock, my heart-
felt thanks for being my main source of information about the
world of prostitutes in Glasgow, especially given her role as Senior
Investigating Officer in so many high-profile murders of street
women during her career; to Katy for sharing her stories with me;
to Annabel Goldie for a great day at the Scottish parliament and a
lovely lunch; to Alistair Paton for his continuing help with guns;
to David Robertson for a good chat about forensic chemistry; to
DC Mairi Milne and DI Bob Frew for keeping me right with the
details; to Detective Superintendent Derek Robertson for ideas
gained during a great lecture at the Scottish Medical Legal Society; to Dr Marjorie Turner for being such an ally to both me and
to Rosie; to Ian Dutfield at Mercedes-Benz of Glasgow for sending
me all the brochures and not minding that I didn't want to buy a
new car; to the staff of the Malmaison Hotel for being so helpful
and for the great gingerbread men; to the staff at the Blythswood
Square Hotel for allowing me to poke around; to John (the one

and only bird man) for the photos of the Monte Carlo Rally and for alerting me to the waxwings in Blythswood Square; to Philip and Elena for letting me use her maiden name; to Caroline for being such an enthusiastic editor; to Jenny Brown for always being there to support and encourage me; to Moira who makes my life so much easier; to Kirsteen, Sally, Vanessa, Thalia, Madeleine and all the staff at Little, Brown who conspire to make it all happen, especially to David Shelley who believed in me from the beginning; to Sophie Neal for forensic advice. To my family for not minding having a mad writer amongst them, especially to Donnie who loves me even when the red mist descends . . .

Keep reading for an excerpt from Alex Gray's
next riveting novel featuring DCI Lorimer

The Swedish Girl

Available from Witness Impulse Winter 2018

Prologue

October

THE OLD MAN grasped the head of his walking stick, feeling its curve snug within his palm. A glance at his hands might have revealed the yellowing knuckle joints and dark, mottled skin, the fingertips stained ochre from years of rolling his own cigarettes: signs of old age and decay along with the necessary stick. With his free hand he pulled open the green-painted door of the close, letting it fall shut with a slam behind him. For a moment he paused in the shadows of twin hedges that flanked the pathway, fingers fumbling the buttons of his jacket. Then, turning into the street, he blinked, dimly aware of the lamps beginning to glow with a faint amber light against the deepening blue.

Twilight was not his favourite time of day. The setting sun was a glare against the lenses of his thick spectacles, any peripheral vision merely grey-hued shapes leering at him from the buildings on either side. Yet he had to be out; had to make this slow journey from his home to the corner of the street.

Earlier, an insistent voice had made him put on his raincoat, wrench the walking stick out from its place in the hall stand and make his painful way down several flights of stone stairs leading to the street. That same voice had made him swallow down a thin line of phlegm, making him feel the dryness in his throat, inviting him to slake this nightly thirst. It was a voice he always obeyed.

The sound of laughter made him falter for a moment and look up. They were there again, those young hooligans from across the landing, sitting outside the pub as if they owned the place. And, although it was not a summer's evening, he saw that the girls were clad in skimpy blouses, the young men sitting hunched towards them, wavering lines of smoke rising from their cigarettes. He would have to pass them in order to reach the pub door, make a detour around the table and chairs that cluttered up the pavement. For a moment he wanted to raise his stick and shout curses at them, tell them to clear off, but instead he lowered his eyes and shuffled past, hoping they might leave him in peace.

As he passed them he could hear whispers, but not the whispered words. Then more laughter, raucous laughter like crows squawking above a rubbish tip, the sound of it following him around the corner and on to the threshold of the Caledonian Bar. He could feel his heart thumping and, as he imagined their eyes turned to watch him enter the pub, the blood flushed his cheeks into angry spots of colour. But then the loud beat of music from an unseen source drowned out everything as he peered into the gloom, searching for a vacant seat. Even before he took his customary place in the corner the barman was pulling his first pint.

'There, Mr McCubbin. A wee packet of crisps as well, eh?' Ina, the barmaid with the purple hair, was smiling down at him, laying his pint mug carefully on the paper mat. 'What d'you fancy the night? We've got in some nice ham-flavoured ones,' she went on, shaking her head as the old man chose to ignore her, lifting the glass to his lips and drinking deeply.

'The captain's in one of his moods,' Ina remarked sourly to Tam, the barman, who merely nodded at the old sailor and directed his glance at the next customer with a tilt of his chin that served as a question.

Derek McCubbin sat still, his back to the window, listening to the familiar jangle from the taped music, sighing into the night as distant images from seafaring days long gone flitted across his vision. For it was more than a mere physical thirst that drove him here night after night; the drink helped him to forget his age and infirmities, old memories smothering this present wretchedness, memories that could almost make his bitter lips twist into the grimace of a smile. They would replenish his glass a few more times during the evening before the old man made his way back along the street, tapping his stick against the cold hard stones.

OUTSIDE THE PUB Kirsty Wilson shivered.

'Want to go in?' the other girl asked her, running her fingers down Kirsty's bare arm, making goose bumps appear along her friend's skin.

'Och, it's just that old man across from our flat,' Kirsty replied. 'Gives me the creeps.'

Eva Magnusson took her hand away, reaching up instead to smooth her own fine blond hair as the wind began to blow the dust around their feet. 'Thought you were cold,' she remarked.

'You feart of Mr McCubbin?' the big red-haired boy opposite them laughed suddenly, stubbing out his cigarette on the metal ashtray. 'He couldnae hurt a fly, that old codger.'

Kirsty wriggled uncomfortably. Rodge was right, of course. The old man was just that: an old man who didn't see too well and who needed a stick to amble along the street every night.

'You shouldnae be like that, Kirsty,' another of the boys protested mildly. 'D'you not feel sorry for him, all on his own like that?'

'Och, he's probably got other old men he meets in the pub every night,' Kirsty said, sensing an argument beginning and knowing she was going to be worse off if she didn't capitulate right away.

Colin shook his head, pressing home his point. 'He's always on his own. I've seen him,' he added thoughtfully.

'Poor old Daddy No Mates!' Eva pulled a face then laughed and the others laughed with her as they always did.

Kirsty sighed quietly. Eva was the acknowledged favourite of their group whom everybody adored. Even the girls from uni didn't bother trying to compete with her because what was the point? Colin, Gary and Rodge pretended that they were cool about living in the same flat as Eva Magnusson but Kirsty knew fine that any one of the three would hop into bed with Eva given half a chance. Especially Gary, she thought, watching the dark-haired English lad narrowing his eyes as he smiled over his glass. Colin and Rodge weren't Eva's type at all: Rodge was like a great bear, more at home on the rugby pitch than in the classroom. Or the bedroom, come to that, she grimaced, remembering a recent drunken night that neither of them ever spoke about. And Colin Young was just too nice for a girl like Eva Magnusson; too nice and too normal. *The boy next door*, Eva had called him once when the two girls had been discussing the lads, and she had made it sound like a sort of insult. No, Kirsty told herself, that wasn't fair. Eva was never unkind about anyone; that was what was so endearing – and maddening – about her. You might envy her Scandinavian blue eyes and silvery blond hair but you simply couldn't dislike her.

'You've just got a suspicious mind, Kirsty,' Gary told her. 'Like your old man.'

'Aye, well, maybe,' Kirsty agreed. Having a dad in the police force was what had swung it for her in getting a place in Eva's flat, she was sure of that. Mr Magnusson had been well impressed when she'd told him that her father was a detective sergeant in Strathclyde Police.

'Ever think of joining him?' Rodge asked. 'Not a bad job for a lassie nowadays.'

'No.' Kirsty shook her head. 'I'm more like my mum. Definitely going to be in the hospitality business. Preferably somewhere warm.' She shivered again and looked up at the darkening clouds.

'You should be your own person, Kirsty!' Eva said suddenly. 'Don't let your parents dictate your life for you.'

'Aye, you get a wee place on the Med and we'll all come for holidays,' Colin joked, glancing from one girl to the other, eyebrows raised in surprise. But the Swedish girl's smile was back almost at once, her sweet expression belying the vehemence with which she had spoken.

'Come on, let's go back to the flat,' Eva said, getting up and looking for the pink cardigan that had slipped off the back of her chair and was lying on the ground.

'Here.' Colin scooped it up and wrapped it around her shoulders, a simple gesture that would have impressed Kirsty but that Eva only acknowledged with a faint smile as though it were her due.

'Five go to Merryfield Avenue,' Colin murmured as he fell into step with Kirsty, Eva and the others already several paces ahead of them.

Kirsty looked at him sharply. Did he think they were kids playing some sort of a game? Well, if that's what he really thought, he was happy enough to take part in it, wasn't he? Or was his remark directed more towards Eva? Kirsty followed her flatmate's wistful gaze. There was no doubt in her mind that Colin Young was well and truly smitten and for a moment she felt sorry for him.

'C'mon,' she said, linking her arm in his. 'I'll stick the kettle on and make us all a cuppa. Okay?'

Colin grinned at her suddenly. 'Know what, Kirsty Wilson? You're going to make someone a great wee wife one of these days.'

Chapter One

DETECTIVE SERGEANT ALISTAIR Wilson drained his mug of tea and gave a satisfied sigh.

'Good day?' Betty asked with a smile.

'Aye,' her husband replied, leaning back on the kitchen chair. 'Just like old times,' he murmured.

'Fancy having Lorimer back in the division again,' Betty remarked. 'You were all pleased to see the back of Mitchison when he got his transfer, but I bet none of you ever guessed who his replacement would be.'

'No. Thought Lorimer would be up in Pitt Street for a good while longer when he made detective super. Cutbacks.' Alistair shrugged as though that single word explained away the myriad changes within the Strathclyde Police. He picked up his empty mug.

'Another cuppa, love?' Betty asked.

'Aye, why not,' the detective sergeant nodded. 'Hear anything from our Kirsty today?' he asked.

Betty Wilson shook her head. 'She's awfully busy. All these assignments. Wasn't like that in my day. We had a lot more practical stuff to do.' She wiped the table top idly with a flick of her cloth, folded it neatly then laid it across the side of the kitchen sink.

'Well if she turns out to be half the cook you are, pet, she'll be doing fine.' Alistair patted his wife's ample bottom affectionately as she passed his chair.

'Don't know if that's what our Kirsty wants,' Betty replied. 'Think she has her sights set on something more to do with the hotel trade.' She bit her lip. Kirsty had been glowing with enthusiasm on her last visit home, telling her mum all about the opportunities for graduates that lay overseas. Although it was still only October she had already applied for summer jobs next year in hotels as far apart as Mallorca and the Channel Islands. It was something she hadn't told Alistair yet. Kirsty was his darling, their only child, and the thought of her spending months away from Scotland would hit him hard, she knew.

'Well, she works all hours at the weekends in that hotel to pay her rent, doesn't she?' Alistair replied. 'And look at the tips she gets from some of those visitors!' he added, a note of pride creeping into his voice. 'Ach, she'll do well, will Kirsty, wait and see.'

'PENNY FOR THEM,' Maggie Lorimer said, looking at her husband who was gazing into space as they sat on either side of the kitchen table, the remains of their Sunday dinner between them.

'Just thinking that it was good being back amongst the old crew, actually,' Lorimer said, stretching his arms behind his head and yawning. 'You don't realise how much you've missed them till you go back.'

'And *they* welcomed *you* with open arms,' Maggie chuckled. It was no secret that her husband was popular with the other officers in the division.

'I think so,' he said lightly. 'Anyway, now that the posting's been confirmed that's them stuck with me.'

Maggie Lorimer picked up the newspaper she had been reading, the smile still on her lips. His promotion had been well deserved even if his career path had been somewhat circuitous.

After serving in his divisional HQ as a DCI, William Lorimer had been promoted to detective superintendent and seconded to the Serious Crimes Squad at police headquarters for the first half of the year. However, massive changes to the structure of the force and budgetary constraints had resulted in the decision to mothball the unit, and he had waited for several anxious weeks to find out if he was to be posted back to his old division in place of the outgoing detective superintendent, Mark Mitchison.

I'll see what I can do, was all that Assistant Chief Constable Joyce Rogers had told him. But it had been said with a knowing smile and a tap to the side of her nose. Och, it was as good as his, Maggie had insisted, back in the summer when they had taken their annual trip up to Mull for a much needed break. And she had been right.

Now he was back in Stewart Street it was as if he had never left the place.

Maggie thought about the city centre police headquarters for a moment; a squat low-level building huddled amidst tower blocks yet standing out with its bright blue paint and that customary chequered strip. It was close to the motorway on one side and to the top of Hope Street on the other, yet Maggie Lorimer had never once set foot inside A Division, preferring to meet her husband after work in one of the small bistros that were a short walk away. *You don't want to see what goes on*, Bill had said to her once when a high profile prisoner had been detained there. And he was right: Maggie listened to what her husband told her, accepting that there would always be a lot left out of any story involving serious crime and glad that she saw a different side to the man who dealt with criminals in his working life.

What neither the detective superintendent nor his school-teacher wife could have guessed at that moment was the effect that one particular crime would have on them both.